LUSH LIVES

A NOVEL BY

J. VANESSA LYON

ROXANE
GAY
BOOKS
New York

Epigraph courtesy of Jennifer Tseng.

FIRST EDITION

Published simultaneously in Canada
Printed in the United States of America

This book is set in 10.5-pt. Berling LT Std
by Alpha Design & Composition of Pittsfield, NH.
Designed by Norman E. Tuttle at Alpha Design & Composition.

First Grove Atlantic hardcover edition: August 2023

Library of Congress Cataloging-in-Publication data is available for this title.

ISBN 978-0-8021-6198-7
eISBN 978-0-8021-6199-4

Roxane Gay Books
an imprint of Grove Atlantic
154 West 14th Street
New York, NY 10011

Distributed by Publishers Group West

groveatlantic.com

23 24 25 26   10 9 8 7 6 5 4 3 2 1

To my own great-great aunt,
JAG officer Lt. Colonel Lucille Caldwell
(1909–1978).

Sudden Onrush of Affectionate Feeling
an erasure of Nella Larsen's Passing

A queer outpouring of pent-up,
Terrible, wild, queer, peculiar
Caressing. Those queer eyes!
Black, strange, languorous eyes,
Set in that ivory face.
Easy on the eyes.
Queer prick of satisfaction.
A kiss on her dark curls.
A queer choking in her throat.
Shunned fancy.
Queer & black,
The feeling passed.
She could not define it.
I am so lonely, she thought.
She was bound to her.
Queer to think
Of never seeing her again.

—Jennifer Tseng

Chapter 1

G lory was determined to make it, and she had. The appraisal of at least some of her great-aunt Lucille's things would happen today, before another week, or month, slid by. Now that she was here, though, taking a seat in the cramped little vestibule felt like a punishment. Like being sent to the principal's office. Or the Department of Motor Vehicles.

The arrangement of the reception area at the top of the stairs was haphazard. More musical chairs than the first impression a pretentious New York auction house should want to make. Maybe it was always this way, but Glory had a feeling the close quarters were even closer today because it was a "Walk-In Wednesday." Free appraisals. Drop-ins welcome. Welcome to wedge yourself into a corral of orphaned antiques with a bunch of other hopeful strangers sitting knee to knee. She looked for an indication that the place was worth the wait but found instead, randomly stacked on the hunter green walls behind the mismatched chairs, a dozen ostentatiously framed but indisputably crappy Victorian landscape paintings, each with its own brass plaque and metal-shaded light. The floor, a checkerboard of buffed black and white, seemed to dare her to cross its gleaming surface.

However claustrophobic, the foyer of Madeline Cuthbert Auctioneers LLC was appropriately intimidating simply for being what it was—a gateway to the kind of old Manhattan firm with unpaid interns and tastefully hand-drawn advertisements in the style of a *New Yorker* cartoon. A business that sold mostly dead white people's valuable things to the mostly white people who wanted to buy them. Glory knew she had every right to be there. But even as she was announced by a two-toned door chime, the receptionist, a dark-rooted twentysomething engrossed in her multiple screens, failed to register her presence. She hadn't even looked up when Glory repeatedly excused herself to take the only open seat in that steerage-like space. There was no choice but to balance the heavy liquor box she'd been carrying on her lap.

Once she was settled, legs together, elbows tucked tight at her sides, Glory cast a furtive glance at the seven or eight other people around her. They might have been nice enough, nodding and rolling their eyes in shows of camaraderie. But she wasn't in the mood for small talk. Or any talk. Unlike her mother and sister, she didn't feel compelled to make people comfortable through the performance of neutral chatter. Everyone was busy anyway. Some were texting, others reading. One, a middle-aged man in a sweatshirt, was clipping his nails into the soil of the potted ficus beside him. Snap, snap, snap.

The room was windowless, warm, and stuffy. As soon as Glory's rear hit the seat cushion, she'd wanted to lay her head down on the box and sleep. This was her own fault, really. For painting through the previous night and into the next afternoon, forgetting that today was the only day you didn't need an appointment for a free appraisal. By the time she'd remembered, traffic was too bad to get anywhere fast by calling a car.

In a matter of minutes, she had dropped her paintbrushes into a coffee can of turps and thrown what she hoped were several representative specimens from the estate into the first container she could find, a Johnnie Walker carton left over from the wake. Then she'd rushed out of the house without a coat and hustled over to 116th to take the train downtown.

Lucille had been dead for close to six months. But only a few weeks ago had Glory found the energy to unlock the door to the attic at the top of the brownstone's spiraling staircase. Knowing that her great-aunt had died in her own bed, Glory couldn't easily get herself to enter Lucille's second-floor apartment, let alone that spidery storage space where she seemed to have secreted away the most personal belongings from her past.

It was sad and unnerving to think about a lonely woman's last breath being taken in what was now Glory's house. It couldn't have been the first time someone died there, and Glory didn't believe in ghosts. But she did respect the mysterious power of places and things to retain vestiges of the people who possessed them, to radiate the almost palpable charge of their previous owners' feelings. With limited experience in the world beyond her home, her great-aunt Lucille had surrounded herself not with people but with objects. If she'd made a museum of her life, Glory was now its reluctant curator.

To Glory's right, a woman, carrying a logo'd purse that wasn't quite deep enough to conceal her offering of an ornate silver candelabra, rose when beckoned. She'd hardly been there long enough to do the paperwork. But just like at the DMV, there didn't seem to be any rationale behind the auction house's intake process. After filling out the questionnaire they'd been given, the people in chairs were definitely not being called in order of arrival. It all seemed arbitrary. Completely at the whim of the gossip girl behind the desk. This would-be greeter had barely offered a thank-you when Glory returned her clipboard. But she did seem to be reading the completed forms. And by some dubious algorithm, she also seemed to have determined the likely return on time invested in those who were seated in her midst.

One by one, almost everyone was instructed to proceed to a room down the corridor where a specialist in X or Y or Q would be happy to reveal their fate. By 4:45, even the brown-haired brother-and-sister-looking couple with the plastic laundry hamper (who had arrived long after Glory) were directed to see someone down that hallway. Only fifteen minutes remained, and Glory could officially feel her blood coming to a steady simmer. She didn't like to make a scene, but she hated to be ignored.

A door slammed somewhere deep in the building's bowels.

Minutes later, the nail clipper, making a hurried exit, nearly tripped over Glory's boots on his way out the door. Chin to his chest, he muttered a slew of obscenities as he walked by her, still carefully guiding his submission—something thin and rectangular wrapped in a striped bedsheet—through the door to the lobby. Once he was gone, the receptionist glanced up from her computer, mechanically sweeping the room like a Cylon.

Only two contenders remained. Aside from Glory, Cuthbert's other potential client was a pink-faced, expensively suited older man who had placed a large, faded-turquoise Tiffany box on the chair next to him as if it were his companion.

"Sir, if you'd like to go ahead," said the receptionist in the most dulcet of tones. "Just down the hall to the right, our specialist in decorative arts will see you."

"No, no," said the fellow in pinstripes, waving his hands. "I believe this young woman was here before me. I'm a retiree with a punch bowl. I can come back another day if need be."

Glory was relieved to be able to return the man's empathetic smile.

The girl at the desk raised her barely there eyebrows. As Glory set the box on the floor, a few stray beads of dried paint popped off her gray coveralls. She suddenly realized her hands, too, were stained with still-moist oils. Come to think of it, she more or less reeked of minerals and solvents.

"Oh, I'm sorry," the receptionist said merrily. "I didn't see you. How can we help you today?"

Before Glory could answer, a woman around her age, maybe a little younger, emerged from the mysterious hallway. She had to be close to six feet tall, and she wore a tailored navy skirt suit over a kelly green, nearly see-through chiffon blouse with a flouncy bow. She walked over to the receptionist and leaned the silver-handled walking stick she'd been using against the edge of the desk. While the woman was making a series of rapid entries on her clipboard, a thick lock of her strawberry blond—or was it more like French ochre—bangs kept getting in her eyes. Each time it did, she pushed out her lower lip and blew it off her forehead, not seeming to care if her professionalism took a hit.

"I'm sending three and four to Nicholas," the woman said, evidently referring to the numbers assigned to the prospects she had already seen. "Is anyone else good for me?" she asked, turning to the odd couple still sitting there. The redhead gave them a disarmingly friendly smile. Her tone and the mischievous look in her eyes were sexy and suggestive, and Glory found herself hoping she was their intended target.

"I was just, um, determining that," said the receptionist. "This . . . woman hasn't told me what she brought in."

"Because this woman's presence wasn't even acknowledged until this nice man pointed it out," Glory said. "Even though she was here first."

The tall woman's smile disappeared and her green eyes, trained now on the receptionist, went cold. She came Glory's way and stuck out her left hand.

"Parkie de Groot," she said solemnly, as Glory stood. "I'm so sorry. Please accept our apologies, I can't imagine how that happened. There's no excuse for it. But if you still have time for an evaluation, we do, too."

Glory nodded. The woman's name was ridiculous in a way that seemed almost strategically engineered to offset her good looks. But her sincerity was a nice surprise. TBQH, the Parkie package as a whole was worth waiting for. In the first place, those hips.

She shifted her weight from one stockinged leg to the other. "Why don't you show me what you've got? It's not as if anybody here goes home at five."

Glory thought better than to respond to that request, so she bent down and hefted her box onto the chair. She flipped open the cardboard flaps, but as soon as she had, a wave of embarrassment overtook her and she immediately wanted to close the box back up. This initial surge of discomfort was followed by the more unseemly feeling of being ashamed to be embarrassed to begin with.

These were her family's things, not hers. If what was in the box wasn't valuable, it shouldn't reflect on Glory—though she couldn't help feeling it would.

The redhead looked so eager. Standing there with her eyes darting from Glory to the open carton. Glory thought about telling her to forget about it. She could come back another Wednesday. In a dress. Freshly showered. With the good stuff.

Under the auction house's harsh lights, Lucille's things now seemed woeful in a way Glory imagined they might not seem if she were white with a social registry name. And it was worse with the eyes of the old man and the receptionist now upon her, in addition to the interested gaze of Miss de Groot, who looked on encouragingly as Glory pushed aside the loose balls of crumpled newspaper shoved into the box for protection.

"I really have no idea if any of this is even worth showing you," Glory said apologetically as she pulled out a tarnished coffeepot engraved with Lucille's geometric initials.

The redhead's face fell almost, but not quite, imperceptibly. She sat down stiffly in the neighboring chair.

"May I?" she asked.

Glory handed over the coffeepot.

"How stylish," she said, sounding almost as if it were an insult. "So. This is a very nice piece of 1930s silver plate. But being plate, it's not something we would normally offer at auction. Most of what we sell from this period is sterling, or of that grade. You know, Jensen, even Spratling, Christofle. French Deco is sort of our signature. But yours is attractive, isn't it? Looks like it was well loved."

What a condescending little . . .

"Is there anything else you'd like me to see?" the obnoxious woman named Parkie asked, handing back the coffeepot.

Glory set down her stylishly worthless piece of nothing and felt around for the scrapbook and French enameled boxes and porcelain vases she had also packed. Not only was this a waste of time, it was humiliating. The redhead was acting as if, obviously, Glory had heard of those Deco designers—she had. But then she also implied Glory couldn't tell silver from silver plate—she couldn't.

Still.

"Anything *else*? I mean, nothing that's worth your time," Glory said.

"I don't know about that. I saw on the questionnaire your great-aunt lived in Harlem? Was she there a long time?"

"A century, basically."

When Parkie whipped her ponytail around to see if Glory was serious, there was real curiosity in her eyes, like a kid about to hear a ghost story.

"No way."

"Yep. Lucille's parents died young. She and her sister inherited the same brownstone where they grew up. They stayed on the second floor and rented out the apartment downstairs. According to family legend—which is basically stories my grandfather told my dad because, as someone new to the family, he believed them—a few famous people lived in the rooms downstairs. Possibly, though no one can prove it, Cab Calloway when he was home between gigs. Duke Ellington came by for parties, supposedly."

"Holy shit. That's amazing," Parkie said.

"Amazing isn't worth much, I guess."

Across the room, the phone rang. The receptionist answered, closing her eyes after enduring the first few seconds.

"So sorry to interrupt," she said when the noise of a muffled diatribe had ceased. "Parkie, I have Madeline from Miami and she's wondering if you have a sec to update her on the Flagg estate."

Parkie straightened in her chair at this announcement, and Glory could almost see the anxiety start to seep out of her scarcely visible, increasingly colorless pores. When Parkie turned to get up, her flashing eyes met Glory's and both of them looked immediately away, as if they'd been privy to something they shouldn't have.

"Ms.? I'm sorry, I don't think I got your name," Parkie said, pretending to look for it on her clipboard.

"Gloria Hopkins."

With the receptionist watching, the redhead was back in customer-service mode. Glory had liked her better when she let her patrician but pliant features show how she really felt. Excited, annoyed, flustered. And, it seemed to Glory from the way she'd listened when she talked about Lucille, interested.

"Perfect. Miss Hopkins, again, I'm really so sorry for what happened before. I'm afraid I have to return this call from my desk. But if you'd like to leave the box and your number with Olive here, I promise to have whatever else you brought in evaluated and call you myself with the results. Would that work?"

"That would work," Glory said. "Thank you, Ms. de Groot, I appreciate it."

Glory would appreciate it even more if Parkie de Groot was the kind of woman who popped up on one of the apps she'd been meaning to get serious about, though she wondered if the appraiser's chilly magnetism would come across digitally. For the briefest moment Glory considered asking Parkie for her number—in case she had any questions in the meantime. But she had her business card now, so asking for her cell might seem too thirsty. Better to wait until the redhead made the next move.

Parkie was on her feet now.

"Well, have a nice evening," she said.

"I will if you will," Glory replied inexplicably.

"With this call I'm about to do, not likely."

And with that, Parkie adjusted her flouncy bow against her chest and smoothed her pencil skirt over her shapely hips, only to disappear down another mysterious hallway, leaving Glory, the nice old man, and Olive, the prejudiced receptionist, to conclude the business of the day.

Chapter 2

Parkie headed around the corner wondering if today would be the day. She could hear the voice of her old boss—not Madeline but Parkie's direct supervisor—as if it were last week. Which it practically had been. "We arrive at zee hour de la poulet danois, no?" he would taunt Parkie over the partitions of her cube. It was a diet disguised as a breakfast game of chance of Parkie's own devising, but he was the one who christened it "Danish chicken." The rule was that she could get a Danish, her favorite, only when the mock Starbucks a few feet from Cuthbert's entrance had the cherry kind. This was hardly ever the case by the time Parkie was sent down there. After she'd finished her emails and calls. And primarily to pick up a couple of her superior's favorite chia-hemp maple drops, which looked even more unappetizing than they sounded.

Today, alas, was not to be the day. Today she played Danish chicken and lost.

Parkie filled her travel mug, leaving room for the consolation of extra cream. She placed it carefully upright in her Studio Museum tote bag, between her water bottle and rarely read novel, and sent herself back to work with no dessert.

Parkie wished the woman with the unsellable coffeepot had seen her Studio Museum tote bag. Was that so wrong? She was hot. Alluring in a still-waters-run-deep kind of way. The tote bag could have broken the ice. Could have given them something to talk about besides how impossible it would be to sell the woman's estate at auction or anywhere else if the worn-out plate pot was the best she could do. Parkie couldn't very well tell her she "loved" Harlem. Or that the contemporary artists she followed were mostly Black. There wasn't a way to say it that didn't sound gross.

Parkie hit the wheelchair door button with her elbow and entered the lobby, where Vince, a guy maybe in his sixties with a face like a boulder and a bald head under his porter cap, shot her a grin.

"No jackpot today, huh?"

"No joy."

"So, uh, Miss de Groot," he said, after chivalrously yet unnecessarily coming around to call the elevator. "I hear from a little birdie you got an auction on the way. About time, am I right?"

The elevator descended with its usual pre-opening jitters.

"Mr. Sweeney, that depends," Parkie said. "Maybe so. Maybe no."

*

Parkie's first big break at the auction house came in the form of the Flagg estate. In order to start at Cuthbert's the previous year, she'd happily departed the commercial gallery world—where her duties were mainly coffee runs, educating her brainless managers, and chatting up the older, mostly male tech moguls and investment bankers who could afford the art. None of it was unexpected in a position for which the primary qualification was "an excellent memory for faces." The title on her new business card was "junior specialist." At the time, she'd thought it sounded unquestionably more impressive. A vast improvement on "gallery assistant," even if the gallery—yes, it was *that* one—was a huge name.

The gallery position was one of those first real jobs well-connected girls like her often fell into a few years out of college when they were finished waiting tables or being baristas, skills she, too, had long-ago acquired. Someone from her parents' life had made a call, and before she knew it, she was moving into a junior one bedroom near stodgy Yorkville and trying to take the train to midtown every morning. And taking the train *was* trying. Ultimately, the absence of elevators that reliably worked rendered public transportation impossible for someone who couldn't climb long flights of stairs. This made the Upper East Side a pretty ridiculous place to live. But that was another story—one that began her deeply dependent, even codependent, relationship with Lyft and Uber. If you're disabled in NYC, you better have money.

But where most of her friends had either moved on or moved up from their entry-level jobs, Parkie had made the gallery her personal purgatory. For three years. She'd told herself that the contacts and proximity to big-name artists would give her the knowledge she needed to run a gallery herself someday. Meanwhile, she'd mainly spent her free time going to bars and brunch with the other disaffected kids in her circle and, with exasperating regularity, striking out on dating sites where people either wanted to hold hands and light candles or not speak before, during, or after sex.

But that was then. The job at Madeline Cuthbert Auctioneers, though slightly peripheral to the gallery dream, was an overdue vertical career move. She was pushing twenty-nine and she had a lot of lost time, and raises, to make up for.

And yet, as Parkie quickly learned, she'd accepted a job with little room for upward mobility. Her department head at

Cuthbert's was a fellow named Armand Villars de La Mortemart. La Mort, as everyone called him, was in charge of "Contemporary." To Madeline, this meant everything made between 1945 and now, except photography, which had its own specialist. Although he seemed as comfortable chatting up the guys from shipping as the billionaire consignors of prestigious estates, Armand was said to be a self-exiled French noble, next in line for a château and a title. He wore bespoke suits tailored in a style that was slightly too young for a man in his early fifties, and his careful, haughty manners and short temper made working for him a roller coaster—though an often entertaining and always educational one.

Like so many people there, Armand seemed to know everything. Not only about artists and their genealogies from Cubism to Pop to K-art and Adrian Piper but also about the finer points of furniture and jewelry, even couture, which, except for certain Met Gala standouts, he considered faddish.

Parkie liked being Armand's lieutenant and she'd gotten very good at it. At this point in her career, however, she'd been wondering what to do to get noticed on her own and how she might get promoted. There could be only one senior specialist in Contemporary. There was only one La Mort.

Until, quite unexpectedly, something happened.

About ten days ago, Parkie had arrived at work with what Armand termed "the most creative pairing you Americans 'ave ever made"—the toasted bagel and lox she customarily brought him on Fridays—to find a Post-it note stuck to her computer monitor.

"Family emergency. Returning to Foix. Flagg is your golden ticket. Don't f∗ck it up!"

Parkie dropped her cane in the blue-and-white Chinese-export porcelain umbrella stand beside her desk. Just last month she'd found it tied with a big yellow satin bow and waiting for her, a thoughtful gift from Armand to celebrate her one-year anniversary at Cuthbert's. Now here she was, unwrapping Armand's bagel and sliding his requisite chopped red onions into the wastebasket with her finger, careful not to lose all the capers. She sat down to collect her wits and took a warm, cream-cheesy bite.

The Flagg estate. Managing a big account and generating huge results were how you got ahead at any auction house. But Cuthbert's was small enough, "nimble" enough, as Madeline liked to say, that rising through the ranks could happen pretty quickly if you got your hands on a whale. As a senior specialist, you could call the shots on your own auctions—decide how to position them. Maybe even, as Parkie had been fantasizing lately, create themed specialty sales that would appeal to more adventuresome buyers—boutique auctions with transparent titles like: *Contemporary Black Artists* or even *1960s Political Ephemera*—and manage those with your own team. Those senior-specialist dreams might just come true if Parkie showed Madeline the money by successfully handling her first high-profile consignor.

Why, oh why, did it have to be this one?

Armand had presciently taken Parkie along for the original meeting with the estate lawyer at the Flagg family's co-op on Fifth. She'd never been in that particular building but she had a friend who'd grown up on the twelfth floor of the only slightly less famous one next door. The Flaggs' apartment was an opulent prewar compound with mosaicked bathrooms and staff quarters with more bedrooms than some dorms she'd been in. Even Armand was momentarily speechless when the doors of the private elevator opened.

To hear him tell it, he was not so much impressed as irked. His chief complaint was that most of the good Louis XV furniture and Georgian silver had already been claimed by the family—descendants of some robber baron or another who went down with the *Titanic*. When the most recent widow, Nancy Beth Flagg, died a few months earlier, the apartment's walls were said to display a major collection of Abstract Expressionism. A zip painting by Barnett Newman, a Pollock, a handful of works by de Kooning (him, not her), a monochrome by Ad Reinhardt. This good art, however, had been quickly and gallingly entrusted to one of Madeline's archrivals—whether Christie's or Sotheby's or Bostwick's or Peacocks, nobody at Cuthbert's had yet determined.

Madeline (or, more precisely, Armand and Parkie) had thus been called in to hoover up the leftovers—in other words, the relatively low-value crumbs the other auction houses couldn't be bothered with, since the real money would be made with the splashier art and antiques.

Luckily for Cuthbert's, the Flagg place had more crumbs than a derelict Pain Quotidien.

Still, Madeline's having saddled Parkie's boss with Flagg struck her as something like retribution. Other than the now absent modernist paintings already stolen by their competitors, it was unclear to Parkie what in the Flagg estate warranted bringing in Armand.

When she asked him, he would say only that his best guess was, if you really wanted to extend the crumb metaphor, Madeline subscribed to the mouse-in-your-house theory: there's never just one. If these people had such amazing mid-century abstract paintings, they probably had other, perhaps hidden, contemporary treasures—a few of which may have slipped past the fine French furniture and European dec arts experts the other houses would have sent along with the painting appraisers. Whatever Madeline's strategy, Armand and Parkie and two other junior specialists had ended up spending a full week of twelve-hour days on the premises cataloguing every hotel ashtray and paperback book and Steuben lamp. Every gilded mirror and reproduction Ming vase. And every mediocre hunting print, knockoff cocktail dress, and machine-made rug they could get their tape measures around. The property was still being catalogued, mostly by the interns. In the end there had been so many credenzas full of matchbooks and playing cards and golf tees and boxes of expired condoms—usually tucked behind the remotes—they'd had to throw it all in bins for sorting back at the auction house. La Mort might be a thing of the past, but everyone was still talking about Flagg.

*

Parkie missed Armand. But as she approached her cube, she was glad to hear the distinctive voice, think Capote with a soupier drawl, of her favorite colleague. His name was Nicholas Burdine and he was a bearded, prematurely donnish, bow-tie-wearing millennial who had studied at Winterthur and worked after that at a small house museum in Paris. Parkie hadn't known him well before that week at Flagg, but they knew each other better now.

At any given moment during that marathon of cataloguing, Nicholas was one of a quartet (the taciturn rugs guy was there, too) heard intoning into Dictaphones as they worked their way out of the vast apartment's nautilus shell of chambers. Armand had assigned one of the front bedrooms to Nicholas, who, as Cuthbert's most junior specialist in Continental Furniture, was "plum delighted" to be released from his cubicle for a week.

And now here was Nicholas holding forth from the desk across the room from hers, his round, woolly face peeking over the grid like a sheep with Shakespearean ambitions.

"And sooo . . . Friday morning of our mad dash to the finish line finds yours truly, per Armand's orders, entrusted with the description of what the great man identified as 'the last of the beets and bobes.'"

Everyone laughed on hearing one of Armand's favorite, nearly unintelligible English expressions.

"Picture, if you can, little old me, adroitly crouched near the window in guest bedroom number three, holding on to a pretty—but not authentically period—leather-topped marquetry desk so I can get to this clock-cabinet thing on a bookshelf. La Mort is looming over me like the grim reaper himself. 'Urry up. Uurry up. Vite!' But I want. I must. Get myself a better look at this charming little instrument shoved in there between *The Fountainhead* and Danielle Steel. I know I should be going faster. Write it now, read it later. But it's a sweet little revival piece. And I think it deserves its due."

At this point, Parkie, who was coming up behind Nicholas, had appeared in most people's sight line. She stood for a moment as they watched her watching him pantomime.

"So what do I do next?" he asked. "I pull out one of those blameless little drawers for a quick inspection."

Parkie had to because she knew it was coming.

"A boy can learn an awful lot from the chamfering of bottoms," she mouthed, lip-syncing her friend's tongue-in-cheek creed.

There were howls and even a few tears from the cubes, where people were already beside themselves.

Nicholas turned around, crimson-faced.

"Don't knock it till you try it, Parkie the Great," he shot back.

Parkie rapped her cane theatrically on a massive crate someone had temporarily deposited in the hallway.

"Anyway," Nicholas sighed. "I turn on my little machine and I say, 'Item three million four hundred thousand and nineteen point five. A Louis XV–style bronze-mounted cartonnier with clock, possibly tulipwood or pearwood, nineteenth century, having a suite of seven drawers lined with marbled paper surmounted by a clockface and stamped on the interior.' Then I go to open the clockface. And I'm still recording—I can play it for you if you hang on—and I make a noise like I just saw the ghost of Freddie Mercury and I say, 'The case apparently hiding two red, white, and blue USB drives!'" He pauses for effect. "And then I say, 'Well, I'll be a *son of a gun!*'"

*

Needless to say, what was on those not exactly antique data storage units had since initiated a Justice Department investigation into the dealings of Flagg Pharmaceuticals. The first scandal broke when it was revealed that the Flaggs lobbied throughout the 1990s to create a drug monopoly. Add to that raising the cost of one of their most in-demand medications, a treatment prescribed to people with HIV and other autoimmune diseases, by around 4,000 percent. Flagg's bid to please shareholders rocketed the cost from the less than a dollar it took to manufacture a single pill to the several hundred you needed to buy one.

The second scandal came when Cuthbert's lawyers determined that someone at the auction house had leaked the contents of the USB drives to the *New York Times* and *The Economist*, both of which picked up the story and ran, and ran, and ran with it.

But only *after* the auction was announced.

The same auction was now generally referred to by Cuthbert's employees as "Parkie's sale." The auction of the belongings of a family who had decided to make lifesaving treatment impossible to afford for people dying from AIDS and HIV, many of them gay.

At the behest of its owners, Parkie had seen and even done some questionable stuff at the gallery. But thus far in her plodding but not-without-incident work life, she'd never personally felt so professionally fucked. These people were awful.

Getting saddled with such a nefarious client put her in the textbook definition of a double bind. Asking to be taken off the account would not only catapult Parkie out of Madeline's good graces, it would probably mean the end of her career—a career at Cuthbert's or anywhere else with Park Avenue clients who had also done some not-great things to make their money. Not asking to be taken off the account—going along to get along at Cuthbert's—would mean . . . Well, it would mean making choices Parkie didn't want to think about. And definitely not with Madeline watching her every move as if the whole thing were a protracted audition. Her version of probation. Or pledging. To Parkie, it was more like what her Calvinist forebearers called "swimming a witch." If you sink and drown, they find you innocent. If you float, they pull you out of the water and burn you at the stake.

Chapter 3

Outside the auction house it was early-fall crisp and not yet dark. Glory thought about heading back to the nearby subway stop but decided to walk over to Seventh, where she could get the 2. It was embarrassing. Some days since moving to Manhattan she was overwhelmed by the train. She walked long, smelly blocks in the heat merely to avoid the complicated and unair-conditioned business of changing lines. Besides, when she walked, she felt a sense of rediscovery. After so long in SoCal, Manhattan was a culture shock. Dogs and their people. Daring double-parkers and the duets of taxi and truck horns. The city-wide imperative to cross against the light. Enough storefronts and shoppers to make you believe retail wasn't dead. And so much overeager, wishfully autumnal street style. Tweeds and boots and wool on a day like today, when the air had been spicy and warm. There was nothing about it like LA.

"Everything you need is in the attic," Lucille had written to Glory in one of the few cards she'd ever sent her. One line scrawled in shaky blue fountain-pen ink on linen stock embossed with her monogram. The envelope came certified about a month before Lucille died, when Glory was still living in Echo Park, where she'd been since not finishing her MFA at Cal Academy. She had no intention of leaving the West Coast at the time and definitely no earthly idea that she would be the one—out of all of them—to inherit her prickly aunt's New York property.

Now that she was here, it was a relief to be able to do what she wanted when she wanted, but it was lonely, too, to be in a city and not know people—to be going home to a big empty house. Riding the crowded train uptown made Glory feel even more alone. When she stepped out into the commotion on Lenox, she had a sudden feeling of confusion. The halal food truck, the silver graffiti on the boarded-up grocery store. The men of all ages gathered under the scaffolding in a pungent weedy cloud. None of this was familiar. Glory wondered if she'd gotten off one stop too soon until she realized she'd simply come up a different staircase than the one she had begun to think of as hers.

Two blocks over, the brownstone's street was quiet as always. When she walked past the old man who sat on his stoop in the afternoons, he gave her a reserved nod, which seemed like progress. Glory could feel him watching from down the block as she once again fumbled forever with Lucille's ancient lock to get into her own house.

It would have been nice to be glad to be home. But the house was often dark, and the air inside felt stale and heavy after that morning's rain. Glory felt heavier, too. Like a familiar malaise was gaining on her. Like, as soon as she stopped moving, the what-am-I-doing-here dread would catch up. If it did, there was no chance of getting any work done. Any of *her* work done.

Maisie, Lucille's petite tortie, another unforeseen bequest, peered around the doorjamb and rubbed her face aggressively on the molding.

"Aw, come here, Maise," Glory called to her, squatting to extend a hand. "A girl could use a friend right now." The cat, in response, sat down, licked her mottled paw a few times, then sashayed back down the hallway as soon as Glory stepped toward her.

"If that's how you want to be," Glory said. "I'm not going anywhere, and she's not coming back. Them's the facts. So you might as well get used to it."

Diffident Maisie wasn't helping her mood. And neither had the trip downtown. Glory's back was still up from the auction house. She should have known going there in dirty coveralls with a box full of worthless tchotchkes might not end well. But she was surprised how much it pissed her off to hear Aunt Lucille's coffeepot relegated to the shameful category of "well loved," which was clearly no better than "nothing special to begin with," which was not all that different from "junk."

It might be accurate according to the auction house's standards, but it still wasn't true.

She glanced around at Lucille's beautiful, timeless foyer. The powdery walls painted the shade of eucalyptus leaves. The gilt-trimmed moldings and polished marble floor. The entry was the picture of refinement, cold and a little tight but very impressive, just like Lucille.

What would the redhead have to say about Lucille's things if she could see her house? Glory knew the big ball of anger currently lodged in her throat was just "sad pretending to be mad," as her third-grade teacher used to scold. It hurt to acknowledge the indignity of walking into Cuthbert's even if the good-looking woman with the kind eyes and the attitude had tried to salvage it. Glory was this close to unleashing what would have been another admittedly self-indulgent flood of all-purpose tears—for her dead aunt, for her once-again singlehood, for the career that wasn't. But this time she didn't let herself cry.

This time, Glory didn't even stop in her own apartment. Instead, she went straight upstairs. There was still so much to unpack. As in actually unpack. Closets and suitcases and cupboards full of potential remained to be explored, their contents unearthed.

Pretty Parkie de Groot had no idea.

*

Half an hour later, Glory was making some headway with Lucille's "house papers," labeled as such and assembled by year in roughly eighty manila folders shoehorned into a two-drawer filing cabinet that lived in the little dressing nook outside the bedroom. For the ease of it, Glory pulled out one of the deep drawers and set it beside her on the floor so she could spread the contents around her as needed.

Everyone in the family knew Lucille had found a way to stealthily amass enough to live on quite comfortably for all those years. Still, when the lawyers told her there was an inheritance, Glory imagined she might receive a few thousand dollars—whatever Lucille had set aside after the bulk of her money went to the animal-shelter people. Maisie was the last of a long line of very appreciated cats. But the portion of the estate left to Glory, along with her beloved feline, turned out to be this three-story Renaissance Revival on an upscale, locust-tree-lined block near the subway. Six blocks from Morningside Park. Four blocks from Melba's. Somebody left Glory a mansion in Harlem. It felt too good to be true even as she sat on a thick Chinese carpet on what was now her own hardwood floor. She still couldn't figure it out.

Of all of them, Glory was the weakest link to Lucille. She'd always felt that way. Lucille was crotchety. Mercurial. As everybody knew, she could be downright mean. Shoes unpolished, hair not combed—jeans instead of a party dress—Glory had felt the bite of her wrath directly. And Glory's mother, related to Lucille by blood, had endured her share of harsher blows (which, her mother being her mother, Glory figured she probably deserved). But rightly or wrongly, by the time of her death at the grand old age of 101, Lucille was all but estranged from her Hopkins kin. Which made leaving the brownstone to her youngest grandniece a real shocker.

Especially to Glory. Glory who had been sullen at family gatherings when they still lived in New York. Glory to whom Lucille had rarely spoken as an adult. Glory who had abandoned the law to become a painter, failing to succeed at even that, and disappointing everyone.

Glory sighed and returned to last year's folder, realizing she hadn't paid the least bit of attention to the stack of invoices and quotes she was flipping through. Homeownership was overwhelming. It might sound like everything she'd ever wanted, but having real estate in the city was not turning out to be as glamorous as it seemed. Sure, the brownstone was in reasonable condition for its age. But it was no show house—no Sub-Zero fridge, no rooftop deck, new skylights, or secret garden. No refinished floors or resuscitated plaster.

Or updated heating or bathrooms, for that matter. She was staying warm enough so far, but winter was coming.

Glory wasn't sure how long she'd be able to afford to stay in the house. As the new owner, she would have to decide what to do with it before something she couldn't recover from happened to the roof or the foundation. Or, she thought, as a missing pane caught her eye, before something happened to one of the lovely leaded-glass windows that were precariously adorning just about every room. Next to failing as an artist, and dying alone like Lucille, being bankrupted by the house had quickly become Glory's worst fear.

For now, though, the brownstone would have to be home. And she wasn't going to feel bad about it. Enough for one day, Glory decided, slipping the folder back into the drawer and muscling the drawer back into the cabinet. When she went to turn off the light, a glint of silver caught her eye and Glory noticed a group of frames she hadn't seen before. Although there were several of them, they'd been easy to miss. Almost hidden, she thought. You had to stand directly in front of the mirror—maybe getting dressed—to know they were there.

Now here was a fun fact: Lucille had been in the army—surely a partial explanation for her no-bull, drill-sergeant demeanor. Among the suite of deckle-edged photographs, Glory could easily pick out a striking Lucille looking lipsticked and sharp in her monochrome military uniform. On either side of her, in their own frames, were faded snapshots of nurses who must have been wartime friends, in starched white caps. Larger than all these was a matted newspaper article off to the side with Lucille's name highlighted in yellow—a story about the 404th AFS Band—the first and only all-Black women's Army Corp orchestra. In which Lucille had apparently played the clarinet. On a base in Iowa?

And Glory thought Lucille had never left New York.

After the war, circumstances must have changed. Personal or military, Glory didn't know. But the lean, feeble aunt she'd known as a child was nothing like the gregarious, fun-loving party-girl sister her granddad had told her father about while he was alive. That vision of Lucille hardly resembled the recluse who, according to the neighbors, hadn't gone past her front steps for more than a few hours at a time since the early Reagan era. All those years spent living in the same apartment. No wonder her things were well worn.

The sky had gone electric pink and purple, but from Lucille's narrow bedroom, Glory couldn't see the setting sun. It occurred to her that in a couple of weeks the sky would be completely dark at this hour. That notion filled her with a sudden desire to catch the last of the fleeting light outside. Beyond the dusty trappings of lonely old ladies who couldn't get past their thresholds. Into the liveliness of nature. With people and flowers and birds.

*

The top of Central Park was a straight shot down Lenox, which she was still learning to call Malcolm X. As soon as Glory crossed the boulevard at 110th, she felt like a fool for not spending more time there when winter was around the corner. But for now, and for fall, the park was almost tropically lush. The walkways were canopied by dense deciduous groves, and the tops of the emerald hedges snaking along the reservoir had been trimmed Disneyland-round. As she followed the path beside the water, Glory smiled at the many flavors of velvety coleus, a favorite of her mother's. There were borders of pistachio cherry, watermelon lime, and one she really liked in deep ruffled raspberry trimmed with banana.

Glory had lived in Harlem until she was nine. But when her father, a sports doctor, was offered a prime position in Denver, they'd moved out west. Her parents bought a big house in a white neighborhood with broad lawns and mansions with deep, shady front porches instead of sunny stoops. Glory went from being one of the many to being the only one. Denver was where she grew up. She couldn't remember much about her New York life before that.

A bicycle bell signaled its approach from behind, and Glory's mind snapped back to the present. The path she was on was about to spit her onto the hustle and noise on Fifth, which was not at all what she wanted. Up ahead she saw an opening in the tall hedge, like a parted curtain. Just inside was a formal gate. And when Glory passed through the wrought iron and down a few stairs, she found herself in a park within a park. It was a modest manicured garden paved with blue slate squares. There was a shrubby, quartered flower bed and, along the periphery, several long, glossy black benches that reminded Glory of beetles. The garden's focal point, burbling sedately on a stone base, was a figural fountain. From the shiver along her spine, Glory realized she'd seen it before.

She hated this fountain. And she thought maybe she always had. It was certainly possible—her parents and grandparents must have walked Glory and her sister, Grace, through this part of the park enough times when they were kids. It might even explain why Glory's mother was always taking the girls to the Botanic Gardens in Denver, which didn't feel at all like Central Park.

Glory had nothing against water features in general. But this particular fountain consisted of three bronze maidens gripping each other's hands in a ring, maniacal grins plastered across their sharp-featured faces.

Even now, looking at it as a grown woman, she was instantly back with the mean white girls in primary school. Glory'd never wanted to go to private school in the first place, but her parents hadn't given her a choice. Coming from the East, they were used to thinking of public schools as being dangerous and "not up to par." It wasn't until Grace reached high school age that their mother realized public education was almost uniformly excellent in gentrifying, boomtown Denver. The country-day girls were the ones whose parents didn't want their babies mixing with "urban" kids like Grace and Glory. Remarkably, the children of these people weren't all bad. Odd thing was, Glory vividly remembered the ones who were; being nasty about her hair, making her feel less-than. Implying she was out of place. Which, as she looked back on it now, coming from here in Harlem, she absolutely was.

Considering the sculpture as public art, from an artist's point of view, she was struck by its unabashedly pornographic flavor. The sculptor apparently wanted his subjects to look like participants in some kind of flapper wet T-shirt contest. They all had on long, modest dresses—yet the fabric was slipping outrageously off their shoulders and hips, revealing shapely naked breasts, long, smooth thighs, and almost shamefully melon-like asses. Glory couldn't believe how many young women, most of them Black women, kept taking selfies in front of it.

Three near-naked white girls dirty dancing at the edge of Harlem.

Round and round we go, Glory thought, smirking to herself as she watched from the bench. But then a picture of the redhead—tall, white as can be, undeniably handsome Parkie de Groot—appeared in her mind's eye. It had been a while since she'd felt that kind of immediate and unquestionable physical attraction to another woman. She hadn't liked the verdict on the coffeepot. But with her take-charge manner and businesslike ways, Parkie was nothing if not sure of herself. For someone so young, she was as self-possessed as a mother superior. Her shit seemed very much together. Was competence Glory's catnip now? She had unfinished business with a woman she'd just met. For once, that might be a nice change.

Chapter 4

More than a week had passed, and ever since that Walk-In Wednesday, Parkie had been, as Nicholas teased her, "burning the midnight oil at both ends." The truth was she'd been working without ceasing out of something like gratitude for not having to confess how behind she was on Flagg the day Madeline chose to check up on her. After Glory had gone and Parkie was on the phone at her desk, their connection had been terrible—probably because Madeline was on a speedboat. The call dropped while Madeline was mid-excoriation, not to be picked up again, because the next morning, she had gone on an African safari for almost a week. But Madeline was stateside now, which meant, of course, she was back in Florida.

Her call first thing was therefore no surprise to Parkie, who knew her boss would try to catch her unawares. This was why she'd come in an hour early and was able to intercept the call before Olive had even had her first Nespresso. As per usual, Madeline launched into her rant of demands without so much as a "hello." She was never more punishing of her employees than when she returned from vacation.

"You saw the story in *The Economist* while I was gone?" she bellowed. "Of course you did. *We all* saw the story in *The Economist*. I'll say this once, Parkie. Whatever is on the cover of *your* catalogue had better goddamned not have anything to do with goddamned Flagg Pharma. Message received?"

Parkie assured her it was.

"You've got to find something from *before* they bought the drug company. Whenever that was. And you need to be sure. When was that, anyway? I hope for your sake you're on this."

Parkie summarized what she knew of the ins and outs of Flagg Corp's suspiciously timed hostile takeover of another firm in the mid-eighties.

"Great," Madeline said, as if she'd finally been given useful intelligence. "A big-name bauble they inherited from their globe-trotting parents—or even better, their parents' parents, the *Titanic* people. Just find something nobody can say they bought with the drug money."

Parkie could hear the sound of seagulls in the background on Madeline's end. She was always going off to Florida—she said Miami but who knew? It could be Mar-a-Lago, as some of her coworkers joked. Parkie's family had a place on Fisher Island, and the one time she'd been down since taking the Cuthbert's job, she found herself constantly looking over her shoulder, lest Madeline suddenly pop up like yet another Whac-A-Mole in frosted lipstick. It was just her kind of place.

"How can we spin these people?" she was asking. "Old New York? One bad apple? I don't have to tell you we need this sale to exceed estimates. Where did they make their money originally?"

"I've been getting into that," Parkie said. "They go back to New York in the eighteenth century. It's looking like wine and rum—"

"Perfect," Madeline interrupted. "Go with that. Everyone loves booze. Help Kiki with the backgrounder for the press kit and make it about their long-standing entrepreneurial roots in the city. How they laid the foundations for Forbes by selling the libations we all love to drink."

"But they also, you know, sold enslaved people. That was actually their main business. And, you know, the enslaved people made the rum to begin with."

"Did they?" said Madeline. "I guess they did. Well, shit."

"I was wondering if the Flaggs would consider giving up on the idea of a single sale with their name on it," Parkie said. "Couldn't we sort of intersperse their property with other, less controversial consignments over the next few months? We have a couple of other nice sales that would work pretty well with their things."

God. Had Parkie really suggested that? Pouring a little bad wine in with the good wine and hoping nobody would notice. It would sure make life easier for her.

"I had the same thought, of course," said Madeline. "But the kids are really digging in their heels. They think, and I can't say they're wrong, they've got plenty of friends out there and people who admire their family as an example of the American dream. Glamour. Luxury. *Town & Country*. Deb balls and so forth. In their minds, it's as big as the Jackie Kennedy sale. Or the Duke of Windsor's."

Parkie couldn't refrain.

"That's a bit of a stretch, isn't it? Jackie Onassis was famous for actually doing admirable things in the world."

"It's not a stretch to them. *Your* clients," Madeline snapped back.

"Your drink's getting cold, Madster," said a gravelly male voice on Madeline's side.

"Listen, Parkie. Honestly, I don't care how you do it. Just find a way to get the contents of that apartment estimated and catalogued and photographed and into the right buyers' hands. Pick out a sexy cover lot that will sell for ten times the estimate because everybody's seen it and everybody wants it. We'll do a big glitzy preview. Right before Christmas when people are feeling festive and in the mood to dress up and spend money. That's almost two months away. I'm sure even our dogged communist press will have lost the trail by then."

Madeline took a sip of something, swallowed hard, and sighed. "I've got to take another call," she said. And the line went dead.

*

During lunch, Parkie stayed at her desk pulling comps on a set of titanium and gold-plated golf clubs. Armand had stumbled upon them, in what everyone else assumed was yet another of the Flagg family's coat closets, before he left. A similar set had sold at a regional house in Boston for around $45,000. Their value was good news—it would definitely kick up the gross sales. Though the question remained: Would buyers beware of shiny toys obtained with pharmaceutical blood money? Or would the prospect of striking a ball with the club that had touched the hands of a ruthless CEO make that particular lot all the more desirable? She needed the stuff to sell. The trick was to keep its history out of it.

Parkie was just about to write up a draft description of the golf set to pawn off on her colleague in Sports and Memorabilia when an email notification popped up on her screen. The name of the sender, harlemglorious, didn't ring any bells at first.

When it did, Parkie sighed a quiet "Fuck me," instantly remembering she hadn't gotten back to the smoking-hot woman with the box full of nothing who'd come in the previous week.

She reluctantly clicked on the message.

Dear Ms. de Groot,

It's been a week, and although you may have forgotten about me, I have not forgotten about my property. However worthless some of my great-aunt's things might be, I hoped you would at least honor your promise to follow up on the others. Anyway, I'm not willing to leave the box with you any longer. Can you please arrange to have it available and suggest a time to pick it up?

Thanks (for nothing),

Gloria Hopkins

Double fuck me, Parkie thought. This "glorious" woman was not playing around.

And Parkie knew she had it coming.

If it hadn't been for the soul-sucking, day-devouring Flagg nightmare, she would have looked at whatever was in the box herself and made sure she had something nice to say about it, even if the contents wouldn't so much as qualify for Cuthbert's monthly low-ticket household sale. Let alone a catalogue auction. Instead, she had dropped the ball, for which Gloria Hopkins had every right to be angry with her—and with awful Olive, who had gotten them off on the wrong foot in the first place.

She grabbed her walking stick and headed toward reception.

As always, Olive was texting away while simultaneously doing something Parkie had no doubt was probably related to getting a job somewhere else. She could hear how many calls were coming through unanswered until the third or fourth ring. As soon as Olive saw Parkie whip around the corner, she slid something off the desk and into her drawer. That and her unnatural flirtatiousness only heightened Parkie's displeasure.

"Hey, Parks, another gorge suit," she said. "What can I do you for?"

"Hi, Olive. Have you still got that box belonging to a Gloria Hopkins out here?" Parkie asked. "The one you were supposed to send back to me to look at after last week's Walk-In Wednesday?"

Passing the buck never felt so good.

Olive winced and swiveled in her chair.

"Let me . . ." she said, throwing a worried glance around her desk. "I think I . . . just give me a minute. If you don't want to wait, I can bring it back so you don't have to get someone to carry it for you."

"Carry it for me?" Parkie said.

"I mean," said Olive. "I just meant. I could do that if you wanted me to. Not that you couldn't find a way to. *You know what I mean.* Anyway, if it's that box full of newspaper, it doesn't seem to be here anymore. I could swear I saw it on Friday. But then the cleaners came in over the weekend. Lemme call shipping."

Parkie took a cleansing breath. If this racist, ableist b had lost someone's property on her watch, there would be hell to pay. And not just for Olive, as Parkie well knew.

The good news, according to Olive, according to shipping, was that the cleaning crew never threw anything away at the auction house without clearance from somebody who had flattened out every sheet of paper and popped every bubble first. Less helpfully, any unspoken-for boxes found lying around were essentially tossed into a dark and poorly ventilated room on one of the auction house's largely empty upper floors. "The grave-yard," as people called it, was a theoretical lost and found where uninventoried, unclaimed objects went to live out their days or at least die in peace, so unlikely was anyone to disturb them.

Parkie had been there only once.

On her first day, Armand had made a big deal about the recent consignment by a Russian noble of a Fabergé egg that had somehow been misplaced at Cuthbert's. No sooner had he shown Parkie her desk than he sent her to the graveyard to double-check that the egg wasn't hiding in an unclaimed shipping box. About an hour after she'd gone up, he came to find her. She was sweating, crazed, and frustrated, surrounded by towers of cardboard, looking as if she'd lost the storied needle. She could too easily remember jumping out of her skin at the sound of Armand's convivial smoker's laugh, tears streaming down his cheeks as he waved her back into the hallway to inform her that this was all just "Russian roulette," a Cuthbert's hazing tradition—other than what was on her face, there was no lost egg.

Those were the days. Parkie glanced at the vintage watch she wore, a Patek Philippe that had belonged to her grandfather and kept perfect time. It was nearing six, and she'd been ordered by client relations to stop by an opening in Chelsea, where the business office thought she might be able to "connect," as they put it, with the newly appointed woman gallerist—who was "not married" and "around her age." Madeline had gotten it into her head, because Parkie had put it there, that they should be cultivating more contemporary galleries as clients.

She would absolutely take a trip to cold storage in search of Gloria from Harlem's box.

Cross her heart.

But it would have to wait until tomorrow morning, after the opening. Parkie couldn't afford to be on anyone else's shit list right now. And besides, after yet another full-tilt day she definitely deserved a drink.

It was pretty, strollable evenings like this when Parkie most missed walking as long and as far as she could, whenever she wanted to. The air was brisk, but the light at that magic hour was splendid. Mellow autumnal reflections multiplied in mirrored windows. Pigeons fluttered at advancing shoes. People were moving as one giant organism. Flowing everywhere from all directions in that way that made her feel, or used to make her feel, part of an important production. In this hamlet of corporate America, the collective delirium of being off work for the day with the end of the week in sight was unmistakable. It manifested in searching gazes, luxuriant vaping, rapid-fire FaceTiming, and, depending on what was next, the slowness or quickness of strides.

Maybe she would try walking for a while.

Parkie had managed to stay off her feet for most of the day and was feeling relatively good and pain-free. Enough not to use the stick for a few blocks, maybe as much as half a mile. Then again, she'd need to deal with crowds once she got to the gallery, too—and with a drink in her hand. Better to conserve.

She was finalizing her game plan, propped against Cuthbert's building's granite facade—pretending to herself she hadn't made the decision to call a car—when a guy in a suit with no tie, probably in his forties, walked up to her.

"Are you okay, miss? Can I help you with something?" he asked.

"Do I look like I need help?" she answered cheerfully.

The smile left his face. "You're standing here in the middle of rush hour leaning on a cane, looking like you might be lost. So sue me."

"Would that I could," Parkie said.

"What a bitch," he said, and stormed off.

There had been times when an exchange like this would have thrown Parkie for days, maybe weeks. She could call up similarly scary and maddening—truly traumatic—incidents with depressing facility. And the worst thing was, remembering one often brought the others back in quick succession.

But today, she was pleased to note, she felt refreshingly impervious to this bullshit.

It had been more than four years, and countless therapy sessions, since her accident. She was relatively comfortable, given her frequent discomfort, with her life now. And she knew, though it wasn't something she always wanted to admit, living with a disability had toughened her up in certain regards. A younger, able-bodied Parkie would probably have broken into tears right there on the street if a stranger called her a bitch—not that she could imagine that happening without the cane and the unwillingness to play damsel in distress.

But now, having seen how readily people gave in to their savior complexes around disabled women, she didn't care if demonstrating her agency emasculated random passersby who assumed she was in trouble merely because she used a stick to walk with. Some people might need to be shielded from the thrilling velocity of a midtown rush hour on a beautiful autumn day, but a die-hard New Yorker like Parkie wasn't one of them.

Chapter 5

As far as Glory was concerned, Chelsea was a shitshow. More evil than necessary. Or so she liked to say. Any artist knows that being seen at a New York opening is more important to some people than seeing the art in the show. Glory'd done her time in these hangarlike former factories with mostly white men's names attached to them. She'd tried to make nice with the directors and gallerists calling the shots and shooting stars into the heavens from the walls of a few white cubes between the High Line and the Hudson. The more decrepit and unassuming a gallery looked from the outside, the more glam and gazillionaire backers it had and the less Glory saw a place for herself or her work there.

"Think of it as your job," Courtland, her brother-in-law, was always telling her. "I have to go to the bank every day and keep track of the markets, and you have to go to openings and introduce yourself to at least—*at least*, Gloria—five important people."

So here she was. Showing up late enough to her "job" that the current had reversed. More people were now leaving the gallery than entering it. Glory could hear them all around her making plans for drinks and dinner or a quick in and out at one last show now that it was pushing eight. The intimidatingly good art minimally adorning the walls around her was by a genius painter in her late forties—a queer Filipina from Chicago, someone Glory very publicly admired on social media but was privately insanely jealous of. She made big paintings. Painterly paintings where you could see the brushstrokes. Large monochromatic silvery or gold or rose-colored tondos about feathers and insects and shapes she invented. They'd shaken hands a little earlier, but Glory was too shy to properly introduce herself or express anything she really felt. Or even to let the woman know that she had championed the work for a long time before she got famous.

To her utter surprise, she had been personally invited to the show and an "intimate" dinner after by a woman named Manya Shah, the much-talked-about British Indian upstart curator and Moulton & Freer's incoming director. According to social media, Shah had been tapped to be the gallery's heir apparent and future new principal. It was the job opening everyone was talking about: a bid to be the next James Moulton, one of the dealers who had made Chelsea the center of not only the New York contemporary art world but the global art market. The dealer who had also run his own gallery into the ground financially for no forgivable reason. While he lived the high life in London, Moulton & Freer had gotten stale and his rivals had produced ever fresher, harder-hitting shows. The person in Shah's position would be under tremendous pressure to return M&F to its onetime status. The New York crowd was already expecting blockbuster shows from her. She would have to deliver.

Glory had yet to meet, or even see, Manya Shah. But she dared to hope the dinner was a prelude to inviting her to be in Shah's first American group exhibition—especially if she'd seen the current work Glory had up in a tiny gallery downtown. Though that was expecting a lot—it had even taken Glory a few trips up and down the block to find the entrance to that space.

Maybe she was being naive about the whole situation. Shah had probably asked local relatively unknowns like her just to create buzz now that she had made landfall on American shores. Media relations, nothing more. Glory was thinking she might opt out of the dinner when she saw the crowd near the door begin to part in an organic, oddly patient fashion. What, she wondered, could have such a civilizing effect on a roomful of unfed and tipsy New Yorkers?

When a tall, colorful form emerged from the breech, Glory couldn't not do an obvious double take. Wasn't that the woman from the auction house? Who was Glory kidding? It wasn't as if she didn't remember her name. Wasn't that Parkie de Groot? It fucking was. And here she came.

Glory stayed where she was, willing to be clocked trying to catch Parkie's eye. But before she got much closer, Parkie was accosted by a long-haired guy in Gucci sneakers and a puffer jacket. He went in for a hug and was fended off, though he got Parkie to chat for a few minutes until she moved away from him and her eyes went straight to Glory's. Parkie broke into an unreadable smile, only to shoot her gaze past Glory as if she hadn't recognized her after all.

A girl walked up to Parkie with a tray of wine, and she took a glass of red, quite possibly using it as an excuse to face the other way as she drank. But now Glory was undeterred. Damn, she looked even better tonight. Strong and solid in her pencil skirt with legs that went all the way to the floor. The woman had swagger to spare. For a second, Glory felt just a little bit guilty for sending her such a mean email that morning. But no, she'd been blown off by Cuthbert's long enough. The redhead deserved it.

That didn't mean Glory shouldn't say hello.

"Ms. de Groot," she intoned in a lower-than-usual voice as she came up beside Parkie. "Did you bring my box?"

Parkie visibly froze before downing what was left in her glass. Then, slowly turning around to face Glory, she made what was clearly a heroic effort to look happy to see her. Glory decided not to take it too personally.

Glory knew enough about clothes to see that she was wearing vintage Chanel, her pink suit jacket blatantly open over a diaphanous green blouse that revealed the lace bra underneath. Glory momentarily forgot what she'd said.

But then she remembered.

"You could have just answered my email."

"I feel like whenever I see you, I'm going to have to start by apologizing," said Parkie, all batting eyelashes and fake-nervous smiles. "But again. I am so sorry. And I can explain. Sort of. Except, I can't really. It's been a week and it's been a day and basically I just fucked up. I take full responsibility."

Glory hadn't expected the candor. Which was impressive. She was impressive. "Is Parkie your real name?" she asked.

"What do you mean 'real'? It's a nickname but it's still real. Is harlemglorious your real name?"

Touché.

"People have always called me Glory," Glory answered. "Since I was born, practically. Have they always called you Parkie?"

"It's short for Parkerson, so yeah, they pretty much always have."

"Wow. Parkerson. Really? For a girl." It was kind of a turn-on, actually.

Parkie caught her eye in a way that made Glory feel approximately fifteen.

She held Glory's gaze with her sparkling, mesmerizingly flecked irises and wouldn't let her go. Like some sort of lesbian mind control.

"If you give me until the end of the day tomorrow," Parkie said. "You have my word I'll find out everything I can about your box. I mean, the contents of your box." She failed to stifle a laugh. And what a laugh—it was a small, hoarse chortle. Almost a bark. Glory instantly wanted to hear more of it.

"You're in way too deep with that one," Glory said. "Good luck getting out of my box anytime soon."

More chortling. Parkie's face was radiant now. The appearance of a single, very distracting dimple had Glory briefly considering full-on flirtation for the first time in a while. It would be way too simple to get shameless with this woman.

But really. She was serious.

"Really, though, I'm serious," Glory said. "Can I rely on you this time? If it's more bad news, that's fine. But you should know, I have an entire house full of stuff. What I brought you is just a taste. Some of it is worth more than that coffeepot, believe me. And there's so much of it, someone will want to take the trash with the treasure. I just need to decide what to do. I can't keep it all."

"I promise," Parkie said.

Glory looked toward the bar. Parkie's glass was empty. Obviously, the thing would be to ask her if she wanted another. Before she could, however, she noticed a woman fast approaching them from the back of the gallery. She was coursing through the remaining visitors with an ebullient "cheers" here or a boisterous "lovely to see you" there. She was attractive, to use a word that suggests conventional beauty, though Glory didn't see it that way. In fact, she was having some difficulty believing that she and Manya Shah were both thirty-five, something she'd read in one of the half a dozen articles she'd perused online. Shah might look younger, but she carried herself like a movie star or someone highly accomplished despite their youth. It occurred to Glory that she was about to be in the company of two rather exceptional, and rather exceptionally sexy, women. Simultaneously. Things were looking up.

Manya, who couldn't have been more than five two or three unshod, wore what could only be described as a little red dress with six-inch and sinister-looking black Louboutins. Her shiny bob allowed for gratuitous hair-flipping, and she had walked, more like strutted, right up to them like she owned the place. Which, if *Art Weekly* could be believed, with the help of a couple of backers, soon enough she would.

"Well now, ladies," she said in a pert British accent, glancing at Parkie's walking stick and pointedly choosing not to reach for either woman's hand. "Manya Shah, at your service. Welcome to you and your lovely date. Apologies it's taken an eternity to come over, but I had to assure the critics that if we have anything to say about it, Glory Hopkins will have a solo show with us before this time next year."

"Oh my god. That's . . ." Glory stumbled, unable to process this information. "Miss Shah, that's, wow. That would be fucking unbelievable."

Manya Shah arched her eyebrows.

"I'm sorry," Glory said in her Come to Jesus voice. "But that is exactly what it would be. Miss de Groot is definitely not my date, though. It'll just be me for the dinner. Minus a plus-one."

Although Parkie smiled, Glory knew she was probably just as embarrassed. She also looked incredibly confused.

"More cause for celebration," said Manya. She riveted her silvery brown eyes on Parkie, who smiled back and let Manya look, Glory thought, for a little too long before she responded.

"Wait," Parkie said to Glory, her cheeks pinking. "You're *an artist?*"

For someone who was clearly intelligent, Parkie did a damned respectable clueless.

"Yes," Glory said. "I am indeed an artist. And here I thought you were hoping to run into *me* tonight. That's not why you came?"

"No," Parkie said a little too fast. "But I would have. I absolutely would have. It's just. I actually came to introduce myself to Ms. Shah. For Cuthbert's. I had no idea you were an artist."

Manya looked amused.

"Brilliant," she said. "So, let me get it sorted. You"—she gestured to Parkie—"came to tell me what's afoot in contemporary art on the secondary market."

"And you"—she pointed to Glory—"thought Miss Cuthbert's here was stalking you for a rendezvous, when she appears not to recognize one of the most important emerging artists this side of the pond?"

"Close enough," said Parkie.

"I wouldn't say you're one hundred percent off base," Glory conceded.

"I could apologize, but I think that pond-traversing ship has sailed," Parkie said to Glory. "I'll leave you both to it. Obviously, I'm off my game tonight. Congratulations on the show, Ms. Shah. Next time you see me, I promise not to be a disappointment." Then she turned on her heel and headed back through the crowd toward the exit.

"Bit dramatic, isn't it?" Manya said to Glory once Parkie was out of earshot. "I wasn't being flippant. It really is so American to dispense with the niceties. Knowing nothing about a person, you assume you can win her over by sheer force of personality. Or in this case, a very good suit. Yet for us, personality is so often the least of it. Substance over style is what I'm after."

"Maybe that works for white people. But if I had to rely on first impressions to get ahead in this game, I'd be in serious trouble," Glory said. "And charm is not exactly my strong suit."

"I'll be the judge of that," Manya said, grinning. She put her hand on her hip for emphasis. "Anyway, you're not the *you* I was thinking of. Only, coming from London, I suppose I don't think of Black and brown women here as representationally American. Until Kamala, your own people haven't thought of you that way either. Not in any respected or welcomed sense. BIPOC women, queer BIPOC women, are still firmly entrenched at the bottom of the food chain—no matter how much visibility some individuals seem to be getting. There's no shared power with that; no solidarity. We're often quite petty and cruel to each other on the way up. I would have said that's what your praxis is dismantling, as it were. I've seen the way you speak up for other artists some might consider your competitors."

All right then, Glory thought. To meet a dealer who not only might understand what she wanted to do with her art—as it were—but be able to voice it so clearly and unapologetically was something she'd been waiting for since she'd started showing.

"Thank you," she replied, giving Manya Shah one of her "I see you" looks through her specially thick-for-tonight lashes. "It means a lot that the work communicates that, even without my dynamic in-person personality to back it up." She managed an awkward laugh.

A silent, about-to-be-uncomfortable few seconds passed as they sized each other up. Finally, Shah let her full, very glossed lips curl into a smile. Glory was warmed up now. She nearly allowed herself to reply to the signal the woman was sending by telegraphing back her own response: Message received stop. Your place or mine stop.

But could she?

Objectively, there was no question the sex would be incendiary. Culminating-in-an-inferno incendiary. Manya seemed like the kind of woman to whom Glory was so often, and so regrettably, drawn: intense, funny, direct, emotionally all over the place, and almost inevitably a powder keg. A kind of volatile that Glory found tantalizing until it left her steeped in anxiety. Manya would be quick to pick a fight so she could make up afterward. Though, appearances to the contrary, she might not necessarily be the one who ran the show. Which could be a dealbreaker for Glory, who liked it when the attitude in public matched the attitude in private—even though she wasn't sure that could be said of herself. Regardless, the woman would be trouble. She was a walking, sweet-talking red flag.

Glory was midway through a cost-benefit analysis of giving in to temptation when she realized Manya had grabbed her hand and was dragging her across the room.

"I want you to meet some fairly marvelous friends of mine," she said over her shoulder. "From my old life. She's adorable and he's a surgeon, actually, but close to Midas as . . ."

In the opposite corner, Glory saw an unseasonably tan, gray-bearded man gesticulating to a young blond in a very tight dress who seemed to hang on his every word. After living on the edge of Hollywood, the combination of older man and younger woman was not one of Glory's favorites. It was less about the age, or even the gender, differences between these couples, and more about trading one kind of power for another. But she still wasn't interested in being touched by Manya's Midas.

"I'm so sorry, Ms. Shah," Glory said. "I'd love to meet your friends. But there's something I have to take care of. I'll be right back."

Though she made no reply, Manya glanced over her bare shoulder with the type of eviscerating, pillar-of-salt look that confirmed Glory's every suspicion. She didn't appreciate not getting what she wanted and didn't care who knew. But neither did Glory. Jerking her hand out of Manya's grip, she set her glass on a passing tray, and half ran, half walked to and through the front door.

It was now cold and dark on West 22nd. The multistory industrial building opposite Moulton & Freer glowed with large squares of light, each gallery window its own theater of animated silhouettes. Even at street level, these crowded spaces generated sweating glass and close air tinged by smoke breaks and cheap-wine breath. Chilly or not, going outside was refreshing. Like diving into a pool. As soon as Glory hit the sidewalk, she looked quickly in either direction. Parkie would have made a right if she was planning to wait for a car at the busiest intersection.

And sure enough, Glory easily located her unmistakable form under the streetlight on the corner across from the gallery. Parkie's head was bent toward the dim light of her phone, and her cane was tucked under one arm as she typed. Glory ran across the street and down the sidewalk toward her.

"Parkie!" she called once she was in shouting distance.

Parkie dropped the hand holding her phone to her side and peered into the deepening darkness.

Glory caught up to her, realizing she hadn't rehearsed what to say as was her habit when she knew she might choke.

"Hey," she said.

"Hey," Parkie responded with an unexpectedly shy smile.

"So. I have to get back to the gallery and talk to some more uptight British people in a few. But I was wondering if you'd maybe be up for a nightcap, like later, I guess. That's assuming you don't want to come to the dinner with me and . . . Manya Shah."

"Hard pass on dinner. I need to do my homework before I go back into the shark tank. Thanks, though. But yeah. A drink later sounds nice," Parkie said. "Where?"

"I'm assuming you live uptown."

Parkie rolled her eyes. "And I'm assuming you live in Brooklyn."

Glory could feel her face doing that painfully transparent thing it did when she liked someone. Smiling between words. Glancing at the sky. Frowning.

"Wrong," she said.

"Oh, right. Harlemglorious. I am so incredibly slow on the uptake where you're concerned. I don't know what my problem is."

"New territory?"

"You mean girls?" Parkie said. "Nah. Not new at all."

"I mean Black girls," Glory said.

Parkie smiled the dimple smile.

"You might think so. I couldn't possibly say," she said.

Unhelpful. Did it mean Parkie only dated Black women? Had never dated a Black woman? Or did it mean, as was most likely, she didn't want to talk about race? Good luck with that, Glory thought, nonetheless willing to leave it there for now.

"All right then. Okay," she half laughed. "To be determined."

"Totally happy to come up to Harlem," Parkie said. "There's nothing good near my place."

"Despite my scarily prescient college handle," Glory said. "I don't really know it that well anymore. I haven't been in the city long. Or in a long time, I guess. But there's a spot I think you might like. I'll send the particulars if you give me your number."

Glory produced her phone and started to hand it to Parkie, realizing at the last minute that Parkie's hands were full.

"Sorry," Glory said, accepting Parkie's instead. "I'm not big on schmoozing. The plan is to peace out of the dinner on the early side. I know it's a school night. But tomorrow is Friday, don't forget."

"I'm on a deadline, so it's all the same to me right now," Parkie said. "I'll probably stop by the office. Maybe grab something to eat at my desk first."

"That's grim," said Glory. "All work and no play, Parkerson. We can't have that."

Parkie let out a "hah."

And just as she did, her Lyft pulled up to the corner.

"I'll see you in Harlem then. Glorious," she said, closing the door before the car sped off into the night.

The timing was certainly right, Glory admitted as she walked back to the gallery. She'd stayed in LA when she knew she needed to be in New York—and now, one decimating breakup later, here she was. In the end, LA's parochial contemporary art scene hadn't done her any favors—though Glory received attention from a few Brooklyn dealers once she got work into a group show at Vander Vliet Newsom, the big-name Chelsea space a couple of blocks away. That was last fall with nothing since. She was in a much less fancy group show that had been up for a while. Nothing major, just two paintings in a Black-owned space downtown. But she had the feeling it could be a turning point. Being based in Harlem—going to as many shows as she could and meeting other artists and dealers—might finally be getting her seen the way she wanted. As an artist who happened to be a queer Black woman. As someone whose paintings were more than palatable abstraction or autobiography.

After Lucille went on to her reward, it hadn't taken much to get Glory to pack up her shit and U-Haul said shit to NYC. Back to the neighborhood she'd been born in. Where she would miraculously have a place of her own. A place she could not only work in but live in rent free. She was counting on the estate to keep her head above water while she got her life—and her career—going for real in Manhattan. Manya could help with that. And maybe Parkie de Groot could, too.

Chapter 6

When Parkie's Lyft pulled up to the address Glory had sent her for a place called Boulevard Bistro, she was flattered to see her waiting on the corner. She'd put on a frayed and faded denim jacket over the dark blue vintage cocktail dress Parkie had admired at the gallery. The V-neck bodice fit Glory like a glove, which meant she'd probably had it tailored, as Parkie did with her suits. It occurred to her she almost never wore dresses. Even with heels Glory was shorter and, judging from her calves, more muscular, too. Standing there with her Goyard bag over her shoulder and her legs primly crossed at the ankles, she looked like such a girly girl at first. But then, as soon as the car stopped and Glory could see it was Parkie, she bounded over to open the door in what Parkie chose to take as a polite rather than a disempowering gesture.

"So, tonight of all nights, looks like they're closed for a private event," Glory said once she'd given her a hand out of the Lyft. "A stag party or some nonsense. Which sucks because they have a great bartender."

"Plan B?"

"Undoubtedly," Glory said. She raised one eyebrow in an expression that struck an impressive balance between naughty and solicitous.

"Which is?" Parkie asked, pulling her coat a bit tighter.

"My place. It's about six blocks from here."

"Too far to walk for me tonight, but I'm fine with that."

"I figured we'd call another car if needed. It's a brownstone, and there are stairs to my studio on the first floor. Eleven to be exact. With a sturdy cast-iron railing."

"Did you know that number before tonight?" Parkie asked. This was definitely thoughtfulness. Even if there were ulterior motives. And she hoped there were ulterior motives.

"I did not," Glory said, getting her phone out. "But I like to be prepared for any and all eventualities. If the stairs are a no-go, I can easily find us another spot."

"I can do that many stairs as long as they're well lit."

"Right under a motion detector," said Glory. "Two minutes on the car."

Parkie de Groot, you are actually going home with someone beautiful and smart and accomplished, she squealed inwardly, feeling especially proud of herself for wearing matching lingerie that day. She honestly couldn't remember how long it had been.

*

Glory's brownstone was pretty spectacular. It was in no way renovated, but that allowed all the original details to stand out both singly and together—the way the architect had surely intended. Except for the painting studio part, it felt like stepping back in time. When Glory explained how long the house had been in their family, Parkie realized she hadn't quite grasped that Black people had owned big, fashionable houses in this part of the city for at least a century. Glory told her with obvious satisfaction that Harlem's Black population went from about 30 percent in

1920 to 70 percent in 1930 and that her family had bought the house in 1919, as one of the first African American families to worry the Italian and Jewish immigrants who lived in Harlem into moving somewhere else. "Proudly bringing you white flight until people started buying round-trip tickets," she'd said with a completely straight face.

"My family hasn't owned the same house for anywhere close to that long. But they definitely flew to the suburbs," Parkie said.

"Where you grew up, right?" Glory said. "How far back do your people go in New York? Or shouldn't I ask?"

"If you can believe my dad, he can trace the de Groots back to the New Amsterdam days. But I'd guess my grandparents moved to Greenwich, which, yes, is where I grew up, in the fifties. I don't think anyone knows where the original de Groots lived. Probably just as well. But your aunt must have been, well, for lack of a better word, rich. This place is a showstopper. Do you know who designed it?"

Glory looked around. "I'm sure it's in the files somewhere."

"But it's yours now?" Parkie asked. "The whole place?"

"For better or for worse," said Glory.

Partly because of the genealogical chitchat and partly because they were obviously both nervous, they hadn't made it out of the half-light of the frosted glass globe suspended from the entry's high ceiling. On the mahogany table between them, there was a crystal vase of fresh flowers—stalks of yellow gladiolas, pink roses, and white peonies dense as crinolines. With the door closed, it was nearly silent, except for the competing ticks of the clocks. Not knowing what else to do, Parkie snuck a look at Glory in the spotted mercury of the pier mirror. She looked like a model from a sixties magazine.

"How could there be a worse side to *this*?" Parkie said, her voice full of marvel. "It feels like walking into a Henry James novel."

"The one about the formerly enslaved women who owned a mansion?"

"Right," Parkie said.

There it was. She'd had a feeling Glory would find a way to get back to her comment about dating Black women. Parkie had no problem having that conversation. She just wanted them to get to know each other a little better first.

"Maybe more like walking into the house Edmonia Lewis would have bought here. If she hadn't been in Rome with the 'marmorean flock,' shaming the boring male sculptors. And creepy Hawthorne."

"Yeah, I like that much better," Glory said. The lines in her forehead deepened into what might have been regret for coming at her, though Parkie wasn't expecting an apology. "And props for knowing who Edmonia Lewis is. She's actually someone I want to make a painting about someday."

"I wrote a paper on her in college during my eminent queer-Victorians stage."

"You may know more about her than I do. That could come in handy."

"I'm a handy sort of girl," Parkie said.

At last, Glory slid open one of the giant paneled pocket doors that led to her studio/living room. Parkie followed, taking a seat on the worn green leather sofa as Glory switched on various lamps around the space. What struck her immediately, even in shadow, was the presence of three or four enormous rectangles of canvas tacked to thin wooden strips on the walls. Judging from her own height, Parkie figured most of them were at least seven feet tall. Thickly layered in patterned and printed paper, they were complex and tactile and, she thought, seemed to walk an interesting line between figuration and abstraction. On one canvas, she could easily make out the décollaged form of a woman's breasts and hips, but there was nothing more particular or personal than that. If it was a portrait, only Glory could say who the sitter was. The paintings—did Glory call them "paintings"—appeared to be in various stages of completion, though she knew enough not to say so.

"Try to ignore the art," Glory said, following her eyes. "Rule number one of visiting Glory's studio: we never talk about the art in Glory's studio. What are you drinking? I dare you to come up with something I don't have or can't make."

"Now I'm intimidated," Parkie said.

"Took you long enough."

Glory was standing at a vintage drinks trolley in the corner, shaking a tray of ice cubes into a metal bucket.

Underneath those coveralls she'd worn to Cuthbert's, Glory had the kind of figure Parkie would have died for when she was growing up—opposite hers in almost every way. Glory was maybe five five at the most, and her hips were slim and her breasts were high and perky and her ankles were tiny. At almost five ten, Parkie was just plain bigger on all fronts, but not in the places she'd ever wanted to be. Her own hips were broad to the point of making her less hourglass than pear-shaped, despite taking a D cup. And even before the accident and during sports, she'd never had the kind of muscle definition Glory had. Everywhere.

"It did take me a while," Parkie responded, making no attempt to disguise what she imagined her face revealed, "but I'm plenty intimidated now."

"Because you were making assumptions before, weren't you? And you thought I was some kind of, what, delusional low-rent player with champagne wishes and caviar dreams?"

"Oooh. Harsh," Parkie said. "Definitely not that. Or at least not any more than I think that about most of the people who come in on Wednesdays. Or any appraisal day when I'm in some church basement in Bronxville or Ridgewood. Most people have no idea what things are worth. That's quantitatively the truth."

"You can't put a price on sentimental value."

Glory speared three green olives with a toothpick and dropped them into her martini glass. "There. I've made my bed. Time for you to make yours."

"How about a boulevardier?"

Glory sniffed. "Not bad. I'm relieved. If you'd said a cosmopolitan, this date would be over before it started. Bourbon or rye?" Without turning fully around, she gave Parkie a quick smile over her shoulder.

She wants me to know she's in charge, Parkie thought, finding the notion amusing.

"Surprise me," she said, smiling to Glory's back. "So, you think this is a date?"

"It's something," Glory replied, twisting the cork off the Basil Hayden.

*

By the second round, they were postgaming the Chelsea opening, and in Glory's case, the aspirationally outrageous dinner that followed with Manya and her "old friends." As fate would have it, the same couple Glory tried to avoid in the gallery were the only other attendees of Manya's intimate gathering. From the way Glory recounted their practiced swinger moves, Parkie was almost sorry she had declined her invitation. She hadn't trusted Manya Shah not to call her out again in front of Glory, but it might have been worth it to see her A game.

"So then, who was graybeard? Manya's ex-husband or her ex-lover?" Parkie asked gleefully. Glory's deadpan delivery had kept her laughing for the length of the surreal dinner story, which involved embarrassingly on-the-nose song requests and way too much Cristal.

Parkie stretched out her legs. She was resting her face on the sofa's cushiony arm, the better to watch Glory, who was perched opposite her on a club chair that felt painfully far away. When Glory leaned forward for emphasis, Parkie could see her breasts settle into the cups of her bra. Now was probably the time to get romantic. But the mood wasn't quite right. They were still too giggly.

"Graybeard was the ex-husband. But they were both at the opening because the ex-husband married the ex-lover, who looked about twenty-five and was introduced to me as Lady something!" Glory said. "And they purposely sat themselves on either side of me at the restaurant with the DJ."

"Not okay!" said Parkie.

"Oh, it was definitely not okay."

Glory hitched up her dress and slid her legs out from under her, seemingly unbothered by the possibility of flashing her guest, who was certainly not bothered by it either. She reached for the empty water pitcher and swept into the kitchen, passing through what used to be the dining room but was now evidently just another storage space for her giant, unfinished canvases.

Glory continued with the story's epilogue from the sink. Parkie heard her twist out another tray of ice cubes as the water ran.

"She paid for everyone's dinner except the ex-husband's!" Glory said loudly. "Which was just awkward. Then, when I was trying to leave, they were talking about me 'heading out to the clubs' with them and things got even weirder. They say you can't alienate the collectors, but I was not going anywhere off campus with those two. I'm just hoping Manya was wasted enough to think everything went really well. Even without us all in a daisy chain right about now."

Glory turned off the water.

Parkie swung her legs around and sat up. Then she slipped out of her suit jacket, toed off her shoes, and stretched out again on the sofa.

"Come back here," she called in the direction of the kitchen.

The Joan Armatrading album they'd been listening to— Glory had a turntable and an enviable vinyl collection—had her in a good place. Open and patient. At this hour on a weeknight, her desires were modest. Nothing needed to go beyond the living room. A little kissing. *Maybe* a little fooling around. Then she'd go.

But while she had assumed Glory would use her home field advantage to make a first move of some kind, it was obvious by now she wasn't going to. Glory would be that kind of a bottom. Audacious but fundamentally passive. Even if all they were going to do was make out, it was go time. Parkie had an early start at work.

Glory walked back in, took one look at Parkie, and accidentally sloshed water over the sides of the pitcher. But then, she calmly refilled her glass as if Parkie wasn't suddenly less dressed, her see-through blouse revealing what she hoped Glory might want to see. Parkie pulled her knees in to make room at the end of the sofa, which seemed to surprise Glory—who needed a pat on the cushion to actually sit down. Parkie slid her feet into her lap.

"It's getting late," she said. "I should probably head home. Unless you want me to stick around for a little while."

Might as well put the ball in her court.

She made to get up but Glory started rubbing her ankle—the good ankle. It was a funny thing to do but it felt nice. Her touch, as she ran her small hand up Parkie's calf, was curious but gentle.

"I hope it's not *too* late," Glory said. "I shouldn't have gone on forever about the dinner." Now her hand was just inside Parkie's skirt, where she was tentatively running her thumb along her inner thigh. Parkie still had stockings on. But her panties, if Glory ever got that far, were already wet. Underneath the nylon, she was positively throbbing from all the hesitancy and waiting. And fuck did she want to change things up. To speed things up. With Glory on her back, Parkie could straddle her and unzip that tight dress. Go straight to her lips (Parkie liked a logical progression). Then she could peel back the bra and kiss her there, too. But it was never going to happen. Not with Glory's hand in a holding pattern between her knees.

"I'm making this awkward," Parkie said. Gallantly, she thought. She drew her knees back to get her feet on the floor and sit up. Regain control.

"No, it's definitely me," Glory said. "Out of practice, I guess."

Parkie thought not. But then, she couldn't get a read on Glory, who now seemed a little shut down. And from her sigh, frustrated. Mostly with herself for all the hemming and haw-ing, Parkie hoped. Too much rye and not enough necking. Let's bring that grandparental favorite back. Necking makes a hot date hotter.

As soon as she was upright again, Parkie reached for her shoes to signal that it was now or never. In apparent response, Glory scooched down on the sofa until they were thigh to thigh.

It seemed like the time for a do-over, so Parkie dropped her loafers and put her arm around Glory's waist and pulled her toward her until their lips were an inch apart. Glory closed her eyes and Parkie admired the glimmering turquoise shadow on her lids. But torquing her pelvis into that position sent a shooting pain down Parkie's leg. She had to shift away.

"Why is this so motherfucking hard?"

It was all Parkie could say and she'd raised her voice when she said it. This was sheer exasperation, especially for a controlling top. And it seemed so unnecessary when they'd been making eyes at each other all night.

Glory stood up. "Hold on," she said. Then she started hiking her dress over her hips as if she had the sudden urge to go skinny-dipping. Her blue thong perfectly matched the dress.

"Can I sit on your lap, or will I be too heavy?" she asked.

"You? Try me. I just want to kiss you."

She gingerly climbed astride Parkie, balancing on her knees at first. Parkie found herself level with Glory's breasts, close enough to press her face into her cleavage.

"Sit," Parkie said, settling for a quick kiss on Glory's chest. "It's okay."

She could feel Glory take the weight off her thighs as she settled more heavily onto her lap.

But they were both still wearing clothes. It was one of those terrible moments when the tension and the awkwardness, rather than progressing into breathless, wet-spot-on-the-sofa-level sex, merely stayed tense and awkward. Suddenly, Parkie was conscious of the strenuousness of their maneuvering and how it must seem even clumsier and less sexy to Glory. The magic was gone. And Parkie knew her slightly pissed expression gave it away.

But then Glory took Parkie's hot and bothered face in her hands and gave her the sweetest look. Like Parkie had baked her a layer cake or assembled her Ikea bed frame.

"You look way too mad to kiss me," Glory said.

"Wrong," Parkie pouted in response. "I'm just really tired now."

"I feel like I exhausted you. Which wasn't my intention."

Parkie groaned. "You didn't. It's not like that. Believe it or not, I do want to do this. But I have to be in really early tomorrow for a conference call with my boss, who's got a red-eye to catch, and if I don't sleep, I'm useless at the office. And I'm not thinking I'll sleep much if I stay. I don't even have my outfit for tomorrow picked out. And I have a client meeting."

If this race was to the finish, Parkie thought, she'd need an earlier start time.

Glory looked like she didn't want to look surprised. But she couldn't hide her disappointment. It showed in her knitted brow and the pursing of her red lipsticked lips. Parkie was disappointed, too. But sometimes you just have to call it a day.

"All work, Parkerson. I'm sensing a pattern," Glory said, followed by a good-natured laugh. "But I am actually too proud to beg."

She was on her knees again, evidently preparing to swing her leg over Parkie and get up. But Parkie surprised them both and pulled Glory back onto her lap. She gently brushed her hands back and forth over Glory's thighs, cold now with goose bumps, and she watched Glory watching her with wary eyes.

"In my defense, from what I can see, you're not exactly crushing work-life balance here in your . . . studio. I'd say we're both pretty into what we do."

"I was pretty into *you* just now," Glory said.

Then Parkie kissed her. And the thing was, Glory's lips were ready. Soft and giving and warm. Soon she was running her tongue over Parkie's teeth and biting her lip and they were lost in the kiss together as if it had been the easiest thing in the world. And Glory was panting and Parkie was bucking against the lace-covered pussy pressing down on her and they were getting a good grind on until it quickly became clear that if they didn't stop, somebody was going to come fully dressed, and that simultaneous realization caused their eyes to fly open, and they both had to laugh.

"Okay. I give," Parkie said, letting her head fall back but keeping her hands around Glory's waist. "But make no mistake. I'm going to hold your box hostage until I can see you again."

"Never gets old, does it?"

"It really doesn't," Parkie said. And she let Glory know with a swat to her ass that it was time to get off now and let her go home.

Chapter 7

The front door latched securely, and Glory watched through the glass as Parkie got into the car she'd called to make sure she got enough beauty rest. Sleep was the last thing Glory wanted to imagine.

What just happened?

And what didn't? Glory Hopkins lost her nerve was what. She wasn't exactly shocked that flirty, professional Parkie was a top—really more like a domme on good behavior, she suspected. But she couldn't believe she'd started something only Parkie could finish.

Because with her last girlfriend, Alicia, Glory was always in charge. Her household responsibilities—someone had to keep the lights on and buy laundry detergent (and do the laundry)—had devolved into oversight of all aspects of the relationship. Especially sex. Which was not what Glory signed up for when they'd started dating. In the beginning, Alicia exuded control. But in the end, all that bravura was merely sound and fury signifying the avoidance of responsibility. Who'd have guessed making actual love requires honest communication? Whereas, by the time Alicia left her (via text), they hadn't had a real conversation for weeks.

That whole last year, if Glory had wanted to get off, she had to spend half the night—or the week—rigging the outcome.

Laying the groundwork. Executing. And then Alicia would act as if she was doing Glory a favor, especially if the strap was involved.

How Glory thought she could manage Parkie from below was, in hindsight, a mystery. Parkie wasn't merely a woman who made it clear she got what she wanted. It felt like she had something to prove. Maybe to Glory. Maybe to herself.

She was funny and intelligent and she obviously liked sex. But Glory also suspected Parkie was the kind of WASP you tend to encounter in certain cultivated East Coast circles, interesting and emotionally complex but in predictably entitled ways. Arrogant women with tunnel vision who were effortlessly competent and secure, but only as long as things went as planned. She'd fallen under the spell of women like that at Penn. But Glory wasn't going to trip about that right now. She'd dated white women. And nobody in the family needed to know about Parkie. Lord.

They hadn't even slept together.

*

Morning came way too soon. Glory had stayed up fantasizing about future dates with Parkie much longer than she should have.

She splashed cold water on her face and brushed her teeth. Showering would have to wait because this trifling post-hookup afterglow, this can't-stop-imagining-Parkie's-head-thrown-back-in-ecstasy had to stop. It was time to get back in the studio.

Once she'd put on fresh coveralls, Glory brewed coffee and did a few yoga stretches. The light would be good in the front parlor for another three hours or so, and she needed to seize this fucking day. Seize it like Parkie had seized her ass with those strong hands. Goddamn, goddamn, goddamn. This wasn't like her.

Glory was smiling, sighing—and rolling her eyes at herself—as she set up her paints on the table. The unlikely canvas she felt like working on today was the one she'd caught Parkie sneaking peeks at. Frustrated with the shape it was taking, she'd hit a wall with it a few weeks ago and hadn't touched it since.

Hands on her hips, Glory took a moment to pull herself together. There was something going on with bodies in her work these days. That was new. In LA, when critics had written at all, they'd backhandedly praised Glory's work for its "respectful take" on mid-century modernism. For the seeming absence of narratives or history or figures—allowing beholders to simply appreciate "a visual meditation on form and color eschewing a message"—as one reviewer ignorantly put it. They always tried so hard not to see what they didn't want to. Because abstract or not, Glory Hopkins was a painter who was also a Black dyke, and that story, her story, was right there on the surface for anyone who knew where, or how, to look.

Lately, however, undeniably human forms seemed to want to make themselves known. Not surprisingly, they were women. Robust, life-size figures with ample breasts and plump bellies. Women with patterned skins unearthed beneath the layers of newsprint and glossy paper typically plastered on her canvases. It was like her flour-and-water glue had inadvertently generated viscera for these women, stabilizing contours that were jagged but delicate to the touch. She had to admit, it was a little like the old Michelangelo story—the bodies were in there, it was merely a question of freeing them.

Glory dropped her arms and walked into the living room to take down the canvas that had caught Parkie's eye. Holding the giant rectangle out stiffly in front of her, she carefully walked it sideways into the parlor and tacked it to the wall there, stepping back to consider what to do.

The smallest kernel of a plan for next steps had begun to form when her phone pinged.

She must well and truly be in another headspace this morning if she forgot to silence her phone the way she normally did.

It was the notification for a call not a text, but she let it go anyway. That much she owed her practice. Forget sex. It was time to be in the moment in her studio. Glory blew out a deep breath and stood up straight. She rested a palm on the cold, rugged surface of the painting, listening for what it might want from her. Without thinking too hard about it, which rarely helped, she tore off a patch of the colorful Godey's fashion print embedded in one corner.

All these years later, such tiny acts of iconoclasm—destroying someone else's art—filled her with both guilt-laced delight and adrenaline. The thin, colorful strip of antebellum paper spiraled to the floor like a cinder.

Her phone signaled a left message.

Parkie. That was the first thought that went through Glory's mind. It had to be her. Who else would be calling? If it were a family member or an emergency, the caller would keep at it until she picked up. While she was waiting to see if they did, Glory grabbed a thick tab of papier-mâchéd vintage wallpaper in the upper-left corner and dragged it down. The tear made a long, rough-edged diagonal divot straight across the "shoulder" of the form taking shape in the middle. She stepped back. The rip had stopped more or less mid-chest, where the heart would be. It felt like the first decent choice she'd made with the piece.

"Good," she said to herself. "You can do this."

Maybe hers didn't have to be one of those tediously tragic situations where any incursion on art—sex, love, affection, happiness—by life, calls for a choice between them. Maybe she could be distracted, very distracted, by her attraction to Parkie and still have creative ideas. It didn't have to be all drunken fights, abject silences, and sloppy, stressful fucking like it had been with Alicia. Although, she had to admit, that miserable existence had generated some solid paintings.

Glory walked over to her phone. Why not face the music? If Parkie had left her a message, hearing that voice—that hoarse, classy, sex-infused voice—might be the best thing to keep Glory's creative juices flowing.

It would get something flowing.

She clicked on a message with a Manhattan area code. Better not be Parkie canceling the Saturday date they'd agreed on. That jacked-up thought had only just entered her mind. She waited.

"Good morning, this is a message for Gloria Hopkins from Leo Wallford at Sarkisian midtown. I know this is unorthodox and I apologize in advance, but I'm about to leave for an extended trip to China late tomorrow and I find myself really wanting to do a studio visit with you before that. I very recently learned you're based in the city now. Is there any possible way we could connect in the next twenty-four hours? Again, if I weren't going to be out of pocket for close to a month, it could wait. But, things as they are, I don't think it can."

The man left some contact info and apologized again before signing off.

What was this life? What was this day?

Sarkisian's four galleries—the New York ones—were the anchor exhibition spaces of perhaps the most famous international art dealers in the world. The phrase "blue-chip gallery" had been coined for—and probably by—Sarkisian. A show there translated into almost immediate critical and economic success. It was a white-owned, majority white-run gallery but one with a growing list of BIPOC artists and gallerists.

Glory listened to the message again. A studio visit. From Sarkisian. There could be only one reason for it. She was being considered for representation. Considered enough for the director to pay her a visit in her studio sometime the next day.

It wasn't a booty call from Parkie. But it was the next best thing. Glory shook her head a few times and allowed herself an adolescent giggle that soon turned into a full-blown shriek.

*

A phone call later, Glory learned that Leo Wallford was willing to take a trip uptown pretty much whenever she could fit his visit in. He sounded older, maybe in his fifties. And he sounded straight if she'd had to guess. Like a guy with a sailboat and a vintage Mercedes and a wife who wore Valentino and lived solely on nuts. Businesslike. But gracious. She thought it best to have him at the house while the daylight was strongest. It would have to be early in the morning. Glory made the appointment for the next day at 8 a.m. Wallford would undoubtedly be flying business; he could sleep on the plane.

Between the time she scheduled the studio visit—a respectable forty-eight minutes after receiving the message—and tomorrow morning, there was a shitload of preparation, which, as her mother would say, was a polite term for it, to accomplish.

The apartment was clean enough; she'd never been the type to live in squalor. But she really ought to have more new work—or the appearance of new work—to show the guy. The more old stuff she pulled out, hanging smaller stretched canvases onto preexisting nails in the walls and setting the larger, heavier pieces directly on the floor, the more insecure she began to feel about her recent paintings, which now looked to her as if they'd been made by someone else.

The new work peeled back her own layers, or so they would say. It resembled the real world. It mimicked. It seemed. Sure, the old work was less original, but it kept its own counsel. It was restrained. Inscrutable. The old abstractions—if she was paying attention to the critics—were unproblematically meaningless.

Where there was nothing to identify and no story or sell-out social realism, Glory had thought there might also be safety. For white artists there was. In their reviews, they got "clean," "incandescent," "austerely lyrical," "cerebral," and "pure"—while her work was derided for being too much like what had come before. Essentially they'd accused her of aping the modernist canon. Even so. That was the work Sarkisian knew about. Showing them the new, more representational paintings wasn't a risk worth taking.

At times like these, Glory wished she had more friends. Disinterested friends. Regular friends. Friends who had the benefit of not being artists. She didn't have all that many who were, in fact. But the people she got closest to—mostly in LA—were all "creatives."

Of this set of artists/friends, there were a few people who didn't show in galleries much whom she could always call with bad news—gossip about MFA students who slept with their married professors or gallerists who'd been recorded saying something super offensive about their clients. Or lowlife dealers who scammed insurance companies—and their unwitting artists—by staging robberies from their own galleries. That one was something.

Bad news is always good currency. But it would be rude to randomly call a forty-year-old you sat through crits with and who currently works as a production assistant to ask for pro tips on dealing with a studio visit from the director of the gallery that routinely generated six- and seven-figure sales for "emerging" artists via a single museum-quality exhibition.

Which left Glory with the only friend-like, nonartist person she sometimes resorted to when she needed a reality check on another reality—such as the parallel universe that was the New York art world ecosystem.

Courtland. Her corporate banker brother-in-law was a refreshingly plain dealer, possibly, Glory thought, because he was handsome but not vain and seemed totally happy to be outshined by his obscenely glamorous wife. This was Glory's flawless sister. Grace was the undeclared childhood favorite who had sealed the deal by moving back to Denver after studying in New York and Oxford. Back in Colorado she had blossomed—with her own completed JD—into the rarified creature that was the Black, female party strategist, settling down with a big porch of her own within a few miles of their parents. The one good thing about that situation was Courtland, who had fast become the only member of Glory's family she semi-regularly talked to.

Glory dialed Court's number hoping, given the time difference, he would already be at his big banker's desk with the view of the mountains, guiltily washing down a square of high-calorie crumb cake with his customary quad Americano.

"Lost your passport? Transmission blown? Need a gumbo recipe stat?" Courtland said without a hint of drollery as soon as he picked up. "Because, you know, normally that's all I'm good for."

"Aw, don't be that way, baby," Glory cooed back. "And no. None of the above."

"Hey, Court, we're gonna let these gals play through," someone shouted on Courtland's end of the line.

"Thanks, bro. But I'll pick up," Court yelled back before resuming in his regular voice. "Then you must need a refi on that money pit. Rates are at an all-time low. Ask me how."

"No again. Are you seriously playing golf with your banker buddies? Could you be more of a cliché?"

Although Glory's mother had once described his jock side as nonexistent, Courtland was the best cook in the family. He'd honed his craft in Atlanta and everyone relied on him for food advice. But he was incredibly helpful in other ways, too, and always willing to step up for Glory. Grace didn't deserve him, in Glory's opinion, and he didn't deserve Grace.

Glory decided to let the "money pit" comment slide—it was only Courtland's way of reminding her that sour sibling was beyond consoling since she'd learned her little sister got a three-story house in New York City and she didn't get shit.

"I have a studio visit with an international gallery. Tomorrow," Glory said. "I do not want to sound like a child about the money part of things. I need you to tell me what questions to ask."

"Work," Courtland said. "So, Adam Warner or Sarkisian or . . ."

"You're even better than they say."

"If it can be merged or acquired, it's in my wheelhouse. And your art-dealer friends are right there beside me. But that's great, really. Congrats, Glo. You may not need that refi after all."

"You do know my house is paid off, right?"

Courtland laughed. "For now," he said. "But I'm serious, Gloria. You better shore up some savings for when something goes wrong with that place. Because mark my words, with a house that old, it will. You get yourself a decent girlfriend yet? Tick tock—and I don't mean TikTok."

"You don't even know what TikTok is. And you sound way too much like the enemy. Why a girlfriend? So she can pay to fix what hasn't broken yet? I hope you get kickbacks from all those insurance agencies you do business with. But I hear you, Dr. Doom. I did have a lovely white lady over recently, but it's way too soon to sound the alarm. Speaking of money pits, how's everybody in color-blind Colorado?"

"You go, Glo. Your radical interracial love affair is safe with me. I hope she treats you like the queen you are, though, unlike certain no-account women I know. This one needs to hold you up, not drag you down. And being a good earner wouldn't hurt. We're peachy keen out here. Grace has a confab with the Dems in Five Points tonight, so I'm gonna go play some poker in the suburbs. Let's see, your parents are, inevitably, your parents. They're fine. And it's still sunny here every damn day. You should visit, sis. If you get this deal, maybe you can finally turn a corner with my in-laws."

"They won't give a rat's ass about that or anything else I do unless you tell them to. And what if I don't get it?" Glory said. "Whether I sign with them or not, I am making a perfectly good living as an artist. No husband, or wife, needed. They can step the fuck off. They saw one show two years ago and they think anyone can do what I do. Glorified paper-shredding, Priscilla called it, if you'll recall. Which Dad found hilarious. I have nothing to say to either of them until they apologize."

"Okay, okay," Courtland said in his talk-you-down bass. "You don't have to tell me your work is legit. I'm on your side over here. A studio visit from Sarkisian is an achievement in itself. No doubt. Getting in with a gallery like that—a solvent gallery like that—could really put you on the map. But they aren't exactly the Peace Corps. Here's what you need to know."

Chapter 8

When Madeline was out of town, most Cuthbert's employees went home for the day approximately fifteen minutes after her executive assistant—who was also one of her spies. Tonight, everyone was gone by six, which left Parkie in charge. As if. But it did leave her with free range, a perk she had come to enjoy. With nobody to monitor her movements, Parkie usually made the glass-walled conference room, aka the lobster tank, her after-hours office. There was no phone in there, which was ludicrous, but the room was almost soundproof, which made it a good place to play music and hunker down with comps (she preferred to sift through actual bound catalogues with color photographs and results lists tucked in the back).

It was nearly eight o'clock when Parkie realized she'd forgotten to do the one thing she had her heart set on when she walked into the office that morning: find Glory's property. Her days often went that way at the auction house. Task lists and requests from higher-ups could easily get sidelined by a new estate in need of an emergency appraisal or an old estate that suddenly generated a new problem. The Flagg estate checked both boxes. While she and Armand and company had superhumanly met the first impossible deadline, other impossible ultimatums immediately followed. Flagg was the gift that kept on taking: one issue after another had come up with this freaking estate from the minute Parkie collapsed at her desk at 8:36 that morning, still wondering if not staying longer at Glory's was the right decision. After that, Flagg had sucked up her whole day.

Now, almost twelve hours later, fed and watered, she would normally be getting her second, much-needed, junior-specialist wind. But today, good Christ was she tired.

Only after she had enlisted Nicholas's help with the contents of an abandoned storage locker accidentally discovered in the basement of the Flaggs' co-op, and only after she had put out a PR fire about the late Mrs. Flagg owning a Rauschenberg painting with an endangered species glued onto its canvas (she did, but it didn't go to Cuthbert's), did the sickening realization dawn on Parkie that she hadn't (a) heard from Glory since she'd wrenched herself from her glorious sofa the previous night OR (b) taken the time to find the property she'd promised to evaluate before their date tomorrow.

But as Parkie usually had cause to remind herself at this point in the day, it wasn't over yet. Normally, working late wasn't so bad. Especially when it only meant researching a consignment or typing up overdue descriptions. On those nights she could order in and expense it. Sometimes, other people staying late even went out for beer or wine and they camped out together in the tank. Nor, in Parkie's case, was there a love interest to disappoint. She really didn't mind giving her best years to Cuthbert's as long as she got promoted in return. Preferably before the other junior specialists—none of whom, save maybe sometimes Nicholas, worked as hard or as long as she did. If anyone was keeping track of her hours, Parkie figured she had to be home free.

Only tonight had she made a rare tactical error.

Because tonight, working late wasn't yoking it up with an IPA and a burger. Tonight, working late meant taking a trip to the graveyard. After hours. Late on a Friday, when she'd likely be the only employee anywhere in the building.

And Parkie was dragging.

She knew she wouldn't make it long on so little sleep. Given the fitful night she'd had dreaming of what might have been, she might just as well have stayed at Glory's and made her own wishes come true. Her goal for tonight was to be at home in bed before the night-shift security guard showed up around ten.

What she really wanted was to go again. To say yes to taking off that blue dress so they could wake up wrapped around each other under Glory's sheets. It was extremely unlikely she'd go up to Harlem after work, but entertaining the possibility was getting Parkie through. Tired as she was, sleeping anywhere would be fine. As long as it wasn't on the eighth floor.

*

At 8:28 Parkie was still at her desk putting off going upstairs when a text pinged.

I'm thinking 67 Orange St. My hood again! Since you're taking me I thought I should get the ok.

A carnal tingle from last night shot through Parkie on seeing Glory's name. In her mind's eye she got a flash of the bashful, asymmetrical grin that felt like a victory each time it made an appearance.

Hi lovely! she typed, before backspacing over the last part.

Hi. And hah. I *have actually been to that place. It's great. Even better with you I'm sure.

Miss you already. Backspace, backspace, backspace. Easy there.

How was your day?

Glory was typing. But she too must have rethought her response, since the dots disappeared for a second.

All good. Really good.

Working now and may be offline for a while which is kind of how it goes when I'm putting work together for a show.

But I can't wait to see you again. Is 9 too late?

Fingers crossed it won't be too early, Parkie thought. She could use all the time she could get to find that damned carton.

Perf! See you there tomorrow at 9 ☺

xoxo

--xPdG

Seeing Glory again was worth a trip to the graveyard. If Parkie wanted to have something to tell Glory on their date—as she promised her she would—she needed to find that box. She grabbed her phone and, per custom, left a note she hoped wouldn't be her last on a Post-it stuck to her computer: "Friday 8:45 In cold storage."

*

Parkie had never been a particularly fearful person. Reckless was more her style. And although people at the time kept telling her recklessness had nothing to do with the hit-and-run that left her with a shattered pelvis, a junk drawer's worth of compression screws in her hip, and chronic pain, she had often chosen to frame it that way. After the accident, complete strangers were always asking what had happened to her, as if they, who had no clue about any other part of her life, had every right to know why she walked with a cane. After Wesleyan but before the gallery, when thinking of herself as disabled was new, she tended to answer the question with a joke: *What happened? So yeah. Basically, I went into the street one night to see if there was a car coming and, guess what? There was.*

A car speeding around a corner on a winter evening in the Village. A car coming from the wrong direction on a one-way street. Yes, she'd had a couple of beers. Yes, she was in a hurry. But no, she hadn't gotten a look at the vehicle heading straight for her at twenty miles over the limit. If Parkie had been oblivious, the driver was criminally so. But nobody had the right to bring it all back; she didn't give a shit that they were "just wondering."

Things had changed a lot since then, Parkie reminded herself as she rode alone to the abandoned eighth floor. With a lot of work, she had regained the boldness of her youth; little things that happened almost every day taught her not to back down from a fight or scare easily. Why should tonight be any different?

The thing was. With the sun good and down, it would probably be a little scary up there. The windows on the upper floors of their unkempt building were the thick, opaque, whitish ones with lattices of electrical wire running through them. As Armand had once confessed to her, however, the wires were no longer connected to an alarm, which made the security windows that much less secure. Natural light never had a chance on the eighth floor. No one would see you—or hear you—up here.

Parkie stepped off the elevator and quickly found the overhead switch before the doors closed. She fished the key out of her pocket, walked down to the third door on the left, and unlocked it. When she felt around for a light switch on the cold walls of that cell of a room, she found none. Which was bad because, that far away from the elevators, it was dark.

Breathe.

Phone.

Thankfully, a quick sweep with her flashlight revealed a rhizome of strings hanging from the oddly high ceiling of the small room. Because: a single ceiling light clearly ran the risk of compromising the graveyard's B-movie spookiness. Slicing her hand through the air in search of whatever lifeline she could find, Parkie yanked on the lights one after another until the room was more or less on view.

"What the entire actual . . ."

On the positive side, Parkie's previous trip to the graveyard had prepared her for what to expect. On the negative side, the room formerly known as cold storage, though clammy and cold, had nothing whatsoever to store. It was empty. Barren aside from a wall of rusty shelves. Nary a yawning box or partially popped sheet of bubble wrap in sight.

"FUUUUhhhCK!!" she shouted.

Wrong room?

She unclenched her fist. Someone had neatly written "#6 [cld stor]" on the little paper string tag attached to the key that had imprinted itself in her palm.

So no.

However wrong things looked, this was the right place. Or vice versa.

Further good news/bad news: No mouse-poopy mountains of boxes to go through meant no conceivable reason not to get the hell off that floor at her earliest convenience, to use one of her least favorite polite business expressions.

Back at her desk and out of breath, Parkie considered where this left her. In something like quicksand seemed accurate. It was past nine now. Obviously, she had about twenty-four hours to find Glory's lost property or a valid excuse for not finding it that wouldn't make a date number three about as unlikely as Armand's coming back from France at *his* earliest convenience—ideally, to take Flagg off her docket.

She had to get her hands on Glory's box. Parkie half smiled through a gaping yawn.

She would do that tomorrow.

Weekend or no, Parkie's eternally scaffolded, standard-issue courtyard building was deathly quiet. She felt guiltily glad Theodore, her favorite doorman, would be "back in five minutes," because even an abridged soccer update was more than she could handle tonight. She didn't get her mail, or drink a beer in her grandfather's tufted leather chair. She didn't even shower off the graveyard grime. She went directly to bed.

Another typical Friday night chez de Groot. Only this time she had pushed herself too hard. Given the hours the job demanded, it was always a danger. In this case the radiating pain told her she'd better be extra careful if she didn't want to put herself in the position of needing more assistance from Glory, especially during the sex she hoped they'd be having, than she was willing to ask for.

*

The next day, thank god, because you could never be sure how long it would take to recover, Parkie felt rested. Better. Ready, in fact, to get shit done. Starting with what her mother always recommended when she or Hendrik, her older brother, lost something: retrace your steps. Failing that, as her father would add, speaking from his juridical vantage: follow the chain of custody.

Thinking back to Walk-In Wednesday a little more than two weeks ago, Parkie was sure the box went first to Olive, who claimed to have kept it at her desk. After that it was supposedly picked up by either the cleaning crew or some other well-meaning employee, and presumably deposited in the now-empty grave-yard. At that point the trail ran cold. And although the last thing Parkie wanted on a Saturday morning was go back into the office to search for Glory's lost belongings, she was prepared to do so, as long as she had a better idea of where to look next.

It wasn't completely out of line to contact a coworker over the weekend—Madeline had no compunction about calling Parkie at any hour of the day or night; weekend emails from her were a given. Junior as Parkie was in the firm, though, it probably wasn't the best idea to do unto others. She wasn't anyone's supervisor as of yet.

Screw that, she thought, and fired off a text to Olive.

The question, given her reliable deceptiveness, was did Olive actually put the box somewhere near her desk or was she just saying she had?

I really don't remember.

& I so don't apprec. being txtd abt wrk on the wkend.

Parkie had responded with something *Sopranos* to the tune of, *Do you know what happens to people who lose clients' property before it's even been catalogued?* Generously peppering her threats with phrases like "massive insurance payout" and "mandated wage garnishments."

Fine.

Olive wrote, about thirty minutes after Parkie's last text:

I think it MIGHT have gone to Dr. Kenniston's office.

The venerable Eleanor Kenniston was Cuthbert's rare books and manuscripts specialist. She was known for finding valuable property in the most unanticipated places. Kenniston would have been interested in whatever was in that box only if she thought it was worth something. It might not be bad if Dr. K., as everyone called her, got involved in Glory's property—and it might even make sense for the obvious reason. But Glory was Parkie's client, and Parkie did not want to give her up to another, more senior specialist—never mind a department head—even if she personally didn't know a thing about rare books.

The intel from Olive was shockingly helpful. Dr. Kenniston was always generous with her knowledge. She was also widely observed to be a workaholic. If there was anyone from Cuthbert's Parkie could semi-safely disturb on a Saturday—who would either not mind or consider it appropriate—surely it was Kenniston. Parkie remembered she had her number from last year's holiday party, when the two of them were inexplicably charged with organizing the food for the reception.

"Come on, come on," Parkie said to herself, anxious to hear the brisk Barbadian accent of her proper, decades-older colleague.

"Is that Miss de Groot?"

"Yes, hi. Hello, Dr. Kenniston. Good morning."

"Good morning to you."

"I am so sorry to bother you on a Saturday. But I'm kind of in a conundrum with some property Olive seems to have mis-placed, and I wondered if you might know where it's gone to."

"Mis-placed. Miss de Groot?" said Dr. Kenniston, sounding a little too captivated by the consonance.

"Yes."

"Go on," she said. "Happy to help if I can." There was rus-tling and the muffled tinkle of ice cubes dropping into what was almost certainly a nonempty glass.

"Oh, thank you. I really appreciate it. So, a potential left a box with Olive about two weeks ago. There was some silver plate, some porcelain, and maybe a leather-bound scrapbook or two from what I hear. Does that sound familiar?"

"Let me tell you how it sounds, Miss de Groot," Kenniston said without a pause. "The scrapbook, as you call it, might be quite a find."

Parkie glanced at her watch. It wasn't quite eleven o'clock. Apparently, Dr. Kenniston was a day drinker. Parkie knew as well as any other watcher of *Antiques Roadshow* that a scrapbook of rarities might be worth more than a run-of-the-mill old master. It all depends on the scrapbook. And now that Parkie knew more about Lucille, anything seemed possible. But how long had Dr. Kenniston been on the case? And why hadn't anyone told Parkie?

"I see."

"Mind you, Miss de Groot, I haven't gone beyond the first third. But those early pages are what I would call encouraging. Someone slipped onionskin sheets between every sheet of that scrapbook. Onionskin with Italian watermarks. How appetizing it sounds. The interleaved pages point to a very exciting possibility."

"They do?" Parkie said.

"As I said."

"That's . . . fascinating, Dr. Kenniston. Would you care to elaborate?" Parkie wasn't expecting the circumspection, which led her to think whatever bread-crumb trail Dr. K. was following must be pretty promising.

"At this juncture, no, Miss de Groot. I will tell you only that of all the little-known and under-researched Harlem Renaissance authors—the women most of all—one or two names managed to find a place in the sun, so to speak. We know them from little things like the imported paper they used for their letters or the ink with which they filled their pens. If my instincts are correct, this writing relates to one of these women. I'll know more when I've read more."

"Understood," Parkie said. "Sooo," she continued tentatively. "You're thinking this is something historically significant? Literarily significant. Have I got that much right? Do you think the scrap—I mean, the papers, are worth something?"

"Do I think they're *worth* something?" Dr. Kenniston echoed. Her cadence was slow and her tone, as Parkie realized too late, was deeply offended.

"A lost manuscript from the Harlem Renaissance. Oh, Miss de Groot. Let me tell you, to many people, this scrapbook would be worth a very great deal indeed. All the more so if we had some notion of its provenance. But I don't suppose *you* can tell me anything about that."

"About the consignor, you mean?" Parkie said, taking a breath before answering the question.

Of course, she could tell Kenniston about the book's owner, presumably Lucille. But she'd be able to tell her even more after her second date with the owner's grandniece. Madeline was always saying their business was a team effort. But everyone knew the bonuses and the promotions—and the special-interest pieces in the *Journal*—went to the specialist who got there first. It was all about the discovery.

"No, Dr. Kenniston, I'm afraid I can't."

Parkie's lie made for an easy end to their conversation, after which, she suspected, Eleanor Kenniston would continue refilling her glass and sifting through the pages of the scrapbook—for the privilege of which Parkie guessed Eleanor had gone against Cuthbert's Holy Writ by removing consigned property from the premises. Her excitement about the discovery was evident. Who could blame her? A find of the sort she described might provide a fitting end to the woman's career.

As Armand told the story, Dr. Kenniston had been something of a prodigy as a girl, becoming the youngest literature professor at the University of the West Indies at Cave Hill. It was there she met her botanist husband. But after following her spouse to the States at the height of the culture wars, she had fallen into the auction house job through a series of unforeseen events including his sudden death and the failure of their adopted US institution to award her tenure. That meticulous, conservative Kenniston was too revolutionary for promotion during those years—if that was the reason—seemed hard to fathom. Her ways were outmoded even for Cuthbert's, if you asked some people. Armand, for one, had grudging respect for Dr. K. But as far as he was concerned, she was a prudish killjoy. The encyclopedic older woman at the end of the hall was not someone he deigned to work with if he could avoid it.

He called her "the headmistress" behind her back.

She also happened to be Cuthbert's only Black employee outside the shipping department. Kenniston was a former professor who frequently suffered the kinds of daily slights college students were now taught to recognize as microaggressions. "That older Black lady is so articulate," or something like it, was a phrase Parkie had heard from clients more than once. "You'd be articulate, too, with a doctorate in English literature," she'd once told a guy at a preview as Armand practically peed his pants.

For a tiny subculture of New York dealers and collectors, however, Kenniston was a god. She was pretty funny, once you got to know her. A fixture of rare book societies and literary salons across the city—she had become the doyenne of all things engraved, hand-colored, and penned with flourishes, especially in the eighteenth century.

Parkie imagined that getting the odd invitation from the NYPL must be nice for her. But former academic or no, like the rest of them, Kenniston wanted to make a career-defining move in the auction world. Why shouldn't she generate a cover story of her own? And before her retirement from Cuthbert's—which Madeline had recently announced would be shortly after Kenniston's sixty-fifth birthday, now less than six months away.

Parkie hadn't set out to lie to someone she respected—a woman who was also her direct superior. As soon as she learned more, she swore she would communicate it in full to Dr. K., knowing that, in the seeming absence of family in the States—work was probably all Dr. Kenniston had. These days, work was all Parkie had, too. But she wasn't going to let it stay that way.

Chapter 9

Dinner with Parkie was shaping up to be the best date Glory could remember. She told great stories and Glory liked the way their conversation had slid seamlessly back and forth from serious to silly to sexual over the course of the past couple of hours. They were nearly finished with dessert when Glory finally forced herself to bring up the appraisal.

She didn't want to break the spell. Kissing Parkie on the sofa, and dinner tonight, had left Glory feeling abnormally optimistic. Now that they were together again, she wanted to learn everything she could about the woman who was making her feel this way—Parkie's likes, her fears, her obsessions. The direction she liked the toilet paper roll to face.

Up to the moment the entrées had been cleared and the server had left the table, Glory had given herself permission to revel in all of Parkie's, well, everything. With her own ripped jeans, slingbacks, and vintage flowery Etro blouse—and the nervous narration she wouldn't be able to slow down if she tried—Glory was pedal to the metal on flirtation tonight and she didn't care if Parkie saw that. She was even wearing her horn-rimmed glasses, in hopes Parkie had a soft spot for reserved, rather bookish girls, which was how she had always thought of herself.

"I see you went for truth in advertising," she said, trailing her eyes over Parkie's notched lapels. "That's a great suit on you. Understatedly elegant but authoritative."

"*But* or *and*?" Parkie smiled. "Thank you. It's my favorite. I only wear it on special occasions."

"Wow. No pressure," Glory said.

"None," Parkie responded. "Tonight has already been very special."

A teenage expediter with a hint of a mustache arrived with their plates and promptly mixed up the order before leaving the check in front of Parkie.

"Now why would he assume I wanted the key lime pie?" Glory asked Parkie while the kid was still standing at the table. "Don't I just scream tiramisu?"

Glory made an exaggerated gesture of exchanging their plates and sliding the check her way.

"You do now," Parkie said with a raised eyebrow. "Did we just get racially profiled? In Harlem?"

"You just got the benefit of no doubt," Glory said. "And I admit, sometimes that gets to me. But where were we before I lost it a little?"

This was the catch, Glory was thinking. The one thing about Alicia, who was Dominican, was that these little incidents didn't need to be workshopped with her. Parkie seemed to get it. But of course, she'd never really *get it* get it.

"Something tells me he won't make that mistake again," Parkie said. Then she slid her fingertips across the table to Glory's, allowing them to touch.

When Glory looked up at her, she smiled a small smile. "So how are things at the brownstone? Did you have a nice day offline?"

"It was good," Glory said, realizing that Parkie had made things okay without saying a word—which was enough to remind her what else had happened that day. The call she'd screamed out loud about, causing Maisie to pinball off the living room furniture for a solid five minutes. Was it possible she had imagined the call? The call from out of nowhere, with the director of Sarkisian willing to work around his China trip to see what's good with Gloria Hopkins?!? Was that how dreams came true? You got tapped, set a meeting, and suddenly your life became reposted Polaroids by Hilton and picnics at Yaddo with Nona Faustine?

"I had some interest in my work—totally without warning—from someone who could be, let's just say, useful."

"Manya Shah has her finger on the pulse."

Damn. Glory had completely forgotten that Parkie was standing at her side when Manya made her also out-of-the-blue solo-show invitation. Early on at the awkward dinner after the opening at Moulton & Freer, Manya had seemed close to informally asking Glory to join the gallery. But she'd quickly become so occupied with the appetites of the insatiable Brits—or maybe she was just too busy sating her own—and nothing had come of it.

"I forgot you were there for that," Glory said. "I definitely respect what she's trying to do with M&F. But it's early days. We don't know each other yet. She might be blowing smoke up my . . . *arse*. Or trying to impress you."

"That, I seriously doubt," Parkie said, slipping effortlessly back to business. "I mean, if she takes over M&F, she could be the only woman of color to be a partner in a Chelsea gallery. Seems like she's here to shake things up in a meaningful way."

"Guess you did your research," Glory said. "I like her energy for sure. But she feels like a wild card to me. Women like that are always a handful."

It was an asinine thing to say to someone you're hoping will go home with you. These were, in fact, her feelings about Manya. But what the hell was wrong with her for sharing them with Parkie?

Three. Two. One.

"How so?" Parkie asked flatly. Her eyes went from so-into-you green to oh-no-you-didn't hazel in the time it took Glory to swallow.

"She strikes me as the volatile type was all I meant. Not: I'm the expert on hotheaded women."

"But you've seen one or two in your time," Parkie said. "What about me? Am I a handful?"

QED on that one, Glory thought.

"You. Are sooo much more than a handful in the best possible way?" she said.

"Are you *asking* me?" Parkie said before taking a long sip of her wine.

"No, daddy," Glory answered, fighting a smile. "But I do have a question. What's the word on the appraisal?"

Now the light in Parkie's eyes flickered off again. Or was it the change of subject that shifted the energy? Glory hadn't given her a reason to blush. It must have been something else.

"And we were having such a good time," Parkie said through a heavy sigh.

"That bad?"

"Merely inconclusive."

"Meaning?

Parkie took a bite of pie, obviously stalling. Glory, who'd had exactly two bites of her dessert, loaded her spoon with cocoa-dusted mascarpone.

"I had this for the first time in Venice," she said. "At Harry's Bar. They supposedly invented it. Every version I've had since has been better than the original. Including this one."

"Huh," said Parkie. "I knew it was Italian. I would have guessed it was maybe from Rome or Tuscany. But then I've never been north of Florence. I always go south."

"Is that so?" Glory filled her spoon again. She brought the creamy custard to her lips and finished about half of it.

"Taste this," she said, extending what was left on the spoon to Parkie.

Parkie leaned forward to let herself be fed.

"That's good," she said, licking her lips. "I do love to end the night with something sweet."

Glory opened her mouth in mock surprise at the innuendo.

"I see what you're doing, Parkerson," she said. "But we're not leaving this restaurant until you tell me what the deal is with my . . . property. I know you know something. And I think I've been very patient. What's so inconclusive that you couldn't tell me about it before tonight?"

Parkie took a breath. "At first we sort of lost the box. That, I can honestly admit, was Olive's fault."

"What did you just say to me?" Glory squinted. She didn't want to blow, but she was about to blow.

"But someone found it," Parkie jumped in. "Not me, though. For a hot minute, it seemed like it was sent up to storage on the abandoned eighth floor, which we call the graveyard because whatever goes up there never comes down. Only senior staff are supposed to have access but my old boss gave me his key. I keep it in my cube."

"Not helping, Parkie. Not helping at all. Is this a joke to you?"

"No, of course not. Sorry," Parkie said.

Glory decided in that moment that if Parkie didn't tell her the whole truth now, their next date might be never.

"What I'm saying is I actually went up there last night. To the graveyard. Which is not something I will happily repeat. And it wasn't there. So, this morning, I put the screws to Olive at home and she told me the box was intercepted by our specialist in rare books and manuscripts."

Glory didn't mask her impatience. Did they play hot potato with everyone's property at this place or only the Black people's? On some level Glory had supposed she'd be disappointed by Cuthbert's. Just not by Parkie. Especially now.

"*Intercepted*? Don't fuck with me, Parkie."

"Okay," Parkie said. She sat up straight enough for her suit jacket to cover up her cleavage again. "It's not that I don't want to tell you what I know. I'm just not sure what that is. Your silver and the porcelain—with this nightmare client I've got, I still haven't had a chance to look at it. Or have someone else look at it. They could be valuable. But the sleeper is your scrapbook."

"With the pictures? I knew it. I knew those people were famous. If you guys could figure out who they were. Because I have no idea. And neither does my family, who acts like Lucille was some kind of debauched side piece whose man done gone. Even when she was alive, I don't think my mom said Lucille's name once without making a dig. We'd ask her what she meant and she'd just shake her head and tell us it wasn't our concern.

But now that it suits them, they're telling people Lucille knew Langston Hughes and rented my apartment to Josephine Baker."

Parkie's eyes widened. "Did she?"

"Who knows? Honestly, I never got along with Lucille. I was a tomboy as a kid, and she came down hard on me for not being ladylike. 'Unpresentable' was her word. Which was funny since my mother thought that was what Lucille was. Priscilla and my sister are nothing if not presentable."

Glory couldn't remember any stories about famous tenants Lucille might have told the girls when, as children, they were occasionally summoned to one of her intimidating teas. Looking back now, she felt bad at how fiercely she'd resisted spending an afternoon with her prissy sister and the scary old woman in the big dark house with the music. She could hear the music in those memories. Lucille's floors vibrated with the lazy, lilting brass and bass of a big-band orchestra whenever they were there. A pricey Swedish turntable and speakers she must have purchased sometime in the eighties filled the rooms with an endless sequence of dance tunes. Songs with confusing titles like "Begin the Beguine." Singers whose old-time crooning went right along with the refined tinkle of a silver spoon in a translucent teacup. Judging from her closet of carefully ordered vinyl, Lucille had loved all kinds of music, but swing and jazz standards looked to have been her go-tos.

Glory remembered her little-girl self thinking how funny it was to hear a song about taking a train up to Harlem when you were already *in* Harlem.

She threw back the last of her martini. Glory hadn't meant to bring her family into it. Parkie regarded her with an anxious expression, as if trying to gauge the damage done.

"I'm not sentimental about history," Glory said. "To a gallery or a museum, that scrapbook is vernacular photography, right? If those snapshots could be in an archive somewhere or in someone's dissertation, I don't want them rotting in my attic. I don't think Lucille did either."

"I think maybe they could be. In an archive. Or, at least, our specialist does. Her name is Eleanor Kenniston. She'll sound British when you talk to her but she's from Barbados. She has a PhD in lit, and she knows about basically anything that's been published in English. She thinks what's in the scrapbook could be, I don't know, significant. Valuable even."

"She does?"

"Yeah."

Glory relaxed. "Well, that's a relief. For a minute I thought we were gonna have to part ways. But that's good news, right?"

Parkie looked her dead in the eye.

"It could be very good news. And it sounds terrible. Because it is terrible," Parkie said. "But I didn't want to tell you, because I don't want to lose you. As a client, I mean. New business is proprietary at Cuthbert's. I'm junior and I'm trying to make senior. I wanted you as my client even though I had no idea what you had. You saw, I didn't even think what you brought could be worth something. Which was shitty. And for which . . . I'm really sorry."

She gave a small nod as if to signal that she was finished speaking. Parkie was full of surprises. It's one thing to admit you'd almost lost someone's valuables. It's another to admit you tried to steal their business from a senior colleague.

"It was pretty shitty," Glory said. "But I appreciate that you told me. And why shouldn't I be yours—your, uh, client? If I sign with Cuthbert's, I'll request that you service the account—emphasis on *service*—problem solved."

"You would do that?"

"Why not? I mean, unless you don't think you can handle it."

Parkie bit the inside of her bottom lip and Glory watched her jaw tense.

After a few seconds she said: "Honestly, I'm not sure I can. I can't, actually. It's not my area. It shouldn't be me. Plus, I think Dr. K. needs this. It's funny. I've been trying to figure out how to make sure I have my cake—that's you—and eat it, too—that's being on your account—and I just this second realized there's no way I can do both. Which is fine. I'll ask Dr. K. to take over your estate and we can keep it simple. Business over there, pleasure over here. At your service. Just like Manya."

Glory savored her last bite. After a rocky last few miles, they had arrived at that critical post-dessert crossroads. The moment when, even without the Cuthbert's fiasco, she'd planned to explain to Parkie why tonight might not end where it seemed like it was headed. But that was before Parkie apologized. It was also before Glory watched Parkie walk into the restaurant that night. Before she'd watched her survey the tables until she caught Glory's eye, flashing her that broad, confident smile like there was nowhere she'd rather be.

Parkie looked hot. Parkie was hot. With her hair down and her blouse unbuttoned almost to her navel in what Glory now gathered was sort of her trademark, she was nothing if not drop-it-like-it's-hot hot.

More importantly, the woman had just fallen on her sword for Lucille's estate when, as she'd demonstrated more than once, her career was the most important thing in her life—something Glory had zero trouble relating to. All of it together was what made dating Parkie worth considering. What happens, Glory wondered, when two self-sufficient, work-obsessed women get together? Alicia was the opposite of Parkie. She'd been perfectly willing to live off the fruits of Glory's hustling and hard labor while doing next to nothing to get her own career off the ground.

"What's tomorrow like for you?" Parkie asked. Her jaw was relaxed again and she looked relieved. Was she going to be asked back to Glory's brownstone?

This was Parkie's implicit question. And goddamn, did Glory want to invite her. She could feel it between her legs and somewhere more cerebral, too. But tomorrow morning was the visit from Sarkisian. Not only could Glory not fuck that up, but she wasn't sure she wanted Parkie to know it was happening.

The more she thought about it, telling Parkie her good news could be a bad idea. From what she'd gleaned from their conversations, Glory was fairly sure Parkie had gotten her start at Sarkisian's Madison Avenue location. That *it* was the gallery Parkie referred to their first night as something like "the underworld corner store where sellouts get their wings."

For this alone, Glory couldn't have Parkie anywhere near the brownstone when Wallford showed up. And since it was the weekend, there would be no excuse for hustling her out of the apartment for work if she spent the night.

"To be honest," Glory began, hoping she would stay that way, "I've been thinking about sleeping with you since you sat down. After what you said about giving up my account so Lucille's estate would be in good hands—I really, really want you to come over so I can properly thank you for looking out for me. But I have a thing tomorrow early, and I need to bring my A-game for it in a way I just don't think I'll be able to if we fuck all night."

Parkie's eyes narrowed as a small smirk lifted the corners of her mouth.

"That's a bit presumptuous, don't you think?"

Glory reached across for her hand.

"I hope not. And I really hate to ask, but can we rain-check? Just for a day or so. I have got to get some work done this weekend, and I'm behind already and this thing tomorrow may put me more behind. When that happens, I'm the last person you want to be around, trust me."

"It's my fault," Parkie said. She had this adorable way of cocking her head before she spoke that made it seem as if she was about to reveal some great truth. "I've kept you out of the studio with all my lost-box nonsense."

"No, you haven't," Glory told her. "It's me. When I get into these production holes, I just need to make sure I hit some goals, and I'll be back to as normal as I get. If you give me a couple of days to get right with the world, I promise I will make it up to you."

"Sure," Parkie said. Her eyes suddenly looked shinier than they had mere seconds earlier. She turned abruptly toward the window and parted the metal shades with her manicured fingers, peering into the darkness.

"Venetian blinds," she said. "I wonder who invented these."

Chapter 10

There wasn't enough vanilla ice cream and root beer in the world to drown Parkie's sorrows. But she had plenty of both on hand, so she gave it a try. The root beer float was a de Groot—get it?—family tradition going back at least to Parkie's grandparents. A gallon or two of vanilla ice cream and a six-pack of organic soda were the only truly reliable constants in her refrigerator, and while she knew that was embarrassing, adding a second dessert to the night's transgressions was no more terrible than coming home alone. No worse than not getting to hit rewind with the woman whose kiss you had spent the day fantasizing about; who made you wet with a skeptical laugh and a frown.

Parkie was blushing in the privacy of her own home.

She both did and didn't want to blush over Glory. And she both did and didn't want to feel choked up like this. It was painful to feel vulnerable again. But the good kind of pain. The first few confusing weeks of seeing someone new were so pleasantly destabilizing. Parkie liked it when there was a valid excuse for losing her composure.

And Glory had her right there on the edge. Their goodbye at the restaurant came with a quick kiss but no specific plans to be in touch. Not even about Glory's property, which was Parkie's bad, since she'd altruistically, and as it now seemed, quite stupidly, taken herself off the account. And for what?

The *Sex and the City* episodes that offered solace in difficult times provided none tonight. And anyway, were there ever any Black characters on this show? Even gay old Cynthia never got anywhere. Why had she ever liked it?

Maybe Glory had texted her by now.

Between are-you-still-watching? and her first and second float, Parkie was so desperate for deliverance that she clicked on a message from an unfamiliar sender who was actually Nicholas, her Francophilic, slightly younger colleague at work. He never emailed her from his personal account. But tonight he was asking, preceded by needless apologies for writing (way) after business hours, if Parkie had made any headway with choosing the cover lot for the Flagg catalogue, about which she'd asked him a few days earlier. His job, per Madeline, was to vet whatever Parkie came up with. Ensuring, as previously demanded, that there were no obvious connections to the Flagg family's reprehensible drug—or slavery—monopolies.

It hadn't been easy to find a good candidate for the cover photograph, especially from items in the estate dating from either the beginning or the end of the family's history. But Parkie had eventually decided on an enameled lady's watch by Van Cleef & Arpels inscribed "AF from KvM." From what she could tell, the watch had been given to one of the daughters of the *Titanic* victims sometime in the 1930s when the Flagg girl in question traveled to meet poor but aristocratic suitors in London. It all reminded Parkie of an episode of *Downton Abbey*, and if her mind went there, hopefully, so would their nostalgia-drunk bidders. The relatively undistinguished keepsake they'd found at the bottom of one of Mrs. Flagg's jewelry boxes would be presented as a costly and enduring token of a transatlantic prewar love affair.

People can't get enough of that stuff.

The watch was historical yet modest in scale and seemed innocent of blood-money origins whether Caribbean or pharmaceutical. Nicholas's email was asking if Parkie knew if Madeline had signed off on it, which would mean he could start expanding his catalogue entry and writing up any additional copy for the press kit.

As both a lark and a means of waiting out her indigestion, Parkie responded to his message at nearly one in the morning. Almost immediately, to her astonishment, Nicholas wrote back with several questions.

It's Friday night! What is ***wrong with us? she appended to the last part of her detailed response, to which Nicholas wrote back, *Switching to text to answer that one.*

A few seconds later, Parkie received a series of lengthy bubbles on her phone:

Marx-loving graphic-designer boyfriend called me "pathetically obsessed with my pretentious proud boy dead end job" before letting me "discover" him cheating with a Tinder guy. Bf left because I have no life and now I have no bf either. Not sure what I think will happen at Cutthroat's if I keep working like this. It's not as if I'm on the fast track to head of department. Or even senior specialist :#

Sorry about bf! His loss, no question, Parkie texted back. *Similar for me. Went on date with potential client, then gave client to Dr. K to avoid conflict of interest. Then date pretty much ghosted me. In person. Because: work stuff! Thought sexytime was a sure thing. Also thought nobody worked more than us.*

Domage! Nicholas wrote. *And, wow, I'd say that blows but . . . schadenfreude, anyone? Sounds like you did the right thing, tho? Can you ghostbust him on another pretext? Need to "finalize transfer of account," etc.?*

Dude. She's a she. Have we met?

Srsly? Hadn't the foggiest. Now I really want it to work. Maybe SHE has real, actual stuff to do. Maybe SHE's got a pathological—or economic—need to succeed? Can't imagine what that would be like :0

Parkie had to take a second to respond to that one.

Maybe. She does work a lot.

The reply from Nicholas was instant.

She may not be ghosting you at all. And you'll never know if you don't try—as my grandma used to say right up until I tried kissing boys in high school. We can't end up mean and bitter and wrinkled like Madeline. Or Armand. Or Dr. K. (Actually, Dr. K is more wrinkle-free than permanent press, have you noticed?) Somebody has to find their forever home. Report back on Monday! I'm going to bed!

*

When Parkie awoke on a bright, cold Saturday morning, it was almost noon. As always, she reached for her phone as it lay charging on the painted antique chest that also served as a nightstand in her tiny bedroom. There was an email from her mother about Christmas and New Year's—would she or wouldn't she be joining her and Daddy and her brother and his fiancée in Florida? There was also a message from her first college roommate, who was getting married in Belize next summer. And something from a woman she played soccer with and sort of dated, who was having a baby again. And then there was one from Madeline: Did Parkie arrange a time to shoot the watch with the photographer, and was that kid who did the French stuff working on the copy with Comms? And if he wasn't, tell him he should be.

But nothing from Glory. Not even the "sorry again I couldn't sleep with you when I really wanted to" text she'd been holding out for.

Parkie stretched. The generalized stomach upset was still present. And it wasn't from too much lactose.

No, this was the sickening sensation of having fucked up. She'd obviously mishandled things with Glory more than she thought; she shouldn't have been such a baby about the early start when they were on the couch. And maybe she shouldn't have confessed to all the misdeeds at work. Because the woman who couldn't get enough of her only a few nights ago had been perfectly happy to send Parkie home alone after their second date. Without so much as an "I'll text you tomorrow" or "Let's try for Monday."

What comes around, Parkie thought.

She hadn't been ditched for a while. In fact, Parkie was typically the bad guy. La Dumper not la dumpee. For at least a year now, nobody was worth her time. Or her emotional energy. It didn't help that where dating was concerned, she'd become as wary as a spooked horse. An apt simile if there ever was one.

For the origin of that wariness, as Parkie knew, was her relatively long-term entanglement with Loden Bradley. That relationship, her last real one, had conveniently gone to shit, like a cheap appliance under warranty, around month thirteen.

They'd met at an opening at Parkie's old gallery. It was exhilarating in the beginning. Loden FedExing her tickets to Aspen or pulling up in her restored Wagoneer to whisk Parkie away without warning for a weekend on Fire Island. They were rarely on their own, though. Loden's equally established fortysomething finance friends were always in the background. Loden had boundless energy. She was athletic. Sophisticated. The blue-eyed, shot-swilling, poker-playing, snowboarding devil-may-care sexy older sister everyone wanted to sleep with.

And Loden, as would be revealed, was good with that. She had a very hard time saying no.

Until she broke up with Parkie. Over the phone. At the precise hour Parkie was packing for their belated first anniversary trip to Saint Kitts. "We can't do this anymore, Parks. You're sweet and so pretty," she had said. "But I'm bored. Nobody who's with you should be bored."

That call had sent Parkie into a spiral of self-loathing that resulted in a general swearing off of women. She'd given Loden too much control. Being that passive had even bored Parkie, truth be told, especially during sex. Which was the only thing they both enjoyed doing together, most of the time. In the beginning Parkie had relished being the nubile May to Loden's seasoned December. But by the end she had started to see Loden and her shallow, blissfully ignorant friends as immature, at times cruel—and frozen in their twenties in ways she hoped never to be. Wannabe millennials. Perish the thought.

Glory was unlike any of the women Parkie had been with. And not for the reasons Glory seemed to suspect. Parkie had dated pretty widely across race and ethnicity, even in prep school, where the girls were effectively brainwashed with multicultural twaddle about all being the same "underneath" as long as they stayed thin and personable and feminine enough. She guessed she could have told Glory this, but she hadn't wanted to seem like she was trying to score points. There was also the fact that Parkie had never moved beyond the hookup stage with any member of her rainbow coalition.

She had to remind herself that being with Glory made her— or would make her—part of an interracial couple. It was different for her than it was for Glory. Parkie knew that. And while it was premature to be talking about being together—her whiteness and Glory's Blackness had already come up.

Glory was openly bitter about being dropped into a homogenously white world when her parents had moved their family to Colorado. That experience didn't make her comfortable in all, or nearly all, white spaces now. But she wasn't always comfortable in Harlem either. Glory seemed to be amused by Parkie's curiosity about certain (to her) unfamiliar aspects of Glory's everyday life. Her affinities, her assumptions—her beauty regimen. In fact, Glory's often difficult upbringing in a place that sounded a lot like Greenwich had probably rendered Parkie's questions that much less surprising—maybe no less annoying either.

It was funny—not comical but unaccountable—that after so many college seminars grounded in gender, race, and class, the adult Parkie felt a little unprepared for seriously dating a woman who wasn't white. Learning about someone's experience isn't living it. She knew that, too. Maybe the reality was that she felt more willing to hear about Glory's life than Glory was to hear about hers, which had its downside, too. So far, she'd tried to follow Glory's lead.

And look where that had gotten her.

Parkie was on the point of caving—scrolling through Instagram was merely a pretense for having her phone in her hand—when, just as she was about to do something she'd promised herself she wouldn't, Glory texted her.

I didn't sleep :(Did you?

Not where I wanted to, Parkie wrote back. *But I have an idea.*

Chapter 11

Glory loved the tranquility of her South Harlem street, all the more so on a Saturday afternoon when the neighborhood was still waking up. Sometimes she painted for hours while listening to music—Jessye Norman or MJQ or Bach. But today she'd been working steadily in silence since dawn.

At first, she didn't give any thought to the sound of a car screeching away from the curb outside. Then something, who could know what, made her put down her brushes, wipe the wet paint off her hands, and walk into the foyer.

Through the sheers gathered across the front door's narrow windows, she caught a blaze of color at the bottom of the stairs. She immediately recognized the tall, shapely figure and its sharp movements. Glory grimaced at her giddy expression in the mirror.

"Parkie," she said aloud. "What are you about to do to me?"

She watched through the glass for a moment as Parkie set down some of what she'd been carrying on the stoop and prepared to come up. Glory swung open the door, ran down the steps, and grabbed the bags.

"Oh, yay," Parkie said, beaming. "You *are* home."

"You could have called first," Glory said, relieving her of an armful of flowers and inhaling their heady scent as she scaled back to the top.

"I thought you might not pick up," Parkie said. "Or you'd tell me not to come if you did."

"Did you bring food?" Glory asked with faux seriousness.

"Korean barbecue. Which I hope you like. I figured maybe you hadn't eaten anything real since our dinner."

"It smells terrific. And I haven't. Eaten, I mean."

Glory stopped to wait at the top of the stairs. Normally, the last thing she would want was an interruption of these, her daylight working hours. But all she could feel as she stood in her doorway was the excitement of watching Parkie get closer.

"Welcome back," Glory said.

Once they were inside, she led the way into the kitchen and Parkie followed.

"Just give me a few minutes," she said as Parkie hovered near a chair.

"You're working." Parkie looked like the possibility had just occurred to her. "Of course, you're working. I should let you work."

Glory rolled her eyes in response and deposited the bags along the tiled counter.

"Have a seat," she said. "Be right back."

There was a trumpet-shaped green glass vase Glory remembered Lucille using for roses and she suddenly felt compelled to find it. The big crystal vessel in the entry had served its purpose since long before Glory's time. Moving it might disturb some celestial harmony. The vase Glory had in her memory was something she'd seen on one of the side tables when she was a kid. It was simple but she liked the fan of flowers it produced. She found it upstairs, all the way in the back of one of the high cabinets in Lucille's kitchen.

Once back in her own kitchen, Glory filled the vase with warm sugar water, as she'd been taught, and started snipping off the ends of the rose stems at an angle. They were long but not the thornless and overbred commercial kind. The large petals of these flowers were supple and peachy yellow with a bleed of dark pink along each edge. They had the look of the old hybrids her mother cultivated in Denver. Glory thought they might be Peace roses, and they smelled as divinely complex as a sachet.

"That's a very pretty vase," Parkie said.

"Don't bother trying to make it something it isn't," Glory answered. "I like it no matter what."

Parkie lowered her head and looked up at Glory through her eyelashes like a remorseful puppy. "I meant it. I like it, too," she said. "Are you hungry? Everything's still pretty warm."

"I could definitely eat," Glory said. "This always happens. I don't feel hungry until I remember how long it's been since I had food. Then I can hardly stand up."

"I know the feeling," Parkie said.

Glory finished assembling the roses in the vase. "Was that bad?" she asked. "I mean, was it ableist to say that?"

"Some people would probably think so," Parkie said. "Not being able to stand from self-inflicted hunger is a little different from not being able to stand from a congenital condition or an injury. Didn't bother me personally. Not like 'crippling.' Or 'lame.' I reliably go off on that."

"Like if someone said 'Torpedoing an otherwise perfect second date is so lame'?"

"Exactly," Parkie said. "Torpedoing an otherwise perfect second date is pathetic, whereas technically, I *am* lame. But that doesn't make me pathetic."

"Me, on the other hand . . ." Glory said. She had started opening the takeout cartons one by one to see what was inside. "Bibimbap! I love this."

The downstairs kitchen hadn't had an update in probably fifty years. Surely the height of fashion when it was done up in yellow and gray, the rental apartment's dark and defenestrated kitchen had always depressed Glory. She remembered playing spy games under the big table as kids—hiding their faces against the cold metal legs until Lucille got wind of it and shouted them out.

But now, with Parkie in it, the dreary room suddenly seemed warmer and brighter—even the wan overhead fixture and the old refrigerator struggling in the background almost felt cozy. And Glory thought Parkie was different there, too, without her armor of couture and stockings and chunky gold jewelry and long, shiny shoes. She wasn't softer, exactly, just more relaxed in the way she held herself.

Her cheeks glowed from the climb up the front stairs and Glory could picture her as an athlete. She always seemed so ready. Game for whatever. Glory watched Parkie's eyes flicker across the room, presumably attempting to take in whatever traces of Lucille she could find.

She piled their rice and egg and sprouts on two large plates and they ate in pleasurable silence.

"Look at these roses," Glory said, setting her chopsticks on her plate after a few minutes. "When I go through the park, I can't walk past the roses without stopping to smell them. Cliché or not. And these are perfect. Long-stemmed no less. Like you." She leaned toward the vase. "Thank you, Parkie. I don't deserve them, as you've rightly pointed out."

Parkie raised an eyebrow. "I love roses, too. Maybe we can go to the park together sometime. We both live so close to it."

"Your park is not my park, though," Glory said.

"I like your end better. You've got salsa dancing at the Meer, which I find much more interesting than CrossFitting at the reservoir."

"The Meer. You must feel right at home."

"If you ain't Dutch, you ain't much," said Parkie, finishing her rice. "My grandfather used to say that. And not in an ironic way."

"I didn't know *meer* meant 'lake' until I overheard some guide telling a bunch of tourists about the 'legacies of New Amsterdam' a couple of months ago when I was walking home. It's obvious now, but growing up I never thought of Harlem as having anything to do with Europe. And definitely not Dutch people. Did they tell you there was slavery in the North in school?"

Parkie shook her head.

"Me neither," Glory said. "I mean, there were only ever like two other Black girls in my grade, anyway. We didn't want to rock the slave ship."

"I took an intro history class freshman year called Imagining Colonial America. It wasn't until about the last week we got to imagine the Lenape Indians. Most of us never knew 'Manhattan' was an Indigenous word. I just had to inform Madeline that the Flagg family—this terrible consignor of mine—made their money selling enslaved people just to get her to put the brakes on a press release about their awesome entrepreneurship as eighteenth-century rum dealers."

"Jesus. Good for you," Glory said, refilling her plate.

"I love this place," Parkie said, looking at the food containers. "And it's conveniently close to my sad little cave. I'm there like once a week."

"For the record—and before you make any more polite conversation—I'm glad you came over. I wasn't kidding about being distracted by you. I was just trying to find a way to . . . manage that, I guess."

Parkie had on tight yoga pants and a concealing hoodie. Her hair was in a loose braid and she wore just a hint of mascara and lip gloss. Glory watched her throat contract as she downed half a glass of water. The woman even made swallowing sexy.

"I get it. I'm just not used to being . . . rebuffed," Parkie said. Her glass made a loud rap when she set it down on the laminate. "However distracting you might have found me, I was really looking forward to fucking you and instead I had to go home alone and eat all the ice cream in my freezer."

"That sounds like a close second."

Parkie looked up from her plate. "It wasn't."

Glory felt her cheeks warming.

"I should have been the one coming to your place with flowers and dinner. Now I'm down by two. What can I do to make amends?"

"I almost lost your aunt's property, so I'd say we're even," Parkie said. "Anyway, I hope your big morning went well with me safely out of range."

This was her opening to tell Parkie about Sarkisian. She knew this. But Glory couldn't get herself to kill the vibe.

"It was fine," she said. "I got a chance to show some new work, which I think went over well. And I learned at least two people, counting me, have seen my group show downtown."

"Make that three," Parkie said.

She couldn't believe it.

"*You* saw the show?"

"Why wouldn't I? It's not like I expect to rate a studio visit. I really, really like the new work, Glory. I was moved by it, if you really want to know. I think the figures—if that's what they are . . . Those textures. So beautiful. Painful. Visceral. All the things. I had a moment with them for sure. The guy at the desk didn't know what to do with me."

"I can't believe you saw the show," Glory said. The first few words came out so dry she had to start over. "Thank you. I'm not sure yet about this new direction, though. And you don't have much to compare it with."

"There is a thing called the internet," Parkie said with a laugh. "I looked at your past reviews, Hyperallergic, Culture Type, the usual. Besides, you forget I was in the business. I'm pretty surprised my old bosses didn't have you on their to-exploit list. Not that they don't routinely miss some very obviously amazing people. Lucky you, as far as that goes."

Here was another chance to speak now.

"You are the sweetest," was all Glory said. She wasn't trying to disturb Parkie's enjoyment—or her own—of the moment with a decision that was sure to annoy her. "It means a lot. It's just so hard to know what you need to do to get where you want to be sometimes. When I wasn't showing, I just made the art I wanted to make. Now whether or not I want to be, I'm influenced by the dealers and the critics and the market. Sometimes I'm in the middle of making work and I have to stop and ask myself, Is this you? Are you making something you have to make? Something you can't not make? It's like I have to step outside myself to see what's in there. And even then I can't always be trusted. I could really use a good dealer."

"Maybe. Sometimes they just get in the way, though," Parkie said. "I don't know how people stay creative under those pressures. Nobody talked about that kind of thing at my old job—shock, surprise. I think some of their artists were perfectly happy to cater, or try to cater, to what the market wanted. It's not the same in the auction business—we *are* the market, at least part of it. But sometimes I wonder how far is too far, too."

"Yeah, but then you do the right thing," Glory said. "Like last night. I mean, you said it—if there's something valuable in that scrapbook, having me as a client would be good for you. You know it, and now I know it, but you gave that up anyway. Basically, you're my hero. It's pretty fucking valiant."

"Let's not get carried away," Parkie said in her work voice. "When you think about it, I have a fiduciary responsibility to the auction house, too. If your aunt's estate isn't handled by an expert who'll get the word out to the best buyers, we make less money. How do you know I'm not just looking out for Madeline's bottom line?"

Glory finessed her last mound of carrots with her chopsticks.

"Because I've seen *your* bottom line," she said. "And it's fucking superb in those yoga pants."

Parkie groaned but couldn't hide a smile. "As soon as I get in, I'm going to make an appointment for you with Dr. K."

"But you'll come too, right?"

"I mean, I could join, I guess. If you want me to. And if she doesn't mind."

"I do want you to," Glory said. "Know what else I want?"

Parkie's eyebrows shot up.

"For you to strip down to the lace I know you're wearing under that Lululemon performance of giving no fucks—so we can continue what we started on the couch."

*

But instead of going back to the living room, they stumbled out of the kitchen in the other direction—to Glory's bedroom, where, after making out for maybe one minute, Glory hopped around on one foot trying to get out of her coveralls while Parkie laughed at her from the bed as she calmly removed her own clothes. It felt different this time. Coming up to Harlem and bringing Glory flowers—and going to see her show—had to be a declaration of intent beyond a couple of unconsummated two-night stands, didn't it?

Despite their missed connections, previously prudent Parkie had gone ahead and put herself out there, which had to be a good sign. It was true Glory felt like there was something almost transactional about Parkie's courtship style, as if she knew what it would take to close her. And, as of now, had done just that.

Parkie was thoughtful and she paid close attention. But she didn't seem the type to bare her soul. Of course, the reticence of a beautiful woman only made Glory want to work harder. It was a tired old script but one she'd had trouble rewriting. The truly hard thing would have been telling Parkie about Sarkisian so that the first sex they had would be honest. Instead, avoider of relationship conflict that she was, Glory took the easy way out. The easy way that would inevitably become the hard way if things kept going well between them.

Parkie looked up from the edge of the bed, arms behind her, breasts thrust forward like a dare. Her pale belly—which showed the remnants of definition, but was not so defined anymore—was framed, as predicted, by a sheer white lace bra and matching panties. Standing in the corner in her underwear, Glory felt frozen. What she wanted was to go over there, drop to her knees, and bury her face in the ginger-freckled softness of Parkie's skin. When she involuntarily licked her lips, Parkie just chortled a little and flipped back the covers.

The afternoon light that made it downstairs was at its strongest. Though the room was dappled with white patches of sun, it could have been dawn just as well as dusk. Aside from a blue-and-gray Chinese rug whose twin was in Lucille's bedroom, two metal bookshelves, and the Mexican door-as-table she'd moved from LA, the space was empty. It was private and peaceful and exactly how Glory wanted it to be.

"You're the one unsettling me right now." Parkie laughed. "With all your shyness and sweet talk. Get over here."

"Parkie, I . . ." Glory started. When she came within reach, Parkie pulled her in and Glory rested her hands on her shoulders. But Parkie just took them off again and kissed her fingers, frowning.

"No more talking. Get into bed."

Was there something newly present in Parkie's teasing eyes? Or maybe newly absent?

Whatever it was, combined with her horny impatience, made Glory want to put anything she was tripping on on ice. Given time and the whole picture, Parkie might even understand about Sarkisian—she had to know that as an artist sometimes you only had one shot. You can't miss your shot.

But all that would have to wait until later.

Here and now, she had Parkie de Groot in her bed.

The second Glory got under the covers, she was pushing into Parkie's warmth and the supple, muscular body that seemed to radiate something like bliss or contentment. Her hips, that soft stomach. Immediately, she had to kiss Parkie's breasts, which were stacked on each other as she lay on her side. They were heavy and firm and speckled like the rest of her, and Glory found herself licking, then biting, then fiercely sucking until Parkie cried out—more surprised than hurt, Glory thought, since she also told her not to stop.

"I want to go down on you," Glory said.

"I want you to," Parkie said, though she put her tongue in Glory's mouth again as soon as she said it, simultaneously slipping off her panties.

Glory broke away and kissed a path down Parkie's stomach, momentarily detouring back up and kicking off the two heavy quilts, which now felt maddeningly unnecessary.

She didn't want to go too slow—but when her roving lips found a different texture of skin near Parkie's right hip, Glory lifted her mouth, unsure what to do. These were her scars. She had seen them partially when Parkie was sitting on the bed, but she hadn't known where they stopped and started. And she'd forgotten to ask if she should—she didn't even know what. How had she not asked?

"You okay?" Parkie said.

"So okay," Glory said. She put her lips back on the shuddering skin of Parkie's inner thigh, and Parkie responded by spreading her legs a little wider. She had started to make low encouraging sounds after each kiss. And she was also very wet.

Glory didn't want to be weird about it either way—to seem like she was ignoring the scars or only paying attention to them. She decided to do what she wanted to do, hoping she'd be able to sense if things were off.

Meanwhile, Parkie, who seemed to be getting impatient again, was pushing herself up on her elbows, as if to survey Glory's progress.

"How about I move down to the foot of the bed," she said. "If you don't mind being on the floor. It won't take long, I promise."

Had Glory ever before known what to do next?

She rolled onto her side, carefully avoiding Parkie's legs, and shimmied back up the bed.

"I'm not in a hurry," she said.

Parkie's broad smile seemed genuine, even a little out-of-it and dreamy. But she also looked like she needed to get off—and wasn't entirely sure this was going to happen anytime soon.

Things were beginning to resemble their previous nights together, when Glory had needed to just fucking make something happen, but hadn't. This time, she was not going down without a fight.

"I know I'm doing it again. But I really fucking want you, Parkie," she said.

"Put a pillow on the floor and take me then," Parkie said. "I won't break. I want you there."

By the time Glory grabbed a sham, Parkie was sitting on the edge, knees defiantly together.

Glory teasingly pried them apart and went back to work. This time, she rubbed Parkie's inner thighs until she relaxed, keeping her gaze on her pussy the whole time, which was almost unbearably arousing and seemed to get Parkie back in the mood, judging from the little thrusts she was making.

Her encouraging noises resumed.

Parkie wasn't shaved, as Glory assumed she would be, and her pretty auburn curls were fine and inviting. But her skin was cool—probably as much from the chill in the room as the pace of play. When Glory finally got to nuzzling her, Parkie clapped her legs against her cheeks and started to whine and goad her with intermittent "yesses." Glory kept her mouth closed—she practically had to—and breathed Parkie in until she let go enough for Glory's tongue to dart in and out of her entrance a few times. She tasted like the ocean, almost briny, and Glory wanted to drink her in. After tonguing her clit, she shook her whole face against

Parkie, vibrating words she knew she couldn't hear until Parkie gripped the sheets and moaned. And moaned. And moaned.

After, they slid back under the quilts and Glory laid her face on Parkie's chest.

"I'm glad you live alone," Parkie said, rubbing Glory's shoulder.

"I'm glad I live alone, too. I could listen to you do that all day. But nobody else deserves to."

"Not for free anyway," Parkie said.

Chapter 12

Parkie was pissed. She'd done everything within her power to be planted at her desk—prepared to duck immediately into the back stairwell for a quick make-out session—when Glory came in for her meeting with Dr. K. It had been two nights and three days since they'd been together, and Parkie had given Glory explicit instructions for finding her personal cubicle among the hive of identical white-walled desks designated for the junior specialists. She wanted so badly to see her today, and ideally to have lunch.

Then she'd gotten a call.

And a rather bewildering one at that.

"Miss de Groot," said the sonorous contralto. "Manya Shah at Moulton, Freer & Shah. We met briefly, if you'll recall. You didn't know who Glory Hopkins was and I was a bit jet-lagged and I believe we had what you Yanks call a communication breakdown."

It took Parkie a second, but only a second, to place the caller and the night of which she spoke. The night she had taken Glory out after the gallery opening to introduce her to a pair of oversexed collectors with whom she had previously been in relationships, plural. *That* Manya Shah.

"Yes, Miss Shah, how nice to speak," Parkie said, going full Kensington. "How may I be of service?"

"Yes, pray how?" the voice tutted sarcastically. "Only, I've just sold some rather excellent paintings to a client who wants to deaccession a number of much sleepier things in their vault—sort of so-so French Impressionists, nothing the least bit stirring. Late Renoir and other disasters. And I thought, p'raps hit reset. I knew you probably wanted to talk about Cuthbert's Contemporary and I was pretty beastly about it all the same."

"No, no," said Parkie. "It was my fault. I had no business coming unprepared. I was in the middle of handling a very large estate—the Flagg sale coming up in a couple of weeks is mine—and I made the mistake of trying to stop by before I knew . . . anything, really. Which is embarrassing, since what we're best at at Cuthbert's is handling clients. I would hate for you to get the wrong impression based on our first, truly unrepresentative inter-action. But anyway, it's good of you to think of us for your client's needs. I'd love to meet with them. We have an Impressionist and Modern sale coming up in March."

"You," said Manya Shah. "To be clear, I was thinking of *you*. Come and have a drink with me tonight. We'll discuss further."

Danger.

Danger, danger, danger.

"I so wish I could," Parkie told her, the soul of equanim-ity. "But I have something tonight." Yeah, she thought inwardly, a date with knowing better. Personally, the smart move would be to very subtly aim Manya Shah in the direction of another specialist. Just make herself unavailable. Professionally, however, this was business, and you never knew where a connection like this might lead down the line.

"Or now," Shah fired back. "Come and have lunch in an hour. I'll have my assistant tell you where. Until soon, Miss de Groot."

About fifteen minutes later, someone named Martin called back from the gallery with the name of an Italian restaurant in Chelsea and the time of their reservation. Parkie had planned to try to get Glory to go to the French bistro down the street. But there was no chance of that happening now.

*

Lunch was at a little place with black awnings and picture windows. Exactly the kind of deceptively casual spot where even those walking by have an unobstructed view of who is dining with whom.

Like a queen among her courtiers, Manya Shah was seated at a round banquette, surely the restaurant's most desirable table. Parkie wondered how she'd managed to rate, for a weekday lunch, in so short a time. But then again, as Shah rose to greet her with a both-cheeks air kiss, she imagined it hadn't been all that hard to start making a name for herself in New York. Shah was young enough to be counted a striking beauty and experienced enough to be taken seriously in business. And then there was not only the accent, but the words that came with it.

"You're looking sexy for a Tuesday," was how Manya Shah chose to greet her.

Parkie was not unaccustomed to compliments on her appearance. But while she generally brushed them off from men, she was sometimes brought up short when another woman said something brazenly flattering. Surely this was flirtation. And that was no way to do business.

P'raps clients were related to differently in London.

Feeling herself pink up, she went with the reliably benign but gracious "You're very kind."

"So you've said," Shah replied. "Is that American for 'thanks but piss off'?"

"I don't know about American. I think maybe it's New Yorker for 'What am I supposed to say to that at a business lunch?'"

"Mmm, I see. Because even if you thought I, too, looked sexy, you couldn't say so because of the Protestant work ethic or *The Scarlet Letter* or whathaveyou."

"Something like that."

"I knew this would be a very instructive meal," Shah said. "As recompense I've ordered a prohibitively expensive bottle of wine. The Weberian in you won't say no to that, will she?"

No sooner had Parkie assented than a server appeared from the wings to fill her balloon glass with tasty-smelling, garnet-colored red, a luscious balance of tannin and fruit that made you want to kick off your shoes and sit on the floor, starting with the first sip.

Between the drinking, ordering, and eating that followed, Manya Shah made a series of rapid-fire mostly off-color overtures, which Parkie duly deflected by way of heavy-handed changes of subject and feigned obliviousness. Once their salads and small plates of pea and potato gnocchi and carpaccio arrived, Shah had effectively conceded, skillfully worn down by Parkie's seemingly endless supply of non sequiturs. There was then a cease-fire for the entrées, when conversation was conducted on the neutral ground of Italian cities and museums—Shah being a fan of Genoa and Milan and Parkie preferring Tuscany, but eager, she said, to see Venice.

Over panna cotta, Parkie delivered her official Cuthbert's pitch. They then moved on to the fine print of standard contracts and desirable contacts and how their two outfits might be of economic use to each other. Comfortable in the realm of commerce, Parkie finally began to relax a little.

It was then that Manya Shah went in for the kill.

"You're single then?"

Parkie had to smile. If only to acknowledge that she'd been hooked, lined, and sinkered by the best.

"I'm not, actually."

"Married, engaged, exclusive, periodically bored, long-distance relationship? Give me some sense of what I'm working with. I rise to a challenge."

"Not married. Not engaged . . ." Parkie stopped. She and Glory certainly hadn't talked about seeing—or not seeing—other people. But exclusivity was, no question, what Parkie wanted. The very thought of Glory with another woman made her ears burn and her stomach ache, something she wouldn't have predicted until her body started to do those very things as she sat there.

"Definitely exclusive," she said firmly. "Your persistence is flattering. Very. And yet I'm off the market. New blood, though. Word travels fast. I can't believe you're not already inundated with offers from New York's finest."

"I'm bi, so 'inundated' is an understatement where the offers are concerned," said Manya Shah. "But well done, you. I hardly noticed when you made this about my dating proclivities rather than your own sex life, which I trust is sufficiently exceptional to merit monogamy at your tender age."

"You are just bad," Parkie said.

"Only one way to find out," said Manya Shah.

*

Hours later! Back at the office, things were whirring along at a speed for which Parkie was definitely no longer equipped. At lunch, the first two bottles were followed by a smaller one of golden apricotty Vernaccia di Serrapetrona—Parkie had ordered a plate of rustic hazelnut biscotti to go with it—and she now found herself weaving through the cube hive with no real sense of what to do next or how to do it. It was only when she landed at her desk, dropped her walking stick with a loud clank into the umbrella stand, and lowered herself less than gracefully into her chair that Parkie realized she was inebriated.

Being drunk at work wasn't a problem, in the sense that Madeline, for all her inhumane and occasionally illegal workplace practices, was always all about the client. Had Parkie called her up to announce she'd just spent the afternoon in a steam room with the new principle of MFS, her boss would probably have suggested Parkie move the next phase of the talks to a suite at the Pierre, on Cuthbert's dime.

In fact, Madeline seemed to have derived the main points of her business plan from soap operas and early Bond films. She was Parkie's parents' age, possibly a little younger. But her way of running the firm bore an uncomfortable resemblance to the first season of *Mad Men*. At Cuthbert's, showing the client a borderline felonious "good time" was deemed an acceptable means of winning business. As long as you won it.

Wining and dining to the point of passing out? No harm, no foul, as long as they signed.

What felt less okay to Parkie was that she knew she'd forgotten something important she needed to do but she couldn't remember what it was. Lunch had lasted until midafternoon, stretching almost to the cocktail hour. Now it was late. Practically the end of the day.

And which catalogues had she promised to send to Manya?

Midway through formulating an answer, Parkie became aware that beneath her desk her legs were stretching her slim skirt to its limits as they bowed lasciviously open. She looked around to make sure nobody was looking, which of course they weren't.

But why had she agreed to lunch, again?

Right. Yes. To secure a consignment of mediocre paintings toward future dealings with a new dealer. She had agreed to lunch with the intractable Manya Shah in order to get a leg up—that is, in order to get a lead—on the sale of some bad Impressionist art.

And she had positively answered in the negative when relentless Manya Shah asked her out yet again as she helped Parkie into the gallery's own chauffeured Mercedes for her courtesy ride back to work.

Hadn't she?

There was a postcard on Parkie's desk. It was the promotional mailing for the group show Glory was in—and the gallery had chosen a detail of one of her paintings. She'd never imagined that the lunch would go so long. Despite earlier assurances, she'd gotten Glory to agree to meeting Dr. K. without her, which she felt would let them get to know each other. She had also made Kenniston aware of her willingness to sign Glory over to her as a client. But Parkie was sure she'd be back before Glory had left the building—even if they wouldn't be able to go to the bistro, Parkie planned on seeing her.

She hadn't checked in with Glory that morning—and Glory hadn't contacted her either. Already in this early stage of whatever they were doing, Parkie had learned that Glory wasn't the most consistent communicator. Not in the immediately responsive, pick-up-your-phone-while-on-the-toilet way most of her former friends were. Glory was a few years older than Parkie, it was true. But most thirtysomethings she knew were no less symbiotically attached to their phones than their younger siblings.

Not so Gloria Hopkins. Glory posted merely sporadically. She was not always on the grid. She texted when she felt like texting. And she answered, it seemed, only when she felt the time was right.

But those communiques, too, were few and often frustratingly far between—even in the midst of a conversation, she would sometimes drop out for ten or fifteen minutes, leaving Parkie staring at the screen in anticipation of a simple yes or no.

Neither did Glory call much.

Which Parkie didn't do so often herself. But so far she was finding it difficult, by which she meant unendurable—especially when they had just spent the night together—not to hear anything from Glory until the next day.

Theoretically it was leveling up to go from wondering if they'd see each other again to dying to know at a given, irrational moment whether Glory felt about her the way she felt about Glory. But as far as she could tell, the only reward for her advancement was more irrationally anxious moments.

The fact that they had kissed each other goodbye on Glory's doorstep didn't reassure Parkie when she woke up all by herself days later. By then she could easily let her mind trick her into believing the whole thing had been a lucid dream. That Glory had never said, "I can't wait to see you again, P," as she tipped Parkie's chin down to her for one more toothpasty kiss. That she hadn't stood there looking mildly indecent in her striped washable-silk robe as the sun rose, waving after Parkie's Lyft—while inside, Parkie sat in the back seat happy-crying because Glory had informed her she, too, would be counting the hours until they were together again. On a morning like that, Parkie'd partaken in whatever kind of Danish she could get her hands on—feeling hungry for anything and everything, barely able to concentrate on whatever she needed to catch up on. Barely caring about whatever deadline she'd been chasing the night before.

Glory hadn't texted since the night before, when they both stayed up later than they should have flirting with each other and coming close to sexting but not quite going there, which made things more suspenseful in a way—as foreplay for another time.

Today, Parkie knew Glory would be excited to meet Dr. Kenniston.

She had way too much on her hands with Flagg, anyway— the sale catalogues had been mailed this week, and the preview was being mapped out downstairs even as she sat there at her desk wondering what to do with the next hour. She couldn't go home. A premature departure was more likely to be noticed than someone downing Alka-Seltzer at their desk.

She hadn't allowed herself more than a glance through the new catalogue, a glossy copy of which sat beckoning on her desk.

Her catalogue. The one with the understatedly elegant ladies' pocket watch on the cover.

The first Cuthbert's catalogue listing Parkie de Groot as the contact for the sale. No, no, they couldn't take that away from her. She considered giving the thing, which was about as thick as *Vogue*'s fall book, the once-over. But to skim it now, even soused, was to invite the sudden appearance of typos and misprints. It always happened that way, no matter how hard the staff proofed the galleys. A missed accent or a mixed-up caption or wrongly labeled illustration—worse still, the wrong estimate, especially if it was too high. There would be errors. There always were. And someone was bound to bring Parkie's mistakes to her attention soon enough.

Chapter 13

Never say never, Glory was thinking as she walked down the hallway to which she hadn't gained access on her first visit to Cuthbert's. After the appraisal day, she'd vowed not to return. But that was before things got going with one of the firm's star employees. The meeting had seemed so important when Parkie explained who this Dr. Kenniston was. But now Glory found herself hoping it wouldn't take too long. She was there for Lucille, but she was also there for Parkie.

When she knocked at the slightly ajar door, a chipper, rather birdlike voice simply called out: "Come."

Eleanor Kenniston's office was exactly what you'd expect from an expert in rare books. Not only was it wall-to-wall and floor-to-ceiling with shelves; it was appealingly messy, with a small table and four chairs at one end and a little stand with a steaming electric kettle at the other. The herbal scent of tea hung in the air—and something spicy, too. Ginger, Glory thought.

There were books in every direction, Books encased in cellophane or brown-paper dust jackets; books bound in blue or stamped with gold on buttery red calfskin; new books that seemed to be about old books. And stacks and stacks of auction catalogues, mostly from other houses, from what Glory could quickly ascertain.

In the middle of this nest of reading material, which Glory found strangely comforting, even familiar, sat a striking woman. She was long waisted, slender, and upright, with a bob of soft white curls framing her deep-set gray eyes and brown face. Her features were serious in their resting state. She looked pensive but also kind.

Glory entered the room dressed not in painters' coveralls but in her most conservative dress, a patterned Alice + Olivia she'd found at Bergdorf's one flush and hopeful afternoon. Kenniston looked up at her brightly and smiled, making Glory feel instantly at home. She couldn't believe this was the same place of business where she'd been passed over by the little brat at reception, who hadn't seemed to recognize her today. That was weeks ago. Glory's world felt completely upside down—maybe even downside up—now.

"Good morning. I'm Glory. Gloria Hopkins, here for an eleven o'clock."

"I see that," said Dr. Kenniston, indicating the empty seat at the table.

She had to be in her mid-sixties from what Parkie had said. It wasn't that Glory didn't believe it. Though smooth, her face was slightly drawn in a manner that suggested the endurance of a not-always-easy life. While she knew other women that age with a similar bearing, Glory had to admit none were as flat-out lovely as Dr. Kenniston.

She sat down.

"Tea?" Kenniston asked. "I've just brewed some for myself."

"Oh, I'm fine, thanks. And thank you for seeing me. Parkie—Miss de Groot—tells me you've made some discoveries about my scrapbook?"

"Miss de Groot. Well. So you do know each other? I wasn't altogether sure. At first, she seemed a little unclear about the manuscript's origins. But it belonged to your great-aunt Lucille, is that correct?"

In an attempt to give a thorough answer, Glory provided a condensed version of Lucille's biography, stopping to answer Kenniston's questions several times along the way. She already seemed to know things that Glory might have imagined were true but that had never been verified, either before or since Lucille's death, by anyone in the family.

Kenniston had determined, for example, that Lucille formed friendships before the war with people like Helene Johnson and Ariel Holloway, youthful upstarts at the time, who would have been about ten years her senior. There were photographs of these and other women in the scrapbook. Women not well known today beyond scholarly circles. But during Lucille's teens and twenties, as poets, playwrights, and musicians, they would have been local celebrities—even beyond Harlem.

As they were talking, Dr. Kenniston retrieved the scrapbook from what might have been a small safe behind her desk, opening it on the table. She slipped her finger about halfway in and flipped back the pages. Glory was surprised to see two gossamer-thin sheets of paper covered in dense script floating over the book's thicker black pages.

"Does this writing look familiar?" Kenniston asked calmly.

Glory peered down at the tight, almost calligraphic penmanship on the page. She thought about the card she'd received from Lucille—and the notes and letters she'd recently rifled through in the attic.

"Nope. It isn't Lucille's writing, that's for sure."

The sparkle in Kenniston's eyes seemed to briefly intensify.

"No," she said. "I thought not."

Glory moved closer to the transparent page.

"Doesn't look like a letter," she said. "Too many quotes."

Instead of answering, Kenniston carefully turned the page to reveal another filmy sheet adhering to the other side.

"These handwritten sheets are interspersed between the heavier, you might say, protective, scrapbook pages. Hidden, I would go so far to claim. The static holds them in place. It's rather ingenious. As you can see, the writing is minute and it's taking me some time to get through it. But if the number of pages is any guide, there should be about one hundred sheets. Roughly the length of a novella, in other words."

"And that's . . . something?" Glory said.

"It could be," said Kenniston. "Of course, it all depends on who wrote it. It might be the most luminous and original prose in the world, but unless I can attribute it to a well-known literary figure, it's of little value. To the market anyway."

"Any leads?"

"I wish I could say with certainty," Kenniston said. "It's too soon. But there is what we might view as circumstantial evidence. There's the setting, for one: a Lower East Side hospital near the end of the war. World War II."

"What does that tell you?"

"Assuming it's fiction, nothing," Kenniston said. "Unless, of course, there are obvious autobiographical elements in the story— which was often the case for Harlem Renaissance writers. It may be the case for all writers. And then there are the house parties."

"House parties?"

"Whist parties. Rent parties. Lots of characters in one scene, some fairly recognizable, I think."

"They still have rent parties in Harlem, you know," Glory said. "Next time I hear of one, I'll invite you. They're usually worth the trip."

"I might take you up on that. I can't imagine I'd have to go far."

"Do you live in Harlem, Dr. Kenniston?"

"Since spring of 1987. I'm in Graham Court. Do you know it?"

In fact, she did. But only by reputation. Through a story she'd read in the *Harlem Times* about the fiftieth anniversary of a neighbors' association in an exclusive, Gilded Age apartment building—whose tenants included Black actors, publicists, musicians, and designers, as well as a growing number of Clinton-inspired white people of means. Some people said it was the Dakota of Harlem; other people said the Dakota was the Graham Court of the Upper West Side.

"I do," Glory said. "But I've never been inside. My house is only a few blocks away—I walk past your place all the time. We're both not far from the Studio Museum."

"I can see the crockets of St. John the Divine from my bedroom window. You'll have to come over. You and Miss de Groot would be very welcome. It might be more conducive to this detective work to be more social about it. Only seems appropriate somehow."

*

Disappointingly, and really, infuriatingly, Parkie was out on an appraisal by the time Glory left Dr. Kenniston's office, information Olive seemed a bit too eager to deliver. On being told, Glory rooted around in her bag for a stray business card—she could never manage to keep them in one place. Instead, she found a postcard from the show. She took out a pen and wrote, "Sorry I missed you," with a quickly sketched rose on the back. She handed the card to Olive and asked her if she'd make sure Parkie got it when she came in.

Olive looked down at the image on the card. She seemed frustrated that it revealed so little about the woman standing before her whom she might have seen before, though she couldn't recall where. She agreed to do what was requested of her. But Glory had her suspicions.

Dr. Kenniston—Eleanor, as she'd insisted—gave Glory homework. She'd written down ten or so names on a sheet torn from her datebook and asked if Glory would take a look through the letters and books and whatever else she could find of her aunt's things, for evidence that Lucille had possible connections with any of the women on the list.

Glory was feeling energized from their meeting. She could tell that Dr. Kenniston—Eleanor—already had a theory about the manuscript. When she talked about this or that poet or journalist, it was as if she had read their work or known them as friends. Glory hadn't done the math, but she was thinking now that some of the women, even the ones older than Lucille, could still have been living in Harlem around the time Eleanor moved there.

Maybe she really had known them.

After all, the age gap between Eleanor and Glory was not much bigger than the one between Lucille and Eleanor would have been.

With this new knowledge of Lucille's social circle, walking into the brownstone gave her a feeling of pride; a greater sense, if not of ownership, than of belonging. As soon as she shut the door behind her, Glory slipped out of her constraining silk dress and into coveralls. But rather than going back into the parlor that currently served as her preferred workspace, she ran up the stairs to Lucille's apartment.

Opening the door—silently greeted by the scent of perfume not unpleasantly mingled with the lingering aromas of home-cooked meals—was always the hardest part.

Glory stood in the middle of Lucille's living room, allowing her eyes to alight where they wanted to. It was funny how much more feeling, how much more affection, she had for her aunt now that she was gone. Being with her things, living in her house, Glory felt connected in a way she never had when Lucille was still grudgingly willing to make an appearance at family gatherings all those years ago, sticking to herself in a corner, waving off an invitation to play cards or watch a movie. She must have been so lonely, Glory thought suddenly. All those years without anyone to share this with.

She glanced from the writing desk to the wing chair to the fireplace mantel, with its collection of crystal paperweights and silver candlesticks and colorful enameled boxes, when something soft brushed against her shins. Glory jumped a good three inches off the floor. But it was only Maisie the cat, who had somehow pushed her way through the pocket doors downstairs, understandably eager to return to her former home. Maisie sprung onto the little chair at the desk and promptly drew herself into a ball, nesting her nose in her tail and closing her eyes as if she'd been sleeping there all day.

Glory had a sudden vision of Lucille at that desk, sitting and writing letters when the girls were first brought in by their father. Of her aunt not stopping to greet them until she was finished with whatever she was doing. Today, for the first time, Glory felt she'd been given permission to see what was inside those mysterious desk drawers. Permission from one Dr. Eleanor Kenniston, in the form of an assignment, in fact.

When she pulled out the chair, Maisie gave her what she decided was a feline look of approval before jumping down to free up the seat. The cat wandered a few feet away to Lucille's big chair and assumed the same position there.

Glory placed her fingertips on the desk's cool surface. Something told her she should start at the bottom. When she opened the lowest drawer, the room filled with the fragrance of tea roses. Unlike harder surfaces, paper, as Glory knew better than most, has the ability to hold on to scent long after it's been applied, years later, even decades. This girl never gets sick of roses, Glory thought, riffing on a line from a Gwendolyn Brooks poem that sprang to mind. In this case, the source of the scent was a cache of fat stamped and addressed envelopes tied up with crisscrosses of thin navy blue ribbon into bundles of maybe five or six letters each. It was a deep drawer and Glory figured it had to be holding at least a dozen of these bundles. The handwriting on the top ones, those she could see, wasn't the same for each bundle, though all the envelopes seemed to be either to or from Lucille. There was something uncomfortable about reading another person's letters. Or ought to be. If a word like "voyeur" existed for reading, it would fit the act perfectly.

From the moment Glory untied the first ribbon and removed the first scented, cream-colored sheet from its envelope, she felt she was trespassing. Invading someone's sacred and much-treasured privacy. Eleanor must know the sensation well, she assured herself, as the page she'd removed and unfolded attempted to return itself, clamlike, to its formerly closed-mouthed state.

She picked up the letter, glancing again at the envelope.

The return address on the back was faded and difficult to read, but the envelope was postmarked Des Moines. Glory took a deep breath and slipped her finger under the flap, wondering if Lucille had ever imagined that anyone who wasn't the intended would read what she was about to discover there.

Chapter 14

Dinner had already been delivered when Parkie got to Glory's later that night—showered, changed, and sober, now that she'd been away from the office for a few hours.

The first floor of the brownstone had the productive energy of a workshop. Its shotgun of small rooms was a material culture chaos of semidry canvases, piles of torn magazines, rivets, bicycle chains, and an old sewing machine that looked as if it were spewing stitched newspapers. As a place to live, the apartment was less than welcoming. As the studio of an up-and-coming artist who'd been offered a solo show, however, Glory's place felt exactly like it should.

She came to the door in red coveralls, a change of pace from the gray ones Parkie had most often seen her wear. Parkie hardly made it inside before Glory pushed her against the door, draping her arms over Parkie's shoulders to kiss her on tiptoe. It felt to Parkie as if they'd been apart for a lot longer than fifty-two hours. Give or take.

"Don't worry," Glory said as soon as Parkie laid hands on her hips. "The paint is dry—I haven't worked on anything since I got home. Too busy in the archives upstairs."

"I can't wait to hear all about it," Parkie said, stifling a low-blood-sugar yawn. "After we eat?"

Glory led Parkie into the kitchen, where the pizza was warming in the oven and the caprese salad was staying cool in the fridge. She produced a couple of plates from the old cupboards with the scalloped trim that Parkie loved. Like so many things in the apartment, even the regular dishes were formal and decidedly retro—the plates were delicate, gold-trimmed Limoges porcelain with a sap green Greek-key border. The charred thin-crust pizza looked a little out of its element.

Parkie sat down and Glory disappeared into the pantry, returning with a bottle of Barbera.

She set a wafer-thin etched glass in front of Parkie.

"Oh, geez," Parkie sighed. "I think I'll abstain. For now, anyway."

"Whaaat? You're hungover from last night, I bet," Glory said, laughing. "I knew you were drunk—it made you nasty."

"I was not drunk. And I'm always nasty."

Glory smiled as if she agreed. "Are you sure you don't want just a little glass?"

"I'm sure," Parkie said. "I got a little overserved at lunch, actually."

"Yeah. And you stood me up," Glory said. "What happened there?"

Parkie had hoped they wouldn't arrive at the subject of lunch quite yet. But it was just as well. From now on, she really wanted to be honest with Glory.

Besides, it wasn't as if she'd done anything wrong. It was a client meeting. Nothing more. So why did she feel so guilty?

"About that," Parkie said. "I cleared my calendar because I thought we could go to lunch when you finished, and then I got the oddest call."

"From?"

"Manya Shah, actually."

"As in, my future dealer Manya Shah?"

"I guess she figured out why I wanted to talk to her in the first place—there was an *ARTnews* article about Madeline breaking into contemporary art about two months ago—and she asked me to lunch to talk about doing business."

"But that wasn't the only thing she wanted you to do, right?" Glory said, sitting down. "So she gets you drunk and acts like it's all just British business as usual. You can't tell me she didn't ask you out." Her expression turned almost respectful. "That bitch has skills."

"No, I can't," Parkie said. "And she does. But I said no. And no. And no. And I also said no to drinks tonight—that's why I went to lunch. Seemed like the path of least resistance, but that was before I knew who I was dealing with. She's very . . . persistent."

"Like a cat with a mouse. If you're trying to make me jealous, you're doing just fine. Did you tell her we're, um, seeing each other?"

"You mean, does she know the person I said I was, um, seeing is you?" Parkie said, looking heavenward. She was damned if she had and damned if she hadn't.

"I didn't tell her it was you, because I didn't want it to hurt your relationship with the gallery. And with her, too, I guess. If 'relationship' is the right word. And you have no reason to be jealous," Parkie said, taking a moment from her pizza to give Glory a sincere and, she hoped, enamored look.

"Fuck her," Glory said. "Hitting on people's girlfriends. Not that we're. Not that we're not—"

"Exactly," Parkie interrupted. "Not that we're not not. Anyoldway, I didn't tell her, but only because I didn't want to set her off. She reminds me of basically every high-strung girlboss I dated in college. It's all fun and games until you cross them—whatever that means on a given day."

"So she's *your* type?" Glory was only half kidding, and Parkie knew it.

"*Was* my type," Parkie said, reaching for Lucille's ebony salad tongs to lower another serving of dressed cherry tomatoes, basil, and fresh mozzarella onto Glory's plate. "Before I knew better. Before I knew about you."

"An upgrade, then."

"Economy to first," said Parkie.

"Enough about Manya Shah," Glory said. "I was pretty sure her name would come up tonight—I was going to tell you she finally called to officially offer me my solo show. Little did I know she'd be nosing around my boo the next day."

"I know, she told me. Congrats. It's so exciting! So . . . does this make you my bae? I've never understood how that works exactly," Parkie said, taking another slice. "But yes. Enough of Manya Shah. I want to hear about your appointment with Dr. K. I've only been admitted to her office once—and I was not asked to sit down."

*

About an hour later, Glory sat cross-legged on Lucille's living room floor with Parkie on the couch nearby. Around each woman, tidily laid out like a game of solitaire, was a group of open envelopes, the contents of which they were mostly reading to themselves—stopping every few minutes to recite aloud a line that struck them as important or interesting.

"This one is about having lunch with someone named Claude," Parkie said. Your aunt says Claude told her she could be a lot happier if she "embraced things as they are." He said she should let go of pleasing the Miss Annes—and the talented tenth. He says he's thinking of leaving Harlem and he wants her to find some happiness before he goes."

"Claude. No idea. What's the date?" Glory asked.

"Nineteen forty-two."

They had been at it since just after dinner, when Glory had asked if Parkie wanted to see some of the letters she'd been reading at Dr. K.'s request.

She seemed nervous about asking Parkie to come to the second floor—which didn't need to be a big deal but had almost turned into one because Glory wouldn't simply come out and ask if Parkie could handle the stairs.

Lately, the only time her disability came up was during sex, when, for example, Parkie had to suddenly ask Glory to move a little or tell her that a certain position wasn't good for her. So far, Glory seemed to take the cue not to let it hold them back. But Parkie wished she would just ignore her when something hurt a little—it wasn't like sex couldn't be that way for everybody.

Parkie stretched out her leg to nudge Glory's rear with her toe. It was nice up here. Quiet and calm. Hardly as creepy as she'd feared from the way Glory described the overwhelming presence of Lucille's meticulously assembled possessions. Parkie had a thing for objects. You had no business working at an auction house if you weren't intrigued by an old skeleton key or charmed by a mislaid souvenir from a stranger's long-ago travels. Parkie liked the sense she was getting of Lucille's personality from merely existing among her stuff. As if Parkie were the ghost in these rooms, attracted to a blown-glass bird or a marble lamp for reasons unknown—or possibly, she considered with a thrill, owing to the psychic strength of Lucille's enduring attachments. Or even of her awareness of Parkie's sensitivity to them.

She squinted at the letter in her hand. "I think this woman was writing to Lucille from New York when she was in the army in Iowa. Sounds like she was a nurse—she's talking about her shifts and a new chief working on her floor. She calls her a 'beautiful, dusky woman,' who she thinks always looks 'very commanding in her uniform' and is 'somehow marvelously enigmatic, like a Russian empress incognito.' No name. But she calls her 'the author.' So that's interesting."

Glory slid closer to Parkie's legs. She wondered what they would do tonight.

"Yeah, seems like Lucille had a few nurse friends from that time," Glory said. "Eleanor thinks the pages in the scrapbook are maybe a short novel—maybe something unpublished. She was pretty tight-lipped about it. I bet she knows who wrote it. I think she's worried someone will scoop her on it. Or steal it. Your business is crazy."

"Um, yeah, it is. Houses try to steal clients all the time when they get wind of what somebody has who's working with a competitor. We're all striving to give sellers the best terms for access to the best buyers—even though a lot of those buyers are the same people, so it's really all about us. I'm sure Dr. K. does have a theory. But she's careful," Parkie said, looking over at Glory. "Also, *Eleanor*? Really?"

Parkie had stopped home to change into sweats and a T-shirt. The back of Glory's hand began moving up and down her calf the way she liked.

"Yes, 'Eleanor' is what she asked me to call her," she said. "We're close that way." Glory squeezed Parkie's thigh and Parkie jumped from a sharp and sudden pain. It was over almost before it started but on reflex she jerked her leg away.

"Oh my god, babe, I'm so sorry. That was so fucking stupid of me. I wasn't thinking," Glory said, looking like she'd just pulled a chair out from under her. "Are you okay?"

"It's fine. I'm fine." Except, Parkie thought, she obviously has no idea which side my injury is on. "Really. You just surprised me and my arthritis is acting up, if you really want to know the sexy truth. Not exactly pillow talk, but that's what it is. It's new. They said it might kick in a few years later, but I've been hoping they were wrong. Anyway, sometimes my hips and knees hurt these days. You didn't do anything. When you started touching me I could have said something. But I liked it. Anyway, what does Eleanor think we should do now? Did she ask about other scrapbooks?"

From Glory's concerned, not-so-fast expression, Parkie could tell she wanted to ask more questions. But Parkie wanted her to let it go, so she gave Glory's shoulder a squeeze, adding another, "Really, I'm fine," to drive the point home.

"She didn't ask about other scrapbooks," Glory said, getting the message. "But when I told her I thought there were definitely letters *to* Lucille and maybe *from* Lucille from the time of the war, she couldn't hide how excited she was. She asked for permission to transcribe the pages she has, which I gave her, of course. She uses dictation software—who'd a thunk it? Before I left she gave me a list of names and asked me to see if I could find evidence that Lucille knew anyone on this list."

"She is smooth," Parkie said. "Normally, the first thing we'd do is ask to see more. I wonder why she didn't. Speaking of seeing more. It *is* a school night. And even if we go to bed now, that doesn't leave a lot of time for actual sleep."

Again receiving the message, Glory gathered her envelopes together and began to retie their blue ribbons. Parkie gathered hers and did the same.

*

"I looked up Black nurses during World War II," Parkie said, setting down her phone when Glory climbed into bed beside her.

"Thousands of Black nurses were rejected as a class by the army when they tried to enlist. Did you know that? Even when there was a shortage, good old progressive Roosevelt wouldn't let the military accept them. A lot of women apparently worked at city hospitals because they weren't as segregated. That seems like where Lucille's nurse friend from the letter would have been— maybe even a hospital right around here. Love that she calls their friend 'the author.'"

She was eager to get things back to normal with Glory and hoped a light tone would help.

"Eleanor is going to lose her shit." Glory chuckled.

"If we can prove someone wrote to Lucille about having a writer as a friend, I think she'll have to tell us who she thinks wrote the hidden novel."

"A friend and maybe more," Parkie said. She didn't want to push things too far with Glory on this—she knew her family was already weird about Lucille. But it seemed to Parkie that the woman who wrote to Lucille was nursing a serious crush on her new colleague.

"Nah, I don't think so," Glory said. "Things were different then. Women wrote to each other like that. Terms of endearment. If you knew Lucille. On that, you're just wrong."

Their love train had been derailed a few times that night by awkward exchanges like this.

Manya Shah's inappropriate behavior wasn't the best way to kick off a date, though seeing Glory get very jealous very fast was a fitting reward for coming clean. The thing when Glory squeezed Parkie's leg had also been weird. But then she had never told Glory where not to touch or when. Or why. Glory had almost six years on Parkie, and she liked to think of herself as a woman of the world. But she was gentler and more careful by nature, too. With Glory, Parkie hadn't worried about consent or things getting too rough (could they?) or anything else to do with the physical side of their relationship. As to her disability, she simply hadn't felt like providing operating instructions.

So far, everything about sex with Glory had been great.

She wasn't going to let that change.

Glory's bedsheets were as ice cold as her skin. So much for the radiators—on Glory's floor some rooms were approaching hot while in others a light coating of frost had formed in the corners of the windows, like fake snow sprayed on a storefront. In the parlor, you could see your breath if you got too close to the glass. As bad luck would have it, Glory's bedroom was one of the colder rooms and, even under quilts and an added down comforter, the two of them could hear each other's teeth chattering.

"I'm sorry, P.," Glory said. "It's the fucking North Pole in here tonight. I'd turn up the heat but it won't do much good, and honestly, last month's heating bill was almost two grand. It's killing me."

"Christ," Parkie said. "I don't think I've ever paid separately for heat in the city. That's the worst. Don't keep it warmer than usual for me. I'm not as delicate as I look."

Glory laughed before turning to Parkie and pulling up her T-shirt. When she started on her breasts, Parkie shivered at the shock of a hot tongue on her skin. She wished it could be every-where at once. After that, a frozen Glory wasted no time wrap-ping herself around Parkie. She slung her leg across her torso, a sweetly possessive move that warmed them both up until, for Parkie, the pressure there began to build unpleasantly. It didn't feel great. But the last thing Parkie wanted was for Glory to stop sucking and kissing her like that. Girls loved to say they could almost come from what Glory was doing to her nipples, but with Glory, Parkie really, easily, could. She was that close.

Without asking or telling, Glory abruptly shifted her leg off Parkie, leaving a chilly space between Parkie's hip and her own warm stomach.

"What is *wrong* with me?" Glory said, pulling away at pre-cisely the worst moment.

"Oh my god, why did you stop, honey? That felt so good."

"Because I was hurting you," Glory said. "I can tell from how you're tensing."

Parkie felt her gut seize. Was it irritation? Was it shame? Pure sexual frustration? Exactly how could Glory tell? And why didn't she trust that Parkie knew her own body better than she did?

"What the hell? You weren't," Parkie said crossly, because she was that annoyed. "Anything but hurting me. I was about to come from that. I don't need you to try to protect me from my own pain. What you were doing made me feel better, not worse. I'll tell you if I need you to stop."

Glory rocked back on her side.

"Fuck," she said. "I know I keep getting it wrong. But honestly, I think I have a decent idea—except for when I grab your leg without thinking—of when you're not feeling good. Physically, anyway. I don't want to cause you pain. I don't think you always tell me when I am."

Parkie's head thrummed. Her heart was beating too fast. She was getting thick-throated. Choked up.

So fucking irritating.

Nobody had ever said it like that before. And it was true, in fact. She didn't always tell Glory. Or anyone else. She didn't have to if she didn't want to.

But damn.

For a while after the accident Parkie had been unable to dominate another woman in bed the way that had come naturally to her since sex in high school. But eventually Loden's boredom with their relationship had extended to the bedroom, where Parkie had become the bratty bottom. Ironically, while part of her initial appeal to this woman almost twenty years her senior was that Loden perceived as her docile, what she truly wanted from Parkie was to be disciplined; not merely spanked on the ass, but taken charge of. And, when she wasn't gracing the pages of *American Banker*, told what to do by a twentysomething.

And so, at the height of their sexual and interpersonal dysfunction, Parkie had found her top skills again. That relationship had swallowed up a year of her life, but at least it helped her get her groove back. Parkie had been more or less stoic, to her mind the bare minimum of being domme, with every woman she'd slept with since. She'd never mentioned her pain—and the women had never asked.

It's so very inappropriate to have visions of girlfriends past while you're with somebody new in the present. But Parkie couldn't help it. It was like a shopping-comparison pop-up in her psyche. There was selfish Loden, the old model. And here was Glory. Beautiful, brilliant, sad-eyed Glory, genuinely concerned for her health and happiness. And here was Glory's strangely charming, weirdly safe-feeling minimalist bedroom. And her body under these nice quilts and her always tender touch. And here they were, pain or no pain, about to have really good sex, Parkie would have speculated. It was lovely on the face of it. But made her mad just the same, when matters concerning sex weren't dictated by her.

Still. When was the last time any woman had tried to understand? This might be the first time she'd ever wanted someone to. "Come back," Parkie said, reaching for Glory in hopes she'd kiss her chest and nestle her face in her breasts again.

Glory shifted over a bit hesitantly. But then she settled her cheek near Parkie's heart and moved her body close enough so that they were touching again. Parkie inhaled the scent of Glory's shampoo and felt some of the tension go out of her. She pulled the top quilt over their shoulders.

"I know you probably want to know what happened to me," Parkie said. "But honestly, I just haven't wanted to talk about it. Not because I don't feel safe with you. I know you don't want to hurt me. It's just, once we have that conversation, things will change. You'll see me differently. And right now, I don't want that. I love things the way they are."

Glory stayed where she was for a few long moments. Then she moved up to Parkie and kissed her on the lips, pressing their chests together.

"I love things the way they are, too," Glory said. "But so you know, I'm ready to hear whatever you want to tell me if and when you want to talk about it. I haven't asked, because I thought you'd say something at some point. Can you at least give me the lingo? 'Person with a disability'? 'Disabled person'? 'Disability rights.' I've been listening to podcasts but nobody agrees on the terms."

"'Disability justice,'" Parkie said. "I'd say don't get me started, but since you did, I don't mind being called 'disabled.' I can call myself a 'crip,' but you can't unless I say so. I have a disability. I use a cane. A mobility aid, if you want to get clinical. I *have* chronic pain, I don't *suffer* from it. I mean, I do, but I hate that phrase. And I'm apparently getting arthritis. That's lesson one. And you were right, by the way. There was some pain for me with your leg like that. I'm not used to someone being able to tell. Should be a good thing. But when you said you knew what was going on with me, I disconnected for a minute. No one can experience what I'm feeling, you know? Mostly, my situation—the scars and the limp and the pain and the cane—is just me. It's just there. And I'm fine with that most of the time. I've learned how to work with it."

"No argument here," said Glory, sliding lower again. "So I should go back to sucking your tits?"

Parkie grinned at her and Glory looked up with only a hint of the confusion and embarrassment Parkie had hoped to avoid. It was awkward, but she'd seen worse. "Are you asking?" Parkie said, and they broke into laughter.

Chapter 15

Where progress to completion was concerned, Glory never set goals for her work. If she was in a good place, she could paint for hours, even days, without stopping for more than a couple of bathroom breaks and a few spoons of peanut butter. Maybe a shot or two of bourbon if she noticed the sun had gone down. At other times, she'd dutifully set aside an afternoon or a day or a weekend only to have to quit when she realized she simply couldn't find a way into the work; couldn't tap her source.

When that happened, it could feel like she might never make anything decent again, the worst fear of all creative people who have tasted success, whether on their own terms or in the larger arena of critics and the public.

Glory had started painting with newfound energy the morning after pizza night with Parkie. And she hadn't stopped in the day-plus since. She knew she should be keeping in better touch with Parkie. But when she was flowing creatively, clocks stopped working like they usually did. Plodding, incremental time felt like minutes slipping away as quickly as they added up. Knowing when to stop wasn't possible—she had to keep going until she couldn't. Until the time she had ran out.

It wasn't that Parkie wasn't on her mind while she worked. It was more like there was hardly room for anything but Parkie.

In the middle of pasting down and tearing up magazine pages and mixing paint, Glory caught herself immersed in filmic flashes of their time together. How they laughed and how easy it was to talk to her. How Parkie knew exactly how to touch her and how indescribably hot it was to give herself over to Parkie's control.

Thoughts of being with Parkie more often and for longer filled Glory with all sorts of frightening hopes for the future.

She was falling for her. No question. And she was provisionally okay with that. Admitting it seemed like what she needed to do to become productive again. Once that energy was accessible, she had no choice but to ride it. Like one of those eighty-foot waves she'd seen the great woman surfers take on in Portugal when, instead of working, all she could do was watch C-list sports coverage late into the night.

Glory had always found it exhilarating to push past her limits. And she was happy with what she was making, a five-by-seven canvas half an inch thick with paper and pigment. On its uneven, slatelike surface, thick-waisted forms overlapped. Torn contours coursed through the substrate in tiny, jagged ravines, revealing the fragile layers underneath like the geology diagrams they'd studied in school. It wasn't finished but it was close. And it looked as distant from her old work as she felt.

She was satisfied with this one, in that she could stand to look at it, which wasn't always possible. Glory wished she'd been anywhere near this finished when Wallford had visited—of all of them, this painting was the closest to what she'd claimed she would finish for her first solo show with his gallery. Now it looked nothing like it had when he'd seen it.

Which reminded her that she hadn't heard back from Sarkisian since the short but exuberant email Wallford had sent her from the airport. "Let's be in touch very soon," he wrote. "I'm every bit as taken with this work as I'd hoped." She'd admittedly let these words and all the other nice things he'd said go to her head a little, imagining a hardcover monograph, even a two-floor exhibition. Branding. Documenta. Biennials. She had let herself feel significant—just for a few days—because she was sure his implied offer of representation was on its way.

Only it wasn't.

Meanwhile, where Sarkisian was dragging its feet, Manya Shah had gotten her ducks in a row. She was coming for Glory, and as Manya herself had said, once her quarry was in her sights, there was "simply nowhere sensible, or defensible, to hide."

Having arrived at a possible stopping point—knowing when to say when being at least as important as having a good idea—Glory stepped back from the canvas. Yes, she thought, this painting, my best painting, is done.

A few seconds later a flash on her phone screen caught her eye. It was silenced, of course. But those soundless notifications were still hard to miss in one's peripheral vision. Anyway, she should probably be checking back into her life. Checking back in with gorgeous, irresistible go-getter Parkie. Maybe she would show Parkie what had kept her occupied the past couple of days. After a celebratory dinner together. Tonight.

When Glory picked up her phone, she saw, not unusually, that she'd missed a shit ton of messages. Dozens, in fact. The odd thing was, a few of them were from old friends and acquaintances—people she hadn't talked to in forever. Odder still, there were two messages from Courtland. And five from Parkie.

Glory tasted acid in her throat and felt time slow down the way it does when something terrible happens. It was selfish to drop out the way she did. But if they needed her, she thought people would keep trying. Right now, it looked like they had.

Suddenly sensing that something in her life would be very different when she finally put down the phone again, she wasn't sure where to begin.

Given that he was family, she started with Courtland.

Straddling a stiff wooden chair she'd pulled in from the dining room, Glory clicked on message number one and pressed the speaker icon.

"Glo. Court. Hey, sis, wow. I mean, that's how you know you hit the big leagues though, right? Call if you want to. I have no explanations but I do have theories."

What? Glory thought, scrolling quickly to her brother-in-law's second message.

"Gloria. Do not ignore me, child. I know you're not letting this fool fuck with your psychology. Call me. Or no more financial advice."

In his philosophical, big-picture way, her brother-in-law had hinted at what she'd be dealing with. She momentarily considered a Google search. But Glory was sufficiently actualized to know that she needed a filter. Maybe a few filters. The last time she'd had a review, Alicia had to read it to her. One sentence a day.

She went to Parkie's message next. At this point, all she could hope for was something from Parkie to mitigate two messages from Courtland that sounded like there was a version of her out there she would not like; something she'd need to go dark for. Maybe recover from.

Parkie rarely called. But she occasionally had—mostly with a graphic narration of a sex act, which Glory desperately hoped this would be.

"Hey, babe," Parkie started, sounding artificially casual. "Sorry it took me so long. I just saw the thing this morning. And I figured you might call me. But since you haven't I'm a little worried. So call me, will you? Just leave a message. Or text if you want."

Shit. This was not good. Though unbridled terror was rising in her soul, Glory had no choice but to go to Parkie's next message.

"Glory, please call me." Tone not so casual. "This is nothing. In the scheme of things, it could even be a positive someday. I know you know that. But call me."

Onto number three.

"Now I'm mad and worried. If I don't hear from you before the end of the day, I'm coming up there. It'd be sooner but Madeline's in this week and I have to personally stage this fucking preview for the fucking Flagg sale. Let me know you're okay. Just do that. Please."

She texted Parkie.

So sorry, P. Just got messages, will call soon.

She dialed Courtland.

At first, she got voicemail. Then a couple of seconds later, he called her back.

"Dude," he said.

"Okay, Court. Listen, believe me when I say I have no idea what's going on. I've been in the studio for like forty-eight hours straight, totally offline. So just tell me what the fuck is up—no jokes."

"Oh shit," he sighed. "Seriously? Okay, okay. Lemme just say it. *New York Times* review yesterday. The group show. Your work. Not ideal."

"What?!!!" Glory exploded into the phone. "Was it Martha?"

"Not Martha. One of the other ones. The other old ones. Total dick move on his part. Which is why I was trying to get ahead of you overreacting and remind you that any press is good press in that town. Moreover, this guy wouldn't know a diaspora from a diaper—and he's even more full of diarrhea where your stuff is concerned. 'Vapidly overdetermined'? 'Played out'? 'Derivative'? Hell no. Assclown needs to go."

Glory momentarily guffawed against her will. But as soon as her lips returned to normal, everything in her head went buzzy and white.

"You there?"

"Yeah. Court, thanks. Lemme . . . lemmee. I need to see it. I'll call you when I—"

"Whenever. I'm here. Grace has read it but I don't think Priscilla and Ed have. But Glory, Glory, Glory. You're too good to care what the critics say. I need to go make some more money now so I can afford to acquire," Courtland added, ending the call before she could respond.

*

Bad reviews almost always feel more personal than good ones. They can make you uncomfortable in your own skin—and other places, too. Those bias-laden judgments and memorably ignorant quips can skunk your favorite spot to read a book or taint the purity of your bath time. Since reading "the thing," as Parkie called it, Glory couldn't seem to find a place in the house—upstairs or downstairs—to call her own.

"Just don't tell me it doesn't matter," was the first thing she said when she opened the front door. Parkie's eyes were red, her face a little puffy, which could only mean she must have had a pretty serious cry at some point, or points, during the day. Parkie didn't respond to Glory's rudely confrontational greeting other than to set her stick in the corner so she could put her arms around her. Enveloped in Parkie's suited embrace, Glory relaxed for the first time since hearing the messages. She pushed her cheek into

Parkie's chest as if she could hide there, listening to the reassuring rhythm. Feeling cared for. Protected. As if nothing could touch her as long as Parkie held her like that.

Glory had been so mind-numbingly consumed with fury since she'd found the review—which included images of her work alone—she was astonished to find herself breaking into tears. Before they were even out of the entry. If she'd thought *that* would happen, she might never have let Parkie hold her. In fact, she might not even be crying if Parkie hadn't started kissing her temple with her soft Parkie lips. If she hadn't let Glory's defensiveness and petulance roll right off her back like the rock she was.

Once Glory stopped sniffling, Parkie took her arm and walked them into the living room.

"I think you've actually lost weight since I was here," she said as they sat down on the green sofa. "I'm going to order something. Should I choose or do you have a preference?"

Food. Glory considered. What a novel idea.

"No, baby. You pick. I don't think I should be allowed to make any more decisions. 'Whatever made Hopkins eschew her signature abstraction,'" she said, quoting the review, "'we can only hope she makes an about-face. Inchoate politics and storyboard figuration are not what her fastidious technique is cut out for.'"

"Oh, honey. Nooo," Parkie said, spreading a hand over Glory's thigh. "That drivel does not deserve to be memorized. He's just wrong. He's an uptight, white-facing asshole and he's always wrong. And what's also wrong is the *Times* sending the least appropriate reviewer to cover that show. Martha would have done a better job."

"The world may never know," Glory said. "Since that was probably my last *Times* review. Maybe my last show."

Parkie slapped her leg.

"Okay, now you're just being ridiculous. A review in the *Times*, even a less-than-glowing one by a reactionary cipher, is far from being the kiss of death for a rising star like you. Have you talked to Manya about it?"

"I didn't even know that review existed until about three hours ago. So no. But I'm sure she'll be calling any minute now to unmake me an offer. Along with any other no-longer-interested parties."

Parkie frowned in confusion.

"But right now, I really, really don't want to talk about it, P. I mean, we can eventually. But not tonight. What I really, really *do* want is a martini. Six olives. Followed by a very quick dinner and you fucking me doggy style until I can't think straight. And did you say you were staging your big preview already? How come this is the first I've heard about that?"

Chapter 16

What Parkie really, really didn't want was to talk about her preview.

"I dunno," she said as carelessly as possible. "It's strange. If you'd told me last year that I'd be overseeing my own Cuthbert's preview, I would have started screaming and told you to shut up. But now that I'm doing it, it's not at all how I thought it would be."

"This is your nightmare client with the five-thousand-item estate or whatever, right?"

"Five hundred items. But that's a lot of lots."

"But you're in charge of all of it, like the boss bitch you are, right?"

They were still side by side on the sofa, but Glory hadn't been looking at Parkie directly. There was a strange, aggressive energy coming off her tonight. Elbows out and hands butchly gripping her wide-open knees, Glory was the one who looked like a boss. But she was also a consummate stroker of the domme ego. All it took was a handful of words and Parkie's libido went into overdrive. She wanted to lean into Glory but she only made a "hah" sound in response. "Not only am I in charge, I'm responsible. It's like the sale is now about me personally. Which I definitely did not want."

"Because they're pretty awful or because their stuff isn't good?" Glory asked, finally turning her way.

Parkie wondered if Glory would understand why she had to have the Flaggs as clients. She wondered if Glory had all the information, if she'd see that as a junior specialist, Parkie had her hands tied. That she had to play the cards she was dealt. Until they got where they wanted, they both did.

But if Glory didn't see it that way, what then?

Glory put her hand on Parkie's back and rubbed a few circles. When Parkie looked in her direction, she could see that Glory's bottomless eyes were full. Full of affection. Even when she was so angry about the review. Full of attraction—a kind of interest and arousal Parkie wanted to reciprocate.

"Everything about those people is terrible," she said. "And I sort of wish—I don't know."

"That you didn't have to choose?" Glory said, taking Parkie's hand as it lay in her lap. "Between getting ahead and doing what you know is right?"

Parkie didn't want to be looking into Glory's eyes when she answered her question. She brought Glory's fingers to her mouth and kissed each knuckle before she said anything.

"Yeah."

"Seems like you make all the right choices, babe," Glory said. "You have a moral compass as your guide. I love that about you."

As soon as she said it, Glory pulled her hand away and put it in her own lap, as if the gesture would erase the words that preceded it. She probably wished she hadn't said the l-word. Not that Parkie had taken it as a confession. You can love something about someone without being in love with them.

"I mean, aside from the hotness, it's one of the things that makes you such a force. You take the high road," Glory corrected herself. "Even when it's not the easy road, which I guess it never is at a place like Cuthbert's. Or the art world. I don't know why

I thought I could make it by staying true to my vision. Who gives a shit about my vision?"

Parkie didn't respond to the first part, the part about her ethics.

"We both know it's not the same for BIPOC artists," she said. "Either critics hate on you because they don't have a context for work by people who aren't white, or it's the Kara Walker syndrome. You make something radical and honest about white racists getting a sick sexual charge from looking at Black pain. Then white people thriving in a society built by slavery grab it up for hundreds of thousands of dollars and hang it in their living rooms."

"And their bedrooms, probably."

"Oh, definitely their bedrooms," Parkie said, grateful for the new direction their conversation was taking. "I have absolutely seen her work in people's bedrooms."

"So, what can I do? The joke's on me for thinking I was on to something. I do feel like I need to see another estate for comparison with Lucille's though," Glory said with a quasi-serious look. "Am I invited to your preview?"

They were again holding hands. But this was something Parkie had not considered. Glory was always so busy, Parkie just might have secretly wished her new girlfriend? would forget that she had a huge, career-determining auction coming up. On the positive side, Glory had been listening. Realistically, though, where the preview was concerned, she could only hope Glory might fall into another of her production holes once she went back to work again.

"It's open to the public," Parkie answered with a hand squeeze. "They all are. I'll be working the floor the whole time. But of course you are invited to my preview. It's Friday."

"Is it black tie?"

Parkie laughed. "No. But I like the sound of that. Madeline likes to do an invitation-only pre-preview though. And she's for sure going overboard with the conspicuous consumption theme on Flagg, so that part is cocktail-attire-ish. But there will be other sales, babe. And it's not a fair comparison."

"Because my aunt was just a little old Black lady from Harlem?"

"Because your aunt had much better taste."

*

In the auction business, as Madeline liked to say, perception is reality. Architecturally, Cuthbert's wasn't much—its soot-streaked, base-model Beaux Arts building was old but far from distinguished or special. The drop-ceilinged offices and drywalled sales rooms were out of date and small. But these same qualities lent the auction house a rarified and exclusive air when you tried to find it—the only external indication of Cuthbert's presence was a lightly engraved, envelope-sized brass plaque on the facade. There weren't even any visible street numbers until you got into the lobby, where Mr. Sweeney's desk was emblazoned with numbers in gold.

In line with Madeline's "style," Cuthbert's had its own way of doing things. Rather than making her sales more accessible to a wider segment of society, or even more New Yorkers, Madeline's impulse was to separate the wheat from the chaff with a dress code and a chamber quartet while skimping on the quality but not the quantity of the champagne. She also provided a top-shelf cash bar for those who knew well enough to look a gift horse in the mouth, which meant the crowd got pretty loose pretty fast.

Even pre-previews were all-hands-on-deck, with Madeline's favorite caterer providing a battalion of fresh-faced servers. In addition to she-who-must-be-obeyed, who worked the crowd like a popular incumbent, the complete staff of appraisers and specialists were unleashed on the previewers, having memorized the faces and tastes of the city's famed underbidders and most acquisitive collectors of whatever was currently on view.

Madeline had a flair for creating a buzz. One way or another, Cuthbert's previews were always an occasion for the society pages. Scores of prominent New Yorkers were loyal to Cuthbert's on principle.

The Manhattan rooms of the much bigger houses of Sotheby's and Christie's—originally British but since sold and bought and now in the hands of French billionaires—were modern and minimalist. By contrast, Cuthbert's was stubbornly outdated and, as some would say—and others had—*out of touch*. Stuckbert's. Like an embarrassing relative who refers to "the Blacks" or uses the expression "light in the loafers" or consistently tips 15 percent. And that was just Madeline.

Though public by necessity, the auction world is elitist by definition. Cuthbert's was immured in an American idea of classiness inspired by a made-up idea of Britishness. Like the old Polo store. It was the commercial equivalent of the flocks of Gilded Age New York socialites who had descended on England in the nineteenth century, eager to lend patina to their shiny new American money by dropping it in the coffers of a destitute and inbred British aristocracy. The Americans got the status and the Brits got the cash. And so it was unto the Age of Meghan Markle.

It was rumored that Madeline herself was born a nice Polish girl in some Midwestern city like Chicago, possibly Detroit. She had married and married and married again, keeping the second name even after the third divorce. Thanks to her devoted base, she'd stayed in business since the eighties. Over the years, she'd been on the cover of *Time*, worked as a spokesmodel for mink coats, and chaired more charity dinners and show-house committees than Parkie could shake her stick at (a line Madeline had, true story, used during one of their recent staff events).

No one was therefore more astounded than Madeline to see that some people, a great many, in fact, were locked and loaded on this winter night to go to war with Cuthbert's, whose Flagg sale preview would be their battle royale.

*

Parkie, too, was armed, though she was equally unprepared to go to battle that night. Instead of her typical dark tweed Chanel with the green fringe, she'd decided to go icy monochrome. Her hair, recently cut to shoulder-length, was swept back from her forehead and duck-tailed with just a bit of product. Her makeup consisted of only a wash of pink across her cheekbones. This made her changeable eyes, which tonight looked more gray than green to her, stand out, especially against the cream-colored skirt suit she was wearing. The only point of slight contrast was her trademark chiffon silk blouse in a shade of pink even paler than her cheeks.

"You look like a supersize vanilla milkshake. With a cherry on top," was what Madeline cackled when they ended up together in the elevator. Standing side by side, Parkie thought they must resemble rival rulers from a Pixar movie, though she couldn't say for sure who the good queen was.

Madeline's skirt suit, which consisted of a thick basket weave of black satin and lamé strips, set off her unnaturally metallic pageboy. She wore the cobalt-framed, cobalt-lensed cat-eye glasses for which she was known and a trio of enormous sapphire-and-pearl-encrusted jewels on her ears and wrist. She was Palm Beach tan, as if airbrushed. And her breath smelled of gin and cigarettes.

The elevator ride was slow motion.

"Love the Fendi," Parkie managed. "Reminds me of the Boulle desk. You're taking the sale, I assume."

Madeline was scrolling through her phone, though everyone knew there was no signal in the elevator.

"What?" she said pissily. "Yes, of course I'm taking the sale. I have a spotter lined up already. It's really just too complicated with your, your, uh, cane, up there. I worry it's going to slip off the stage and bonk someone on the head."

Before Parkie could respond—and this time she was determined to respond—the elevator doors jerked open and the two of them were confronted by a fireworks of camera flashes amid a wall of handheld phones.

"Ms. Cuthbert! Ms. Cuthbert!" someone called from the second or third row of what Parkie could only understand as reporters. Madeline stood beside her clearly stunned and unable to move either forward or back.

"The HIV/AIDS activist group ACT OUT claims to have spearheaded the protests outside your auction house tonight. Care to comment?"

"The what?" Madeline rasped. "What the hell are you talking about?"

The reporter turned to the camerawoman beside him and asked her if she'd caught the exchange on film. She had.

Meanwhile, Kiki, Cuthbert's sleek blond media director, materialized at Madeline's side, whispering in her ear. Parkie didn't know what to do or where to go. It had only just dawned on her that her sale was evidently the center of a protest, or protests, if she had heard the reporter correctly. Her pulse pounding in her ears, she tried to step away from Madeline, thinking she could slip between the less-organized-looking people at the edges of the press corps and into the stairwell. Or even the coat check room. But as soon as she made a slight movement to the side, the crowd of journalists tightened their circle like a shark ring, hemming her in.

"Isn't that the head of sale there?" someone with a British accent asked, pointing to Parkie. She turned away, but not before several cameras flashed in her face.

"Ms. Cuthbert, Flagg Pharmaceuticals, the company owned by the family whose property Cuthbert's has been promoting, continues to produce Imunoglix at a price point consumer advocates have described as unconscionable and immoral. Will the revenues you generate at next week's auction make the rich richer and the poor—and sick—sicker and poorer?"

Again the blond whispered in Madeline's ear.

Madeline leaned in. To the first microphone she could find.

"Cuthbert's is not in the business of commenting on our clients' business practices," she said. "What I can say is that art and commerce are intimately connected. Don't let anyone tell you they aren't. This wouldn't be the unequaled city it is without the fortunes and philanthropy of old New York families like the Flaggs. And this week anyone with a paper paddle will have a chance to take home a part of that history. That's democracy! Now if you'll excuse me, I've got a preview to get underway and my own successful American business to run." At this point the blond grabbed Madeline's sleeve and, with the help of two of the biggest guys from shipping, they were escorted out of the lobby and into the salesroom.

Chapter 17

Glory's Lyft was stuck in traffic.

"Something going on where you go with many police," she was informed by the driver, a young guy who had been listening to death metal on the radio at a comedically low-decibel level.

"Like an accident?" Glory said, feeling a jolt of panic.

The guy began talking more quickly into his headset in a language Glory thought might be Ukrainian. He broke off the conversation to answer her.

"Not accident. Demonstration. Protest."

No, Glory thought, the driver must have it wrong. They were only a few blocks away, but she did not want to de-glitter her Miu Mius by walking that far. She hoped Parkie would understand. What was Parkie wearing? Glory mused, feeling suddenly very eager to see her in one of her flawless suits—and to get her out of it when they got back to her place. Soon.

They hadn't attended anything social, any type of real event together since Manya's Chelsea opening. Which didn't really count—although they talked about that night as their first date. Life had been too chaotic since to do anything but dinner out. Glory was glad she'd pushed Parkie about getting her into the pre-preview; she wanted her to feel supported tonight.

Another fifteen minutes went by, and they were hardly any closer to the building. Ambulances and police SUVs were double-parked everywhere. They finally crept around a corner where Glory was astonished to see a huge crowd come into view—not thousands but definitely hundreds of people chanting in front of Cuthbert's. Local network news vans were poised around the periphery with reporters in the streets under microphone booms.

Glory thanked the driver, who encouraged her to "Fight the power" as she got out, and started walking with no small trepidation around the ubiquitous police officers and toward the sign-waving throng.

It was only when she was in the heart of the protesters that the words they were chanting made any kind of sense: "Cuthbert's is care-less!" alternating with "Flagg desecration heals the nation!"

It was dark out, but the block was well lit.

She tried to slip between a group of mostly young men waving their signs and chanting. One of them offered her a cardboard mock auction paddle with "Auction = Death" printed on the pink triangle on its face. She accepted it unthinkingly and kept moving forward. Glory had almost reached the doors, which presented a new problem, when she began to put it all together.

She noticed an older man standing off to the side, homemade sign dangling from his elbow while he stopped for a swig from his thermos. He was chic, a stocky Black man in a black cashmere fisherman's cap, black Hokas, and a long, black wool overcoat.

"Excuse me," Glory said, approaching him. "What is the protest about?"

He gave her a disappointed look, eyebrows raised.

"Nineteen ninety-two," he said. "I'm twenty-five, my boyfriend is dying from HIV. He needs the Flagg drug Imunoglix, but it's like ten thousand dollars a course—that would be like fifty thousand today. He can't get it. Nobody can. And they all die. Honey, that's what the protest is about."

He said the words without a hint of melodrama. But as Glory stood looking down at the sidewalk so she could put her ear nearer to his mouth to hear, she felt the heat of rising tears burning through her chest. When she looked back at him, he seemed to appreciate the strength of her reaction.

"I'm sorry," she said. "I should know that."

"You're young," he said with a wide smile. "Now you do. I realize it's ancient history. We're here *tonight* because the president of Flaggcorp is the son of the woman whose estate this is, and he's made it known to the 4chan, QAnon dark web crowd that he'll use whatever he makes from the auction to fund the run he's about to announce for governor. And he is one scary son-of-a-bitch, I can tell you. Jim Crow will not be a thing of the past if this man gets elected."

"My girlfriend works in there," Glory said, almost in a daze.

"Well, if you'll pardon my French, that's fucking treason," he said, growing more animated. "Flagg launched a full-scale assault on the gay community—poor people. Black people. For that alone this place should never have accepted their business. But this. This is a flat-out deal with the devil. Madeline Cuthbert. Caveat fucking emptor."

He slid his thermos back into the deep pocket of his coat. The man was probably a famous lawyer. Or a restaurant owner. Maybe a writer. His presence conveyed a life lived fully—being fully lived. Here he was on the streets doing the real work. With Glory getting more emotional about his dead lover than he had. Goals, she thought. But also, she didn't want to lose Parkie. She needed to know Parkie was safe.

"If you go in, you'll have to cross our picket line," the man said, giving Glory a strangely nonjudgmental look. "And once you've crossed the first line, it just gets easier and easier."

*

Glory had texted Parkie from the car before she got there.

On my way, beautiful, maybe we try your place tonight?

She was still standing outside, hovering at the edge of the paddle-generating subset of the ACT OUT group, who had now changed up their chant to "Going, going, dead! Going, going, dead!"

Every time Glory looked at her phone and saw that Parkie hadn't responded, her emotions ricocheted from relief to worry to hopelessness. What was Parkie doing right now? She had to know this was going on. And most gutting of all, how had she neglected to tell Glory that these clients were those people?

Glory tried to think whether in any of their work conversations, Parkie had provided the kind of details about the Flaggs that would have led Glory to expect something like this. She'd called them "terrible." And she'd said, in that maddeningly alluring, Connecticutty, Parkie way that they were the descendants of robber barons who "were themselves really just pirates on a grand scale, if you think about it."

Truthfully, Glory hadn't paid much attention to the details.

The city was full of people like that. The art world was full of people like that. Old New York, and before it New Amsterdam, was subsidized by the Dutch slave trade and the British slave trade, culminating in the US plantation economy, which had relied on New York banks to do their deals. Brooks Brothers manufactured the clothes enslaved people wore—and Glory had more than one of their button-downs in her closet in Harlem.

But the details seemed more important now. There was no way she was going to cross the ACT OUT picket line. Not even for Parkie. Which left her feeling both sorry and angry to have found herself in this position. What for her white girlfriend must have been the middle ground between rock and hard place.

Poor Parkie, she thought, wishing she could lean up to whisper in her ear that it would be all right; that she knew she was in a really tough spot. That she understood.

Did she, though?

Yeah, right, scolded a little voice in her head. Poor, perfect—privileged—Parkie. From the looks of things, when it came down to it, the almighty dollar and her own career were what mattered most. Glory had believed Parkie was made of better, tougher stuff. And Parkie had let her. Even when, all along, she knew she was contributing to something truly despicable.

Glory tried to imagine herself in Parkie's size-ten Ferragamos. There had to be limits, didn't there? There had to be a point beyond which you wouldn't go for work. If something you did upheld something wicked, made it stronger, you had to say no.

She realized Parkie wasn't perfect. Who was? But, fuck. This was beyond terrible. And she wasn't sure how to feel about Parkie now that she knew about it.

Glory looked again at her phone.

Nothing from Parkie. But there was a message from her mother, which, finding herself in a profound state of confusion, she decided to listen to. Glory'd barely pressed play when a youthful protester slammed into her shoulder, looking askance at her for taking a break from social justice for a phone call.

She stepped away from the crowd, steeling herself for a recording that was fifty-six seconds long.

"Hello, Gloria, it's me. Sorry about the nasty review in the *Times*. I've always liked that critic, so I can't say I wasn't surprised. Anyway, I'm sure it was difficult to read. But we can always learn from these things. Even the difficult messages are messages. You know I believe that. I did want to call to ask, if you're coming to Denver for Christmas—and you still haven't told us if you are—that you kindly give me advance notice if you plan to bring a guest. Courtland says you're seeing somebody new and that's nice for you. I hope this one is a little more stable. I shouldn't have to tell you that your father and I are not about to play Guess Who's Coming to Dinner for your latest . . . affair without knowing what we're getting into. We don't need that kind of stress around here. Not this Christmas."

What Glory knew *she* didn't need was the stress of her parents prejudging Parkie. That she undeniably came from money would be to her advantage, as far as Glory's parents went. Ultimately, though, it wouldn't matter how well she dressed or where she'd gone to school. It would only matter that she was white—and was thus an indication of how conspicuously their youngest daughter had rejected all they had imagined for her. Their irony knew no bounds. It was as if, since moving away from Harlem, the Hopkins family was determined to out-Black anyone and everyone in their midst, as if they and they alone were the upholders of the race on the Western front. To many she knew in Denver's comparably small Black communities—and there were suburban and urban ones, both—Harlem was the source of all negritude. As Glory got older, she realized the extent to which her mother played her New York roots to the hilt—like she had come to the mountains to spread the gospel of Blackness as only she could. For all her faults, even Alicia had known better than to go home with Glory—she'd always had good intuition. Before that, Priscilla had subjected her daughter's last white girlfriend to a Thanksgiving dinner that was more like a lightning round of "Famous African Americans" on *Jeopardy*. Glory hadn't even known most of the answers.

In fact, Glory thought, she didn't have to go anywhere for Christmas. She had a home. And she didn't need Parkie or anyone else to complicate her life there or get in the way of her success. She had everything she needed right where she was.

Chapter 18

Parkie had extricated herself from the media circus enough to see that there was no place to go but into the jaws of hell that were the preview itself. The elevators were blocked, and the entrance doors were being monitored by Cuthbert's staff. The stairwell would provide only a temporary hideout, as there was no way she could climb the five floors to her cube.

From the cheerful Vivaldi strains sporadically released into the lobby, she could tell crowds of visitors were pouring in and out of the preview rooms. But although she knew her absence would soon be detected, if it hadn't been already, she did not want to go in.

She had convinced herself that staying physically outside the space that contained the material gains of the Flagg family might somehow preserve her from disgrace. Surely there must be a way to distance herself from all of it. Was any of this really a surprise?

It would be to Glory, she thought. After tonight, Glory would know everything. She'd see that Parkie, with her name literally on this disgusting sale, was in the middle of it all.

A friendly presence appeared at Parkie's side in the person of Nicholas Burdine.

"Holy cats," he drawled. "I guess we should have seen this coming. Maybe not Madeline, but for sure that scary raptor from

Communications. Somebody should have known the chickens would come home to roost."

"That's a lot of animal, and dinosaur, imagery," Parkie said.

"As to dinosaurs, you'll see what I mean when you get in there," Nicholas said. "And you should go soon, too. It's a cluster-fuck. Absolutely teeming with the old guard. I gave out so many cards, I had to go back upstairs for a refill—from the bottle of old Kentucky bourbon in my desk drawer. Shit. Are we awful people? I knew in the back of my head something was rotten about them after the whole USB thing, but I never asked the Google. Pricing AIDS patients out of their meds, though, Parks. Not good."

"I mean, of course it's not good," Parkie said. "It's heinous. But I never asked for this sale, and you know Madeline would have fired me if I'd said I couldn't do it. Armand went MIA, remember?"

"Yes, nutter butter. We were both just following orders. I don't think that's gonna fly with the next Anderson Cooper–loving homosexual I date. Maybe that's why he left. I wouldn't put it past La Mort to grow some integrity for this one thing. He was alive for AIDS."

Parkie hadn't considered this possibility, but it did make a certain kind of sense. Armand had indeed left suddenly. And he had seemed uncharacteristically edgy about being in the Flaggs' apartment from the minute Parkie followed him into their vaulted faux-marble foyer.

But whatever his reasons, he was gone and she was here.

Parkie was the one Madeline had asked to step up after her supervisor's departure. And, like the boss bitch she was, Parkie had handled everything—supposedly with Armand's blessing. From the endless rounds of cataloguing to the decision to re-create the look of the Park Avenue apartment. It was a professional coup, it looked great, and it was all hers.

*

Once she entered the preview, Parkie was immediately sucked into the vortex.

Nicholas was right. The exhibition space was mobbed. In every direction she looked, one of her colleagues was speaking quickly and excitedly to a crowd of entranced potential bidders. Nicholas was now parked before the lots from the former "French guestrooms," as they'd creatively labeled them, giving a lively description of the last days of Marie Antoinette and the roots of the style Louis Seize. Across the room, Madeline was telling tales in front of the painted trompe-l'oeil stone Directoire mantel they had commissioned to serve as a background for the shelves of unexceptional glazed porcelain plates and vessels amassed by several generations of Flagg women.

"Of course what's interesting about all this blue and white, which you're probably used to seeing scattered around the great rooms of those gorgeous English country houses—think Pemberley or even Mansfield Park—is that it was actually made in China for export to the people with good taste who could afford it in the West," Madeline said, following a script she often trotted out. "Sound familiar? And thank god, because I don't know about you, but I never get tired of it!"

Parkie closed her eyes, as if she were about to brave the elements, before making her way to the corner of the floor she'd been assigned to: the mediocre-paintings section, as she called it. The big names had gone to their competitors, but the Flaggs had a lot of wall space to cover in that apartment. Most of their rooms were adorned with turgid engravings and flaking portraits of someone else's vacuous-looking family when they ran out of their own. Parkie headed for the wall of bloodless likenesses.

She alone was permitted to sit down during a preview. And she had just assumed her usual position in the uncomfortable side chair someone always borrowed for her from reception, when a harried Madeline speed-walked over: "Eleanor called in sick, I kid you not. Need you to take books and prints, too. Try to run back and forth."

When Parkie shot her a death glare, she added: "That's no . . . Just do what you can, Parkie!"

This was disconcerting. Among Dr. Kenniston's numerous claims to fame was her perfect record of sale attendance. As far as Parkie knew, she had never missed a Cuthbert's preview.

Never before tonight.

Dr. K. may indeed have been too ill to play her assigned role in the Flagg sale. But Parkie suspected that wasn't what kept her away.

*

The preview ran much later than scheduled. Madeline was happy as a clam at high tide, euphoric from the potent combination of the protest and an unexpectedly large turnout. Not only did she not want the fun to end; she must have hoped that the protesters would cease and desist before the majority of the viewers confronted them on their way out of the building. Champagne was still flowing well past the official 8:30 end time.

But then someone had an idea.

It was Kiki, the blond PR lady who came up with the plan to chain the front doors (for "safety reasons") and herd any departing visitors out through the rear exit by the loading dock, which dropped them near the sidewalk down the street from the official entrance.

This strategy was successful. The oblivious clients, who had managed to make it through the demonstration without knowing what it was about, had even less exposure to the ACT OUT crowds once they trickled out of the alley.

When the musicians were packed up and the staff had furtively finished off the last half-poured bottle of wine, they, too, departed through the loading dock.

It seemed nobody at Cuthbert's was willing to face the principled protesters with their creative signs. Parkie, especially, was relieved not to have to see the faces of the people demonizing the woman who'd hired her—a disabled woman with a cane—for a decidedly public job that required her to actually go places and be seen as a Cuthbert's representative. Not that this made up for any of the things Madeline thought, or said. Or did. And not that Glory would understand Parkie's having made this her rationale for working there. Something Parkie may not have fully acknowledged to herself until now. Glory said she wasn't willing to make the compromises asked of her at law school *or* art school—how could she see Parkie's pact with the Faust of Fifth Avenue as anything but two-faced?

"Y'all are uptown, aren't you?" a bushed-looking Nicholas had asked Parkie when they met at the coat closet. His bow tie was askew, and the hair at his temples was moist with perspiration.

"Wanna share an Uber?"

Parkie was drained, too. Beyond drained, really. She could barely think who she was.

Now was the first chance she'd had to look at her phone (something explicitly prohibited by Madeline during a preview), and she was unprepared to see the screen stacked with messages from Glory. Unprepared and grateful. Unprepared and grateful and forlorn.

"Nah," she answered distractedly, swiping through the messages as she slipped into her coat sleeves. "I've got a couple of things to do before I head out. Thanks, though."

"I hope she's ready to rub your feet," Nicholas said, raising a shaped eyebrow in the direction of her phone. "I was hoping to catch a glimpse of the mystery woman tonight. Did I miss her?"

Parkie forced a smile.

"I don't think so. If you did, so did I."

"Extra points for not crossing the picketers," Nicholas said. He was still riding his own high from holding forth on rococo-painted fans and fire screens for several hours. "I was about to say here's to the freakin' weekend, until I remembered we have to do it all again tomorrow. Think the protesters will be back? I do. Wish I had the guts to call in sick. Kenniston's a baller. Do you think she's queer? Never thought of that until now. Or maybe she lost someone to HIV. That's probably it. She's that Studio 54 generation, right? Can you picture Kenniston at a disco?"

"Did you do blow before this?" Parkie whispered in all seriousness.

Nicholas again responded by eyebrow.

"I think she was married to a man at some point," Parkie said. "Not that that means anything."

"Girl's gotta do what a girl's gotta do," said Nicholas. "Speaking of. I mon go suck it up. Sleep well. And don't forget to enter through the gift shop tomorrow."

*

Parkie clicked into her messages. To read Glory's several increasingly angry texts was to relive the emotional arc of her once and former girlfriend's night. Its hopeful beginnings. Its outraged conclusion.

Parkie couldn't make herself think what the protest might mean for their relationship. But she could feel it. And it felt like being handed an unflattering photograph or hearing a cringe-worthy recording of your own voice. Even if she convinced herself it wasn't the real her, Glory would now know better. Glory's idea of her as innately good, always striving to do the right thing, was way off base, of course. Parkie knew this, though she hadn't done much to disabuse her of it. But Glory wasn't naive. Neither of them was. Still, Parkie realized she'd somehow gotten herself to believe Glory would understand that she didn't have a choice. Not if she wanted to keep her job. Not if she wanted to get high enough up at Cuthbert's to improve things down below. Wasn't that the plan—get in, get promoted, consolidate power, and do things differently once she was in charge? Yeah right. What kind of difference could be made by someone disabled or queer or well read in critical race theory if she was complicit in hurting other marginalized people? By someone who aligned herself with "Big Harma," in the words of one of the investigative reporters given no comment by Madeline. People who tell you to make change from within are already breathing the air inside the bubble. And Parkie had been breathing it, too.

She could have said no to Madeline. She could have said no to Flagg. She'd had a choice and she made it.

Glory had texted her for the last time about an hour earlier—when the protests were still in full swing.

I thought you were better than this. I know you are.

Coming from her it sounded like a break-up text. But it didn't matter. Parkie would take a car straight up to Harlem anyway. She'd bang on the front door until Glory answered. She'd apologize for not telling her about the Flaggs. And she'd explain the trouble Armand had left her in, admitting she knew it was wrong to take on their estate even before the protests. Because she had.

She would kiss Glory hard and they'd crash into her freezing bedroom and warm each other under the pretty old quilts with Maisie curled up at their feet. And everything would be okay. Because she would never make this kind of mistake again.

But of course, it wasn't going to go like that. There was only one valid response this time. Even if it did ring hollow. Parkie typed the three words she didn't want to write instead of the three words she did.

I'm so sorry.

She took a deep breath. And she sent them.

Chapter 19

Glory was making hot chocolate in her kitchen when she got Parkie's apology text.

"I'll bet," she said to herself, staring at the screen, tears clouding her vision. She was tempted to write back. But what was there to say? She was so disappointed in Parkie, it made her feel like all the good things she'd known were possible suddenly weren't. She hadn't thought Parkie was perfect. Obviously, she hadn't. But in her heart of hearts, she believed Parkie was, as she'd written to her, better. Not the kind of woman to compromise her ethics for personal gain. And in such a public way. Even for the health insurance.

The milk boiled over and she burned her thumb taking the frothing pan off the flame.

Glory didn't particularly like the taste of hot chocolate—or hot milk—but at times like these she fell into childhood habits; childhood traditions. Like her mother making hot chocolate when Glory was upset about not being invited to a birthday party. Or had a fight with her best friend. These memories, she realized, were Harlem memories.

Though the drink was watery and not sweet enough, Glory stood at the counter indiscriminately sipping as she searched for what it was about Parkie's behavior, her words, her ways, that warranted putting her on a pedestal. Or, she wondered with a twinge of humiliation, was this merely another case of nobody meeting Glory Hopkins's obnoxiously impossible standards?

How had Hannah—two girlfriends before Alicia—put it when she cheated on Glory with a married professor of theirs at Penn? "You need to believe whoever you're dating is perfect. Because you think you're perfect, too." "Well," Glory had told her, "at least I'm perfect enough not to have an affair just to get a glowing recommendation to a PhD program."

"Trust no one," Glory said to Maisie, who brushed back and forth against her leg when she gave up on the comforts of cocoa and poured what was left down the drain. "Lesson learned."

A few minutes later, as Glory walked into the hallway with a mug not of cocoa but of Scotch, the little cat ran ahead of her the way she sometimes did, up the stairs to Lucille's apartment.

"Oh, Maisie, come on," Glory called to her. "You know I wasn't going back up there. Come down."

Being a cat, naturally, she did not. Glory didn't like Maisie going up there, because she liked to hide in her secret spots and sometimes it was nearly impossible to find her once she had—which made Glory anxious. She liked to know the cat's whereabouts when the house made its mysterious cracks and wheezes and otherwise unidentifiable noises.

It seemed there was no choice but to follow Maisie to the second floor, where she strode arrogantly into the living room, jumped onto the sofa, and curled up against its red arm. Lucille's furniture was upholstered in a plush fabric with a soft pile that must have been very fashionable—and expensive—at the time. It still looked like new, most likely because Maisie and her kind had never been officially allowed to occupy it.

Glory sat down next to the cat. For lack of anything better to do, she reached below for a letter from one of the beribboned stacks still arranged on the carpet from when Parkie was there. As was the case with most of the envelopes, sun had bleached out the address to the point that Glory, without her glasses, couldn't make out more than a few numbers and a New York postmark.

She didn't recognize the writing on this one. If it was from Parkie's pile, that made sense. It, too, could be from the woman who wrote about the "dusky" nurse who'd caught her eye at the hospital downtown. Glory couldn't imagine describing another Black woman as "dusky."

The ink on the page inside was fresher and darker. Dated September 1944, the letter read:

My dear Lou,

    To be perfectly frank, I can't bear the thought of you going overseas. Facing danger there. Though I know how brave you are and that it is what you must want now that things are changing with FDR. My valiant officer. I am here and you there and without my better half in Harlem I am so very lonely. I know I shouldn't let you know—in order to keep morale up. But wouldn't you rather I told you? I hope so. I'm thinking of asking the author to take the apartment. Between us, it's safe to say she's fallen on hard times, though she would never admit it. I believe she may have been quite the sensation when she was young. Must be ten years older than yours truly. Maybe more. Keeps herself fit as a fiddle. But I have reached this conclusion from the odd tidbit dropped thither and yon. When I told her where I live she clammed up about her past! Yet I can see she knows Harlem and is your kind of person, I promise. When you return, and I know you will soon, my darling, we three could have a gay old time

together. She comes here for Sunday dinner whenever
I can get her to take the train and our shifts line up. Tell
me your opinion, it is your house, and you know I would
never take on a tenant without your blessing.

Glory stopped reading, unable to reconcile the information
in the letter with what she knew of her aunt's life. Who was this
woman? Had she been living in the brownstone while Lucille
was in the army?

She jumped off the couch and walked very quickly into
Lucille's bedroom. There was the Deco four-poster with its luxurious quilted-satin coverlet. There, the glazed maple chest of
drawers. And there, outside the closet door, was what Glory had
written off as a sort of personal wartime wall of fame, pretty young
nurses included. She switched on the overhead light.

The photographs were pale and yellowed. But even under
the pebbled glare of the glass fixture overhead she could see quite
easily that the subjects wearing crisp white uniforms in the five
photographs were the same two women. One of them—a blond
with a swirl of movie star waves beneath her nurse's cap—was
white. The other was an equally attractive but more solemn-
looking, somewhat older woman. Even from a creased and faded
snapshot, her dark, dark eyes exuded mystery and sadness. If the
blond was pale and almost certainly blue-eyed, this brown-eyed,
brown-skinned nurse might even be described as "dusky."

In the other photographs, the same two women stood outside buildings on what must have been cold days. They wore heavy,
superhero-esque black capes over their wasp-waisted dresses. That
these should be the women in and of the letters struck Glory
as both too easy and totally impossible. If one of them was "the
author," then who was the Betty Grable lookalike? Could she

possibly be the effusive writer who addressed Glory's stern but eternally ladylike aunt as "Lou"?

Glory's head was whirring so fast she had to lean her shoulders against the wall to fight the vertigo. For the second time that night she'd found herself facing a situation for which she was totally unprepared. She wondered what should, or could, possibly come next.

And then, as if in divine response, her phone and her laptop simultaneously chimed from downstairs with an incoming-call notification: "Doctor Eleanor Kenniston," said the feminized robotic voice. She managed to sprint back down to it just in time to beat voicemail.

"Eleanor, hello," Glory said, slightly winded.

"Good evening, Glory, I hope I haven't caught you at a bad time."

"Oh, no. Not at all. Sorry. I was just on the other side of the house."

"I really didn't expect you to answer, you know," Eleanor said. "Seems nobody does anymore. But I'm pleased you did, just the same. I, ah, I wondered if you'd seen the news coverage of the protests. At Cuthbert's, that is."

"I saw more than the news coverage," Glory said. "I was there." And so was Parkie, Glory thought to herself. Hiding inside, apparently. Being a "traitor," as the man in black at the protest had labeled her.

"Yes of course you were. Well done!"

"Oh, no. Not like that," Glory said. After all, she'd removed herself so far from reality lately, she hadn't even known what the protest was about. "I wasn't protesting. I was trying to see the preview. It hadn't clicked that Parkie's client was *that* Flagg family. And then I got caught in the crowd and met a man who explained it all to me. I didn't want to cross the picket line, so I came home. But it was something. Hundreds of people. Were you in there?"

"No," she said. "Rightly or wrongly, I didn't think I could protest outside, so I did so silently by calling in sick."

"That was noble," Glory said. Now this was a woman with principles.

"Too little too late, I'm afraid. But anyhow, I wanted to assure you that I'd still like to handle your estate if you'll allow me. I've had the things you left looked at and we'd like to send appraisers to see what's in the house. I'm not Madeline. Not by a long chalk. And if I may say so, nobody in this city comes to your aunt's property, to your inheritance, with more respect. And possibly, more knowledge, of her historical moment. Of her culture."

Again, Glory felt a mixture of relief and disillusionment when she realized Eleanor had called to *handle* her. This was client relations. And if she hadn't previously seen and heard Parkie in action, she'd never even have noticed. But like everything transpiring around her these days, the call was just another premise for quid pro quo; another transaction. Making a life in New York is always a kind of business. And doing business successfully requires compromise. How much truer that must always have been in Harlem.

Chapter 20

P arkie leaned on the bell. She'd already rapped several times on the door's wooden frame with no response, and she was too tired to do it again. She was so far on the other side of tired, in fact, she wasn't sure how much longer she could stand there, sciatica screaming, in the biting cold, at half past ten on a wintry December night.

A triangle of light flooded the first-floor hallway. The staircase came into view with Glory quickly descending it. She was wearing the most beautiful, shimmering dress, and she was barefoot, with her hair swept up. To a weary, emotionally spent Parkie, she looked like a larger-than-life Christmas-tree angel.

Presumably for safety's sake, Glory parted the sheers before opening the door, though Parkie was certain she knew who would be there.

The door squealed open and Parkie felt herself pulled inside along with the dry grit of snow in her wake. Now that she was face-to-face with Glory, it occurred to her she might not have the energy for the conversation she told herself she came for. After the day she'd had, her body was about to shut down, and anticipating that was its own kind of stress. Glory wasn't happy. But however done and dispassionate her greeting was supposed to be, she wasn't able to hide the concern in her eyes.

"You're frozen," she said, rubbing Parkie's arms. "Don't take your coat off yet. I was just thinking I should make a fire tonight."

"Do you know how to make a fire?" Parkie asked. She was sure Glory did.

"I grew up in Colorado," Glory replied.

Her tone told one story but her actions told another. Already she had her arms around Parkie, gingerly guiding her into the living room as if she'd been excavated from an avalanche.

She sat Parkie down and opened the flue. Next, she took a bundle of logs from a brass basket Parkie must have missed on her previous visits. After quickly stacking them, she went to the kitchen for a small stack of newspapers, expertly twisting them into kindling-sized ropes.

"Impressive," Parkie said when Glory lit the miniature log cabin she'd constructed. "Now this is what I call a good tinder date."

"This isn't a date," Glory snapped. Parkie knew better than to try to cajole her into a forgiving state with a bad joke. But it was worth a try.

"I know," she said. "It's me coming to apologize in person and maybe even try to explain. Thanks for not leaving me out in the cold."

"You can't help yourself, can you?"

"I'm sorry. I'm so tired, Glory. I don't think I've ever been this tired. I feel drunk and I didn't have a drop of anything. None of us had time to eat. I've had so much coffee I'm shaking."

Glory's expression softened again and she came to sit down next to Parkie as the fire spat and roared into a blaze. She took Parkie's icy hands and rubbed them in her warm palms a few times before replacing them in Parkie's lap like something she had temporarily borrowed.

"What time do you have to be there tomorrow?"

"Nine-thirty."

Glory stared at the flames as she spoke.

"That's not too bad. For Cuthbert's," she said. "I know you're tired. I can see how tired you are. And I don't want to make things worse. But I'm not going to pretend tonight didn't happen. Not this second. Maybe not even tonight. But at some point—sometime soon—I need to know why you did what you did. I need you to explain it to me. Why you didn't tell me sooner about those assholes—about your part in letting those shitty, shitty people keep making money off of so much suffering. You could have told me about it. You should have."

Parkie let the words echo in her head for as long as she could without answering. Of course Glory wanted answers. And of course Parkie didn't have any.

She dropped her face into her hands.

"I know I should have. I wanted to. No, that's not true. I never wanted to. But I knew I needed to. You'd just come right out and say it because you're the one with the compass, not me."

Glory had shaken her head once or twice while Parkie was saying these things. But she still hadn't turned to Parkie, as if she knew, just as Parkie did, that seeing her face—the look in her eyes—would make them both speak differently. Parkie wanted exactly this, but Glory did not.

"Look at me," Parkie said, slipping her fingers into the crook of Glory's elbow the way she sometimes did when they walked together. "They are my clients. And I knew they were shitty. I'll tell you everything. Even if it won't stop us from blowing up, I'll tell you everything. But I just can't do that tonight."

Glory stood up and Parkie knew not to hold on.

"This isn't an all-night fire," Glory said, her back to Parkie. "But I want to keep an eye on it for a while. It should heat up this floor at least. You go to bed. I'll be there in a few."

So often when you anticipate the worst, what you get if you're lucky is something not quite as bad. But this was the opposite of that. Parkie's mind was as desperate for slumber as her body. Maybe this was a form of grace. Being warmed by a fire made by someone who cares enough about you to wait. To wait for you to try to make things right. She would answer all Glory's questions tomorrow. It might mean the end of something she was starting to attach a future to. But for now, as the need to sleep overtook even her sadness and regret, Parkie was just happy to be where she was.

*

The next morning, she opened her eyes to Glory's bedroom. It was dim and freezing as always, except for Glory's hot breath on her collarbone. They had sidled up to each other during the night and now Glory was practically asleep in Parkie's arms, wrist draped over her ribs. Poured into a borrowed T-shirt of Glory's that was two sizes too small, Parkie didn't feel the cold in her marrow anymore. But she was tired and she hoped it was early.

"What time is it?" Glory murmured, like she was reading Parkie's mind.

Her hand trailed down to Parkie's waist and she pulled herself in closer.

"Six-thirty something," Parkie told her when she'd tipped her phone into view.

Parkie let the weight of her own hand settle on Glory's back, keeping it in the safe zone until she could tell where they stood with each other.

"Mmm. Good morning," Glory said groggily. "We have to talk, Parkie."

Parkie made a few noncommittally flat circles in the hollow between Glory's shoulder blades. She was surprised to feel Glory press her face into the compressed swell of her breasts beneath the borrowed shirt.

"You don't want me to fuck you a little, first?" Parkie said.

"What I want is for you to tell me about Flagg."

Parkie stopped the back rubbing but Glory's cheek stayed where it was as if to convey that anytime would be a good time for her to start talking.

"I don't know what you want me to say," Parkie said with the instant knowledge that this wasn't how she wanted to start her confession or whatever it was going to be. She felt a headache coming on. Possibly because she could tell Glory wasn't going to make this easy.

"Don't even," Glory said. "It's not my job to drag it out of you."

As she spoke, she lifted her cheek off Parkie's chest and turned onto her other side to face the wall.

Why was it so hard? Parkie had rehearsed a version of this since before she knew about the protests. In fact, she'd been preparing herself to tell Glory since the first time they'd kissed. And now they were sleeping together and she still hadn't done it. Parkie knew she was a lot of things. But she was not a coward.

Even when she sat up and started talking to Glory's back, Glory didn't turn around.

"I had a chance and I took it," Parkie said. "My old boss went back to France—I told you that—and left me this huge consignor. The Flagg estate, substandard as some of it is, will be a huge moneymaker for us. It's quantity over quality but the money spends the same, as Madeline keeps reminding us. Anyway. Whatever. Did I know that the clients my boss assigned me were bad actors? I can't say I didn't. The whole business is founded on a hypocritical premise—we want the world to know where things come from if we like the pedigree. If not, we hide the trail. But fuck, Glory, you know as well as I do that so many of the big collectors made their fortunes, or inherited them, from poisoned wells. What about when they want to buy your art with that money?"

"Do not try to make this about me," Glory said. "You work for a morally bankrupt monster. The Flagg family isn't just not very nice, they are killers. From what I've learned they're killers."

"So there we have it. You're right, Glory. We both know there's nothing I can say that's going to change whether or not they are or have been killers. Do you want me to leave?"

Glory flipped back over and looked her in the eye.

"No, Parkie, I don't want you to leave. I don't know what I want."

"Do you want me to say I'm sorry for taking them on as clients? That I wouldn't do it again if I had another chance? Because I am and I wouldn't. But I feel like that's not enough for you."

"You're right. It isn't enough," Glory said.

It was strange to have her so near and not experience the aura of Glory's attraction to her—the unambiguous desire she felt for Parkie and Parkie felt for her that seemed to generate its own magnetic field when they were together. Normally, even in public, they couldn't keep their hands off each other. Now, in the privacy of Glory's bedroom, Parkie had to judge if she'd be allowed to come any closer.

Figuring, at this point, she had nothing to lose, Parkie slid over. She cupped Glory's chin, gauged the look in her eyes, and softly kissed her. Glory not only let her, she kissed Parkie back. Yet in the pained, involuntary moan she made when their lips touched and the undisguised aggressiveness of her tongue, there was something novel.

"What if I want to fuck *you* a little?" Glory said, pulling her face off Parkie's.

"Do you?"

Glory fell onto her back and laughed a dark laugh. "Like I said, I don't know what I want. I think I want what I always want."

"Then I'll fuck you until you come for me," Parkie said. "You know I will."

"Do it," Glory said. "And then we'll see how I feel about your apology."

If this was Glory's way of, if not exactly disciplining Parkie, then letting her know she wasn't in charge anymore, it was a spoonful of sugar minus the medicine. Because, as Glory was well aware, Parkie getting her to climax however she wanted her to was one of the ways she stayed in control.

They were still facing each other, though Glory had put her chin in her palm in a show of thoughtful consideration.

"How do you want it?" Parkie asked her.

"With you on your back and me riding your hand," Glory said without hesitation. "With your nipples in my mouth. And you not stopping no matter what I do to them."

When Parkie looked back at Glory, she made sure her pleasure was invisible. She didn't want Glory getting the impression she found this cute, coming from her. It wasn't cute but it wasn't a punishment either. If it would reset the scales, however, Parkie could find another way to assuage her guilt.

*

There was a cool layer of remove in Glory's gaze as she pushed Parkie down and climbed roughly on top of her. Parkie wanted to spur her on, but thought better. Glory, who was anchoring her small hands on various points of Parkie's body, clearly had a plan. She even resisted Parkie's attempt to kiss her—only to let her pussy streak Parkie's torso with telling wetness as she made her way down to her clit.

From there the sex was nonverbal, efficient, and, yes, more than a little punitive.

Glory teased Parkie, coming on not strong but with excessive delicacy and finesse. She licked light circles around her areolas, kissed the sides of her breasts, took just the tips of both nipples between her lips. And then, as soon as Parkie entered her—with three loosely interlaced fingers—she bit and nipped and sucked her nearly to the point of rawness. Parkie let herself squeal and whimper from the twinges of pain even though it only made Glory go further.

After a while Glory gave in to a dramatic orgasm. She came so hard she had to rip her mouth off Parkie's breasts and spring upright. Back arched, she shuddered and jerked as Parkie lay beneath her continuing to make subtle movements with her fingers, waiting an extravagant amount of time to pull out.

"Jesus, Parkie," Glory panted when she did. "How can I hate you after that?"

"I'm hoping you can't," Parkie said. "I fucked up. But I was never as good as you thought I was. Better to know that now."

Glory leaned in to kiss her then sat up again. Parkie experienced the kiss, like being invited to stay last night, as a mercy.

"Well, you're still pretty fucking good. But the Flagg thing really messed me up," Glory said. "I felt like whoever that woman was who took on a client so truly evil there had to be a protest.

A protest! That wasn't the you I know. I still can't believe it's you. At least if you had told me, I could have . . . Honestly, I don't know what I would have done."

"It was me. And I don't have a good excuse, just the background, I guess. It was me, but it's not how I want to be," Parkie said.

Glory climbed off her and lay down.

"I decided I'm going home for Christmas for the first time in a while," Parkie said when she'd gotten settled. "To Greenwich. I need to straighten some things out with my parents. I might as well tell you, now that I'm batting a thousand in bravery, I haven't officially come out to them. It's not like they don't know. They just work incredibly hard at keeping it an open secret. Something they never let me talk about. But I'm going up a full day ahead of the dreaded semiformal Christmas Eve dinner and the idea is to put an end to the de Groot family 'don't ask, don't tell' policy before you can say 'ho ho ho.'"

"Shit," Glory said. "Home for the holidays: A Reckoning. Good for you, baby. But I hope you're not doing this now because of me. Because I for sure don't want to be the bitch who stole Christmas."

"You aren't. You won't be. I don't know if I'll tell them about you or not. But you're not why I'm telling them. I mean, of course you're why. But not the only why. If this is going to work with us, I know I need to be honest with myself. With my family. With you."

Glory reached for her hand.

"Are you going home?" Parkie asked. "For Christmas?"

"See, you are brave," Glory said. "Because I should. I mean, my parents have always been fine with the gay part—it helps them feel like good liberals. But there's plenty of other shit that needs to be straightened out at the Hopkins house. I just can't handle it right now. I'm gonna stay here and make art, I guess. Whatever that means. Christmas kind of snuck up on me. Seems to be a theme these days."

"What do you mean 'whatever that means'?"

"Well, my new stuff is shit, obviously, so I need to figure out where that leaves me. With Manya. And . . . some other people."

"Other people like who?"

Parkie had picked up something like this a few conversations ago, and she was beginning to think there was something Glory purposely wasn't telling her.

Glory sighed and squeezed her hand. They were both staring at the ceiling.

"Sarkisian."

"No! Sar-fucking-kisian!?" Parkie shouted. "Or should I say, *Star*-fucking-kisian? *That* was your studio visit. I knew it. I hoped I didn't know it, but I knew it. Well, first of all, congratulations."

Glory turned her way and put her hand on Parkie's stomach. This conciliatory gesture was unwelcome, and Parkie shifted a little to show it.

"Knew what? There wasn't anything formal until they called a couple of days ago. And that was after the obliterating review. You were busy, I was busy. We hadn't even talked about Christmas."

"Bullshit," Parkie said.

"Come again?"

"You could have told me it was them during any of our many intimate and not-so-intimate conversations over the last few weeks. But you didn't. Why is that, I wonder?"

Glory pulled her arm back.

"Let's be clear, this is in no way comparable with what you did. I didn't want to jinx it, in the first place. Also, I knew you'd basically react like this and I wasn't in a place where I could deal with someone shitting on an offer that could make my career if not change my whole fucking life. Which is pretty much the same thing."

"You didn't know how *I'd* react! *If* you told me the truth about it. Hah. You felt guilty because you knew what a deal with them would say about you. How is that different?"

"It's different because Sarkisian is not Flagg Pharmaceuticals. It's a commercial gallery not a right-wing conspiracy. Maybe it's not run by a queer woman of color, but it's much more diverse than it used to be. You know who's in their stable. And curatorially, there's no shame in working with them. They're single-handedly driving contemporary; they could even control my value on the secondary market."

"Oh, please. You sound like a Wharton grad. Tell me more about the shame part. I wouldn't know, since I only worked for the director there for three years."

"You need to stop," Glory said. She was sitting up with her arms crossed over her chest. Her eyes crackled with fury when she looked over at Parkie, who suddenly wanted out of their way.

Parkie pushed herself up and leaned against the headboard.

"You worked for them a while ago," Glory said. "Especially around BIPOC artists, things have changed there. Which you should know."

Parkie pictured the ever-present flock of skinny, enthusiastic, almost entirely white Ivy League and Sotheby's grads fluttering around the gallery trying to sound impressive. Trying to meet their future employers. Trying to meet their future husbands. The more the girls themselves changed, the more the business stayed the same.

"Here's what I know. They always have, and always will, want certain kinds of artists for certain kinds of reasons. So tell me this: After the *Times* review, did they or did they not inform you that representation—and a solo show—would depend on you going back to your more abstract style. That the new work wasn't consistent with their microwaved new criticism. Read: too figural. Too narrative. Too political. Too full of context. All the things, in other words, that Manya likes about it. That I like about it. Tell me that's not what . . . who was it? Had to be Wallford—said?"

Glory swung her legs over the side of the mattress as if she were headed to the bathroom.

"You know what, Parkie? I don't want to do this with you. And I'm pretty sure you don't want to do it with me. So maybe you *should* leave."

"Maybe I should," Parkie said. "I wouldn't want to *not* say anything I might regret."

Chapter 21

G lory hadn't heard from Parkie since what she was choosing to think of as their mutual decision to take a break, a Christmas break, before trying to work things out under less, shall we say, charged circumstances. It had been twelve days, and she missed Parkie desperately.

She also had to respect Parkie, something she seemed hardwired to do, for not giving in and calling or texting or stopping by. Glory had, after all, essentially sent the woman she was falling for packing. In no uncertain terms, she'd asked Parkie to leave, and leave Parkie had. Parkie, who was nothing if not disciplined. So disciplined, Glory now feared, she might be the kind of woman who is perfectly willing to sever all emotional ties if she feels she's been treated unjustly.

Cut and run.

Glory knew all about that.

Whatever Parkie's endgame, she had certainly called Glory's bluff. It would take something big to get her attention at this point. It would also take an apology. But grand gestures had never been Glory's style. She might have been able to make them her style if she could reconcile herself to Parkie's infuriatingly accurate paraphrase of Wallford's offer. That was another double-edged sword: Parkie was dead-on about Sarkisian, and while that was impressive, it was also humiliating to see herself and her work through their eyes the way Parkie described it.

Parkie had that part right. But Glory's situation was in no way the same. Sure, she'd been in a tough spot with Madeline. But not tough enough to justify what was effectively collaboration with the heir of a far-right dynasty for whom the auction was apparently an insurrectionist fundraiser. Glory was merely considering an adjustment of her own creative agenda in order to align with market forces. It might not be pure of heart but it simply didn't compare.

However. Without so much as a text from Parkie, Glory had started to wonder if she'd been too harsh that night—and the morning after—when she had started to believe their epic makeup fuck would turn things around. Parkie had apologized. Parkie was contrite. And what did Cuthbert's mean in the scheme of things, anyway? As her father liked to ask her when she broke one of her mother's favorite glasses or missed a shot in sports: "In a hundred years, do you think it will matter?"

After days went by with no human contact of any form, Glory could feel herself starting to crack a little—starting to wonder if she'd really said and done what she thought she remembered. Starting to wonder if Flagg was a mountain or a molehill.

It was time to call Eleanor, the wisest single Black woman she knew.

Glory's premise for reaching out, at least initially, was the discovery she'd made about Lucille and the two nurses in the letters from Lucille's desk.

She wasn't sure why she was feeling nervous about sharing what she learned about her aunt with someone she trusted. Even if she'd done something scandalous, Lucille was gone. Nothing could touch her now. And if who she was was someone Glory's parents couldn't handle, then . . . fuck them.

Glory was beginning to think nobody in their family deserved Lucille, including her. But whatever the case, without Eleanor's knowledge and connections, there was only so far Glory could go on her own. While intuition told her where the roads were leading, Glory had to know for sure where Lucille had ended up.

She'd asked Eleanor to stop by on the way home from work. And this was a huge step. Other than Parkie (and Wallford), Glory hadn't invited anyone to the brownstone—not socially. The house still felt more like someone else's than her own.

Which left Glory in a quandary: She didn't want Eleanor to see her work, examples of which were currently dispersed throughout the first floor. Including the bathroom. Nor did she want to give her visitor free rein over Lucille's apartment. She suspected, given Eleanor's age, that many of Lucille's possessions would hold a significance to her in a way they couldn't to Glory; that Eleanor would gain access to knowledge about Lucille simply from being there. After all this time, Glory was finally becoming a little possessive of her aunt and her legacy— she didn't want to feel left out of Lucille's real life any more than she already did.

They were sitting in Glory's kitchen downstairs because, in the end, it seemed the most neutral room in the house. Aside from Lucille's aversion to open shelves and affection for tile, the kitchen gave nothing else away about the landlord. On the big swirly laminate table, Glory spread out the letters she'd described to Eleanor on the phone. She planned to tell her about the nurse photographs on the wall of Lucille's dressing room. But at the last minute, she got cold feet about that. Instead, she decided to see how much Eleanor could put together on her own.

It hadn't taken her long.

As she explained it to Glory, all the letters seemed to be by and/or about three women: Lucille, while she was serving in the army at Fort Des Moines; a nurse writing to her from the brownstone (who signed her letters merely "R."); and a nurse with whom R. worked in Manhattan, referred to by the two other women as "the author."

Even behind her half-moon reading glasses, the curiosity was visible in Eleanor's intent gray eyes as she read and reread the sheets of stationery, arranging them in chronological order when she was finished.

"And you say there's been no mention in your family of someone with an *R* name living here?" Eleanor said.

"And no mention of 'the author.' Or any other author," Glory said. "Did you see the one where R. tells Lucille that the author cooked her a delicious dinner downstairs? I don't know about you, but that meal sounded pretty intimate to me. Then the next one says the author's been staying upstairs to save on the heating bill. Sounds like R. and the author might have been heading in a certain direction."

Eleanor nodded vigorously, patting one of the envelopes. "Yes, yes," she said. "But you saw, I assume, this from the previous week, where your aunt Lucille tells R. she's spending her furlough in Chicago with that *other officer*. The funny one from Ohio. I think maybe R. was not above sparking a little good old-fashioned jealousy in your aunt."

Glory considered what to say before she said it.

"Jealousy."

"Did you never see that side of her?" Eleanor asked.

"The jealous side? Or the . . . are you saying they were?"

"Heavens, Glory," Eleanor said with a chuckle. "I will say it if you won't. I would bet my bottom dollar that Lucille—or Lou—and R. were passionate and devoted, cohabitating lesbian lovers. And had been for some time before the war, if I've read these correctly. Enter the author, and the happy couple is forced to contemplate what her role in their lives might be once Lucille comes home. Or so it seems to me."

Until that moment, it seemed as if Eleanor had always been the woman sitting beside Glory now. Elegant, reserved, white-haired, and careful. So careful. But of course that wasn't true at all. She had been young. She had been happy at times. In trouble at times. And almost certainly in love at times, too. You had to have been in love yourself to discern it in the key changes of a friendship or a letter writer's turn of phrase. Eleanor hadn't needed to see the photographs or even the upstairs apartment to understand Lucille.

*

How the hell did it get to be Christmas Eve?

Glory was so absorbed in freshening up the old work, she'd lost an entire day again. She wouldn't have known Christmas was upon her if her playlist denouement, the entire *Renaissance* album, hadn't come to an end. When the last song ended, it was early morning. Sometimes after an all-nighter, she felt a kind of jittery, can't-stop, won't-stop high set in. When it did, Glory liked to ride what she secretly knew to be the kind of pure inspiration when her choices were beyond her control. Now she was working in silence. Feeling sufficiently energized by the parlor's strengthening sunlight to boldly scrape off most of an illustrated cover of *The Comet* from the surface of a huge, mostly red canvas. There was gold leaf on her sneakers and cerulean blue in her hair, and at the very instant she had stepped away to think what would come next, she heard a loud series of raps on the front door.

People usually used the doorbell, so the impact of the knocking was immediate. She had an instantaneous vision of Parkie, who liked to use her cane to announce her presence on the stoop. Had Parkie waited just long enough for her to begin to regain equilibrium, like a person back on solid ground after months on a choppy sea? Glory hesitated before she put down the pigment-soaked paper she was holding. She hesitated before she wiped off her hands. She hesitated before she ambled, eyes on the floorboards, into the front room.

Before she looked up, she felt her heart shoot into her chest like a rocket. And just as quickly, she felt it nosedive into her gut.

It wasn't Parkie.

Glory knew the feathers and bright green coat right away. It was the woman from the house next door, an elderly retired insurance agent. She was a longtime widow Glory had come to recognize from afar, owing to her baroque taste in hats. When she caught sight of Glory inside, she waved something back and forth as if to let Glory know it was for her. Glory opened the door.

"Good morning, Miss Hopkins," said the woman. "I know it's early but I'm headed up to see my kids in Hartford, and I keep meaning to give you this envelope that mail carrier of ours misdelivered. Looks like a Christmas card. I had it on the hall table and I kept walking right past it. It's been a few days.

Better now than never, I guess!" She offered Glory a large square
envelope hand-addressed in a flowery script. "You have a merry
Christmas, Miss Hopkins!" she said with a wave behind her back
as she started down the stairs.

Glory had barely said hello and goodbye before she was
back inside what felt, by contrast, like the warm embrace of her
welcoming home. Still no snow of consequence, but it was gray,
cold, and windy out there.

A card for Christmas. Tomorrow.

She wished she hadn't heard the rapping. The work was
finally going well again. She'd been in the zone. Mrs. Healey could
have put the envelope in the mailslot. If Glory hadn't thought it
might be Parkie out there waiting for her, she never would have
stopped.

Now the painting magic was gone. The zone was no more.

Still, it was a new day. Glory decided she might as well get
back on some sort of a schedule—something Eleanor had advised
as a way to combat the at-sea-ness of being alone so much. She
shuffled into the kitchen and robotically ground some coffee
beans, filled up the kettle, and opened the refrigerator, hoping to
find the components of breakfast.

The best she could do was two slices of crusty, days-old
bread slathered with butter and peanut butter. Once the pour-
over was ready, she plopped down at the table with the square
envelope.

The return address wasn't familiar, and the envelope's stock
was so heavy she'd needed to wipe off her butter knife to use as
a letter opener. Inside was a single pale-peach card with a combination of handwritten and printed information in a rich shade
of brown. It read:

You are invited to:
      cocktails, revelry, and the twenty-sixth annual
        Christmas Eve for Those in the Know
          Where: At Graham Court No 7F
       When: 24th December, beginning at 8 p.m.
          Dress: Black tie, why knot?

It was signed, "Cordially, Eleanor."

Well, how about that? Glory thought as she propped the card against the peanut butter jar to take a bite of her PB&B.

Chapter 22

Parkie slept in on Christmas Eve. First of all, she was dog-tired. And second of all, her intention was to sleep her way straight through Christmas. She lacked any preferable, less demoralizing options and had, as a result, swan-dived into the depths of self-pity. Her current situation had come about when, one foot out the door to Grand Central, her brother had kindly informed her that, per their mother, their recently divorced uncle, Hugo, was coming to Greenwich this year.

On hearing that news, Parkie had abruptly changed her mind about going home. But not about coming out.

Back in the apartment, fueled by successive shots, she called to inform her mother that she refused to be in the same room with a self-professed homophobe and racist. Her mother, as always, invoked the sacred ideal of family first, and the two of them proceeded to get into a heated argument.

Of course, *heated*, by de Groot standards, wouldn't soft-boil an egg.

Thus, when Parkie had calmly made the point that Uncle Hugo supported legislation that would allow her to be fired from her job because she was gay, Mrs. de Groot implacably countered by asking Parkie if she had any reason to think she was in danger of losing her job anytime soon. When Parkie answered (1) that she didn't, and (2) did she hear what she just said? her mother replied with something like, "Well, Parkie dear, it's Christmas, and if your job is safe and you don't have a boyfriend to be with, you might as well come home and be with your family. Which would make your brother happy. Unless, of course, you'd rather stay in the city eating ice cream all alone."

To which, Parkie had said, "Mother, I believe I would," and hung up.

She'd never before drawn a line like this with her parents. She expected it might feel good, liberating even, to have said what she knew were the right things to say. But they always found a way to push her buttons. Her tender buttons. It was as if she'd shouted the words "Your only daughter is a dildo-wielding, pussy-licking, yacht-club-membership-threatening homo" into a chintz-upholstered void. No surprise, really, since her mother's superpower was unlistening. She had a particular genius, a sub-set of gaslighting, Parkie could now acknowledge, for unhearing and unreacting so that she could simply move on as if nothing had been said or done. Because it hadn't. Her unacknowledged coming-out had therefore left Parkie feeling even more alone. Although she wasn't sorry she had said what she said, she felt sorry for herself for having had to say it.

That phone call to her mother had called for a root beer float.

And now here it was, dinnertime on Christmas Eve, and she was sad and alone and overly carbonated.

Christmas Eve. Her only prospect a silent retreat in her lightless apartment, pummeled by the ambient sounds—which had already started—of other people having fun all around her.

Her phone pinged.

"You're fucking kidding me," an incredulous Parkie said aloud to the screen before answering.

She considered declining the call. Now it was almost too late to answer. She could easily just let it go to voicemail. What if it was an emergency?

"Ms. Shah," Parkie said with every icy ounce of professionalism she could siphon.

"Ms. de Groot," came the facetiously formal reply.

"I hope nothing's wrong," Parkie said.

"Not at all. Except I'm learning the night before is almost as big a to-do as Christmas Day over here. I don't partake. But I had every intent of leaving a festive yuletide message. Guessing if you're picking up, though, your dance card might have an opening. You wouldn't fancy a quick bite, would you?"

How she was able to think and act so fast was a wonder to Parkie, who'd barely had time to follow the first part, let alone contemplate, and reject, the invitation. A strictly unprofessional get-together with Manya Shah. On a holiday.

What a terrible idea.

Worse, from where Parkie was sitting (the crewel-embroidered armchair her mother had donated to this, her first adult apartment), it felt suspiciously like being asked out. Shah had some nerve asking her out. Parkie should decline on principle alone. Just say no. She could be the kryptonite to Manya's fucking Superman.

On the other hand, Manhattan on Christmas Eve might be wonderful. For thousands of New Yorkers, it was just another night—in this case a Saturday night—so why not treat it that way? In some neighborhoods restaurants and bars would be hopping—full of non-Christmas-celebrating people of all descriptions. It could be fun. She certainly hadn't been anywhere unorthodox—besides Loden's bedroom—in Christmas Eves past.

Parkie looked around as her observations began to coalesce into a rationale. Apartments were impossible to land in the city. And this one, in a quiet, respectable building on a floor of grandparents and independently wealthy non-profiteers, was truly a find. Not that she had found it. Either her dad or her mother had known people who knew the people in the apartment next door, who also owned this one, which was inhabited by one of their fathers after his wife died. It was small and dark and, on the days she was willing to admit it, it still smelled like a place someone very old had spent their final years.

And yet it wasn't at all like Lucille's apartment, which was haunted, Parkie supposed, but benevolently. When she was there with Glory, it was like they were protected by a supernatural mosquito net. Glory had laughed when Parkie told her she thought her aunt still might be looking out for her from upstairs. But Parkie believed it was true. Whatever there was in Harlem was the opposite of the claustrophobic, postapocalyptic ambience of her own place—to which she owed her recurring Cuthbert's overtime. It wasn't much to come home to. And it wasn't a place to spend Christmas Eve alone. Not if she wasn't already asleep. Even with Manya Shah, a dinner was only a dinner.

"Why not?" Parkie replied at last.

"Blimey, you don't say," Manya Shah answered, sounding perplexed. "And here I was primed to build an elaborate brief in support of my case. Bit of a letdown, this. Not that I'm complaining."

"Because it sounds like you're complaining," Parkie said to Shah's muffled laughter.

Almost against her will, she could feel her mood lifting. Volatile and intimidating as she was, Manya Shah's company was sure to make for a night before Christmas worth remembering. Parkie hoped going out with her wasn't a decision she'd soon regret.

*

Chop-Shop, the restaurant they agreed on, was a casual Asian-fusion spot in Chelsea they'd both been to before. Parkie noted that it was steps away from the gallery, which made it very easy for Manya Shah to get to, provided she was working, but more of a trek for her guest. The addictive food was always worth the trip and the wait, though—Parkie was a fan of the cloudlike pork belly buns, and everyone knew their drunken noodles were to die for.

Just like the last time, here was Manya camped out at a prime table—a big four-top—in the back of the unaffected, not-very-large restaurant.

She opened her hands across the table in a welcoming gesture.

Tonight, despite the cold, Manya was wearing trousers with just a blouse, unbuttoned about as low as Parkie would have gone for a date with Glory. Parkie, by contrast, had thrown on a green lambswool sweater, jeans, and boots, even though nothing was sticking to the ground yet. Green really does complement a redhead's coloring. And although what she was wearing also showed off her curves, Parkie hoped the very choice of a wool crewneck marked her as unavailable, or at least inaccessible, for the hours to come.

Again, Manya stood to give her a double-cheek kiss, only this time, Parkie felt the actual touch of her lips. She was near enough for the rarified scent of her perfume to reach Parkie's nostrils. Parkie couldn't help taking it in.

"I've fallen in love with this place," Manya said as they sat down. "I think I've tried everything."

"Seems like your standard approach," Parkie said, immediately looking back at her menu.

"You have a very ill-informed idea of me. Is someone feeding you gossip?"

"Just instinct, I guess. You strike me as someone who gets what she wants. But always does the recon first."

"Whereas you tend to trust your aforementioned instinct and jump in with both feet," Manya said, taking a quick sip of her coconut cocktail. "I'm sorry. Poor choice of words."

It was always the most conscientious people who kicked themselves the hardest for getting tripped up by what they feared was ableist language when they were around her. Parkie found it humorous.

"Thanks," she said. "I'm not super sensitive about that semantic level. I still can and do jump in with one foot. I got in touch with your Renoir people, by the way. Thanks for that." She took a sip of the cocktail Manya had ordered for her. "So. How goes the gallery biz? Excited about your first killer group show? I can't imagine running a space like that in a new city. Your artists must really trust you to follow you."

"It goes," Manya said. "And yeah. Wherever you are, you have to have an eye and a sense of how that translates. In the end, it goes down to the courage of one's convictions. If I believe in an artist and what they're doing, I will go to the brink for them. I'll stay with them even when they're feeling blocked, you know, or trying out something that I don't think—or they don't think—is working."

"Sounds like you're very loyal."

"Incredibly," Manya said, looking Parkie in the eye. "It's one of the things I pride myself on. In all facets of life."

As she was talking, Parkie thought she spied a glimmer of something in Manya's expression—a bad memory, maybe, or something that still pained her. As if she'd accidently bumped a bruised spot she already knew was there. It occurred to Parkie that she might have misjudged Manya, something she was really hoping not to find out. Not tonight.

"Anyway, how goes the married life? I will say, I'm surprised you're not with your unnamed spouse tonight. Does she celebrate Christmas?"

"I never said 'married.' I was seeing someone and we're taking a break, I guess. Otherwise, I wouldn't have come to dinner."

"Because you think I'm out to tick you off my Christmas list, as it were."

"You really are shameless," Parkie said with a good-natured nose-crinkle. "Like I said, I think you're used to getting what you want, whether it's the best table in a restaurant or dinner with someone who has previously, and repeatedly, refused your invitations."

"I did want to see you again," Manya said, smiling. "I had fun at lunch. You're intriguing. Smart, heart-stoppingly toothsome, and, I'd wager, still rather humane under it all. Among other things. Can you blame me?"

*

It wasn't the kind of restaurant where you linger for hours, even if, as Manya quickly had, you've become one of the best clients. After they finished the mango crème caramel they'd agreed to split but that Manya had wolfed down on her own, it was still quite early, not yet nine.

Parkie wasn't interested in going to a club. Or even a bar, necessarily. She was trying to assess Manya's game plan, which seemed not so much a question of *what next* as *how soon*. So far, the night had largely consisted of Parkie suppressing her emotions. She agreed to dinner as a diversion. Or possibly, as an affirmation of her suppositions about Manya Shah, the London Lothario. Contrary to what she'd experienced over lunch, Parkie's aim was to find Manya off-putting and her conversation, at a minimum, fatally narcissistic, somehow offensive, or merely uninteresting.

Instead, Parkie had been rapt the entire time. Her stories were funny and strange, increasingly self-effacing as the dinner wore on, in a completely endearing way. Her manner was refreshingly candid. Her confidence, enticing.

And Manya's undisguised attraction to Parkie, far more than flattering, made her feel as if she'd been given a glimpse of the road not taken. She'd wanted to take that journey with Glory, of course. Until she worried she wasn't good enough for Glory, only to find Glory had a double standard where goodness was concerned.

Parkie had been holding out hope that Glory would try to reach her. She'd awakened each morning desperate for an overnight text saying she was ready to talk. In her dream of what would happen, they would both apologize—Glory for not admitting Parkie was right about Sarkisian. Parkie for not telling Glory the whole truth about the Flaggs. And possibly, for taking them on as clients. Though that part was really between her and her maker, she'd come to realize. If someone was owed an apology for managing Flagg, it wasn't Glory.

Almost two weeks had gone by since that morning in bed. Glory showed no desire to reconnect. Nor, following Nicholas's stern advice, had Parkie made any attempts to contact her. Tonight, come what may, she'd planned to text Glory a Christmas greeting.

But then Manya had called.

"Something on your mind?" Manya asked. "I was kidding, of course, about the clubbing. But you must know a nice little boite for a drink. I think we've about worn out our welcome here."

"I don't spend much time in this neighborhood," Parkie said. "You've been great with the choices so far. Do you live close? I'm uptown."

"The gallery keeps an apartment on the High Line, so it's just a few blocks away if that's relevant. One doesn't like to presume."

Parkie would have thought presuming was one of the things Manya liked to do best.

So tempting to let it play out. But so too soon. Even if tonight was going somewhere with Manya, an idea she currently didn't hate, Parkie didn't want them to move too fast. In addition to being tacky, a hookup tonight could taint Christmases future.

Manya politely excused herself to check her phone and began speedily typing something lengthy to someone somewhere who must have known she was always working.

Parkie checked her own messages.

No texts from Glory. No calls from Glory. No new IG stories from Glory.

Not having anything else to do, she opened her company email, where she was basically flabbergasted to see a new message from Dr. Kenniston. A must-click.

The message had arrived while they were eating. It read:

Miss de Groot. I know you sent your regrets RE: my Christmas Eve gathering. But if you happen to find yourself unexpectedly in town, don't feel as though you can't still join us in Harlem. Graham Court, apartment 7F. Things usually go quite late. —EDK

"Sorry about that, lovely," Manya said, putting her phone away. "Crisis averted. These jackals of yours are going to make keeping that gallery open a struggle, it's been made clear."

"Mine?"

"Oh, you know, your American art mafia. TPTB. 'Poachers' might be a better word."

"Powerful people trying to steal your artists, you mean?"

Manya let her face go blank.

"Let's see how far it gets them," she said.

"I think they better watch their back." Parkie nodded. "Have you been to Harlem yet?"

"Of course," Manya said. "Harlem is where I went first. Why?"

"I remembered a party I was invited to tonight. Could be fun. The host is a woman I work with. She's kind of fascinating, I think the two of you would like each other."

"Even I'm against threesomes on a first date. You won't get rid of me that easily."

Parkie rolled her eyes.

"Definitely not where I was going with that. Should I call a car?"

Chapter 23

What Glory imagined might be a drowsy gathering of a dozen of Dr. K.'s aging book-enthusiast friends was anything but. First of all, the apartment was a palace, with a vaulted great room and long walls of windows on two sides. It was a corner unit, and although the building wasn't more than ten stories, neither were most places in Harlem, so the views of the city's urban landscape of twinkling lights were breathtaking.

The room where most of the guests had gathered near the grand piano was pleasingly but unevenly illuminated by small lamps and candles. The flickering reflections echoed in an army of mirrors and ornamental gilt-bronze fixtures of the sort they sometimes sold individually at the auction house. On the floors, fine Persian rugs of different sizes were tossed over a straw-colored marquetry pattern. Above, cove ceilings over persimmon-colored walls displayed delicate plaster moldings. There were attractive objects everywhere, yet nothing was the least bit garish or overdone.

Although it was hard to know where to look first, few guests could enter without being bewitched and bewildered by the books. Rather than the few lengths of painted shelves one might see in the den of a prewar Park Avenue apartment, Dr. Kenniston's living room was flush with books on all four walls. Each towering built-in was graduated in scale with studded grosgrain ribbon trim edging the shelves. The effect of the multitude of candlelit spines, with their thickly stamped titles and variously hued leathers, was a carnival of color. Her Cuthbert's office looked like a bookmobile by comparison.

It made you want to pull something off the shelf and read it on the spot.

Or at least it would have if it weren't for the party itself, which was undeniably lit.

Glory was still standing in amazement like a swimmer on the shore when Dr. Kenniston glided over to her.

"Glory," she exclaimed with touching enthusiasm. "What a surprise! I'm so pleased you were able to come. And how well you look."

"Tuxedos are easy." Glory laughed, taking in Eleanor Kenniston's lavishly beaded, undoubtedly couture red gown—she was the one who looked fantastic. Glory said an internal prayer that she might look half as good as Eleanor when she was twice her current age. She was straight out of a movie.

"Drinks are being concocted in all four corners," she said. "But I highly recommend the house toddy, which is only available in the kitchen."

Glory reached for her hand and, feeling unusually bold, kissed Kenniston's emerald ring.

Eleanor laughed bashfully and waved Glory off.

When she returned, a toasty glass mug of spiced rum in hand, Glory scanned the room as she reentered it. When the piano player began to tinkle out a jazzy version of "Greensleeves" on the lacquered Steinway in the corner, she realized she was brimming with good tidings and maybe even a little joy.

And then she saw them.

Near the wide arch she'd also passed through. There they were. Standing arm in arm. Or, rather, one with her arm through the arm of the other, their backs to her as if they'd just turned to greet the hostess.

Eleanor hovered in front of them, facing in her direction. As Glory continued to move forward through a cluster of guests, against her own volition, it seemed, she could hear the introductions.

Here was the voice she'd been missing. The voice she'd know anywhere.

"Eleanor, you look stunning. Let me introduce Manya Shah, the new director of Moulton, Freer & Shah," Parkie was saying. "We were out to dinner—I didn't end up going to Greenwich after all—when I got your very kind message and, without thinking, I suggested we come straight up."

"I may lose my EU passport for violating the dress code," Manya added. "Enormously sorry about that."

Dr. Kenniston's bright eyes jumped back and forth between them. She was, after all, a first-rate appraiser. In no time she appeared to have a decent idea of what was what.

And so, Glory thought, did she.

Manya reached to shake Dr. Kenniston's hand, offering gracious compliments about the apartment. Kenniston regarded her with an expression that Glory read as a combination of "welcome" and "you really, really shouldn't have."

"No, no," she said. "Think nothing of it. It's black-tie optional, of course—merely a sartorial opportunity for those who are so inclined. But unlike dear Cuthbert's, we don't stand on ceremony in my house. Miss Shah, perhaps you'd like to fetch some drinks—the bartender in the kitchen makes a wonderful rum toddy—and then you must tell me all the news from England. Are you a cricket fan?"

"I am when Jofra Archer is involved," Shah replied, receiving Kenniston's conspicuous, if reluctant, approval. "Rum toddy?" she asked Parkie, who nodded with a brilliant smile.

As soon as Manya Shah was away, Dr. Kenniston leaned over to Parkie.

"There's something you should know," Glory heard her say.

To turn around now, Glory realized, would be to create a scene. It would be uncouth. It would be rude. It would be cowardly in the extreme. But goddamn did she want to do it. Anything not to be in the same room with Parkie on a date with another woman, absurdly dressed for the occasion in a sweater and jeans. Not that Parkie couldn't do her absolute worst in a sweater and jeans. But still, black tie ought to mean something.

Usefully, this rare social misstep on Parkie's part gave Glory something negative to focus on. A reason to stay mad. Because at a time like this, she could use all the help she could get.

"Yes, there you are, Glory," Eleanor said unflappably. "I was about to mention to Miss de Groot that you were, much to my delight, present. And now I must take my leave. Try to enjoy yourselves, my young friends. It's Christmas."

Eleanor knew exactly what she was doing. Not long ago, Glory had spilled her guts to the good doctor after they'd spent an afternoon together reading dozens of epistolary variations on the theme of "love may conquer all but that doesn't mean things won't be difficult first." Eleanor, who seemed so chary, even cold, on the outside, was ten times more empathetic than Glory's own mother. Her advice to Glory had been not to give up on Parkie or let Parkie give up on her. Not when she felt the way she clearly felt about her. "It takes time to see the world for what it is and find our place," she had said. "You're both doing that right now. Parkie isn't the only one."

"I thought you were working," Parkie said hesitantly.

"And I thought you were speaking your truth in Greenwich," said Glory.

"And yet, here we all are," said the unmistakable voice of Manya goddamned Shah.

She came up behind Parkie to offer her one of Eleanor's toddies, which Parkie gratefully accepted. Their hands practically caressed each other in the delivery, and Glory got a feeling she did. Not. Like.

It hadn't even been a fortnight!

"Vintage YSL, Miss Hopkins?" said Shah. "Le smoking hot."

"Thanks," Glory said. "I see you didn't get the memo."

"It was kind of a last-minute decision," Parkie apologized. Her eyes were glistening. "You do look amazing."

"We'd no time for a costume change," Shah interrupted, suggesting they'd been otherwise engaged beforehand. "Not that she needed one."

We? Glory thought. Was her girlfriend cheating on her with a dealer now? Could this really be happening?

"You're full of surprises, Parkie," Glory said, trying to keep her voice from shaking. "I think the bed is actually still warm. And really, Manya? So much for keeping things professional. I guess that means something different over here."

Manya's jaw dropped.

"Bloody hell," she said, turning to Parkie. "When you said you were exclusive, you might have thought to mention with whom."

"Not that it would have made a difference, given the *exclusive* part," Glory said. "If I worked as fast, I could have two shows by now. Sort of like you, Parkie."

Coming off "Silent Night," the pianist struck up a keyboard version of "All I Want for Christmas Is You," and a youthful server, who had been standing beside them for longer than was probably acceptable, foisted a tray of bacon-wrapped chestnuts into view.

"Ladies," said Manya, catching both of them in her glare. "This is the second time something like this has happened, is it not? If you two are a couple, far be it from me to get in the middle." To which she added a deadpan: "Unless, of course, that's what you want."

"We don't!" Parkie actually shouted.

"We're not," Glory added just as loudly. "A couple. Not anymore."

"Glory," Parkie said, taking a step away from Manya. Glory hadn't seen this wide-eyed and panicked, possibly guilty, expression before. It was all so disappointing. Parkie was. And she was, too, for putting herself in the position she was in. For being one who got cheated on. For being a fool.

"*What*, Parkie?" Glory said. "No use trying to fix what was wrong with us. Easier to just move on. It's fine if you're not sorry. I'm sorry enough for both of us, believe me. You two have a happy New Year! I'm going."

"I wish you wouldn't" came a voice from beside Glory.

Just then Eleanor put her hand in the small of Glory's back, effectively preventing her from going anywhere.

"Miss Shah was asking about Barbadians, or Bajans, as we call ourselves, and the Harlem Renaissance," she said. "And I said, of course there are people like Paule Marshall—though she's of a later generation than your great-aunt."

Glory wasn't sure what Eleanor hoped would happen by keeping her there for an impromptu lit class. Parkie didn't seem to know either. And Manya certainly couldn't be expected to have a clue. It felt like Eleanor was vamping.

"Refill your drinks and stay for a few more minutes," she said. "One of my cohosts has an announcement."

Manya offered to get more drinks for the three of them. But Glory gave her a steely gaze and said, "I can get mine and I suggest you get yours," before returning to her original spot by the piano.

"How do you say 'cock up' in American?" Manya said to Parkie in a stage whisper. "You're even more complicated than I thought."

The piano player called the room to order with a few arpeggios. An older man in a green velvet smoking jacket appeared in the doorway to the foyer.

"Ladies, gentlemen, and the rest of you, too, may I have your attention, please?" he asked in a low growl. The guests settled into comfortable stances and the room fell obediently silent.

"I've had the pleasure of attending this party for almost three decades, the first few years while Ellie and I were married—though not, predictably, to each other. But all the rest when we were on our own, me down the hall and she right here. Since the very beginning, each gathering has been held with a sort of secret dedicatee in mind, an artist or a musician or a friend in need, for the time of the night when we pass the proverbial hat—we used to pass an actual hat, but now we can't find one big enough!

"Anyway, people who leave before that happens usually place a check in the big pig in the entry if they want to. But nobody has ever been expected to contribute unless they're comfortable. This year, Ellie and I thought about calling tonight a 'rent party,' because in some ways, that's what it is. As most of you know, Graham Court is still a building of renters. Some of us have been here for decades. Some of us inherited our apartments from relatives. But we've never been able to go co-op and we probably never will. A few weeks ago, our housing association was informed that the building has been sold."

There was an eruption of collective surprise from around the room, followed by a wave of demoralized groans and shaking heads, with many guests turning to Eleanor in obvious disbelief.

The man in green velvet continued.

"We knew it would happen someday. I just hoped I'd be dead for it, frankly. But no, I live on and someday is now. If we can get a legal judgment to allow us to continue renting for another couple of years—even until we can try to find ways to buy our apartments—we can stay. As things are now, we'll all have to go sometime in the next three to six months. Could be sooner. So tonight really is a rent party. All proceeds go to the Those in the Know Legal Fund. So let us eat, drink, and be merry, for this may be the last year we partake in Eleanor's celebrated Harlem hospitality!"

*

After the gloomy dust from the announcement settled, people did indeed get merry again. There was dancing and more drinking, and some phenomenal singing from cast members of various Broadway musicals, and a famous lounge act or two as well as a state senator who did a passable Hamilton. At a point shortly after the bad news was delivered, Eleanor herded Glory and Manya and Parkie into her study, a smaller version of the great room, with still more books and bookshelves.

After softly closing the French doors behind her, Eleanor sat down in one of two club chairs covered in what seemed to be a kind of printed toile, only with pastoral-looking Black people—under an arch, in a garden, on a swing. Glory was still trying to get a closer look when she realized Eleanor had left the three of them to find their places on the striped love seat and the empty chair that matched hers. Then Manya pointedly took the empty chair and Glory and Parkie had no choice but to sit together on the small sofa.

"I don't have family," said Eleanor, glancing across their faces. "And my friends are all old. Most of them much older than me. I have money saved, and I will find a place to live. But retirement is nigh. And all this with the building is very upsetting and very sudden. The truth of it is, I could wake up in a few months with no gainful employment and no place to live."

Eleanor stopped to smooth the sparkling fabric over her knees as if the modest hem were in danger of rising on its own. Glory wondered if she would have spoken to them like this if there hadn't been "trouble," or whatever it was, earlier between her and Parkie. Was Eleanor's face more drawn tonight than when they met? Glory thought it might be.

"It pains me to ask you young ladies for help," Eleanor went on when she lifted her head again. "More than I can say. But there's simply no choice. I need your assistance with Lucille's estate. I can't do it all on my own and I don't wish to try. Research is required, and if we don't do it and do it right, Cuthbert's will make a travesty of something unique, to invoke the proper meaning of the word. Miss de Groot, a great deal needs to be done before my mandated March departure. Miss Hopkins, I need your help with finding a new place to live. It's just got to be in Harlem. And Miss Shah, I'm not sure what I need from you just yet. But I'm sure I'll think of something."

Chapter 24

New Year's came and went, and Parkie settled, or rather sank, back into her former life. The old routine of work, work, and, when that wasn't enough, a little work to top it off.

She closed out the Flagg estate, negotiating private sales of the Rolls Silver Cloud and the fourth-rate Remington after the auction. Madeline gave her a small, taxable bonus and a supposed promotion, from junior specialist to specialist in charge, which resulted in greater responsibility but did not result in more money. Per Dr. K.'s edict, Parkie quasi-officially started working on Lucille's scrapbook and the manuscript apparently hidden therein. Eleanor also made her the decider of what property from Glory's house might be profitably sold. It was through the management of the estate, as its specialist in charge, that Parkie endeavored to see Glory, who had not returned her calls since the Christmas party almost two weeks ago.

Parkie made the most of her new role. Knowing she had little to offer, she nonetheless schemed her way into accompanying the decorative arts appraiser tasked with a first-pass evaluation of the contents of Lucille's apartment. But when they arrived at the brownstone, Parkie in Glory's favorite suit, Glory gave them a quick rundown of what was where before announcing that she wasn't planning to stay. In fact, after exchanging a few words with the other appraiser, she attempted to walk right past Parkie, who had followed her colleague into the familiar entry. Parkie put out her hand to stop Glory as she walked past, trying to catch her evasive gaze.

"I miss you," she said, gently brushing her fingers down Glory's arm.

"I miss you, too," Glory replied, heading for the steps. She looked tired and seemed on edge, Parkie thought, almost trapped. Her eyes were mobile and unfocused as she attempted to dodge Parkie—like she couldn't be responsible for what happened if she stayed. Once she touched Glory again—even if it was only her sleeve—it was all she could do not to pull her in and kiss her, whether Glory thought she wanted it or not. Had they been there alone, Parkie would have.

After Dr. K.'s party, riding back to their respective apartments, a worked-up Manya had exhorted Parkie in no uncertain terms to get herself "bloody sorted" where Glory was concerned, for the sake of all their intersecting relationships, business as well as personal. Parkie wondered what, if anything, Glory had told Manya about her offer from Sarkisian.

Precious little, she decided when Manya claimed she didn't like surprises, which surprised Parkie, though she didn't care for them much either. Parkie wasn't sorry she'd gone out with Manya. She had every right to go on a date, given that Glory had kicked her out of bed. Kicked her out of the brownstone so that she could insulate herself with time or space or whatever it was she thought she needed in order not to deal with her feelings, and her failings, and the revelation that they were both only human after all. But she *was* sorry Glory seemed to view her spending time with Manya as a betrayal. And she was sorry Glory hadn't wanted to try, at least, to work things out.

Instead, Glory was apparently no less willing and maybe even more able than Parkie to let a riptide of work drag her under at the start of the new year. For both of them, it was easiest just to give in.

Glory was, Parkie assumed, on a deadline for Sarkisian, for which she'd either be trying to cobble together a convincing body of work from her old portfolio or making a bunch of bland new work in her more bankable former style. Either way, she knew Glory must be full throttle in the studio.

It was a relief merely to see and, however briefly, touch her. But it stung like fuck to spend time in Lucille's apartment without Glory there. Absent the object of her affection, Parkie invented a reason to go back to the office.

By the time she arrived, it was midafternoon, teatime for those who observed. As Parkie walked past Dr. K.'s partially open office door on the way to the mail room, a steamy cloud of ginger slowed her pace.

"Is that you, Miss de Groot?"

Her cane had given her away.

"It is. Can I help you with something?" Parkie asked, reversing course to peek inside the door.

Eleanor gestured her in. Though Parkie was glad for the invitation, she could only hope to keep a lid on what she was feeling since she'd last seen Glory—when Eleanor had been their witness. The older woman was at her little tea table at the end of the room. Parkie, rather than joining her there, pretended to take stock of the contents of the bookshelves, hoping to hide whatever her face might be doing before she sat down.

"I was surprised to hear you'd gone out on the appraisal at the Hopkins's house, Miss de Groot. Quite surprised indeed," Eleanor said between stirring and straining.

Parkie bit the inside of her cheek. "I know," she said. "I know I shouldn't have. She could barely look at me. And then she just left us there. So it was a waste of time anyway."

"You went with the intention of seeing her. To talk, was that it?"

Parkie felt the tears welling.

"We haven't since your party. She's furious with me about Flagg and Manya and some other things I can't go into. She's so stubborn and now she's shutting me out tout court because . . . I don't know. Because I'm not perfect, I guess."

Eleanor smiled over her readers.

"And neither is she. And neither am I. And neither is Miss Manya Shah. But neither is Sarkisian, as you and I know all too well."

This was unexpected. If Glory had discussed the Sarkisian offer with Eleanor, they must be closer than she'd realized. She should be glad about that for Glory's sake—she had so few, if any, friends in New York. Yet despite herself, Parkie couldn't help feeling a pang of jealousy. She wondered what advice Eleanor had given Glory about joining forces with her former employer; Glory certainly hadn't asked Parkie for hers.

"She told you about that?"

"She did," Eleanor said, reaching over to pull out a chair for Parkie. "And we mustn't discuss it without her, but be assured I passed on everything I've learned about them over the years. Especially where Black and brown people are concerned. Anyway. I do have a favor to ask, which, now that I know what you've been up to this morning, might not be something you feel you can take on. If not, I'm sure I can count on you to tell me so. It's just that our fearful leader has only this morning taxed me with a major collection of rare Federalist pamphlets and early documents related to the US Constitution. I think she took real pleasure in it."

"Christ," Parkie said. She sat down and absently took a piece of shortbread from a floral plate, biting off a corner before she spoke again. "For the March sale? Together with Lucille's whatever-it-is from the Harlem Renaissance and all the Civil War stuff?"

"Strange bedfellows indeed. But it wouldn't be the first time."

"How can I help? What can I do?" Parkie was eager for a distraction, though she wondered if what Eleanor requested would be a welcome one.

"I finished the transcription of Lucille's manuscript last weekend. It's really rather extraordinary in its complete form. The story itself, the characters, the plot—they all go to strengthen my attribution. Or so it looks to me. But I would feel more secure moving forward with whatever documentary support we can produce—something for which I simply don't have time."

"So you need me to go to Harlem. To the Schomburg, I'm guessing?"

Eleanor's eyes twinkled. "You know of it?"

"I do. Oddly enough, I did some research there when I was at Sarkisian. They had a client interested in Augusta Savage, so I got into the collection for a while. It's a nice place to work. What would I be looking for?"

Eleanor Kenniston took a sip of her tea, delicately replacing the cup on its saucer.

"I'm going to give you a transcription of what is surely a short novel dating from the mid-1940s, Miss de Groot. And I ask that you read it and cross-reference some of the locations and citations with whatever correspondence you can find at the Schomburg relating to a Nurse Imes. Nurse Nellallitea, or Nellie, Imes."

"Nellie Imes?" Parkie said, the excitement rising in her stomach. "As in Nella Larsen Imes?"

Eleanor clasped her hands together. Parkie hadn't seen her look so pleased since the Christmas party.

"Why, Miss de Groot. I did suspect you'd be able to establish, or not, the connection once you had more information. But here you are, already a Larsen scholar in your own right."

"I'm not," Parkie said. "I'm really not. It's just, ever since I met Glory, the things I do know keep coming up. It's a little eerie, really. On our first date we talked about my Edmonia Lewis paper. And believe me, reading *Passing* my freshman year was absolutely how I started to make sense of my feelings for girls. I read it—and *Quicksand*—in a course called Queer Poetics. But even without that class, I would have assumed she was queer from the way she describes women in those books. The dresses and the voice with the tinkling laugh—remember? To me at that age they read like romance novels. *Passing* is super sad in so many ways. But not that one—I can remember exactly where I was in the library when I read it and exactly how it made me feel. I kept looking around to see if anyone could see me—like my queerness was suddenly showing."

"Did you really have a class like that?" Eleanor asked in a voice more breathless than usual. "Of course, we never would have considered the possibility of her—what you would call *queerness* when I was in the academy. I arrived in the States when she and Zora Neale Hurston were just beginning to be known and studied. And Larsen is still so misunderstood—nowhere near as celebrated as the others. Perhaps for the very reasons you've noted."

"But, oh my god," Parkie said, suddenly vibrating with excitement. "Are you saying this novella of Glory's could be by *the* Nella Larsen? Did she publish anything after her first two books? I thought she basically disappeared."

"The first Black woman to win a Guggenheim was accused of plagiary, as they called it, for a short story she wrote the same year," Eleanor said, thrumming her long fingers on the table. "That was 1930, and as the story goes, she wrote a few more short pieces and revised a novel, but never published another book. A tragic mulatta for the ages."

Dr. Kenniston looked at Parkie directly when she said the last part, and Parkie, thinking she took her meaning, nodded in response, hoping Kenniston understood that Parkie understood, too. As much as she could, anyway.

"Let's see. A lost Nella Larsen novel discovered by you in the pages of a Harlem scrapbook owned by a woman who served in the army's only all-Black female band during World War II. Talk about a way to drop the mic. That would be pretty fucking awesome," Parkie said.

"Yes, Miss de Groot," said Dr. Kenniston. "It would be pretty fucking awesome indeed."

Chapter 25

Glory's breakfast meeting with Manya Shah was at her gallery. Thank God. Even so, knowing Manya, as Glory thought she was beginning to, she'd try to change it at the last minute to a lunch in a quiet café or, worse, to an apology dinner for the Christmas party. With every passing minute leading up to ten o'clock, Glory was prepared for some form of unanticipated foolishness.

Happily, nothing came her way before she got to Chelsea.

Manya had ordered an outrageous assortment of French pastries for the occasion, and Glory was even greeted by a steaming pour-over, which Manya, or her assistant, Martin, had somehow learned was her favorite vehicle for caffeine.

Or maybe, Glory reasoned, momentarily seething with dislike for the idea, Manya had gained this bit of her Glory knowledge directly from Parkie.

"Happy New Year," Manya said cheerily, as Martin closed the door to her office behind him.

"You, too," Glory said. She was suddenly very aware of her less-than-friendly feelings for the woman who tried to steal her girlfriend out from under her. But as she looked around the office, at the large and small canvases by some of her favorite artists, all women of color, Glory took a measured breath and checked herself.

Being where she was this day. This morning. On the point of discussing representation by one of the top contemporary galleries in New York, and therefore, in the world, was something she'd been working toward for more than a decade. Against her parents' advice. After dropping out of a grad program that had become untenable as soon as she wouldn't sleep with her lecherous but very famous adviser. After she'd started out on her own again—still inevitably riding the asshole's coattails—with a tiny New York show, which she couldn't help thinking that the same resentful, highly connected, highly misogynistic adviser had arranged to have panned by the *Times*.

After all this, success was within reach. It was happening. And whatever kind of girlfriend-stealing Lady Casanova Manya Shah might be, she believed in Glory's work. And Glory owed her the honest and forthright conversation they were about to have.

"Please eat as many of these as you possibly can," Manya said, shoving the pastry box in Glory's direction.

Glory settled on a chocolate coconut croissant, happily devouring it with the delicious coffee.

"Right then, not to put too fine a point on it. How goes the new stuff?"

"It goes well," Glory said. "I've been working on a larger scale than before. I'm thinking of it as a series. It's not hyper-programmatic or anything, but basically I'm working through a sextet."

"Oooh, brilliant. Such a lovely word, 'sextet,'" Manya said, seemingly with no humor intended.

"The six is for six women—names to be revealed at a later date. I'm working on the fifth canvas right now."

"Well, color me chuffed!" Manya said between bites of a pink macaron. "Sounds like you're feeling on pace. I'd love to do a studio visit sometime in the next few days or weeks if that's something you'd allow."

"Listen, Manya," Glory said, finally hoping to spit out what she needed to.

"All ears, as they say," Manya replied, blotting her red lips with a napkin. "What was Elizabeth I's motto? 'I see and keep silent.' Not for me, that."

No kidding, Glory thought. Manya was one of those people who could pull the perfect telling, scathing, on-point aphorism out of her ass every time. You always had the feeling you were running to catch up with her. And that was clearly just how she liked it.

When Glory looked up from her plate, Manya was staring right at her.

"I, um, I did want to talk to you about your proposal," Glory said, sounding more unsure of herself than she wanted to.

"The one you verbally signed off on? What about it?" Manya asked assertively.

Glory understood from her tone that Manya knew why she was there and what she had come to say—and didn't have the slightest problem taking her out of the catbird's seat or making this awkward. Her placid expression belied the anger sizzling just beneath the surface.

"I've had another offer of representation," Glory said. "And I did want to talk to you about—"

"About accepting it? Without informing me until now? Yes, I know all about that. I may be just off the boat, but I do have connections. And not just on both sides of the Channel. Do you think I don't know exactly what Sarkisian is up to? I know before they know—that's how predictable and hackneyed they are."

"Manya, really," Glory said. Her ears were ringing. Whatever unwarranted self-confidence she'd brought to this meeting was out the window. Had she really imagined Manya would take rejection well—when she'd been willing to put her reputation on the line by defying the *New York Times*? By offering to show the unpopular work of an emerging artist—the only emerging artist she'd likely present during the next year-plus of programming?

"I . . . Manya. I'm sorry. I know you were willing to take a chance on me and I should have handled this differently. I haven't made a decision. I wanted to talk to you first."

"For a counteroffer. Is that it?" Manya flipped her hair to the side, picked up her phone, and started apparently scrolling through her messages. "To be perfectly honest, Glory. I don't have time for that. I'm not going to make you a counteroffer different to my original offer. You want to talk? Let's talk. I believe in your new work. I was impressed by what I saw downtown. The old work, while competent, fails to rise beyond safe. It's palatable but noncommittal. Frankly, it's a little vanilla for my taste. And certainly not you at your best. I think we both know that. This conversation is about fearlessness and guts—whether you have them, as I had hoped, or whether you don't, as my competitor assumes."

"Okay," Glory said, rising from her chair, feeling like she grasped, maybe for the first time, what it meant to be hot under the collar. "I can see why you're not happy with me. I wasn't so happy with you on Christmas Eve, for that matter. But I'm sorry, Manya. I'm not sure what else to say."

Manya put down her phone and smiled joylessly up at her.

"I only work with a handful of artists," she said. "You could be one of them. It's a crossroads in the career of Glory Hopkins. Sarkisian will set you on one course; MFS would set you on another. Both could be wrong. What I do know is this: I believe in you and what you're doing. As an artist, as a person, as a Black woman, as a queer woman, as a mind and a conscience who knows what needs to be created in this moment. For you. For us. For them. I don't care if I sell a single painting the first go-round as long as I know it's true to your purpose. Your true purpose. I don't give a tinker's goddamn what the critics say. That's the only counter you'll get from me."

Glory had the peculiar and confusing impulse to applaud Manya for insulting her. To thank her for being the kind of woman she had always wanted to be. Even if it made Manya, at best, a formidable detractor. But before Glory could say a word, Manya's phone chimed.

"Hmm," she said, raising her brows at the screen. "Have to take this. I'm sure we'll be in touch." Then she rose from her desk and angled toward the window with a buoyant greeting to the caller.

*

Outside the gallery it was a sunless day with a white sky. The humid air had the edge of a coming storm. Still, Glory felt like she needed to walk for a while in the cold. She hoped a few icy lungfuls would crystallize her thoughts and help her know what to do. No two snowflakes are alike, according to the adage. But Manya's gallery and Sarkisian, both of them art world snowflakes of a sort, were perhaps more alike than Glory wanted to admit. Both were large commercial enterprises, global in reach. Both were darlings of the press; respected, followed—patronized by the "right" collectors, meaning the ones with big money. A solo show with Manya would almost certainly propel Glory into the atmosphere. But not the stratosphere. This choice was about loyalty. But it was also about the kind of art for which she would be known. Possibly for the rest of her career.

Glory wondered what had possessed her to try to tell Parkie anything she didn't already know about her former gallery bosses—that wrong move was not only foolish but insulting, and she didn't blame Parkie for resenting her for it. And then there was seeing Parkie lose her cool like that, which was incredibly sexy. Or would have been if instead of asking her to leave the apartment, Glory had gotten over herself and they'd started fucking again.

Parkie knew what went on at Sarkisian. Glory just hadn't wanted to find out how the sausage was made. A few blocks later, Glory found herself at the 20th Street entrance to the High Line, which, she noted, did not have elevator access.

She was about halfway up the metal stair enclosure when she heard a voice she couldn't immediately place, even though it was strangely familiar. Stranger still was what the voice—male, out of breath, and conspiratorial—was saying.

"At this rate, MFS is about to be FS. To the highest bidder. I don't think even the Shah can keep us afloat if we keep vomiting talent like this."

Glory froze where she stood. That voice belonged to Martin, Manya's assistant, the stylish guy with the platinum-pink halo of a buzz cut that looked so good with his golden-brown skin. Smoke floated down to her.

"Are they all going to the same dealer?" the person with him asked in a sympathetic tone.

"Mostly," Martin said. "I don't know what fresh hell today brought, but I think she lost two yesterday. Moulton left us without a pot to piss in, basically. She just can't compete at this point. But fuck all those motherfuckers. We get a brown woman—a posh AF, brown, name-taking, ass-kicking woman in that white fucking cube—and the big artists jump ship like rats on a rowboat."

Glory didn't catch the response from Martin's conversation partner, since the two of them must have reached the top to emerge into the walkway's meek daylight. Glory stayed put in the stairwell until a couple with a child hoisted on the guy's shoulders needed her to move. When she stepped onto the jangly metal path, she was high enough above the street to discern the brick facades of some of the other big galleries below. She walked across to the railing on the other side and looked out toward the Hudson. The shining, purply layers of the river reminded her of abalone. She thought about mixing the colors.

She thought about Chelsea. How far it was from Harlem. How banal and commercial—and white—it had become. Not Manya, of course. But the pristine galleries with their nonchalant homogeneity and their employees—mainly girls not unlike Parkie. White kids with trusts who smoked weed and loved land art and read *October* and hadn't heard of Countee Cullen.

Glory laughed to herself. Just the other day she'd read that the Oreo was invented in the old Chelsea Market—back in 1912, when it was still Nabisco.

If she'd wanted a sign—this was probably it. But she still had no idea what to do.

Chapter 26

Parkie's Lyft car arrived at the Schomburg Center for Research in Black Culture just before it opened. She'd worked late the night before, still trying to sort out the list of items Nicholas's counterpart, another young appraiser, had made after several hours spent in Lucille's apartment. The range was extreme, as Parkie knew it might be—not unlike the Flaggs', in the end. There were trinkets from prewar Paris that weren't expensive or innately valuable, but which would probably exceed estimates in unpredictable ways. There were regular, everyday things that wouldn't make the cut, and then there were some very good rugs, Chinese porcelain, and actual silver, rather than plate, that would almost certainly bring high dollars.

After what they'd learned about the scrapbook—that it might have been written in the company of these objects from Lucille's long and, it would now seem, colorful past—Parkie was surprised Glory was still considering selling any of it. But she gathered, from Glory's occasionally aired money worries, that things were getting tight financially and that, without a successful show, she could last in Harlem for only so long.

At West 135th, the Schomburg was a mile and change uptown from Glory's brownstone. Its two main buildings were rather awkwardly separated by an open courtyard. The gap was no doubt intended to lessen the curbside shock to the senses of seeing the original building, with its McKim, Mead, and White facade of ivory stone pilasters flanking a Roman arch, juxtaposed with the new one, a sharp and shiny asymmetrical monolith whose mirrored face resembled a retail outlet of some kind. The older—and Parkie thought, better—building was finished in 1904—about a decade prior to the post-WWI era most historians credited with invigorating the Harlem Renaissance.

Did Eleanor know, as Parkie had just learned, that Nella Larsen became a librarian at this very 135th Street Branch, as it was then called, in 1921? Larsen would, Parkie reflected, have been almost exactly her own age when she started working—and writing—there.

Here.

Less than a decade later, when she left her library career, Larsen had completed the only two books for which she'd ever be known. Two short novels generating a level of authorial fame that burned brightly but briefly, failing to run the course of Larsen's lifetime since, as every short biography was keen to note, she died "in obscurity" and nearly destitute at the height of the Civil Rights movement in 1964. She was just a few years older than Eleanor.

Parkie had meant to bury herself in her apartment some evening after work, in order to focus solely on Eleanor's transcription. Barring that, she'd meant to read what she could of it on the Lyft ride uptown. Instead, she'd gotten carsick when she pulled out the stack of fifty-five single-spaced pages that Eleanor, as if she were passing her nuclear missile codes, had placed in Parkie's hands when she left her office earlier in the week.

Parkie hadn't been back to Harlem since the appraisal. Today was the eighteenth day Parkie hadn't heard a word from Glory. Nor had she made any attempt to contact her. Which was, she'd noted as the car slowly made its way up Third Avenue, beginning to feel like a catastrophic mistake. Parkie knew she was in the right. In the end, at least, she told the truth. And while it hadn't exactly set her free, it had righted an imbalance. Glory had formed a ridiculous idea of her that was too good to be true.

She couldn't pinpoint when exactly it was that Glory started seeing her as someone principled and unerring: a Chanel-clad Joan of Arc willing to take on all comers, consequences be damned. She would like to be that woman. She would try. But she hadn't been that woman so far.

Was it when Parkie called out Olive that first day in reception when they met? Was it when she volunteered to give up being the specialist on Lucille's estate in exchange for another date or two? Or when she'd told Glory about her confrontation with the guy on the street who called her a bitch? Or when she'd taken time off work to see Glory's show in a gallery that was hardly ever open to the public?

Maybe she wasn't that bad, Parkie thought with an inward thumbs up. Those were, in fact, real demonstrations of how she could be as a person and as a girlfriend. Nobody does the right thing every time.

And anyway, concessions have to be made. Bills need to be paid. Deductibles must be reached.

These were the mundane concerns, as Parkie had now established, that Glory was also dealing with. Even so. Throwing in with Sarkisian would have moral implications for her future—Parkie could explain that to her. If only Glory would suck it up the tiniest bit and just tell Parkie she was sorry for some part of their last interaction—the not telling her about Sarkisian, the exile from the bedroom—Parkie knew she'd accept the apology. Meanwhile, Glory was a fine one to cast stones from her broken leaded-glass windows. Until she admitted that, Parkie would stay her course.

Besides, she consoled herself, Glory would have to realize that even in the midst of heartbreak, a true woman of principle doesn't give in. Not to a wrenching sense of abandonment. (Parkie was lonelier now than before she met Glory.) And especially not to her own relentless desire. (She'd fantasized—and more—about Glory almost every single night since they'd slept together.) But, and she was firm on this, she wouldn't give in to someone who held her to an ideal. Someone who couldn't admit when she'd made a mistake herself.

*

A number of chatty people were already standing under the marquee-like portico when Parkie had joined them in the line outside the door. Inside, the library hummed with soothing incandescent light and early-morning energy. The woman at the desk asked if she needed help finding anything. But since she hadn't even skimmed the manuscript, Parkie didn't want to bother the librarian with her unformed questions. She wasn't yet sure what Dr. K. thought she would be able to deduce about historical fact from literary fiction. Dr. K., the real specialist in charge, seemed to feel they were close to a revelation. But she wanted something concrete, she'd said. Something to incontrovertibly identify Larsen as the author.

Parkie found an empty table in the main reading room, ringed overhead with the famous Aaron Douglas murals. Completed in the 1930s, these wouldn't have been in the library in Larsen's time, Parkie noted, feeling a small shiver unrelated to the cold outside. She sat down and removed the manila folder that Dr. K. had labeled "Trinity."

Was this an invention of Dr. K.'s? Or would the title, or the reason for the title, make itself known to her by the time she came to the end of the last page?

Again, Parkie withdrew the tidy stack of white sheets and leafed quickly through them, surprised to find chapter breaks. This, too, made her wonder if the novella's organization was imposed by Kenniston's editorial fiat or if such divisions were indicated to her as she read between the minuscule lines of the author's loopy penmanship? Parkie wished she had asked more questions.

She took a deep breath, realizing that her work for the day was to read a short novel. To draw from it what conclusions she could about the writer's biography, her influences, and the sources of her allusions at the time she'd finished writing. To find the terminus ad quem Dr. K. was after from the historical details sprinkled throughout the story.

The first page of the manuscript, quirkily but endearingly printed by Kenniston in Courier, read:

```
                 Chapter One
   If recognition is to be found for the daily
drudgery of bedpans and bloody bandages,
for enduring the patient's rude and heart-
less relatives, for confronting the eventu-
ality that something so mighty, so majestic,
as death can, after routine exposure to its
presence, become typical, even comical—if
such recognition is to be found, it is from
other women; it is from one's fellow nurses.
   Lily Powell had inwardly digested the
first lesson of this gospel of Saint
```

```
Michael's after marrying a doctor. The sec-
ond lesson she was only learning now, fol-
lowing their recent decision to divorce. For
when, having wavered on buckled knees after
dabbing the brow of some pompously complain-
ing, red-faced surgeon—not her husband—for
a half a dozen hours, him not expressing the
slightest awareness that she, too, might
be exhausted, it would be another nurse who
took it upon herself to sweep Lily Powell
off her feet
```

This was how the provisionally titled *Trinity* began. With the character named Lily Powell swept off her feet by another nurse, whose name in the novella was Rita Eastman, an "exotic" choice given the lie (considering the era) by her stereotypically WASP features. Rita Eastman was, according to the author, a little "hard" but "unrepentantly beautiful" and a constant source of hospital gossip. Tall for a woman, and taller than Lily Powell by "a good five inches," she was obviously a stacked, fragrant-smelling, page-boy blond in the style of the wish-fulfilling wives and girlfriends who were meant to be keeping the home fires burning during the war. That the author also went out of her way to describe Rita as tough and pretty but not artificial intrigued Parkie. It was as if Rita's height and her physical strength—she'd swanned in to catch Lily Powell in her arms when she fainted in the operating room—were the subtext beneath the contrivance of her starched curves, flowerlike mouth, and eyes the hue of a summer sky.

Parkie flipped over the finished page and looked up to the Douglas murals. They'd been shaved from the walls of the old building and subsequently mounted and framed in the new one.

From where Parkie was stationed at the edge of the small reading room, she got a general sense of the animated figures in silhouette, their solid brown and blue and purple and green bodies emerging from abstract landscapes of streamlined trees with formulaic leaves that might have been stenciled or machined from metal.

What she was reading felt from a different time. Not this late-Deco, Herbert Hoover, Flapper-girl age but later, during the next war, when nurses became a kind of propaganda, too—symbols of beauty and nurturing and womanly competence. Symbols for whom there were real life models in the world.

It was a point in the story when the attractive Nurse Lily Powell, who, we learn, "had passed as white throughout college, since graduating high school in Harlem," wakes up in the closet of a storeroom where Rita has taken her to recover. When Lily comes to, Rita calls her her "brave beauty" and presses the back of her hand against Lily's cheek. Theirs is not a segregated hospital and it is somewhere in Manhattan. Kicking up the tenderness quotient, Rita then leans in, breasts ahoy, to settle a blanket around Lily's shoulders—but before anything else can happen, an orderly pounds on the door, telling them to look sharp, as there's been a factory explosion nearby and the injured workers are headed their way.

Chapter 27

Glory ran a few errands on her way back from MFS in a semi-conscious effort to prolong her time away from the brownstone. Her studio. Now, home again and too full from Manya's profusion of puff pastry to eat lunch, Glory was impatiently drumming on the kitchen table like she was waiting for something. She felt confused, defeated, and anxious all at the same time. As if the very crossroads Manya mentioned was within the walls of her apartment.

It was nearly two o'clock. The good light had gone but she knew she should suit up, pull out the utility lamps, and get painting anyway. And she would do that if the million-dollar question of what kind of work she should make, if indeed she did start working again, wasn't weighing so heavily on her post-Chelsea.

The fluorescent ring flickered overhead, disturbing Glory's thoughts.

She looked around. Maisie's dish was full, which made her wonder where she'd gotten off to. Normally, she would have greeted Glory by now, especially when her caretaker had been out of the house for more than a couple of hours. As usual, it was frigid, though. Poor thing was probably taking advantage of the more efficient radiators and softer furniture upstairs. Fourteen years ago, Lucille made a rare trip out of Harlem to bring Maisie home as an abandoned kitten from the no-kill shelter she respected. The feisty little animal had spent most of her life in one apartment.

"Mai-sie," Glory called, trudging up the steps to Lucille's. She half expected the cat to rocket ahead of her on the stairs before she made it to the top. But no. Glory creaked open Lucille's front door and stepped into the apartment. Not on the sofa. Not on Lucille's desk chair, Glory noted, standing in the doorway to the bedroom.

"There you are," she said, spying the cat's mottled tail draped over the front edge of Lucille's favorite bedroom chair. It was the twin of the blue-green bergère Glory now had in her own bedroom. The chair over which Parkie had draped her neatly discarded skirt suit on their second unforgettable night together.

"What are you doing up here?" Glory continued. Usually, Maisie would have come running when the door opened. Or at least she'd jump down to greet her when she came into the room.

Glory got a back-of-the-neck chill.

Walking slowly around to the front of the chair, she reached down to pet the little ball of caramel and black fur curled there. But once she was closer, she could tell from the animal's slightly agape mouth and glassy eyes, she was gone.

"Oh no, Maisie. Oh no, no, no," Glory cried, collapsing to her knees with an intensity of sadness she didn't expect. It was all just way too much. The tears took a few seconds to build, but once they started she couldn't seem to turn them off. She knelt there on the rug for what felt like a long time, struggling for breath between hitching sobs that were mostly for Maisie but also for the general state of things, which had been "pear shaped," as Manya might say, since Christmas Eve.

She was an oddly withholding but deep-down affectionate creature. Very smart, Glory had come to believe, probably from living with a woman who spoke to her not as if she were human, but as if she understood what she was saying just the same. Glory never liked cats before Maisie.

Especially after the breakup—was it?—with Parkie, she had come to rely on Maisie's companionship. It helped that they were both essentially nocturnal, finding their creative energy at night. Working was more fun with Maisie shredding a paper bag in the background or racing up and down the stairs making a game for herself with a pencil or one of her toy mice. Sometimes she just snoozed in a nearby corner for hours in what Glory liked to imagine as moral support.

But aside from her many good qualities, Maisie was also the last real, and certainly the last animate, connection Glory could claim to her aunt. Had Maisie been sick without Glory's knowledge? Had she been mortally lonely without Lucille? She had likely lived a good, and surely a pampered, life. A relatively long one. But her sudden death struck Glory as not only a loss but an omen.

Maybe Glory was unworthy of any living being's devotion. Maybe this is what happens if you shut yourself in your house for days on end and put all your time into your work instead of apologizing to your wise and beautiful onetime girlfriend who was only trying to get you to do what's right. But there was *right*—and there was right for her *right now*. She needed Parkie to understand that.

Objectively speaking, nobody in the art world would advise her to choose Manya over Sarkisian. Nobody who wasn't independently wealthy or looking out for their long-term career would. Manya was amazing, Manya was a world-beater. But Manya—or Manya's gallery—was also, it seemed, in trouble. If Glory wasted her one good chance on a show at a gallery that was about to go under—maybe even before that show opened—she would never forgive herself. She could see that alternative history with disturbing clarity: from the moment she told her parents the show was canceled to the moment they told her they'd told her so. Being an artist was pretty much all creative risk and little financial reward. Unless you were one of the anointed—one of the talented 5 percent—you faced a lifetime of late payments, lethal envy, and compromised principles. Of trying to get noticed until you woke up one day—or didn't wake up one day—in complete obscurity with nothing to show for your trouble.

After the sad discovery, Glory had pushed herself a few feet away from the turquoise chair to lean her back against the bed rails.

"What a fucking day," she muttered, pulling her knees into her chest.

It was quiet in the apartment, as always. Scattered shafts of sun flattened the bedroom's afternoon shadows, but it was darker at Lucille's, which felt appropriate. Glory looked down at her phone as it lay by her side on the cobalt and yellow rug with its pattern of peonies. She had a sudden desire to text Parkie, who also liked Maisie, and was a self-described cat person, though she couldn't have one at her place per the landlord's rules.

Parkie would say all the right things.

She would offer to come over and almost certainly offer to help Glory deal with "the body." She'd bring dinner and rub Glory's shoulders and kiss her in all the right places. Then she'd take her to bed and, if the past was any indication, soon she would feel much, much better. If only for a little while.

*

Glory swept the tears off her cheeks, readying herself to get up. Outside, the clouds must have shifted, because a narrow sunbeam that hadn't been there before was suddenly streaming in through the sheers. The wavering light caught something on the floor in its path.

She hadn't seen them when she was sitting perpendicular to Lucille's vanity, a low, pale wood piece with a large round mirror. But as she rose to her knees, Glory spied a small cluster of shiny things on the carpet beneath the left-hand drawers.

She crawled quickly over and stuck her hand into the shadowy gap, feeling around until she made contact, fairly sure of what she'd find. The metal was smooth and cool, and the shapes easy to know. When she opened her palm, there were three rings tethered together with a piece of the same dark blue ribbon used to tie up Lucille's letter bundles.

Three gold rings. Each inset with a trio of small rubies, not much more than chips, centered on the rounded surfaces of their bands. Other than the stones, the rings were unadorned, uninscribed; completely unmarked. Without thinking, Glory slipped one on her ring finger. No luck there—it was too loose. Realizing the rings might be different sizes she tried again, and again. The last one fit as if it were made for her. She spread her fingers at eye level, shifting her hand back and forth to admire the way the little red jewels caught the light.

Her spine prickled. "Well, that's . . . weird," she said aloud. She'd grown accustomed to talking to Maisie the way she knew Lucille had. She was reminded now that nobody was listening.

*

About an hour after she discovered Maisie and the rings, Glory left a message with the call service of Lucille's veteran vet, a grandfatherly-sounding man with a basso profundo named Dr. Price. He called her back immediately and assured her that, given his long friendship with her aunt, and with Maisie, he would personally drive to the house and collect her.

It was late afternoon when the knock came at the front door. The portly fellow with close-cropped white hair was wearing what Glory imagined could double as his church suit, looking dapper indeed for someone who must be in his late seventies.

"Well, I see you haven't changed much around here," he said sarcastically, glancing through the open doors on the first floor as he followed Glory upstairs.

"Not that anyone could tell, right?" Glory laughed back.

"You must miss her," he said more seriously. "I miss her, and I only saw her every year or so. But that was for probably forty years, so, I guess that's a good-enough reason. She was old school. Always tried to get me to stop over for a house call on the way home from work so she could ply me with a cocktail."

"I'm told she did love a cocktail," Glory said.

"A highball," they both said at the same time, sharing a nod of agreement.

"You stay here," Dr. Price said as Glory opened the bedroom door. "Do you have the towel I asked for?"

Glory handed him an old bath towel from the back of Lucille's closet. It seemed like the right thing to use as a shroud. Until she shook the bath sheet out.

"That's funny," she said. "'RWC.' Whose monogram is that?"

Dr. Price smiled at her.

"Rosalind's, no doubt," he said matter-of-factly.

"Rosalind?" Glory responded in utter befuddlement. "Who is Rosalind?"

Now Dr. Price was confused. He took the towel Glory offered him and pulled it up over his arm to get a look at the three initials heavily embroidered at the bottom edge.

"Rosalind Cowles Westerly, of course. I know she was before your time, but you have to know about Rosalind, Miss Hopkins. You can't tell me you haven't heard the stories of those two hosting Coretta Scott King in this very apartment while Dr. King was here to preach at Riverside? Or how they busted into the board meetings at the Museum of Modern Art because there weren't enough Black artists on the walls? Or the parties they had?"

Glory was speechless. Rosalind, aka "R."?

If she was the woman from the letters, the woman Glory thought lived in the apartment while Lucille was in the war—if she was the woman who Eleanor assumed was Lucille's lesbian lover—it just might explain the presence of this inexplicably monogramed towel in her aunt's closet. What it didn't explain was why no one in the family ever mentioned a woman with such a memorable—and aristocratic-sounding—name living with Lucille in the brownstone.

"Well, I better tend to my patient," Dr. Price said.

"All due respect, Dr. Price, but Maisie isn't going anywhere she hasn't already gone. Are you saying you knew a woman named Rosalind lived here with Lucille?"

Dr. Price used the toe of one of his giant brogues to push a cat toy out of his path. "Rosalind must have died in the early eighties. Something like that. I hadn't been in practice for all that long when I first met her and she passed a few years later. But sure, that's what I'm saying. Those two were the talk of the town for decades. A white newspaper heiress from St. Louis and one of the first Black women trained at the Julliard, living as what they used to call 'companions'—not that anyone believed that. Those women had it. Dressed right out of the society pages every day. Even my mother said they were two of the three most stylish women in Harlem. And she didn't cotton to companions, I can tell you."

Glory felt as if she were suddenly underwater, her inner ears whirling with inaudible noise.

"Well, well," said Dr. Price with an air of satisfaction. "I guess your mama never told you that one. Lucille never said anything either?"

"No," Glory said simply. "But you know, I hadn't really talked to her since I was a kid. She never seemed to have any interest in me. Or Grace either. It sounds terrible, but after we moved, I didn't give her much thought."

"Well. Lucille took Rosalind's death hard, as you'd expect. Some kind of cancer. A bad one. That formidable woman did not go down without a fight. And then the music and the socializing just stopped. Ask your father, he knows all about it. Rosalind left my clinic a tidy sum. She was one of a kind. I say a little prayer for both of them these days. All right, let me do what I came here to do. You go back downstairs, and I'll see myself out when I'm finished. It's good to know you, young lady. You take care. Call me when you bring home the next one. This place is too big—and too cold—to live alone in."

Once she thanked him, Dr. Price waited for Glory to reach the first-floor landing. A few minutes after she disappeared into her studio, she heard him descend the stairs followed by the sound of the big front door closing behind him. And then they were gone.

What a lovely man, Glory thought.

She'd learned more about her aunt in a fifteen-minute exchange from Lucille's smitten veterinarian, than she had from her parents. And now she knew why.

Chapter 28

Parkie had tumbled down a few internet rabbit warrens, frantically surfing for a biographical detail here or a journal article there. But she had barely changed her position since sitting down at her table in the Schomburg's reading room. The novella was riveting. And it was hot. She hadn't read *Passing* in years, but she was instantly drawn to the current writer's promiscuously descriptive, often humorous way with words; it did feel familiar, though far more personal than the earlier books—almost confessional, she thought. She saw immediately why Eleanor's intuition had led her to the attribution. Both of Larsen's published novellas featured a woman of color who had a Black parent and a white parent, like Larsen herself. From early in the scrapbook manuscript, it was clear that Lily Powell was another such character, and probably the woman with whom the author, or in any case, the narrator, most closely identified. Larsen was, after all, both the former wife of a doctor and, by profession, a nurse. Rita and Lily were doing the same kind of work Larsen did at the end of the war, after she stopped writing in the late 1930s. Or so the people who studied her seemed to believe.

Larsen's abrupt exit from the writing life was most often associated with the notorious plagiarism scandal that erupted around her last published short story, "Sanctuary." Parkie didn't want to spend too much time on that stage. It was complicated and ultimately sad and infuriating. Some critics thought Larsen had, in fact, stolen the plot of "Sanctuary" from a white British author, also a woman. Others claimed she had brilliantly expropriated, with something like a knowing wink, when she "Blackened" the story by switching out the English location and races of the characters for a setting in the American South. If this was plagiarism, Parkie sniffed, most of the insipidly multicultural adaptations of Regency novels on Netflix and Hulu could hardly be viewed as original. Still, it seemed most important that the English lit crowd claimed Larsen hadn't penned any other stories after the late '30s. What Parkie had been reading was surely set in the '40s—Lily's love of Eleanor Roosevelt and hatred of sugar and coffee rations confirmed that.

Parkie knew in her gut this phantom novel could turn out to be a very big deal merely by existing in the world. One of the articles Parkie found explained that in Larsen's first two books, women moved through a bigoted culture where the way their race was perceived by others, far more than the way they saw themselves, determined their fates. Writing in the Roaring Twenties, before Kimberlé Crenshaw had radically formulated a way to think about, and apply the law to, the crosscutting of gender and race, Larsen was writing that as a form of fiction. She was so far ahead of her time, Parkie marveled. Less intentional, according to the literary historian she'd read, was the undeniable presence in the early writing of women whose lives were animated and given purpose by other women. For Parkie, that queer feeling on the page was enough in some ways, like a secret message written in lemon for the women-loving women who held it up to the light.

But this onionskin story was different. It felt like a queer romance and a race novel that knew what it was. The pages Parkie read were nothing less than a love story between women. It might even be the openly lesbian novel many of Larsen's admirers had longed for, given the obvious homoeroticism of her other two books.

Parkie knew she was supposed to be close-reading for period colloquialisms and historical clues, but it was hard not to lose herself in the characters' lives. Especially because it was becoming increasingly obvious to her that the novella's three main characters had to be based on "the author" and the life she came to share with Lucille and the woman Parkie and Glory had encountered in the letters only as "R."

It was past Parkie's lunchtime and although she hadn't finished the story, she knew she'd need to take a break soon to keep her strength up. Get some air. Maybe find a café or restaurant nearby. One more chapter, she agreed with herself, and she'd stop.

She'd reached what appeared to be another crucial plot point: Following the fainting incident and a couple of cloak-and-dagger rendezvous at the symphony, Rita and the considerably older Lily had started a maddeningly chaste, slow-burn love affair. Chaste, until society girl Rita—who was something of a free spirit and understandably the more willing of the two to take on the hospital and any other establishment—invited Lily to dinner at her "funny old Victorian pile" in Harlem. There, the women had spent numerous cozy nights together listening to the wireless and knitting. Until. One rainy night, they'd shared soup in Rita's kitchen and—the weather being so treacherous—she'd invited Lily to stay over rather than make the long trek back to her place near Gramercy Park.

The ensuing scene was Parkie's favorite so far. The author's description of the women's flirtation finally escalated to wet kisses and feverish "petting," and from there to Lily's shockingly capable and scorching seduction of Rita—which had no doubt brought color to Parkie's cheeks. There were negotiated girdles, fugitive fingers, and the hurried sliding down of black-market silk stockings. After that episode, the story's focus shifted somewhat to the very different status of Black and white nurses at the hospital. And to the growing tensions between Lily and Rita as the war looked to be drawing to an end. When it did, Rita had let Lily know, she would leave nursing to return to her former life.

What that former life had been, the reader could only speculate at this point. The story was punctuated with several well-placed mentions by an avowedly unmarried Rita of a "young enlisted friend." Yet it wasn't at all clear what her relationship to said friend might be—or how his return might affect her affair with Lily. For all sorts of reasons, Parkie didn't want things between the women, who were obviously so right for each other, to end badly.

Tragic endings were, according to the critics, one of the primary faults of Larsen's work. People almost always died and the final act was too over-the-top sad. Extra, and not in a good way.

Parkie's eyes darted briefly around the reading room. It was more crowded now. At the tables nearby some men, but mostly women, sat quietly typing away at their laptops or taking notes as they paged through folders. An older woman on the other side of the room glanced up suddenly, as if disturbed by the heat of Parkie's unseeing stare. She raised her eyebrows and gave Parkie a slight smirk—she could have been in her forties or even early fifties—but Parkie felt the inquisitive opening move in that look. She immediately dropped her own eyes to the neat stack of papers on the desk in embarrassed response, realizing this wasn't like her at all.

*

Back at Cuthbert's, where she was tidying up her library notes for Dr. K.'s review, the ringing phone on Parkie's desk startled her. People so rarely used that line unless Olive passed them through.

"Good afternoon, Miss de Groot," said a melodious male voice. "George Stepton at the *New York Gazette*. I left a message earlier and I'm sorry to pester, but I'm wondering if I can ask you a few questions."

"Yes, hello. I'm just this second back at my desk. Apologies for not getting to you first, Mr. Stepton," Parkie said. She felt a little on edge. Calls of this type, usually from arts and culture reporters, were typically chattier and less urgent-sounding. This Stepton guy, while friendly, sounded on a mission and in a hurry. She looked at her iPhone, sitting on the desk next to the black-plastic office one. Just to see if it would work, she tapped the voice memo button, something she'd only recently learned about from Cuthbert's media relations people, who advised the appraisers never to do what she was about to do.

"Questions about what?"

"Great. Well, first off, I'm wondering if you were aware that the jeweled watch on the cover of your last major auction catalogue—for the sale of the Flagg estate—was a gift to its initial recipient from one of the first Nazi field marshals, a man named Karl von Milch?"

Parkie chortled. "No way. Wait, what?"

"Were you the one who chose the watch for the cover?" Stepton asked, his tone less friendly now.

"I, er," Parkie stumbled. "I was. But, I had no idea. I thought it came from . . ."

Then she remembered. She had been told that the watch was a gift from the intended fiancé, some British aristo chasing after one of the Flagg daughters. She hadn't, in truth, researched his biography or even his name. It was still the early thirties, years from the beginning of the war. It hadn't even remotely occurred to Parkie that Nazis could be involved in that particular English-American wedding. Given Wallis Simpson and the former king Edward VI, that seemed a pretty big oversight just now. She knew she should have watched *The Crown*.

"You thought it came from where?" asked the intrepid George Stepton.

"I mean, as far as I knew, the Flagg girl married a British baron or maybe a marquess or something. Definitely not a Nazi military man. It was the thirties."

"And Hitler became führer in 1933. The English aristocracy was riddled with admirers of Mosely sympathetic to the Nazis. All the way to the top, some say. Some were even suffragettes. Do you care to comment on that?"

"On whether British suffragettes were Nazi collaborators? Or whether one of the Flagg daughters secretly married one of Hitler's field marshals? Or whether I knew about any of that when I chose a cover lot for the catalogue?"

"Take your pick," said Stepton.

Parkie paused. "I have learned that there are historical connections between the Flagg family and slave trading. That they are considered by many to have held a monopoly on lifesaving pharmaceutical drugs with fatal results for poor people and people of color. And gay men, of course. Honestly, family ties to the Nazis don't surprise me much."

"Can I quote you on that?"

She thought about it. Someday, as Nicholas liked to say, the hens would come home to roost. Why not get that homecoming started?

"Yes," Parkie said. "You can."

"One more thing," Stepton said.

Parkie's stomach churned. She was already trying to think what kind of ammunition, precisely, she had just given this guy. Trying to think what, precisely, her next move would be if she were quoted in a story about a Cuthbert's employee—her—failing to do her homework about Flagg's Nazi connections.

"Yes?" she said anxiously.

"Your last name," Stepton said. "That's German, too, isn't it?"

"No," she said. "It's Dutch. Like Bed-Stuy. Like Brooklyn. Like Harlem."

Chapter 29

After Dr. Price took Maisie, Glory had climbed midway up the stairs, felt unable to go any farther, and sat down in the middle of the Persian runner. Now she couldn't seem to get herself up to the top or down to the bottom. The house was all loss and death again, yet she had the impression the staircase was somehow less haunted than the rooms it led to. The space in between seemed like a good place to think.

As of that afternoon, she had assembled the borders of the puzzle of Lucille's life. That was the easy part. What remained was the chaos in the middle, where you had to stumble on a few key pieces to make the larger pattern recognizable; once that happened, the big picture would snap into place.

Lucille had shared the brownstone with another woman. The woman's name was Rosalind Cowles Westerly and she was white. White and rich. White and rich and one of the most stylish women in Harlem in her day. Lucille and Rosalind had been—according to not only Eleanor's interpretation of the letters but also Dr. Price's implication—longtime lesbian lovers. Until Rosalind died, probably in her early sixties, in the 1980s. Maybe even around the time of Glory's birth.

This unearthing of her aunt's sexuality and unacknowledged widowhood answered as many questions as it raised. Why had no one ever mentioned Rosalind? Rosalind, who seemed sufficiently upper-class and undoubtedly presentable enough to meet the reactionary social standards of Glory's supposedly left-leaning grandparents and parents—even if she was white. And more important where Lucille's scrapbook was concerned, who was the brown-skinned author who had somehow inserted herself into Lucille and Rosalind's life—what had become of her and why did her manuscript end up hidden between the pages of a scrapbook in Lucille's attic?

Glory eventually drifted down to her living room, marched straight to the drinks cart, and poured herself three fingers of Scotch, something she rarely did, but which she felt the revelation—and the day—called for. From her taut neck muscles to her queasy stomach and twitching right eye, her body was a mess. She needed to not think about having found Maisie like that. And she needed to not think about Lucille being with Rosalind. Which was really just a way to think about being with Parkie. Or not being with Parkie, as the case, the worst she could currently imagine, might be.

She wondered what Parkie was doing at work today. What she had worn. Whether she ever woke up with her hand between her legs thinking about touching Glory the way Glory woke up thinking about being touched by her. They were going to have to talk, if only to share what they'd learned about the manuscript.

Soon enough, Glory would inform Eleanor that she'd discovered the identity of "R." But she was feeling more guarded about the rest of Lucille's letters now—and infinitely protective of the three gold rings. The only person she knew who would truly understand those was Parkie.

Glory swished the amber liquid in her rocks glass, taking a serious sip. At this moment, she was good for approximately nada. Grabbing her phone absent-mindedly, she checked her email. Sometime after she'd met Parkie, at that early stage of dating when merely viewing your love interest's name in print or their image on social media soothes the horny but insecure soul, she had signed up for news alerts about Cuthbert's. Generally, this produced barely revised press releases relating the results of some record-breaking auction or, less frequently, recounting Madeline's truly vile social life. The subject headings were usually so boring, Glory didn't bother opening the emails, never mind clicking the links. But this alert, which read, "American Aristocrat Promoted Third Reich Gift for Sale to Cuthbert's Highest Bidder," had her full attention.

What in the?

She quickly scrolled through the story, immediately worried about the photographs. She knew there would be some. The *Gazette* sometimes ran stories that consisted only of images—not what you'd call a true photo essay, just a bunch of provocative pictures offered to the tabloid's puerile readership to interpret as it may.

As she feared, about a paragraph into this story there was a sizable color photograph. Landscape in orientation, it featured a younger, deeply tanned Parkie in a white bikini. She was pitched forward from the photographer's overhead perspective, allowing for a salacious view of her cleavage that, under other circumstances, would have had Glory and her phone back in the bedroom ASAP. From what she could tell, someone had caught Parkie vacationing at what was obviously a luxurious beach resort; to her side, a Black man in a stiff white uniform was proffering her a cocktail of some kind from beneath a canopy of palms.

As far as that went, posting the (arguably flattering) Parkie portrait didn't necessarily strike Glory as problematic—beyond the usual objectification and sexualization of any woman thrust into the public eye—and the use of a contrasting Black "servant" figure to prop up all that white leisure and conventional femininity. More of an issue was the suggestive juxtaposition of this photo with a nearly identical but much older one.

Scrolling down an inch, *Gazette* readers encountered a snapshot of a white bikini'd brunette, dating probably from the early 1940s, judging from the cut of her swimsuit. She was leaning forward in a pose a lot like Parkie's. Though she didn't hold a candle to Parkie, the beach looked similar, and she, too, was being offered a fancy drink by a dark-skinned waiter.

Beneath this photo, the caption read, "Hitler's mistress on vacation."

Under Parkie's picture, it read, "Heiress de Groot enjoys the white sands."

"Holy shit," Glory said. "What the fuck?"

It was only then that the headline began to make any kind of sense.

"'American aristocrat.'" Glory said. "Could they be any more ignorant?"

A few lines lower, Glory's eyes were assaulted by a giant pull quote, bolded across the screen in a larger font:

"Honestly, family ties to the Nazis don't surprise me much. —P. Katrina de Groot."

Uh-oh. Now that was not good.

Finally, an airtight, fully justified excuse to contact Parkie, Glory had thought at first. She really wanted to. And she knew Parkie, who was in fact a very private person, would be upset about the negative publicity even if she wouldn't have the easiest time talking about it.

But then there was that quote. Jesus, who says something like that? Glory had to ask. We're talking Nazis for fuck's sake—the day being linked to their shit isn't surprising is a very dark day.

She might have to reconsider. And anyway, maybe Parkie would be the one to call Glory. If only to explain herself. Parkie had to be waiting Glory out. She had to be telling herself that Glory should surrender first because she very mistakenly believed that Glory throwing in with Sarkisian was no worse than Parkie continuing to do Madeline's bidding. Which it was not. Surely it was not.

Hoping to get a clearer sense of the story, Glory did some research of her own.

She quickly discovered that the *Gazette* piece had spawned additional "coverage." And while these stories were posted in truly questionable blogs and on the pages of disreputable media outlets, it was frightening to see how rapidly and rabidly one lie led to another. A publication she'd never heard of, the *New Empire*, published, or stole, a very similar piece, but this time with a photo of a redhead who was definitely not Parkie walking down the street in huge sunglasses, waving the photographer away with her walking stick as if she were some kind of media-phobic villainess. Seeing that, Glory knew she had to talk to Parkie, and soon, regardless of the pull quote.

Maybe Parkie could have found out about the watch being an engagement gift from a Luftwaffe commander to his Blackshirt-sympathizing American mistress. Or maybe she couldn't have. Glory didn't know much about that chapter of history either. But she was struck by the fact that the story of the auctioned watch overlapped with the period of Lucille's life they'd been uncovering—the years before and during World War II, which she had learned were sort of the second act of the Harlem Renaissance.

But that was after weeks of reading letters that had been written during the war; it wasn't that Parkie didn't do her job.

The woman never stopped working, for crying out loud.

If someone had asked, Glory would have told them what angered her about the quote was its offhandedness. She couldn't help thinking it sounded exactly like something Parkie might confess to a reporter, making the most of the careless, fallen-debutante affect that got Glory so turned on when she was saying what she wanted to hear.

On the other hand. If family ties to the Nazis don't surprise you much, you know that's a fucking problem.

Nope. Texting Parkie was not, in fact, going to happen today.

Glory could, however, imagine doing a little debrief of the latest news with Eleanor. She was surprised Eleanor hadn't called already. Knowing it would be no use texting or even emailing her if she wanted a fast response, Glory called Eleanor's direct line. She was waiting for her to pick up when another news alert popped up on her screen: this one reporting Madeline's appointment as finance director for the gubernatorial campaign just announced by one of the Flagg offspring.

At last Eleanor answered. "Hello, my dear," she said breezily. "It's a little chaotic here, as you must realize. Is this something that can wait or . . ."

Eleanor was rarely so dismissive, and Glory found her eagerness to get off the phone irritating. Maybe even suspicious. She wondered if Eleanor was trying to avoid a discussion of Cuthbert's professional ethics with a skeptical client. And this made her want to have that conversation all the more.

"I guess it can wait. You've obviously seen the story about Parkie. I just wondered if you might have some, I don't know, perspective on what she said."

"Well, Gloria, dear, I really think that's something you'd have to discuss with Miss de Groot. She's out of the office now, as it happens. I haven't talked to her since the story broke. But I'm sure she'd welcome a call from you."

"In my present state, I don't think she would," Glory said. "Doesn't it bother you?"

"Doesn't what bother me?"

"Working for a fascist? I'm seeing right this second on Politico that your boss is raising money for a white nationalist. Did you know she has a bumper sticker on her white Range Rover that says 'Black Labs Matter'?"

"I did not," Eleanor said. Her tone was less chipper now. "I wasn't aware she kept a car in the city."

"This is the car at her Hamptons place, apparently," Glory said. She was simultaneously reading the story on her phone. "I was pretty fucking angry Parkie would say something like that. But talking to you, it sounds like it's all in a day's work. I picked Cuthbert's because it was woman-owned. Little did I know what that would mean. Even after everything else with Flagg, I've stayed in this because I trust you and Parkie. But I'm not willing to play games with my aunt's legacy. If Parkie doesn't care about her own reputation working at that place, it's on her."

The words dropped into the silence. A second passed before Glory heard Eleanor inhale and exhale slowly. This conspicuous deep breath didn't seem like a strategy for deescalating. It seemed like a warning to her listener to metaphorically sit the hell down.

"There was a time, and not long ago, Miss Gloria Hopkins," Eleanor Kenniston began low and slow, as if reciting from a book, "when speaking to me like that would have tapped you into a well of rage the depths of which you cannot possibly imagine. I would have told you *my* story. About how I came here just married, daughter of a shopkeeper, having grown up in the twin shadows of the molasses factory where all the Blacks labored and the sugar plantation owned by the descendants of white colonizers. I'd have unleashed a tide of resentment about the jobs I never had a chance at. Ending up in a university department run by racist white men and a handful of racist white women, treated like a student assistant when I had a doctorate in English literature. Deans of the college slipping their hands under my dress in broad daylight and calling me things I wouldn't repeat to you out loud."

Glory had been sitting on the green leather couch with her drink. But she stood up now, still holding her phone in front of her face, as if distance might lessen the force of Eleanor's words. Upstairs, one of the clocks chimed the hour. That, too, seemed like a judgment. By the house and everything in it. Maybe even by Lucille.

Eleanor took a beat before speaking again. Her shaking voice was still musical, almost mocking. "Do you know what it has meant for me that Madeline Cuthbert—on a whim, there's no question about that—decided to hire me for what she thought was nothing? And even though it was twice what I was earning, it *was* nothing. But it was finally intellectual work that allowed me to use my education, and my mind, after my husband died. I finally felt respected. And I have been. Respected."

"Eleanor, I . . ." Glory said. Feeling the heat of shame down to the soles of her feet. All she could hope was to get her apology in as soon as she could. But Eleanor ignored her.

"Thirty years later, I am part of this firm," she said. "And not without something akin to pride, I freely admit. But I also see the duplicity in it. And in Madeline. Maybe that's only because I won't be here much longer. But I do see it. You're not wrong about that. Though I do think the way you put it was unkind. I really shouldn't have to say this to you, but I suppose I do. Many of us have hard decisions to make in our lives. Outside looking in, you can rarely see what's at stake for someone else."

Chapter 30

Only after she had skimmed what seemed to be out there about her did Parkie confront the multiple phone messages and frantic texts and emails from Nicholas, Madeline, and intriguingly, Manya. For now, fortunately, there was nothing from Glory, whom she prayed hadn't seen the *Gazette* story.

Parkie had to call Madeline first. Yet of the three, the only person she could remotely stand the idea of talking to was Nicholas. Parkie wondered if it was even safe to call him. Or should she text? The notion that texts were untraceable seemed, according to TV, to be a myth. But everyone knows phone records and email are standard evidence in a court of law.

She'd start with a text.

Txting only. Seems better. Before you come at me. There was a lot more to what I said.

As always, Nicholas responded immediately, as if he'd been on call.

OMG, PdG. I am so sorry!!!!!! How can I help? And, no joke, Taytay has nothing on you, gur. At least you look AMAZE. #cruelladegroot

Okay. She actually kind of liked that one.

Not sure there's anything anyone can do. I fear even my (ex?) girlfriend would think it's just my latest soulless capitulation to the neocon dark side. Speaking of: Need to call MC now. Advice?

He was clearly handcrafting a response. At length, his advice arrived.

MC tends to think all press is a boon, so prob won't be (that) mad. I haven't TT her either. Think she forgot I was on this. I had no idea, of course. Still trying to work it out. Seems like von Milch was the real lover behind the Brit proxy Adelaide Flagg married. But who could have known that?

Where was that photo taken anyway? (Yours, I mean)

This last inquiry was a little unseemly. Parkie wondered if someone might be asking Nicholas for details and if, perish the thought, he might be trying to provide them.

Can't actually remember—they obvi trolled FB. Vacation with fam a few years ago. Anyway, thanks. Will let you know if/when MC fires me.

*

Madeline wasn't the least bit angry. She had reposted, retweeted, and generally promoted the photograph of Parkie—possessed, she thought, of a certain je ne sais quoi—on every platform she could.

"At some point in this business, something like this is bound to happen," she told Parkie. "Yes, you should have been more careful—rule number one, never say the words 'Hitler' or 'Nazi' to a journalist. In any interview. But we're not college professors here, for Christ's sake. Our business is to know what things are worth in today's market. You did what you needed to do to come up with an estimate, and only a reporter, or the History Channel, could have uncovered the German admirer." Her demonstrative replacement of "Nazi" with the more acceptable "German" was less than comforting.

In fact, after that conversation, not being fired felt like an affront.

But: Madeline down. Parkie had now contacted two of the three names on her "most messages from" list. Which left only Manya Shah. Yet as she prepared to send the shortest and vaguest possible acknowledgment of Manya's several subjectless inquiries, Parkie realized that, besides Glory, the person she most wanted to talk to hadn't made any effort to reach her yet.

Why hadn't Dr. Kenniston sent so much as an email?

Parkie had been purposely offline back in the Schomburg Library when the story broke. But Dr. Kenniston had to have heard the fallout from the *Gazette* grenade by now—she always knew the latest Cuthbert's news. Trying to manage its impact on her own reputation seemed to be one of her coping strategies.

Once she'd gotten home and the hours wore on, however, Parkie hadn't been sure what to do with herself. Going out seemed ill-advised. Not that all of Manhattan was reading the usually laughable *Gazette*, but the last thing she wanted was to be accosted by some asshole with a camera on the street: "Mussolini Sympathizer Buys Bottle of Pinot Grigio!"

Anyway, there were leftovers from the previous night's takeout; it wasn't like she'd perish if she didn't leave the premises for the night. Still, the whole thing was depressing, and being trapped in her apartment only took Parkie to a more hopeless place.

It was just so lonely.

Since she'd been home, nothing about the day, from eating more than one bowl of cereal to finishing the last of the tequila and starting in on the gin, to editing today's notes from the Schomburg—especially this—had prevented her thoughts from boomeranging back to Glory. Once they did, it was impossible to resist the masochistic thrall of reviewing, like a movie montage, their highs and lows together. Not rating an in-person break-up was about as low as one could get. Woe unto Glory Hopkins for throwing in the towel without a fight.

Thoughts of Glory aside, there was a dwindling window of time to nip Manya Shah in the bud, which sounded kind of dirty, didn't it? Unlike some people, Manya had sent Parkie four emails and three abbreviated texts. By all indications, she understood how shitty this must be for her and wanted to help.

Why did accepting her help feel like cheating?

And given Glory's ghosting, why did she care?

Before taking action, Parkie decided to game it out for a change. She could respond to Manya in a couple of ways. The play-it-safe option meant limiting the flow of information from her side. In this scenario Parkie would accept the assistance of a businesswoman who had a sixth sense about media relations. She would politely thank Manya for her advice over the phone, wish her the best with her blockbuster group show, and return to the remastered *Cotton Club*, which she'd rationalized as research for the Larsen novella even though it was really just a way of feeling closer to Harlem.

The second option, the one most likely to transpire if Parkie wasn't careful, was the one she "feared" most. In this version, Parkie would find herself ultimately powerless to resist Manya's most recent, multiple, offers—of dinner, of lunch, of coffee, of drinks at her apartment, of another visit to the gallery, of a mani-pedi, of a bundled-up walk on the High Line, etc. Inevitably, finding herself alone with Manya again, Parkie would cave, as she had come close to doing when they went out before the Christmas party. And why shouldn't she? Glory showed no signs of wanting to know the truth, let alone come to Parkie's defense. Glory showed no signs of paying attention at all. Parkie had been given a bum rap, as Rita and Lily would say. And Glory didn't even care enough to come around and bust her chops about it.

At this point, Parkie had to ask herself, what could possibly go wronger?

*

The next night Parkie met Manya at her 28th Street apartment. Manya deemed Chelsea too active for a private appointment at the gallery. Nor were any of her usual attention-getting haunts an alternative, since Parkie still didn't want to be seen in public.

Moulton & Freer had bought the multimillion-dollar condo they kept for gallery business after selling a pair of town houses, cheaply bought in the '80s, a few blocks away. The building, designed by a famous female architect, was a space-age pancake stack of rounded glass channels adjacent to a cute little Romanesque Catholic church and a high school basketball court. The unignorable edifice was a bit like Manya: Parkie knew she shouldn't like it but she did.

Because the celebrity architect favored an organic, cell-like idiom, there were very few true corners or sharp angles in the apartments. Walls of windows in each room were rounded at the ends into an oval, which stopped the spaces from feeling like a clinic. Even the elliptical lobby resembled the cabin of a giant airplane.

After opening the door with a canary-eating smile, Manya welcomed Parkie into a sparsely furnished living room where the art, more than anything else, took center stage. On one wall, radiating color into the whiteness, was an actual Alma Thomas painting. On another, beside one of Tschaba Self's massive and graphically sewn canvases, there was a large multimedia work with a mystical-looking creature at its center, Chitra Ganesh, Parkie assumed. She recognized the hieroglyph in the hallway as one of Lauren Halsey's; next to it were photographic portraits by Genevieve Gaignard and Fabiola Jean-Louis. Impressed, even as a former gallery assistant, Parkie walked from work to work while Manya poured them glasses of an exceptional grenache she'd been decanting.

"I'm glad you made it," she said cheerfully. "Was the press still camped outside your building or did you sneak out through service?"

"No reporters I could see," Parkie said, unable to generate a laugh or even a giggle.

"Sorry, darling. I'm sure it's been a difficult couple of days. As I mentioned, I've been through just this sort of thing. I will say, our British rags are a good deal bloodthirstier than yours—and a good deal more sexually explicit. Back home, they'd simply have found a nudie of you, smacked black strips on your nips, and splashed it across the front page. Hmm. The very thought. One must admit this preposterous intimation that lounging at posh beachside resorts, almost a century apart, demonstrates a shared affinity for Hitler was nothing if not creative. Top marks for that. A bit too asinine to count as even fake news, I would have thought."

She dropped down to the love seat and motioned for Parkie to do the same. Instead of sitting next to her host, though, Parkie chose an egg-shaped chair near the window, for which she received from Manya a kissy purse of the lips.

"How are you really holding up, ma' dear?"

"My job is not in jeopardy, if that's what you're asking. Madeline is fine with all of it—from the asinine and preposterous photo pairing to the actual history of the watch."

"No shock for the ages there. Why do you think I'm courting you instead of her? Odious woman."

"So there's courting. Good to know."

Manya tilted her glass a few times, inhaled, and took a sip.

"Oh, I like this very much," she said excitedly. "First question: Did you say what they said you said? And second: Were you on the record?"

"Absolutely, to both," Parkie said. "But there was a lot more before the part they printed."

"They quoted you out of context?"

"Oh, for fuck's sake. Of course, they did. Never mind that everyone I know seems perfectly willing to believe what they implied I meant, as if I would actually say something like that. You seem to think so."

"Quite the contrary," Manya said. "All wrong. Initial thoughts were that the Parkie de Groot I know was not that person. I said to myself, and anyone else who would listen, namely Martin, I'd have to hear it to believe it."

A tingle shot up Parkie's spine. Even if it wasn't truly Manya's first thought, it was the kindest thing anyone had said to her so far.

"Thank you," Parkie said. "That actually means a lot."

"Did he interview you in person?"

"No, it was over the phone. I had no idea where he was going. Usually, they just want a few comments about how rare something is and why it sold for so much. He started off friendly, but then he went for the jugular."

"And was he recording?"

Parkie's eyes went wide.

"He didn't ask permission. So I don't think so," she said, simultaneously feeling around for her phone in the leather bag at her feet.

"But I was. I'm so completely out of it that I totally forgot until you asked. I mean, I never listened to it. I couldn't stand to. And I didn't start from the beginning. And I didn't ask him first. So I'm sure it's inadmissible. At least it would be on *The Good Wife.*"

Manya moved a pillow to make room beside her.

"Excellent, darling. That's brilliant. Let the real work begin."

*

Manya listened to Parkie's recording of the interview probably ten times before she came up with a plan. It would need to be leaked, obviously. The only questions were to whom and when.

"It's double jeopardy. But you knew that when you said it, didn't you?"

"Why, because when Madeline hears the rest of it, she really will fire me?"

"I should think she'd have to."

"Bring it," Parkie said. "I've lost everything else. Why not add my job to the list?"

"Surely not everything else?"

Parkie reached for the decanter and refilled her glass.

"Yes, Manya. Everything else. Glory. That *is* what I mean."

"You two are quite the melodrama," Manya said. "On again, off again. One feels one should wait for the all-clear."

She leaned across Parkie to reach the wine for herself. In the process, her sleek dark hair brushed against Parkie's cheek. Almost unconsciously, Parkie leaned back at her—that is, she leaned forward into what was very much Manya's personal space.

Manya abruptly turned Parkie's way. And suddenly, they were nose to nose—breathing and blinking but otherwise statue-still. Until Manya broke the connection with an incredulous little shake of her head.

"It should be abundantly apparent that I like you, Parkie. But you must also know by now I'm not looking for a 'long-term relationship,'" Manya said, delivering the last phrase in a very believable American accent. "I merely want to see what that indifferently professional face of yours looks when you're begging me to make you come. And you *will* do both."

Parkie was on the point, the very knife's edge, of capitulating to herself. Of cupping Manya's obnoxiously arrogant jaw and kissing her.

But before she could, Manya, attempting to set the agenda, showily leaned her way. Blouse gaping, breasts on view; her chic balconette had done its job. The proximity of Manya's clavicle alone should have made kissing her there the obvious place to start.

And she probably could get Parkie to beg.

If Parkie let her.

But she just couldn't. A couch. A few drinks. Undeniable chemistry that made getting together seem inevitable. It was already one of those dating déjà vus. She'd been here—or someplace very like it—before. With Glory. Only after the canoodling that night, she'd gone home with that scarily distinctive feeling she never wanted to admit she'd never really had. The feeling that somehow, someway, sometime Glory would be the one.

"You are the most inspiringly confident woman I have ever met," Parkie said, collapsing against the back of the sofa. "Saying no to you takes the strength of a suspension bridge. Or a dam. But I just can't. I mean, even if Glory and I never see each other again, it's too close. You know her work. You know her. Whatever happens at Cuthbert's, you're the director of a gallery I respect—or will once you take over. And besides, I actually kind of like you. In the platonic sense. Of course."

"In the engineering-analogy sense. Crikey. I knew I'd lost you there at the end," Manya said with a small grin. "That line never works on tops."

So damned perceptive. She leaned back next to Parkie, closer again.

"Can't lose what you never had," Parkie said, not meaning to be catty, but fearing it came off that way.

"I'm sorry," she said. "I didn't mean it like that."

"No, you're absolutely right," Manya said, turning. "One would think you were the only attractive woman, or person, in New York. But I yield. Important to go out on a high note, isn't it? Head up. Dignity intact."

They both laughed.

"And triangulation aside, who doesn't love a highly competitive, hard-fought lesbian match made in heaven? Gives us all hope."

"You'll have to look elsewhere for that," Parkie said. "Glory has had enough of me. Just ask her. Only qualified applicants need apply for that job. If there are any."

Manya shook her head in feigned, or possibly real, consternation, sitting forward as if energized by the news.

"Surely she doesn't think that quote in the *Gazette* is all there is to it?"

"Who knows? We haven't talked in weeks. She's still disappointed in me for having the Flaggs as clients. I can't imagine this will help with that."

"And who is Glory Hopkins, the Dalai Lama? I think not," Manya said, her face coloring. "If she can make compromises, why can't you? And to my mind, yours are much more justifiable. You're only starting out and it's not your company. Business is business. She believes working for Madeline is a mortal sin, then?"

The flaring temper could only mean Manya had found out about Sarkisian. Had Glory chosen a gallery? Parkie honestly didn't want to know. She would be disappointed in Glory either way—for making the wrong decision or for making the right one but not telling her.

"It is a sin of some kind," Parkie said. "Which I realize. Obviously I realize that. Why else would I have said what I said to that reporter? And yes, some of my life choices have been fucked up. But I'm the one who put myself out there with this. I'm the one who'll get fired. Madeline might even give me the 'you'll never work in this town again' speech. She's vindictive like that. She could blackball me if she wanted to. It's not like we're in the same sorority."

"I've never understood American sororities," Manya said. "Though I do fancy the idea."

Parkie flashed her a hardy-har-har look.

"It's just beyond infuriating."

"And then some, I should think," said Manya. "For both your sakes, I hope Glory pulls her talented head out of her talented arse when she learns what you truly told that smarmy reporter. But disapproving girlfriend or no, justice shall be served."

Chapter 31

Glory found herself walking around aimlessly before breakfast. The house was empty without Maisie. It was disproportionately lonely without her cat to share the space; to break the silence with her erratic yowls; to inexplicably skid across the floor or rub against her shins when she stood in the kitchen staring at the pantry shelves, as she was doing now.

Nobody could say that Glory wasn't truly on her own. Not in the world, of course. But in her corner of it. In the part of the city she was trying to call home. In the house where she'd started to make happy memories and feel loved.

Not only by Lucille.

But by Parkie.

When she eventually stopped feeling sorry for herself, Glory made some oatmeal and wandered into the front parlor with her steaming bowl. In preparation for the Sarkisian show, she'd moved most of her new-old work there. Lucille's rose-and-green rhododendron wallpaper was almost entirely obscured by her huge monochromatic canvases. Most rooms were now fully occupied by those well-received early works of hers so sparing with color and paint. So thin and evasive and denuded of everything and anything that looked like something.

She glanced from wall to wall wondering, as she'd rarely done of late, where her old adviser was in all this. He had gotten Glory noticed by the New York dealers—and probably by Manya, too—that much she surmised. That much he had repeatedly told her in his supposedly omniscient, hint-dropping way.

She didn't think about Richardson much anymore. Of course she thought about him constantly. But she didn't allow those thoughts to intrude on her art. How he had impacted her art. She didn't think about him that way. She didn't ask herself if he was the one responsible for getting her to make the work that got her noticed in the first place.

So why was she asking that question now?

Over a year had passed. A handful of semesters and a few school-subsidized sessions with a good therapist ago. It was, she observed, finally possible to look back on the end of grad school without puking. Without literally having to run sweating into a bathroom and vomit because she would feel herself physically and psychologically and immediately back in the studio that night.

On campus for that midnight visit, bottle of imponderably expensive wine in hand. Latent cigar smell in his clothes. The stems of the upside-down glasses clenched between his fleshy fingers. She wished she hadn't had the music on. Her music. Her space. And then it wasn't. In a matter of minutes, he made it his. Tried to make her his.

It wasn't rape or anything like that. She'd told herself this over and over. He hadn't really touched her. And as a result, she hadn't really said anything. She hadn't screamed at him the way she'd screamed into the hot silence of her car after, as she drove home to her shared apartment in East LA. She hadn't told him he was a pig for expecting something from her in return for doing his fucking job.

Maybe he was the one who learned too late that it was possible to veer off a road very suddenly. With no notice. Glory didn't believe she'd given him any reason to think she could be had, by him or any other man. New York galleries, the ones he told her only he could get her into, were all the way across the country—far away from him. He couldn't stop the dealers from knowing about her work; once he'd put his plan in motion, it went, like a wind-up clock until time ran out and she got a show. He couldn't very well take back his praise. Yet even after she left the school, she worried she'd never get away from him.

Only Lucille could have saved her. That was how she had begun to think of it.

The bowl of oatmeal, hardly touched, was cold and heavy in her hands. Rush hour. Such as it was. A car horn outside. Another in response. Then the doorbell rang. The monotone schoolhouse trill never failed so make her jump; and since Parkie came into her life, it never failed to fill her with hopeful expectation. Even when she knew she had no right to feel that way.

Not anymore.

The figure on the stoop was shapely, feminine, tall. But it wasn't Parkie. No, this body belonged to the only other woman whose anatomy was like home to Glory; that familiar. That familial. It was Grace.

"I'm only here for the day," Grace said as soon as Glory opened the door. "BIPOC mayoral candidates. Blah-blah, kill me now. We haven't seen each other in forever, though, Glo. Let's not waste time being bitches."

"I won't if you won't," Glory said. Even when she knew she didn't mean it, there was no resisting Grace's outstretched arms and air kisses; today the nominal pressure of her silky cheek and feather-light embrace felt strangely substantive and sincere. The way comforting feels when you can't admit you needed comforting.

Before they could really look at each other, Glory turned around and started walking to the kitchen.

"I didn't know if you'd be up yet. Are you in one of those preshow nonsleeping phases? You look skinny."

"I did sleep. I'm just up early to work. And how can you tell if I'm skinny under this? You look skinny. Too skinny. I know Court brings home plenty of bacon. Doesn't he feed you?"

Grace smirked.

"That didn't take us long," she said.

They both laughed.

"Do you want coffee? Tea? Scotch?"

"I'd love a pour-over. If it's not too much trouble."

"You, too much trouble? Impossible. Nah. It's fine. I was just about to make myself one. You can't say you never taught me anything."

"I guess that's as good a skill as any. I know I didn't teach you to ignore our mother when she says hurtful or nasty things nobody should even dignify with an acknowledgment."

Glory could feel Grace trying to catch her eye. But she didn't let her. She didn't want her sister's expression—joking, or wanting to take it back, or ready to deny she'd said it—to cancel out the words she'd just spoken: possibly the only critical words from Grace about their mother since they were adults. Instead, Glory said the first thing that came into her mind.

"Why are you here, Grace?"

"Like I said, mayoral-candidate thing. As goes Manhattan, so goes Denver." She laughed.

"If only," Glory said. "I meant, why are you at my house?"

"My little sister the big-time artist moves into her own brownstone in Harlem and I'm not duty bound to drop off a housewarming gift when I'm in town? Did we grow up in the same family?"

"I don't know, did we? Our parents don't seem to recognize me most of the time, so I might not be the best one to ask. But I will take that present. Why are you being so nice?"

Grace accepted the hot cup of coffee and watched as Glory pulled out the opposite chair at the table and sat down.

"Oh, Glory," Grace said, her voice suddenly low and tired-sounding. "This has to stop. I know you've been talking to Court. And honestly, I've been so happy about that. It's like, if he knows what's up with you, I don't have to worry. But I do. You're my little sister. My family. I can't stand that we don't even pretend to care about each other anymore."

Glory had to throw a mental switch to stop her mind from overheating. Was Grace, her perfect sister, who had never—as far as Glory was concerned—tried to understand anything about her, attempting to do that now? And if so, why?

"You know I will always love you on paper. Maybe not in real life, but officially, I always will," Glory said. "But Grace, since when have you cared? Since when have I fit into all those perfect plans you've had since high school with all my mess? Before"—she gestured around the room—"this?"

Grace sipped her coffee. Then she put down her mug and gave Glory a look that said, Okay, I'll give you that.

"Glo," she said. "You know, and only you know, how it was growing up. The difference between us is that I believed, I received, Mom and Dad's uplift gospel. I did what they said. And yeah, they made us so competitive I wanted to beat my own sister at their game."

"And you did," Glory said, drinking from her own mug.

"No, baby girl. I didn't. You dropped out of law school," Grace said. "You did the unthinkable. And you survived. Went out on your own. Made a life. I don't think I'll ever know what kind of strength it took to tell Mom and Dad you were quitting something. You were always strong like that. And I've been so ass-backward, I thought you being strong made me weaker."

In a way, it did, Glory wanted to say. Growing up, praise for achievements felt like a zero-sum game at their house. She suddenly had a painful memory of the two of them sitting in the station wagon after Glory's win at a tennis match, comparing what their parents had just told her to what they'd told Grace (the goalie, of course) after a shutout in soccer the week before.

"Where is this coming from?" Glory asked. "They must have some kick-ass therapists in Denver these days."

Grace sighed.

"No joke, girl. It's amazing what two hundred an hour will get you in that cow town," she said.

For the first time that morning, Glory felt herself wanting to take Grace in uncritically. She became aware of a wish to regard her sister not as an enemy whose flaws deserve detection but merely as a very beautiful woman. Just as she always had been. Runner-fit, she would never be skinny by most definitions—but Glory knew Grace would appreciate her saying she was, with her tailored trousers and plaid blazer and god-only-knew-how-expensive heels. She was so put-together she could run for office herself.

"You look good, Gracie," Glory said. "Younger than me. Happier."

Grace looked down and drank her coffee.

"Wouldn't that be nice," she said. "Seems I missed my chance to do the only thing that counts."

"The only thing that counts? You're gonna be the head of the DNC by forty-five. I have odds on that, so don't disappoint. What are you talking about?"

"Children," Grace said. "We can't have them. I can't have them. And frankly, I don't want them. Which makes me an aberration, apparently. A stain on the family name."

Glory stared at her perfect sibling, to whom it was suddenly important to carefully reposition the salt and pepper in relation to the glass vase of flowers on the table.

"Says who?" Glory said. She could feel the tension closing her throat. Nobody got to shame her big sister about . . . anything. "Mom and Dad? Court?"

"Not Court," Grace said. "He's got nieces and nephews to spare. He gets to be fly Uncle Court. He likes our life. And he knew I might not want a family. I was clear on that even before I knew about my body. But Mom and Dad have just been . . ." She swatted away a rogue tear. "For lack of a better phrase, needlessly cruel about it."

"Needlessly cruel is indeed their specialty," Glory said.

"It's taken me practically forty years to realize what you've had to go through with them your whole life. I'm sorry, Glo. I just didn't want to see it."

Grace had an early-afternoon meeting downtown, so they didn't have much more time to talk. Maybe because they knew it would be brief, the topics of their long-overdue conversation were limited.

"Court says you're seeing someone. What's she like?"

"Gone, as of this moment," Glory said. "We're sort of taking a break or something. I've got this show and she's got this job working for people I can't really handle. Ethically. So . . ."

"Classic Glory," Grace said. "How long did it take you to realize she didn't walk on water? How long is it going to take you to realize you don't either?"

That was the Grace she knew and didn't especially love. Thinking she knew Glory when she hadn't bothered to find out anything about her life since they'd left for college. Just because she wanted to respect the people around her didn't mean she idolized them. Or wanted to be idolized herself.

"I never said I did," Glory answered, trying to keep things easy.

"She's white, right?"

"What does that have to do with anything?"

Grace had stood up and was beginning to walk out of the room, heading for the parlor as she talked.

"Let me see some of this work before I go," she said. "You've dated white women before and you know it makes Mom and Dad batshit even though they won't admit it. How much of you is still worrying about that? And for what? Court says this woman sounds like the first one who might deserve you—and you might deserve. What's her name? Peyton? Chandler?"

"Parkerson," Glory said.

"Oh, that's real cute," Grace said with a husky laugh. "At least I'll never scar a child for life. Parkerson? For a girl? Is she as—what do you call it?—masculine-of-center as the last one?"

"She goes by Parkie," Glory said. "And she's. She's. She's really fucking amazing. Really fucking strong and smart. Funny. And you're half right. For once. I don't care what Mom and Dad think about me having a white girlfriend. But maybe I haven't been see- ing things clearly where she's concerned. Where I'm concerned."

"For once?" Grace said. "You really need to start keeping better track, lil sis. I am way ahead of you on being right."

Chapter 32

Parkie was supposed to be home from Manya's early enough to get her nine hours. Chauffeured by the gallery's driver, she left the Chelsea apartment under cover of darkness. She was full of red wine and resentment. Doing the right thing was so overrated.

Manya hadn't told her how she would leak the story.

She told Parkie, probably rightly, that the less she knew, the better. She also made it seem like whoever she was going to tell would be told in the next twenty-four hours. She wasn't willing to say when. This way Parkie would be surprised, with no need to pretend—or lie.

Plausible deniability.

Manya was turning out to be a very good person to know. If the two of them could get beyond the relentless pickup lines and eye-fucking that were so much a part of their encounters to date, Parkie thought they might even become friends.

She'd had her phone on silent while they were drinking in Manya's living room. But that hadn't stopped her from checking it whenever her host wasn't watching, hoping against hope that Glory might text, or call, or email to apologize.

Of course, she hadn't.

Evidently, lots of people had seen the *Gazette* story. Clicking through the hate messages in her Cuthbert's account and the even scarier expressions of support, Parkie realized that Glory was doing what she'd probably always wanted to do—disappear into her studio with a deadline to meet and little to no contact with the outside world. Finally, she had an excuse to retreat into the solitary existence she'd supposedly treasured before they met. Painting alone for days on end.

Making work instead of making a relationship work.

Believing that was all there was for her.

Days had passed since the story broke, and the more Parkie thought about it, the more she decided a sincere apology was the only acceptable response from Glory.

She'd decide who got a second chance now.

She was honest-to-goodness quoted out of context. Not only had she not done wrong, she'd done right. And Glory needed to understand that. Her inability to be with her, today, when Parkie really needed her, made Glory the one with questionable decision-making skills.

This seemed obvious in the wake of two beautiful bottles of French wine, some Indian snack mix she was now addicted to, and half a pound of hard cheese. She would try to put Glory's cynicism out of her head and get some sleep as soon as she got home.

The MFS Mercedes must have been no more than a mile from Parkie's apartment when a text popped up.

LWBradley.

What the hell?

Loden, in other words. Loden "Will Break Your Heart" Bradley, who had made good on her nickname, what, three years ago now? Loden. The bottom who was inadvertently responsible for Parkie's fire-as-fuck top game.

Parks! Nice bikini! Hope you're giving that Gazette asshole holy hell.

Of course, Loden would have seen the story. It was good of her to reach out.

Responding would only be asking for trouble, though.

Hiya. Glad you like it. The takedown awaits.

A few seconds went by and she relished not caring whether she heard back from Loden. Now, or ever, really. It felt great to feel nothing for a woman she had once worshipped. Someone she had adored with a depth of devotion that was pretty shameful to openly contemplate even while riding home unaccompanied and high on Manchego.

That she'd been so completely enamored of Loden seemed almost inconceivable to Parkie now. What did her first grown-up girlfriend have besides looks, money, and a borderline-contagious "fuck 'em if they can't take a joke" approach to life? So there was that.

By many sapphic standards, Loden was indeed the perfect woman.

Parkie took a moment.

With their year together now a broken-heart-shaped relic of the past, it should be possible to be honest with herself. Loden had, as she now saw, loved her. If only in her own repressed, self-centered, less-than-fully-adult way. Parkie brought out qualities in her that her friends seemed not to see—or want to deal with. But that kind, considerate Loden was the same Loden who bailed on Parkie with no warning. Probably because she was starting to recognize a self with Parkie she couldn't understand and didn't want to be.

Funny. Been awaiting a takedown myself.

Come over. Made some changes.

Parkie knew this would happen. She'd set the trap for herself. And now, that palpitating in her neck. That tension in her throat. Those were Loden feelings. Painful, exciting, "fuck me if I can't take a joke," Loden feelings. And she was every bit as scared of them as she ever had been. But beneath the fear, or alongside it, there was also the voice that would ask Loden to "make it go away, the way only you can." And that, as always, was the voice she listened to.

How many more times tonight could she reasonably be expected to turn down a perfectly good offer of sex? Loden didn't know Glory. No conflict of interest there.

"Excuse me," she said to the driver. "I hate to ask. But can we head back downtown? Something's come up and I need to be dropped in the Village."

*

Loden's apartment, though enviable, was less flamboyant than one might expect, given her seven-figure annual earnings. Hers was an airy but modest two bedroom in a nice co-op building on West 12th Street. She'd lived there since she did one of her first big deals in the aughts, snapping up the place with the cash bonus.

For Parkie, coming to Loden's had always been a kick. Mostly because she'd usually been strongly encouraged to attend, just as she had tonight, at the spur of the moment. When Loden was fresh from a trip or had a night open or a meeting canceled. They'd gone to Parkie's place only once or twice and never stayed the night. Never in a year of dating. But they'd had sex in every room, in almost every corner of every room, of Loden's.

When she opened the door, Loden didn't even try to subdue her reaction. She was wearing a blue-striped men's cotton shirt. It was loosely tucked, as always, into un-skinny jeans draped around her slim hips with a weathered leather H belt so that her waist looked longer and leaner. The thick waves of her once salt-and-pepper hair were completely silver-white now, parted on the side with one wayward lock swooping across her forehead. She was wearing what Parkie always called her old-man glasses.

"Fuck me," she said, blue eyes dancing. "You just get better and better."

Parkie laughed.

She'd be lying if she said it didn't feel amazing to hear this from someone she hadn't been seen by in years.

"You, too," she replied, fully meaning it.

Loden was from Houston. A big part of her appeal, as Parkie was instantly reminded, was her forthrightness. The rest was an inborn charisma that made it hard to separate the way she looked—vital, with glowing skin, great teeth, and breasts like a Greek statue's—from her larger-than-life personality. You just wanted to be with her. Whoever you were. Now it was all coming back.

"Come in and take your clothes off," Loden said mischievously.

She closed the door behind her and walked past Parkie into the kitchen, where there was a bottle of twenty-five-year-old double-matured single malt and beside it a tall carafe of purified water sitting on the slate counter.

"Figured you must be drunk if you showed, so I put together two options, according to your mood. Sober up or balls to the wall, either works for me."

"That's new," Parkie said. "Did we ever have sex sober?"

"Not that I remember. But there's a first time for everything. As you know."

Parkie also knew they could continue in this manner for quite a while. Loden's teasing had always been their form of foreplay.

She slid a crystal rocks glass Parkie's way and opened the Scotch, releasing its ancient cedar aroma. It even smelled rare.

"Two fingers about right?"

"Three would be better," Parkie answered. "As you know."

She couldn't stop her eyes roving. Loden's speckled, manicured hands, unseasonably tan from whatever getaway she'd just
treated herself to, made Parkie feel eager. Eager for whatever was
going to happen between them. And eager to make it happen
soon, before she lost her nerve.

She tossed back most of the Scotch.

Loden followed suit, coming around to Parkie's side of the
kitchen island to put her hands on Parkie's hips. She didn't say a
word or make another move; she simply gazed into Parkie's eyes.
Parkie was unprepared. Loden's expression was anything but prematurely triumphant. It was inquiring. Maybe a little uncertain. Not
like know-it-all Loden of yore. And it made Parkie practically rush
at her, kissing her fast on the lips as if she had finally come home.

They did that for several minutes, exploring each other's
still-familiar teeth and tongues until a fiery pain shot down Parkie's hip and her knee buckled.

"I can't keep this up," she said breathily, through the kiss.

"Sure you can," Loden said. "You are. And it's making me
goddamn wetter than an otter's pocket. I haven't been this worked
up since you left."

Parkie broke from her grasp and got herself onto a stool.
Pain radiated down the backs of her legs. She felt dizzy. And it
wasn't from the alcohol or the kissing.

"I didn't leave," she said hotly. "You left me. You broke up
with me. With a phone call. While I was in the middle of packing.
Do you not remember that? You left me."

Loden came over to Parkie and stood behind her, placing her
weighty hands on Parkie's shoulders in a way that inadvertently
exacerbated the pain.

"Don't," Parkie said.

"Oh please, Parks. Don't *you*. Be so high and mighty. We were in different places, and you know it. Now you're all grown up and I'm . . . Well, I'm still me. But I've never had better sex than we had, and I bet you haven't either."

About this, she was just plain wrong.

Parkie wasn't really into competitively judging sex. It had been good with different women in different ways. But if she had to say, it was never better than with Glory, and here again, now that it came down to it, she couldn't stomach the thought of being intimate with, giving herself to, anyone else. Least of all Loden "We've Been There, We've Done That" Bradley.

Strike two.

"Now I remember. You never cared how I felt when we were together," she said. "Physically, mentally, whatever. Nothing. You could have thought about my actual feelings, you just didn't want to. That should make a onetime thing easy. But it doesn't. I don't want to be with someone who can't tell when she's hurting me."

Loden had removed her hands from Parkie's shoulders soon after Parkie had started talking.

She went back around to the other side of the island. "I never did mean to make you uncomfortable," she said. "Not then and not now. I just get carried away with you. I want what I want. Like always, I guess. But I'm sorry if I hurt you, Parks. I really am."

*

As far as monumental mistakes went, it had worked out all right in the end.

Loden had a freezer full of ice cream. And chocolate sauce. And a microwave.

They'd had a good, at times difficult, talk, being honest with each other about what had gone wrong when they were together and how life had treated them since. The whole time Parkie was thinking, I'll never do this with Glory. We'd never get to this point. She couldn't say why she felt it with certainty, but she did. Loden was at the height of her professional game, a named partner at her firm, yet, as Parkie could have told her, it wasn't enough. She was lonely and busy and hadn't found the time to give dating a fighting chance, settling instead for random and unfulfilling encounters with women half her age when she traveled.

She admitted hoping there might be a chance to get back together with Parkie now that she'd done some emotional work and, she hoped, become a more empathetic person.

"Clearly a bad investment," she'd said. "My life coach took my money and all I got was rejected by my self-aware ex."

"You do seem different," Parkie told her. "But I'm different, too. And let's be honest, I could never keep up with you. At pretty much anything."

"You didn't have to try, sugar," Loden said, the same modest expression reappearing in her eyes. When she brushed a lock of Parkie's hair off her face, it didn't seem like a move, it felt like a friendly gesture.

"I know that now," Parkie said. "But you needed someone to chase you back then. And that was never me."

Loden had sent her off with a kiss on the cheek, sweetly expressing the hope that when the time was right, they might meet again. Neither of them seemed to think this likely, or even necessarily desirable. But they acted like they did.

Parkie got home late, a hangover reporting early for duty in her throbbing head. She took a painkiller, drank about a gallon of water, and went to bed at last.

Chapter 33

After Grace left for her meeting, Glory went upstairs again. Not to Lucille's bedroom, which she now considered doubly haunted, but to the living room with the old hi-fi. She was playing records while she went through the last of the letters. The ones she and Parkie hadn't gotten to, most of which, oddly enough, were postmarked from Manhattan.

Lucille's seriously vintage stereo had to have been the fanciest available at the time; the kind that anticipated the CD carousel, itself the precursor to the playlist. You could stack four or five records at the top of the spindle, and when one was over, the next one would wait for the arm of the needle to retreat before dropping down to play. There was something satisfying about spinning vinyl on a turntable. The stereo's mechanical efficiency was offset by human intervention, a scratch or stray hair or dust mote could generate a repeated word or phrase that was hard not to receive as a prophecy.

Life is lonely again, lonely again . . .

She'd been listening to some of her faves. There wasn't much Lucille didn't have in that closet. The current quartet of albums included Sister Rosetta Tharpe, early Ella, Duke Ellington's *Black, Brown and Beige*, and an album by the tragically short-lived Dinah Washington.

Tharpe's growling, upbeat hymns were over, and the First Lady of Song had begun crooning Billy Strayhorn's wittily heartbreaking ballad. Glory hadn't even bothered to get out of her coveralls. But since she hadn't bothered to work today, it was safe to sit down on Lucille's furniture without the fear of wet paint leaving a mark.

These letters were different from the others. Their finer paper felt more expensive. The hand, though legible, began many regular, mid-sentence words with distracting capitals, and there was a loopy letter *h* that proved challenging. The letters from this writer weren't always dated but rather had phrases such as "Saturday, en route" in the upper-right corner.

They were spare in terms of content with sometimes only ten or so lines on a sheet. Each envelope was addressed to Lucille but most of the letters began, "My darlings," simply signed "N." Glory raced through them. Not because they weren't interesting and often tear-jerking. But because she had, in the back of her mind, a plan to jump into a Lyft as soon as she finished and make it to Cuthbert's before the end of the business day. She couldn't wait to give Eleanor the news. And if Parkie was there, well, who knew?

She was down to the last couple of unexplored envelopes when her eye caught a postmark that was much later than the rest—not from the forties or even the early fifties but the sixties. The faint date within the black circle stamped on the paper was 1963.

Glory retrieved the single sheet from its delicate sleeve and pressed the page open on the sofa cushion beside her.

At home, Sunday twenty-fifth
My darlings,
   Not so long now until I will no longer come to you.
Soon our fireside chats and card games and Sunday

dinners will figure as a single memory. A happy one. We three, together. Nothing in your encouragement, faith, and belief in my abilities fell on unhearing or uncaring ears. For while I may have come off as obstinately devoted to nursing at the expense of writing, it wasn't always or entirely so. When I was not with you or in the hospital; when I was locked up in my gloomy little apartment wondering what had become of my calling—I was re-creating the very best part of my life in words. Whether for you, for myself, or for posterity, by which I mean, women like us, I cannot say.

But something called to me from within myself, even after my humiliation at the hands of the critics and the white people—but also the black ones—who so badly, so determinedly, wished to see me fail. And did see me fail in the making of novels about colored women. What they did not see is what your companionship and trust and, yes, your ardor, returned me to. I know not whether the "scraps" I leave you constitute anything original or good—or if this, too, allows the hard-hearted, modern segregationist to overlook my acquaintance with the literary tradition and my intervening therein. Whether this, too, will secure my reputation as a mere copyist or worse, a thief. I had always wished to tell a story with a happy ending, perchance to redeem my own tragic tale. But I had to live that story first. And I have lived it, truly reveled in it, with the both of you. My first, and last, true loves.

—N

*

When Glory arrived at Cuthbert's, it was nearly five. She walked right past Olive, who, in response to her ice-ray glare, didn't utter a word to stop her. On the ride down Glory had thought about who to see first. She owed it to Eleanor to tell her ASAP about the letter from N. incontestably identifying herself as the author of the pages found in the scrapbook—the "scraps." What Glory owed Parkie she wasn't quite sure, but she knew it was more than she had imagined before she read N.'s letters.

It was heartbreaking to think that N., whoever she was, had stopped writing because she'd been wrongly accused, as the letter implied. That happens commonly enough to artists who aren't white—even though most audiences (should) know that the Beatles, Elvis, even Soft Cell, got their most popular material from Black people. The list goes on and on. And how often are *they* called derivative?

From the letters, it seemed Lou and Rosalind had become N.'s sole source of joy, her emotional sustenance; the only meaningful things in her life besides nursing. Which had become more than a way to pay the bills and maintain a semblance of authority as a brown-skinned woman whose adult life was circumscribed by Jim Crow. According to N., Lucille and Rosalind were the reason she wrote one last novel. A novel that, unlike anything she'd written previously, ended happily. A story in which every word and phrase was alive with the heavenly sensations and unchecked passion women can have with women when that level of devotion, of trust, of what Glory wanted to follow N. in labeling "ardor"—is present and acknowledged between them.

Lucille and Rosalind hadn't saved N. But they had made life better for her, as she clearly had for them—through her way of living in the world. Through her humor, her intelligence, through her art.

Glory got the message. And like many formerly skeptical recipients of epiphanies, it made her feel as if she'd been walking around in a cloud of unknowing for much of her life. Until now, she hadn't known the power of trust and devotion to sail the beloved over life's hurdles. She'd been unable to conceive of being made better at being yourself by someone else's care and belief in you—to the point that they might just tell you things you didn't want to hear when they thought it was the right thing to do.

She only hoped it wasn't too late. Because Parkie could be cagey. She was not only a vigilant self-preservationist; she was someone who, like a character in one of the Laura Ingalls Wilder books Grace had secretly loved so much, would get on with her life no matter what the world threw in her wagon-rutted path. She was in charge. She handled things. And she didn't need help from Glory to get 'er done. This was Glory's takeaway from the past few weeks, and she was a little in awe that it made her want to come for Parkie that much more. To put it all on the line. Whatever that meant.

Eleanor was not in her office.

"She's out. I could have told you if you'd asked," a packing-up-for-the-night Olive said as Glory rushed past her desk and headed down the other hallway that was a shortcut to the cubicle hive and Parkie's desk. "Something about an emergency meeting of her renters' association. Or co-op or whatever. Anyway, she left."

Glory was moving too fast to allow for a response. She rounded the corner with just enough momentum to knock down an oncoming Parkie, who had been, but was no longer, holding a travel mug of mercifully cold coffee in her free hand.

On impact, the mug flew into the air. It sprayed a thin stream of milky brown liquid onto the walls and over the carpet.

And when it bounced back up, it splattered the ruffled surface of Parkie's ivory silk blouse, too.

"God dammit!" Parkie roared from the floor, where she was splayed like a newborn fawn, all extremities and soulful, shocked eyes. Glory offered her a hand, but Parkie had already pushed herself to her knees. By the time Glory had retrieved the renegade travel mug, which had rolled farther down the hall, Parkie had risen to her full intimidating height and was standing in front of Glory, walking stick firmly in her grasp. So firmly.

Parkie's eyes were sharp. Like a green stone cut into facets.

"What the fuck, Glory?" she said, glancing down at her inundated blouse. There was so much coffee—more than it seemed a travel mug could hold—and it was making Parkie's blouse stick to her chest in large splotches on her pale skin, wet enough splotches that Glory could discern which of her La Perlas she was wearing.

Parkie didn't wait for Glory's answer before she started off in the other direction, toward the staff powder room.

"Can I come with?" was all Glory could think of to say.

"I don't know. Can you?" Parkie said as she disappeared inside the door.

With only two stalls, it wasn't a large or updated restroom, as would befit its users. There was a pink-and-gold-specked Formica counter with a pair of sinks and matching Formica-veneered stalls. Unchanged in decades, it was almost a period piece, but for the gingerbready dark wood étagère pushed up against one of the short walls and heaped with hotel toiletries like ex-votos at a shrine. This was a tradition Madeline had started years ago and which was now more a joke than anything else to the generations of female employees who wouldn't be caught dead availing themselves of a miniature bottle of lotion grifted from the Ritz San Diego ten years earlier.

Glory, however, was suddenly glad to have a few dozen brands of bodywash at her disposal.

"Just stop," she said as Parkie began to rip paper towels from the dispenser one after another. "Leave this to me. Artists know all about getting stains out. It's part of daily life for us. Stop with the towels. In fact, just stop everything you're doing and let me help you."

"Because that's what you do," Parkie said.

"I deserve that," Glory said. "Keep it coming."

She'd settled on the clear and citric Bigelow product, of which there were four of five unopened small brown containers.

"I'm not trying to take advantage, here," Glory said. "But you will need to take that blouse off."

Parkie made a curt guffaw.

"Oh, really. Is that your idea of help?"

"It's my idea of getting coffee out of silk before it sets."

Parkie was already unbuttoning. Before she was finished, Glory had moved close enough to nudge Parkie's ass against the counter with her own hips.

"Here, let me get that." Glory tried a smile as she lowered her eyes. "Your hands are shaking."

"Yours would be too if someone randomly knocked you down. Just randomly came at you out of nowhere. Ruining your new favorite blouse."

Then it occurred to her. The accident. Of course. Glory was glad she'd had the sense not to make a joke before she realized where Parkie's mind had gone. Even if Parkie hadn't realized it herself.

Glory took her fluttering hands.

"I know. I'm so sorry, baby. I was in a hurry to catch you before you went home."

Parkie smiled the first real smile Glory had seen from her in a very long time. Even in the cramped and deodorized confines of the Cuthbert's staff bathroom that smile felt like everything she'd been missing.

Parkie reached both arms behind to steady herself against the counter, and Glory wasted no time in unbuttoning the last few of her fabric-covered beads. Parkie slipped the wet garment off her shoulders and threw it into one of the twin sinks.

Glory frowned. She reached for a couple of the brown miniatures and removed their dusty caps.

"Seriously?" Parkie said.

"Of course, seriously. I'm sure that's, what, Givenchy or at least Anne Fontaine right? No more friendly fire. Let me just get it soaking."

She filled the sink with cold water and emptied the bottles of gel, swishing the bubbles around the fabric.

"Now we wait."

"Do we though? You have to find me something to wear. I'm not walking around Cuthbert's shirtless. Still too many paparazzi." Parkie laughed. Then, while Glory was still swirling the water-logged blouse, she came up behind her and put her hands around her waist, pressing her breasts into Glory's back. Glory stopped but didn't move, not wanting to turn around with wet hands. And not wanting Parkie to move either.

A lump in Glory's throat expanded as she shook off the water. Then she took a deep breath and rotated in Parkie's embrace until they were facing each other.

"Are you crying?" Parkie asked.

Although her expression was more surprised than sympathetic, Parkie proceeded to wipe the tears off Glory's cheekbones with her bony thumbs. Her eyes were calmer now.

"I'm . . ." Glory hesitated, averting her gaze. "Feeling some feels. The *Gazette* thing. Wow. What a shitshow. I was really sorry to see that. I know it must have been hard. I'm not stalling, I swear. But I am trying to think how to say the other things I need to say to you."

"Before you do," Parkie said, her hands still circling Glory's waist, "tell me one thing. Are you going with Sarkisian?"

"No. You were right," Glory said, making a point to look Parkie firmly in the eye. "I'm not going with Sarkisian, I'm going with Manya."

Chapter 34

It was impossible to know when Manya would drop the other shoe where Parkie's *Gazette* story was concerned. But in case it was today, she had come up with a "what to wear when you're expecting to get fired" outfit.

Making that selection from her wardrobe had been easy. She needed to convey the impression that she was running the scene. And for that, only leather would do.

Vegan leather, if you're nasty.

She had acquired the garment in question, and a questionable garment it was, via a random lunchtime Saks detour on a day when she was in a scorched-earth frame of mind and wanted a dress for the next time she felt that way. What she walked out with was a form-fitting, long-sleeved black shirtdress with a full, supple skirt. It looked great with her black patent loafers, an unavoidable diminuendo—though the walking stick tended to ratchet the mood right back up there. And anyway, stilettos would have been overkill for business BDSM.

Should Madeline reappear from Florida, this was just what was needed to face her, Cruella de-villain to villain. But if Parkie was vaguely prepared to confront her boss, she was nowhere near ready for the response she got from her fellow employees. Walking into work had been a bit like those scenes in movies where it can go either way for the protagonist: gradually rising applause from across the factory floor or withering looks and mean-spirited whispering as the heroine gradually realizes she's walking the gauntlet to the executioner's block.

People were definitely staring. Beginning with Olive, who gave Parkie an apologetic look while murmuring, "Take me with you?" under her breath as she passed by.

Elsewhere in the office, the other appraisers in the hive reacted in staggered phases. The first group stopped talking when she came in, scattering back to their cubicles like, well, like fearful employees trying to avoid guilt by association.

The second group, the ones with desks closer to hers, mainly peered around the short walls between them to see who was there, as everyone always did when people came or went, greeting her with a variety of looks ranging from awestruck to thoroughly disgusted. It all seemed a little much, given that Madeline had trumpeted the firm's positive take on, if not outright endorsement of, what had been "revealed" in the *Gazette*.

As soon as Parkie sauntered into her cube, Nicholas stood up from his spot on the other side of the grid. He dramatically threw his eyes back and forth to the emergency exit like one of those cat clocks with the swinging-pendulum tail. Clearly, this was the signal for a meet.

Parkie looked meaningfully back. She took off her coat, put down her coffee, picked up the phone receiver, pressed a few buttons, and pretended to listen to her messages. Then, a few minutes later, she rose and, taking the long way around, slipped through the stairwell door in the back corner of the hive room.

Nicholas was already sitting on the stairs, shirt cutely pooching, as he scrolled away on his phone.

When the door shut behind Parkie, he looked up. "Oh captain, my captain," he said in a breathy, mock-swoony voice. "Do I need a safe word for this conversation?"

"I thought I'd go out with a bang," Parkie said. "I just haven't decided who to screw yet."

"She's here all week, ladies and gentlemen," Nicholas said with a friendly smirk. "Fierce. And I would have said nobody wants a piece of that. But then, I work for our employer and she wants a piece of everything."

Parkie looked at the ceiling. "She's still my biggest fan, as far as I know. Loved the pictures. Loved the story. Can't get enough of my totalitarian resortwear."

"Are you saying you haven't seen it yet?"

Parkie knew immediately what he was referring to even though she had no idea what he was talking about.

Manya must have done the deed.

"Seen what?"

"Oh, you're good. Keep that up and you may avoid the ax. So, you had nothing to do with the *Slate* story? No knowledge of how a recording of your *Gazette* interview might have found its way onto their website?"

"Wait. *Slate?* Oh god. Let me see!" Parkie had braced for this. But expecting the worst doesn't lessen the blow when it arrives, it just takes the edge off the shock of it. Mainly, she told herself, she hadn't been wrong to put her trust in Manya.

Nicholas clicked back to the bookmarked front page. Along the margin's list of popular stories was "Cuthbert's Whistleblower Cuts Bait with Morally Compromised Old NY Client." True to their more balanced—and accurate—reportage, the piece provided context for Parkie's sale, including a brief muckraking of the leaves under the Flagg family tree. Within the story, an embedded link took the reader to an audio clip of Parkie's answer to the reporter's question in its entirety: "I have learned that there are historical connections between the Flagg family and slave trading. That they are considered by many to have held a monopoly on lifesaving pharmaceutical drugs with fatal results for poor people and people of color. And gay men, of course. Honestly, family ties to the Nazis don't surprise me much."

"And gay men, let's not forget," Nicholas parroted. "Because, you know, AIDS."

"Fuck off," Parkie said. "So that's that."

"I'm afraid it probably is," Nicholas said. "For both of you."

"Glory's not implicated in any of this. She can still work with Eleanor."

"Eleanor?" said Nicholas incredulously. "I knew Dr. K. had a first name. Just not one that could be intoned by mortals. Her breaking ranks is what probably drove Madeline over the edge. I mean, treachery from you, no big deal. But treachery from Cuthbert's pier of company loyalty months from her apotheosis? I bet MC Hammer went ballistic."

"Okay. Stop. What the hell are you even talking about?"

Nicholas picked up his phone again.

"Right, right," he said. "I keep forgetting you *haven't* seen the story yet. Wink, wink. I think we can drop the pretense. She's too cheap to install cameras back here where nobody can see them."

"Dammit, Nicholas," Parkie thundered in her loudest whisper. "I *haven't* seen it. Tell me what you're talking about!"

Nicholas gave her a worried glance, soft lines beginning to pile up on his forehead. He seemed to know the *Slate* story by heart. With a quick scroll he arrived at a passage that wasn't focused on Parkie alone.

"Third paragraph. 'According to Dr. Eleanor Kenniston, long-time employee and specialist in'—blah-blah-blah, book stuff," he began again, reading from his phone. "'For years, Cuthbert's has worked closely with clients who have questionable backgrounds. But in my estimation, none of those estates or consignors has a history quite as unconscionable as this family's. Just the other day it occurred to me that some of the young men I knew in the nineties had probably died because they were unable to afford Flaggcorp's criminally expensive drug. It's too little, too late, but I thought to myself, I can't ignore this anymore. I can't pretend it isn't connected. It's all connected. Always has been.'"

Parkie wasn't the story's headline, Eleanor was, she thought admiringly. Parkie gave Nicholas a five-minute lead to lessen suspicion of their joint reentry to the hive. As she leaned against the railing while he snuck back in, she imagined being called into Madeline's office by her assistant, summarily facing a one-woman firing squad and being unequipped with an explanation for her disloyal behavior to the firm other than that she, too, discovered she couldn't keep ignoring the past and live with herself. Let alone sleep at night. Not if she didn't want her bed to stay empty.

As Parkie emerged from the stairwell, she heard her desk phone ringing and rushed over to grab it.

"Hi, Parkie, it's Cameron," said the always dreaded voice. "Madeline wants to see you in five. Can you make that work?" She always put it this way, though the answer was never in doubt.

"Absolutely," Parkie said. "I didn't know she was back."

"Well," Cameron said. "She is."

*

Madeline's office was disarmingly small. Facing the doorway like a triumphal arch, her leather chair and desk were claustrophobically

surrounded by tall Napoleonic shelves containing every Cuthbert's catalogue ever published as well as two or three, mostly
ancient, glass and brass business awards.

There were other, larger offices elsewhere on the floor, but
none offered what Madeline so clearly prized about this one: its
closed circuit–like feed of the comings and goings of her staff.
Appraisers are always on the run. But one couldn't easily sneak in
or out of the building without passing the sole office positioned at
the crux of two corridors. From her petite panopticon, Madeline
could, should she wish, accost any of them at any time with an
ulcer-inducing interrogation or a weekend-ruining assignment
or, and this happened all the time, a withering criticism publicly
launched while the door was still wide open.

When Parkie entered, Madeline gestured for her to close
that door.

"Sit," she said. And Parkie did.

"So, loop me in. Is Parkie de Groot my deep throat?" Madeline said with a crocodilian smile. "Have you found religion?
Because there's only one good book here, and it's written in
double entry."

"Listen, Madeline. I don't know what—" Parkie began.

Madeline cut her off. "No, you *don't* know what. You've
done well here, Parkie, and everyone knows you're willing to put
in the hours. Maybe you don't feel loved. We can't have that. If
this is about a raise or a promotion, I can give it a think. But first,
I have a proposition for you, and here's how it's going to work."

Her proposition was not, of course, a suggestion. Not a hypo-
thetical. It was a done deal. And while immediate dismissal didn't
seem to be on the table, it certainly would be, should Parkie not
accept her boss's conditions. Madeline leaned forward on her
elbows, jeweled fingers delicately templed.

"Your little tell-all put us in the doggie doo-doo with the Flaggs. But I'm not too worried about that. What chaps my hide is that you played the race card. For Christ's sake, Parkie, with all the PC ninnies around. You've even got Eleanor about to riot over that. And this I do not need. So. I'm moving up the timeline on this Harlem estate you and Eleanor are bleeding hours on. It's all going in next month's Americana sale, and the two of you are going to give it a big African American dog and pony show so people see we're not burning crosses over here. If, and I do mean *if*, you two can whip that sale into shape. Dredge up some solid interest and I'll think about keeping you around—and not firing Eleanor, as I have every right to do, before her retirement. Questions? Didn't think so."

With that, she picked up the phone.

"Okay, Cam. All done. Get me back to the important stuff."

*

It was almost dark by the time Parkie's Lyft got up to 115th after work. The wintry sky had been gray all day, and the sunset's pink and purple streaks hadn't quite disappeared, leaving the trees and nearby buildings in black silhouette against the cloudy sky. The ride gave Parkie just enough time to question her decision to visit unannounced. It was the only action she could think to take. And she would take it even before contacting Glory about the new sale and the new date. There was still so much she needed to tell Eleanor about her time at the Schomburg.

As they got closer to Graham Court's intersection, Parkie could see that Adam Clayton Powell was backed up with more than the usual traffic, as if something was going on. There were police cars along the median and pulled onto the little triangle of trees across the street. Lots of police. And three or four big trucks, like ship container big, double-parked, with streams of people rushing toward and away from them in every direction.

In the early-evening light, it was hard to make out anything else at first. The unthinkable thought that first crossed Parkie's mind was fire. But as she strained to look up and down the block through the car's window, there wasn't a firetruck in sight. Nor was there the awful presence of smoke or ash in the air to indicate that kind of catastrophe. Thank God.

As the car got as close as it was going to get—so said the driver—Parkie saw that people were moving. Not into Graham Court's archway, but out of it. Whether in uniforms or street clothes, people were streaming from the building carrying furniture and multiple boxes; some carried lamps or small appliances or stacks of clothing on hangers. There was a feeling of urgency about it. As if they were in a race against the clock.

Parkie had to get to Eleanor.

She stepped onto the snow-dusted sidewalk across the street from the building's entrance and very carefully made her way to the drier pavement under its scaffolding.

After inching along, she emerged near the pretty wrought-iron gate and barrel vault over the driveway, narrowly missing an exiting station wagon piled to the headliner with somebody's furniture. Parkie pushed through a crowd of people, mostly professional movers, smoking in the overgrown courtyard. The unusual building had four tiled entries, each with its own elevator bank. And while any evidence of movers or workers was usually banished from the fancier lobbies, all of Graham Court's were now spilling over with residents and their helpers carrying various possessions onto the street.

There were even police officers inside—not a good sign—stationed by the mailboxes. The super on duty in Eleanor's lobby was being overwhelmed with requests, which made it easy for Parkie to slip onto the elevator and up to the seventh floor.

When the doors opened, Parkie was affably greeted by two square young men in brown Cuthbert's uniforms balancing a pair of loaded dollies.

The Cuthbert's guys recognized her and she them. A muscle-bound blond whose name patch said "Atlas" winked at her and said, "You never saw us." To which Parkie gave a succession of quick nods before they exchanged places and she continued down the hall.

Eleanor's door was open, and just as Parkie went in, a few more Cuthbert's people came out.

"Miss de Groot?" came an agitated voice from somewhere she couldn't yet see. Eleanor, dressed to the nines in an emerald green skirt suit, as if she'd gotten ready for work when, as far as Parkie knew, she hadn't gone in that day, appeared in the apartment's rotunda.

Parkie moved in with a half-hug, instantly conscious that Eleanor Kenniston, even in dire straits, was no hugger. Her slight, slender body had tensed up immediately. Though she did seem to like the idea.

"What's going on?" Parkie asked.

"Oh, my dear. The worst has happened."

"What do you mean?" Parkie asked, looking around. "I saw the shipping guys."

"Out of nowhere they order us to vacate in forty-eight hours, supposedly for safety reasons. Suddenly the roof is about to fall in on us, they say. These kind, kind people received a desperate call from me this morning, and they've all come over on their own time to help. Madeline knows nothing about it, God willing."

Parkie wondered what other aspects of Eleanor Kenniston's world Madeline knew nothing about.

"Not two weeks ago we learned we'd almost certainly have another six months before anyone would need to make a decision. Then yesterday, I receive a notice that the building has been sold and the new owners are worried for our safety and the people from the penthouses on down have to pack up and get out. And if we do not? If we do not, they will impose all manner of excessive fines and fees. I'm sure it's not legal, but none of us have the capacity to fight it and pay the legal and these other fees with the money we've saved to move. Those of us lucky to have a savings, anyway."

"Fucking gentrifiers," Parkie muttered. "Sorry, Eleanor."

"Don't be," Eleanor said.

"But where are they taking all your things? Where will you go?"

"Well, that's the one silver lining. I have friends at Peacocks who have graciously agreed to take delivery of whatever I can get over there. You see, I've been in talks with them about selling my books when the time came, and they had already agreed to store them. And whatever else I plan to sell. The good Lord knows nothing I own is going anywhere near Madeline's infernal gavel. With that off-site storage in Queens, they have space for my things. But it was a professional courtesy just the same. And a consolation after being surreptitiously evicted from my home of over thirty years."

"But you can't sleep at Peacocks," Parkie said. "Let me book you a hotel."

"You're quite clearheaded in an emergency, aren't you, my dear?" Eleanor said, placing her hand on Parkie's own as she gripped her walking stick. "I'm not destitute. Not by any measure. Just caught on the hop. I'll book something until I get things arranged. I've been meaning to do that all day. Thank you for reminding me."

"Eleanor, you will absolutely not," Parkie said firmly. "I have a much better suggestion and I won't take no for an answer."

Chapter 35

"Are you sure you don't mind me inviting another woman to stay over tonight?" Parkie asked in a dramatic voice. She was in the kitchen filling a glass of water from the tap and Glory, watching her from the doorway, was thinking how she made even the simplest movements elegant. Or maybe it was just that while Glory was happy to see Parkie in any setting, she looked extra fine, and wonderfully at home, in this one. Parkie was back at the brownstone and she'd been comfortable enough to invite Eleanor to stay there even when she hadn't been able to ask Glory first. It was all so astonishingly couple-like.

"You know it's exactly what I would have done," Glory said. "And I'm sure time was of the essence with her trying to get into the Four Seasons or whatever five-star she had in mind. But when you say 'another' woman, you make it sound like she won't be the only one staying over tonight."

"Do I?"

"You do."

"I don't have an overnight bag. You'd have to lend me something to sleep in."

"Or not," Glory said.

Parkie handed her a glass of water.

"I was just thinking this morning that the three of us needed to get together to compare notes on the scrapbook. Really go through it all. We haven't been in the same room since Christmas Eve. Now here we all are for a slumber party."

They were waiting in the kitchen until Eleanor, who'd wanted to freshen up, came back down from Lucille's. Glory, in the meantime, was resisting the urge to take a few steps toward Parkie and kiss the hollows of her collarbone, just below the heavy gold chain, where she liked to get things started. Yet she was suddenly aware—and Parkie seemed to feel it, too—of a potentially parental level of surveillance with Eleanor in the house, like they'd been assigned a chaperone. They couldn't just start going at it at the kitchen sink when Parkie's superior might surprise them at any moment. It was fucking arousing.

"I can't believe how thirsty I am," Parkie said, turning to refill her glass.

"Me, too," Glory said, pushing Parkie's hair behind her ear. She'd never cared much about hair color before Parkie. But there was something about that changeable, indeterminate hue—now copper, now brass, now a true burnt sienna of the intensity she'd only seen in tubes—that moved her every time.

"There, that's much better," came the singsong voice of their guest by way of announcing her descent. She seemed to be referring to her shower, but Glory wasn't so sure.

Like a child caught red-handed, Glory snapped back into position at Parkie's side.

"It really is pleasant up there," Eleanor continued. "Your great-aunt had very fine taste—and such breadth to her interests. Quite cosmopolitan. At least that's the impression I'm getting."

"A woman ahead of her time," Glory said. "And I thought she was trapped in the past."

*

"Then he said something very like, 'African American writing might be a subject you could teach here,'" said Eleanor, milking her delivery. "'But for the Queen's English and the literary canon, we have a number of tenured faculty who are simply better qualified.'"

She looked from Glory to Parkie for a theatrical pause before erupting into an extended belly laugh the likes of which neither of them had ever heard—or ever imagined hearing—coming from the normally mild-mannered Dr. Eleanor Kenniston.

"So what did you say?" Glory asked, her eyes dancing as much from the cocktails as the fun they'd been having since Eleanor joined them in the living room—she and Parkie on the sofa and Eleanor in the club chair.

"Dr. K. unplugged," she had whispered to Parkie at one point.

"Oh, I may have said, 'I'm not African American. I'm from Barbados. We learned English from the queen herself. Does that qualify me to make half a white woman's salary at your institution?'"

She took a small sip of her old-fashioned.

"Things like that happened all the time when I first came to the States. I expected it because I was one of the darker ones in my family. A true embarrassment to my own great-aunts. They looked white to some of the white people there. Especially the tourists."

Parkie poured more water from the pitcher into Eleanor's glass and gave the last of it to Glory.

Eleanor nodded and smiled in response, suddenly looking, Glory thought, more introspective than before. If she was feeling melancholic, there was good reason for it, several reasons, in fact.

Eleanor looked to Glory. "So. Miss de Groot and I are to be the public face of the estate of Lucille Hopkins. I suppose Madeline gave us both the same marching orders. Even before she called me on the carpet I'd been thinking how much I despise that woman. For as long as I've known Cuthbert's would be my last act, I've managed to put her life beyond the firm in a box. Out of sight, out of mind. Her friends, her hobbies. Even her politics. I'm an incredible coward, really. It's not as if once I'd made something of a name for myself, I couldn't have found another position. I've simply gotten comfortable with my head in the sand."

"We all have to make compromises," Glory said. "I mean, if we were only willing to work for good people and good companies, most of us wouldn't have jobs."

"I've read myself that line for thirty years," Eleanor said. "It may even be true. And it's easy for me to say this now, I realize. But if good people continue to do what bad people ask of them, I simply cannot see things changing. Not fast enough to make a difference for your generation. We make them richer and more powerful, and they use that to take what they want from us. They give us a carrot or a lump of sugar every now and again—or kick us when we're down—because they know we need them, or we think we do, to survive. In the beginning I thought, Who else is going to hire a Barbadian immigrant, verily a Black widow, for her expertise in archival research and rare British books?"

Eleanor turned to face Parkie. "And you, Miss de Groot? What did you think?"

Parkie sighed. "I thought, Who else is going to hire someone disabled and a woman and young—who needs a cane to go anywhere—for a public-facing job with a ton of travel?" Parkie said. "And then I thought, I'm so lucky to get this job. I'll do whatever she wants. Whatever it takes."

Eleanor nodded. "And you, Gloria Hopkins, what did you think?" she asked.

Glory clinked the ice in her drink, staring into the tumbler as she formulated an answer. "I thought," she began slowly. Why was it so difficult to say what was in her head? "I thought, A show at Sarkisian will mean that I'm a real artist. And that kind of acceptance, that kind of outside approval, is the most important thing—it's always been the most important thing to me. To my family. The #MeToo stories and price fixing and tokenism can't hurt me because I'm smart. They're giving me exactly what I want. I thought, I'll finally be in control."

Even to Glory's own ears, the curt laugh that came out of her sounded cynical. But when she raised her glass, Eleanor and Parkie raised theirs back with similarly wry expressions.

"To falling scales," Glory toasted.

"You *are* going to be a star," Parkie said. "Just not their star. You will be in control."

"Honestly, it's like Eleanor said, time to admit my own place in all this. I don't want to keep compromising. Not in this house or anywhere else. I owe that much to Lucille."

"Speaking of dear Lucille," Eleanor said. "It sounds like you've both made considerable headway with the identifications. Parkie linked the descriptions of the book's brownstone to this one, and there's plenty else to suggest that Nurse Lily is the fictional alter ego of Nurse Nella, who appears to have spent a good portion of her later years in these very rooms."

"She never moved here though, did she?" said Glory.

"No," Parkie said. "She kept her apartment downtown, which was closer to the hospital. Living alone might have stopped her from being involved in any kind of scandal associated with the Colonel and Rita. Especially during the McCarthy era."

Parkie had begun to refer to the Lucille character in the novella, a decorated Army officer (who was later unveiled as Rita's mysterious "enlisted friend"), as "the Colonel." She thought it a delightfully butch nickname.

"The Colonel and Rita. You mean Lou and Rosalind," Glory said. "Can you imagine the kind of courage it took to carry on basically a polyamorous relationship in the forties?"

"And fifties. And early sixties," Parkie added.

Eleanor looked at them.

"Oh," Glory said. "Sorry, Eleanor. That's what they call nonmonogamous . . ."

Eleanor cleared her throat conspicuously. "Yes, Gloria. I am familiar with the term. And I know exactly what it means, if you can believe it. But indeed, if the novel is autobiographical, the narrative mirrors the love affair between distinguished veteran and musician Lucille Hopkins, advocate for nurse's rights, and St. Louis publishing heiress Rosalind Westerly—and *the* Nella Larsen. Well. It's almost too incredible, isn't it?"

"Beyond incredible. And the idea that Madeline will probably funnel at least part of the money she makes from selling the manuscript into the Flagg campaign makes me physically ill," Parkie said. "But technically, Glory's under contract. And even if she took the manuscript to another house and I quit my job and you retired early, nobody is going to publicize this like Madeline, now that she's worried about the auction house's rep. And nobody could bring it to market as quickly. Nor would I put it past Madeline to publicly sabotage the manuscript if it were out of her hands by questioning the attribution or undermining Eleanor. Or me."

"Just so," Eleanor said. "Which is why I think we give Madeline every assurance that we've accepted her proposition."

*

Later that night as they lay in bed, Glory came clean. "I'm worried," she said to Parkie, who was scrolling through an influx of messages.

Parkie put her phone down and drew Glory in, putting her arm around her.

"What about?"

"A couple of months ago I got an envelope from Lucille's lawyer. I knew I should have opened it but I didn't. Until last week."

"And?"

"Property taxes. Like fifty thousand in property taxes. Due in four months. Which, I know is nothing for the city. This place is probably worth a couple million, I guess. But I don't have anything close to fifty grand. It's not tomorrow, but that due date will be here before I know it. If I had shown with Sarkisian, the timing would have been great. The money would have been great. Eleanor's idea makes sense, I guess. But any plan that hinges on Manya Shah and perfect timing makes me nervous. Do you honestly really truly think it will work?"

"I think it has to," Parkie said. "Cutting myself off from the trust on Christmas seems like a pretty bad idea to me right about now, too. Ditto the four shots of Patron I did before I made the call. But I'm done with Greenwich. If my parents want to see me, they can get their asses down to Harlem."

Glory kissed Parkie on the little V of naked skin not covered by her own old T-shirt.

"I know that's right," she said.

Chapter 36

Three weeks later, Parkie and Glory waited together in the brownstone's chilly entry. It was a Saturday morning in late February, and it had snowed lightly the night before. The auction was today. Cuthbert's Americana sale would start in just a few hours, at noon, and Parkie had to get there early to troubleshoot and generally be on hand to take inquiries. Glory had made them a light breakfast, but Parkie's normally cast-iron stomach was roiling. She already regretted the second pour-over.

"You're pale today, my love. Paler than usual," Glory said, slipping her arm around Parkie's waist with one of her serious smiles. She kissed Parkie's cheek. "Don't worry. It's going to be all right. And you look great, baby."

Parkie didn't feel great. But Glory's confidence helped her step into the cold with what was at least a measure of courage. She was wearing a simple gray skirt suit, albeit the usual Parisian make, and the icy air instantly shot through the microfibers of her stockings. All it took was the short trip from stoop to car and she was frozen to the core.

So many things could go wrong in the next few hours. Parkie wished she could simply fast forward to the end of the day when, come what may, she and Glory would be together again in the brownstone to process what the fates had allowed.

Cuthbert's was, as usual on a sale day, as frenzied as the backstage of a theater on opening night. The air inside the building was always charged before an auction, and while today's sale was a rather uninspired one even by Cuthbert's standards, a current of expectancy had steadily built around what Madeline had hideously dubbed "Nella's notorious novelette." In the past few days, interest in the lot had grown exponentially and there were now, at 11 a.m., a handful of respectable absentee bids, which meant, to Parkie's great relief, enough potential buyers believed it to be what Eleanor said it was.

The manuscript was number 326 in a sale of 353 lots. It wouldn't come up—or need to be retrieved—for quite some time. Until the auctioneer approached lot number 300, the manuscript was to stay in Eleanor's office, where it had been stored (it was assumed) since the preview. In truth, the "scrapbook" had been kept most recently at Eleanor's—thence to Glory's after the eviction— though Eleanor had returned it to the old safe behind her desk that morning. Parkie now had the little vault's combination, just in case Eleanor couldn't get back there at the appointed time.

Show-woman and businesswoman that she was, Madeline liked to start every sale by taking the podium at her eponymous auction house, asserting the connection like an evil mermaid affixed to the prow of her ship. In a field dominated by jokey and charming men, she had an uncharacteristically solemn but strangely hypnotic selling style. Her auctioneering was full of pregnant, frozen-featured pauses and two-fingered hand gestures suspended in the air. Nobody would deny that Madeline's persona lent importance and drama to whatever came under her purview. She generally slogged through the first fifty lots before handing subsequent sections, where less interesting and often lower-dollar lots were stashed, to a younger, inevitably male protégé.

And so it was today, just as Parkie had predicted.

From the beginning, Parkie, too, had wanted to be an auctioneer; several of the junior specialists went this route in hopes of becoming popular Cuthbert's—and later Sotheby's or Christie's—personalities. But a few months after she'd started, Armand let her know, in the gentlest terms, that Madeline required Cuthbert auctioneers to stand for the duration of their time at the podium; she wouldn't want Parkie to have to "endure" that. Looking back, Parkie couldn't believe she'd accepted Madeline's unashamed, not to mention illegal, decision on the matter. But she had.

Although Madeline had seemed to be avoiding Parkie of late, today she had ordered her to be visible on the floor for the length of the sale. "For all your adoring *Gazette* fans," she'd said. Eleanor was likewise told to stay near the dais, or on the phone with bidders who couldn't be in the sale room or didn't want their identities known. Parkie would be handling phone bids, too.

On the off chance something went wrong with the plan, or someone from the press figured out who she was, Glory wouldn't be at the auction. Parkie had been covertly texting her from the moment she got in, though. She would give Glory a play-by-play in real time when it mattered.

"Next up, lot two hundred twenty-six, a letter from founding father Thomas Jefferson requesting a cake recipe from Paris," said the current auctioneer. His name was Cramer Lyddell and he was a slender New Yorker in his forties with a long, waxen face, wavy hair, and wire-rimmed glasses. Given the audience, he was the perfect choice to move rapidly but genially through the various Federalist pamphlets and constitutional amendments. With a hundred lots to go, Parkie would have to closely monitor Cramer's pace—there were only a few standout items likely to generate the kind of tennis match that could slow him down.

Thirty minutes later, when her phone bidder dropped out, Parkie scanned the room for Madeline, who, happily, was nowhere to be found. Then again, neither was Eleanor, though this was not what they'd agreed on. Cramer was already pushing lot 275. At this rate it would be forty-five minutes or less until the manuscript came up.

Parkie slipped a scrap of paper with "bathroom break" written on it to one of her even more junior colleagues, who gave her a pitying look. She rose to make her way behind the long table of people on the phones, overhearing Nicholas as he flirted unabashedly with one of his bidders.

The hallways were quiet except for intermittent electronic ringing in the empty offices—people always called whoever they knew on staff for unofficial intelligence during a sale. Eleanor had correctly anticipated that Parkie wouldn't have much time, and she was surprised to find that while the door to Kenniston's office had been left ajar for her, the overhead lights were off. When Parkie flipped them on, the first thing she noticed was the door to the little safe behind the desk. It was wide open. And the manuscript was gone.

"There you are, Parkie," said the last voice in the world she wanted to hear.

She turned around to see Madeline in the doorway, grinning one of her awful grins. "Are you looking for what I'm looking for? Listen to this one. Some idiot—who will no longer work here on Monday, I guarantee—seems to have sent the manuscript up to cold storage. Can you imagine? We've got to *show* it to sell it. Be a dear and help me find it, will you? I've never actually seen the thing. If we don't get it down here right away, Cramer may have to spell me when it comes up."

Parkie was speechless. And furious. And very, very freaked out. But what could she possibly say?

There was no universe in which what Madeline was telling her was true. But if there had been, Parkie would have had no excuse not to do as she said. She couldn't exactly tell her employer that this really sucked because she and Eleanor were planning to pull the manuscript from the sale at the last possible minute—while Madeline was on the podium with all eyes on her, unable to protest—and that this newly made wrinkle in their blueprint was most unwelcome. You had to *have* it to pull it.

"Sure, Madeline, of course," Parkie said. "Just let me text Dr. K. in case she needs me. I'll go get Armand's cold storage key from my desk."

"No need," Madeline said, her serpentine eyes flickering. "I have my own key. And Eleanor will be fine. She's on the phones anyway, so hers should be off. Better be. Now come."

This elevator ride was even less friendly than their last one, at the fucked-up preview for the Flagg sale. What goes up, Parkie thought, preparing to elude Madeline as soon as possible. Once she determined Lucille's property was safe, she would find a way to outmaneuver her.

In a way, they already had. There was a built-in plan B. Because, no matter what her boss was up to, with all the interest so far, the manuscript would almost certainly sell above estimate. There might even be a bidding war. Odds were, *if* it came up, the Larsen manuscript would end up with one of the competing institutional buyers—Parkie hoped the Schomburg had the funds. That outcome hadn't sounded bad to Glory, until Eleanor and Parkie reminded her that as long as the manuscript was sold at a Cuthbert's auction, Madeline would make a healthy commission on both ends—a percentage from the buyer and from the seller. Money made on the resistant backs of Black women, as Eleanor had put it, since she now considered herself to be one of them. Plan A, however, was to sell the novella privately themselves after the auction when the interested buyers would be known to them, and the manuscript had been properly vetted by real experts. If Madeline balked, Parkie would keep blowing her whistle while Eleanor and Glory laughed all the way to the bank.

If there was a way to prevent Madeline from profiting off Larsen, they would. If she lost face in the process, so much the better.

The elevator doors opened, and Madeline hurried out ahead of Parkie, heels ominously clicking down the hallway. Muted at that time of day to a urinary glow, the dirty windows around the room's edge failed to illuminate their path. Yet even in near darkness, Madeline appeared to know where she was headed.

Within seconds, she had unlocked one of the line of doors and stepped inside.

"They said it would be somewhere in here," she called to Parkie. "My eyes are terrible, can you see what this envelope says?" Parkie sighed and shuffled uncertainly forward, sweeping the dark as she walked.

There are times when every instinct in your body tells you not to do something. Following Madeline Cuthbert into cold storage was one of those times. But Parkie did it anyway.

This was her first regret when, as soon as she was midway into the room, Madeline came around from behind the door and slammed it shut, immediately turning the deadbolt on the other side.

"You two sit tight," Parkie heard Madeline mutter as the clack of her heels grew softer. "This will all be over soon."

Parkie reached for her phone, ignoring what she knew to be true: there was no signal up here. Nor was the flashlight feature much help in such a pitch-black cavern. But then she remembered what she'd done the last time. By slicing her hands through the air, Parkie found a few of the spaghetti strings and yanked the working bulbs to life.

Now she could think.

"You two." What had that meant? She banged on the walls with her stick.

"Eleanor!" she yelled as loudly as she could. "Eleanor! Are you up here?"

After a few seconds of banging Parkie thought she heard an impossibly small voice.

"Miss de Groot? I'm. I can't see a thing and I'm bleeding quite badly, I'm afraid."

"Shit, shit, shit," Parkie said, dropping her head. How could this be? How could Madeline have known? Spies. Everywhere. The luminous hands of her chronograph told her they had maybe twenty minutes, if that. Parkie needed to get back down there before her number was up.

And now there was Eleanor to think of. If an injured Eleanor was trapped in another room, Parkie would need to get her out first. How long would that take? How badly was she bleeding? And how in the world could she get them both out and make it to the sale room in time?

She swatted around freely with her cane, feeling like she needed to hit something hard and not finding much in the way of candidates. Suddenly, Parkie realized something: this room was full of boxes. And bubble wrap. And not much mouse poop. Despite the bulbs on strings, this wasn't number six. Madeline had stuck her in a different plot of the graveyard. Which meant

Eleanor might just be in the one to which she had a key. If only she could get there.

"Do you think anything's broken? What happened?" Parkie yelled into the door. "Can you breathe all right?"

"Madeline said the manuscript was up here for some out-landish reason. I was suspicious and I said so. Then she just pushed me in," Eleanor said. "Shoved me like a guard would a prisoner. And I caught my arm on one of these jagged metal shelves as I went down. It's quite profuse. The bleeding, I mean. My skin is somewhat thinner than I thought."

Good old Eleanor. How were these women of a certain age so brave?

"I'm going to get us out of here, Dr. Kenniston," Parkie shouted. "Hang on."

"Yes, please do that, Miss de Groot," was all Eleanor said in response. Her voice was even smaller than before.

Go time, Parkie thought, feeling the adrenaline kick in as she hadn't for a very long time. She took a couple of steps back and to the side of the door. Madeline was nothing if not cheap. It had to be one of those hollow-core doors you can buy at Home Depot, didn't it? It had to be the kind of shoddy balsa-wood dollhouse bullshit someone with a temper, or a black belt, or a fucking silver-handled Victorian mobility aid could punch right through.

Parkie switched up her grip on the walking stick, choking down near the rubber tip with both hands so that her beloved swan was at the other, business, end. She breathed out a big breath, yoga-style though her nose, and swung her stick at the center of the wooden surface with every single bit of strength she had.

Chapter 37

When Glory told Parkie everything was going to be okay that morning, it wasn't like she believed it. Call it intuition or second sight or merely lived experience, beating powerful bad people at their own game isn't an easy thing to do. When it happens, there are bound to be casualties. Glory had told Parkie, and convinced herself, that she would be perfectly content to follow what happened to the manuscript—the lost Nella Larsen novel that told the story of her great-aunt's erotic relationship with two unbelievable women—from a remove in Harlem. About an hour after the auction started, she knew better.

Snow had begun to accumulate and the Lyft car, on this Saturday afternoon, was taking forever. It was so slow, in fact, Glory tried to hail a cab while she was waiting. When that didn't work, she'd briefly considered running all the way downtown, which showed her how irrational with worry she'd become. She hadn't heard from Parkie in forty-three minutes. And she hadn't heard from Eleanor in much longer than that.

When she finally got to Cuthbert's, the big sale room was filled to capacity. An overflow of people with paddles and cell phones and Post-it–flagged catalogues had spread into the small hallway outside the glass doors. Glory wove her way through them into the crowded room and climbed onto an abandoned banquet chair in the back corner. Scanning the crowd, she couldn't securely identify anyone except Madeline, who was up there slowly waving like a conductor, her attention fixed on the bidders. Manya was supposed to be here somewhere; if that was her black bob swaying toward her neighbor, she might be in the second row.

The room was a cacophony of whispers. It was humming with suspense. In fact, the air was so electric, Glory wondered if the manuscript had already sold before she got there.

And Madeline had won again.

She couldn't find Parkie, who should be on the phones right now, close enough to get to the auctioneer in time to personally hand her an official-looking form stating that lot 326 had been pulled by the consignor. A notice like that, signed by Glory, would ensure that Larsen's manuscript would not be sold by Cuthbert's. Not today. Not ever.

But Parkie wasn't among the showcase of pretty girls in black with phones plastered to their ears. And neither was Eleanor. And Glory had a very bad feeling not unlike the other bad feelings she'd become attuned to lately, all of which had been warranted in the end, right up to sweet Maisie's death.

Glory stepped down from the chair, and just as she did, a young, bearded white guy in a funny suit backed carefully away from the phone tables and began slinking toward her, clinging to the wall like a cat burglar in a *Pink Panther* film.

"Are you Glory?" he whispered on approach.

"Are you Nicholas?"

"Yeah. Hey, so nice to meet you. Listen. I can't find Parkie," he said. "She left for the powder room—that's what the girls said—about half an hour ago. And she didn't come back. Neither has Dr. Kenniston. There's no way they aren't here for your lot.

Which'll be up in, give or take, fifteen minutes, I reckon. I don't mean to worry you. But I'm worried."

"Me, too," Glory said. "She won't answer my texts."

"Might have her phone off," he said. "We're supposed to. Or she could be somewhere with no service. Which, God's honest, is like half this building. It's pathetic." He cast a quick glance at the phones. "Best get back. Think I've been clocked."

"Hey, can you get a message to someone in the audience for me?"

"You mean one of the bidders?" he said, nervously leaning in. "I can try."

*

Glory returned to the hallway and found the stairwell. She could only hope, first, that the door to Parkie's floor was unlocked and, second, that she could remember how to find Parkie's desk. Fast.

The first thing she realized was that few of the cubes were personalized with more than a calendar or a mug of pens emblazoned with the owner's college insignia. Here and there was a black and white *Vanity Fair*–ish photograph, its subjects posing on beaches or in black tie. But really, if it weren't for the blue-and-white umbrella stand she'd heard so much about, Glory might only have located Parkie's desk by the process of elimination, which she definitely did not have time for. Once she did find it, Parkie's lack of personal effects made her search easier still. There were a few desk drawers and a bulletin board, but Parkie was too smart for anything as obvious as that.

Glory sat down in Parkie's desk chair. It felt like being near her. Maybe the chair smelled like her soap. Or maybe the unergonomic foam seat had molded itself to her beautiful Parkie frame. It was a comforting sensation but it also filled Glory with fear.

If Parkie was in any kind of trouble, she didn't know what she would do. She hadn't even told the love of her life how she really felt about her.

What would be Parkie's clever hiding place? Glory asked herself, swiveling from side to side in the tiny square of space until it came to her. She lurched forward, tipping the heavy umbrella stand on its side. There within the embossed circle of carpet underneath was the key to the graveyard.

Back Glory went into the stairwell and up and up and up she ran. Three flights to the eighth floor. Was that the right one? She prayed she'd remembered. With each floor, the stairwell grew dirtier and darker, until at the top of unlit number eight—even at her exhausted speed—Glory nearly ran headfirst into the metal door.

She turned the knob and then. Sweet Jesus.

Come on!

Of all the doors in the whole unsecured fucking place, this one had to be locked?

"God dammit," she screamed into the darkness, pounding a fist on the door.

"Is that you, Glory?" responded a British voice a few seconds later.

Glory heard footsteps and then, bam, the door flew open and there was Manya. And there, thank God, was Parkie standing next to her. There they both were, silhouettes backlit by a dangling bank of bulbs. There they were. Looking like the powerful women she knew them to be.

The front of Parkie's gray Chanel suit was coated in what looked like sawdust, and there was a run in her stockings three inches wide. "You came for me," she said excitedly.

"I did," said Glory, still panting from the stairs and slightly amazed she'd found them.

"But you have to do one more thing," Parkie said. "You have to go get the key from my cube. Eleanor is bleeding and I can't break down her door. It's an old one and it's metal. I'm worried she's—"

Glory didn't try to process any of what she'd heard. She merely handed Parkie the key, which Parkie handed to Manya, who went running back down the hallway in her thirteen-hundred-dollar pumps like an Olympic sprinter.

"What else, babe?" Glory asked.

"You stay with Manya and Eleanor—Manya went down to call 911 before you came. They should be here soon. I have to get back to the sale. There may still be time."

As they waited for the elevator to thunder up to the eighth floor, Parkie put her arms around Glory. She knew Parkie had to get to the salesroom but she didn't want to let her go.

"I love you," Parkie said, giving Glory a quick kiss near her ear as the doors opened. "Thank you for saving the day."

"Thank you for—" Glory said. It was all she had time for before the elevator slammed shut and Parkie was gone.

Parkie had said something about Eleanor. About Eleanor being hurt? Glory was about to try to find Manya when Manya called to her from down the hallway. It was the right key, and Manya was already kneeling at Eleanor's side, dabbing at the nasty gash still pooling bright red from her forearm.

"Have you got a T-shirt under that?" Manya asked Glory in a remarkably even and pleasant voice.

Glory had thrown on coveralls, without even thinking, or caring, how much she would stand out in the Cuthbert's crowd. No wonder Nicholas had recognized her.

She nodded.

"Take it off and tear it into strips. Do it. And do it quickly."

There was something thrilling about the way Manya spoke to her, the self-assurance behind the request, which was not a request. It was a command. Glory was taking off her clothes and tearing up her shirt in no time.

Once she had done as ordered, she ran the strips into the little room where an ashen-faced Eleanor lay on her back, babbling words that, to Glory, made no sense at all.

Manya doused Eleanor's arm with clear fluid from a bottle she'd apparently removed from her enormous somebody-Italian bag—it looked to Glory like contact lens solution—and cleaned up the wound. Then she wrapped the jagged flap of skin with speed and precision and gently raised Eleanor's arm over her head, speaking to her in the same calm voice.

"You're a jack-of-all-trades," Glory said, deeply impressed. "Good thing you got my message. I never would have known how to do that."

Manya looked across at her with a faraway expression in her dark, intelligent eyes.

"You would if you'd been trained for it," she said. "Back in London. Before all of this I was . . . I am. A nurse."

*

"No, babe, I was still with Eleanor and Manya when that happened," Glory called to Parkie. "We didn't know if you made it before the buzzer or not. Then the paramedics came. So we just went straight to street level for the ambulance. It wasn't until I got your text that I knew."

Glory was still pretty wired. She was having trouble concentrating on the simplest things. Like washing her face and getting ready for bed.

"Where is your . . . ? Oh, got it," she said, finding the tooth-paste in a drawer.

They were at Parkie's. For the first time. And it wasn't nearly as weird as Glory had imagined. With Eleanor at New York Pres for observation, it made sense to decamp to Parkie's, a few blocks away. They were tired and it was closer. Parkie had protested at first. But Glory had always wanted to see her place.

"It was pretty surreal," Parkie said. "I mean, I literally busted out of the elevator when Madeline was giving fair warning on lot 325. It was a good thing we filled out the notice of with-drawal ahead of time. Even though I practically forgot it was in my pocket. I really didn't know if I could do it at that point, physically, I mean. But when Madeline announced lot 326, 'an uncensored *novelette* attributed to Nella Larsen,' I got this rush of energy and climbed up on the dais in front of everyone and handed her the slip. She stared at me like she might kill me with her eyes. But I just stood there beside her for all the world to see. And the room started to get the way it gets when something out-of-the-ordinary happens—restless, almost panicky. And then she said it: 'Lot 326 has been withdrawn from the auction and will not be sold.'"

"My heroine," Glory said. "I wish I could have seen it. But, so then what? I'm surprised she didn't try to push you off the stage."

Glory had finished in the bathroom and came now into the tiny bedroom, with Parkie's double bed all the way against one wall. She slipped off the too-big robe she'd borrowed and climbed under the covers. Parkie slid over.

"Then I actually whispered—or I like to think, hissed—in her ear. I don't even know for sure what I said. But something like, 'You better hope we don't tell anyone what really happened upstairs. Eleanor and I will be in touch about our very, very generous severance packages.' And then I just bounced. Walked onto the street, got your texts, and cabbed to the hospital."

"Boss bitch," Glory purred in Parkie's ear. "Like I said."

"Back at you. How did you know to do any of that? I can't believe you found the key. If you hadn't. God. Who knew Eleanor was a hemophiliac?"

"And who knew anything at all about Manya?" Glory said. She laid her face between Parkie's breasts, rubbing circles on her belly with the flat of her hand.

"You know I like to hear you talk," Glory said. "Whatever you say stays with me. Makes me think. Makes me miss you. I don't know how else to explain it. I remembered about the graveyard and I just knew that's where you'd be. When I sat in your chair, it was like I could feel you hiding that key."

"What else can you feel?" Parkie asked, sliding her hand down Glory's chest, over her stomach, and inside her thigh.

"That I love you, too," Glory said. "And I want this to be the way it always is. Wherever we are. Whatever we're doing. Lifting each other up. Catching each other if we fall. Or if we're headed in the wrong direction. Like I have been."

"Like we both have been. Mostly me, as I think we both know. But I'm done making excuses," Parkie said. "Better together?"

"Yes, we are," said Glory.

It was the first time she'd said the words. But Parkie didn't say them back this time. It'd been the heat of the moment outside the elevator. Maybe Parkie regretted it. Glory repositioned herself so that Parkie could no longer see her face.

"You know I want this always, don't you?" Parkie said. She kissed Glory's forehead and pulled her closer. "Can you do that?"

Glory smiled into the softness of Parkie's skin, feeling her pounding heart, knowing her love was real. Happy to be anywhere as long as they were together. "For you, Parkerson, I can definitely do always."

Epilogue

The show sold out. Manya's idea to coordinate the opening of Glory's first solo exhibition with the release of Nella Larsen's heretofore unpublished last novel proved irresistible to the press. That Glory's home/studio was revealed as the site of the novel's love affair was simply too poignant a coincidence to ignore. Brooklyn bookstores ran out of *Passing*. Even *Quicksand* was selling like hotcakes. The exhibition handily drew the author's admirers to the artist's work and vice versa, which only seemed appropriate, since one of Glory's newest and largest paintings was called *Sanctuary*. If the story with that title proved to be Larsen's undoing, the lovers she'd taken a decade later had invited her into their Harlem brownstone and redeemed the word for her. At least Glory hoped that was the case.

They'd had a huge and very festive opening almost two months earlier. But tonight's invitation-only event was not arranged to celebrate Glory's show; it was a ribbon cutting, sans the ribbon or the scissors, for Shah de Groot, as the new contemporary gallery in Bushwick would be known.

In light of Madeline's nastiness, Parkie and Eleanor had managed to negotiate—no need to call it blackmail—platinum parachutes from their former employer. After that, it only seemed logical for Glory and Parkie to go in with Manya, who had saved much more than the day, given that Eleanor could have bled out on the eighth floor that afternoon. Privately, Parkie told Glory she wasn't at all sure Manya's handful of remaining big-name clients would follow her when she broke from M&F shortly after the Americana auction.

But they had.

There was only one request from Manya when Glory came back with her tail between her legs, apologizing for her misguided near-decision to work with Sarkisian and pleading—truly she had—for Manya to wipe the slate clean. The dealer had taken it in stride; it wasn't the first time. But she was adamant that Glory show her new work and that alone. She wanted only the figurative paintings, to which, this time, for some reason, the *Times* had had a far more positive response.

*

The new space was three times smaller than the old one but, six months later, with backing from an angel or two, Shah de Groot looked the part. It was more their scene than Chelsea. Only Highland Park separated the gallery from Nella Larsen's final resting place.

When Parkie and Glory arrived that night, there were already people there. Unlike Moulton & Freer, the new space was merely a single, low-ceilinged room with a storefront window. They could see who was inside even before they walked in.

"No way," Parkie gasped, squeezing Glory's hand as soon as they entered. It was a buzzy, warm night and they were both dressed for a New Yorker summer: Parkie in white jeans and Belgian shoes, Glory in a striped sundress and heels.

"What?" Glory said. "Has there been a heist?"

"There will be," Parkie said. "That's my Texan ex. That's Loden Bradley."

"Did you invite her?"

"Hell no," Parkie said as they went in. "Of course not."

"Manya," they said in unison.

To be fair, Parkie's business partner wouldn't be doing her job if she didn't realize that Loden Bradley was one of the biggest spenders in American contemporary. Or had been when Parkie dated her, when her tastes—and the reason they'd met in the first place—ran to the predictably preapproved fare at Sarkisian. Still, Parkie thought, good for Manya.

"Well, I guess you better introduce us," Glory said.

She was jealous all right. Parkie knew the look. She knew the furrowed forehead. And she knew the stance, Glory's legs crossed at the ankles, her hand resting in the hollow of Parkie's lower back. Behind-the-scenes possessive, just the way Parkie liked it.

"Plenty of time for that," she said. "Let's get a drink."

With Glory's hand steering her Parkie led them through the crowd.

But when they tried to slip behind Loden, Manya magically appeared next to her and called them back over. Loden was standing in front of Glory's most expensive painting. The one she'd titled *We Three*. It was roughly, very roughly, a version of the graces: Euphrosyne, Thalia, and Aglaia, though its subject could also be interpreted as three ages of women. There was a curvy, dancing youth and a voluptuous middle-aged flower-gatherer, with an athletic figure taking her place between them.

Of course, Loden liked that one. Too bad for her it's sold, Parkie thought, with a touch of guilty glee.

"How does it feel to get what everyone else wants?" Parkie heard Manya say in a voice that was nowhere approaching coy. The woman could make a grocery list sound pornographic.

Loden answered without looking at her. Vintage Bradley.

"Have dinner with me and I'll ask you that very same question," she said with a meaningful pause. "Tomorrow morning."

Parkie laughed an astonished laugh to go with her WTF expression. "*You* bought this?" Glory's hand dropped from the spot above her belt before she'd finished speaking.

Loden turned their way now. And so did Manya. The four women were facing each other, eyes bounding and rebounding from one face—and one body—to another.

"Thank you," Glory said more than a little coldly, Parkie thought. But when Loden extended her hand, Glory reached back and her voice sounded different when she spoke again. "This one is my favorite. May it bring you exactly what you need, as it has for me."

Glory returned her hand to Parkie's back, and Parkie put her arm around Glory's bare shoulders.

Loden's dazzling smile flitted from one woman to the other, before settling, in that heat-seeking way of hers, on Manya.

"One way or another," she said. "I have a very good feeling it will."